*To Mike and Mary Bernice
friends and fellow civilizers
of the barbarian hordes*

UP

HOMEBODY

OTHER BOOKS BY ORSON SCOTT CARD

Treasure Box
Lost Boys
Pastwatch: The Redemption of Christopher Columbus
Saints
The Folk of the Fringe
Ender's Game
Speaker for the Dead
Xenocide
Children of the Mind
Seventh Son
Red Prophet
Prentice Alvin
Alvin Journeyman
The Memory of Earth
The Call of Earth
The Ships of Earth
Earthfall
Earthborn
Cruel Miracles
Flux
Monkey Sonatas
The Changed Man

HOMEBODY

A Novel

Orson Scott Card

HarperCollins*Publishers*

HarperCollins books may be purchased for educational, business, or sales promotional use. For information please write: Special Markets Department, HarperCollins Publishers, Inc., 10 East 53rd Street, New York, NY 10022.

FIRST EDITION

Designed by Elina D. Nudelman

Library of Congress Cataloging-in-Publication Data

Card, Orson Scott.
    Homebody : a novel / by Orson Scott Card. — 1st ed.
      p.   cm.
    ISBN 0-06-017655-5
    I. Title.
  PS3553.A655H66   1998
  813'.54—dc21   97-37627

98 99 00 01 02 ❖/HC 10 9 8 7 6 5 4 3 2 1

Contents

Acknowledgments

My thanks to:

My wife, Kristine, who was my collaborator at the conception of this story; and to Emily and Geoffrey Card, Erin and Phillip Absher, and Peter Johnson, whose comments at the earliest stages helped give the first draft a better shape and substance;

Clark and Kathy Kidd for hospitality and more as I began the second draft; and Kathy again for reading that draft with fresh eyes;

Mark and Margaret Park, in whose guest bedroom I wrote and faxed away many a chapter;

Kathleen Bellamy, my assistant, who always waits to read till last, so she can catch the mistakes that everybody missed;

And (again and always) my wife, Kristine, and my children, Geoff, Em, Charlie Ben, and Zina, who have taught me what a house is for and what a home can be.

1

New House
1874

Dr. Calhoun Bellamy made it a point to stay away from his property while the crew was tearing down the old Varley house. He didn't want to remember scenes of destruction. All he wanted to see was each step in the construction of the new house, the one he had designed for Renée and for the children they would have together.

Architecture was all he had wanted to study, ever since his father sent him abroad after the War Between the States. It wasn't the grandeur of the great buildings of Europe, the cathedrals and palaces, monuments and museums, that made him long to be a shaper of human spaces. Rather it was the country houses of Tuscany, Provence, and England. In his mind they formed a strange amalgam: the rambling outdoors-indoors of the villas designed for the perpetual summer and spring of the Mediterranean, and the bright-windowed tight enclosures in which the English managed to frolic despite the bitter winter and the endless rain. He came home full of ideas for houses that would transform American life, only to find that architects weren't interested in new ideas. No one would take this mad young man as a student. At last Cal settled down to study medicine and follow in his father's footsteps.

But now, with his marriage less than a year away, he was granting himself one last indulgence. In consultation with an architect from Richmond, he had designed a house which seemed to be a conventional Victorian on the outside, but which on the inside preserved some of the ideas he had developed abroad. Nothing too strange, just a different use of space that made him dream of the swirling dancers at a country-house ball, with arches that reminded him of the open doors and passageways of the Riviera and the hills above Florence. The architect tried to persuade him that no one would be comfortable in such a house, but Cal responded with cheerful obstinacy. This was the house he wanted; the architect's job was to draw up plans for a structure that would last, as Cal modestly suggested, until the Rapture.

"Do you happen to know when that might be?" asked the architect, only a little superciliously. "I wouldn't want to waste your money on excessive sturdiness."

"Make it last forever," said Cal. "Just in case."

All that remained now was for the old Quaker family's house, which had been standing longer than Greensborough had been a town, to be cleared from the lot on Baker Street. The city was growing toward the west, and although this was not the wealthiest neighborhood, it was the most tasteful. It was fitting that the son and heir of the most prominent physician in the city should build his bride a house on such a piece of land. The wooded gully at the back of the lot would guarantee privacy and a wild-seeming, natural setting; the large carriagehouse and servants' quarters would separate the house from the neighbors on the one side; and shaded residential streets bounded the property on the other two sides. In effect, the house would stand alone, conventionally graceful on the outside, a place of surprise and enchantment within.

So Cal was not pleased when a servant boy came all out of breath into his offices and insisted on giving him a message from the foreman of the wrecking crew. "You best come, sir. What they found you gots to see."

"Tell them to wait half an hour—doesn't it occur to them I have patients whose needs are urgent?"

The boy only looked puzzled. There was no hope of his delivering the message coherently.

"Never mind. Just tell them to wait until I get there."

"Yes sir," said the boy, and off he ran again. No doubt the moment he was out of sight he'd amble as slowly as possible. That's the way it was with these people. You could make them free, but you couldn't make workers out of them. There was a limit to what Northern arms could impose on a prostrate South.

In truth he had no patients that afternoon and so it was only a few moments before he set out from his office, walking because it was such a fine day. He expected to pass the boy on the way, but apparently he was either more ambitious than Cal had expected or better at hiding.

Cal was not surprised to see the entire crew lolling around–getting paid, no doubt, for their waiting time. But if the foreman was at all embarrassed about wasting Cal's money, he showed no sign of it. "Something none of us was expecting, sir," said the foreman, "and there was nothing for it but to ask you to decide."

"Decide what?"

"I reckon you best come down into the old cellar with me and I'll show you."

With the house a ruin, it wasn't a safe enterprise, slipping down into the darkness of the cellar. Even when they got to the brightly lighted place where the floor above had been torn away, it was tricky walking without banging head or shins into some lurking obstruction. But at last the foreman brought him to a stone foundation wall with a small hole knocked in it.

"See?"

Cal definitely did *not* see. Not till the foreman took out several more stones and held a lantern into the opening. Only then did it become clear that there was a tunnel connecting the cellar with . . . what?

"Where does it lead?"

"Sent the boy down there, and he popped out in the gully. Looks like them Varleys was smuggling niggers out before the war."

Cal tightened his lips. "I hope you'll never use that term in my presence again."

"Pardon me, sir," said the foreman. "I meant nigras."

"I'm not surprised that a Quaker household would break the law in that fashion. I don't sympathize with their cause, but I honor their courage and integrity."

The foreman grinned. "Good thing they moved west, though, don't you think?"

"Without question," said Cal, smiling back, just a little.

"So do you want us to fill it in?"

Cal thought about it for a moment. It was history, wasn't it? Having a tunnel once used for hiding slaves would give his new house a bit of ancient lore. American houses rarely had a sense of age and history. His would.

"Keep it. We'll build the foundation in such a way as to preserve it. Perhaps use it as a wine cellar. Or a root cellar. Don't you think?"

"Whatever you want, sir."

"Keep it."

All the way back to his office, Cal felt the lingering glow of the day's discovery. My house will be new for my bride, but it will also be old like the catacombs of Rome.

2

Rediscovery
1997

The Bellamy house grew old along with the College Hill neighborhood. Prosperity in the nineteenth century had lined these streets with large, extravagantly decorated mansions. But by the time the Great War came, the rich were building their new mansions near the country club in Irving Park, and College Hill began its long, slow decline. While elderly widows continued to live in the houses their rich husbands built them, other homes fell vacant and were bought by entrepreneurs who began renting them out. Soon some began to be redivided into apartments, with kitchens and bathrooms added wherever they might fit. And as the decay grew worse, the rents fell until students at the growing university could afford them.

That was the end of the neighborhood. At first the students were all young ladies and therefore civilized, but no matter how refined their manners, they were transients, and the houses did not belong to them. Then came the end of segregation, and the women's college became the University of North Carolina at Greensboro. Frats and sororities swallowed up the best of the houses near the growing campus. The rest of the houses were cut up into ever-smaller apartments, with students packed in shoulder to shoulder, or so it seemed. They cared nothing for the yards; the landlords seemed to care even less.

All of these things happened to the Bellamy house, including a brief stint as a sorority in the early sixties. But when gentrification came to the neighborhood in the early eighties, the Bellamy house was passed by. In 1987 the aging landlord moved to Florida, and in the vain hope that leaving it empty would help to sell it, stopped renting the rooms. It quickly became a derelict, boarded up, vandalized, lawn gone to weeds and only mowed a couple of times a year. The FOR SALE sign stayed up long enough for the red paint to disappear completely; then it fell over in a storm and no one put it back up again. No one wanted the house, it had been so badly deformed when it was cut into apartments. No one even wanted the land, with its corner location and a gully in the back yard. The landlord forgot he owned the property.

And, as if to rebuke the house even further, the carriagehouse and servants quarters next door remained in good repair. Long since converted into a residence, it was old but well tended, the yard neatly trimmed. It seemed to thrive as the Bellamy house itself withered.

Until the day in August 1997 when Don Lark drove by in his slightly beat-up red Ford pickup, then turned around and came back for another look. He parked on Baker Street, got out of the truck, and walked all the way around the house, sizing it up. He found the fallen FOR SALE sign, turned it over, and took down the name and number of the real estate agency.

The realty had changed names twice since the sign went up, but the phone number was still the same. Don stood at the payphone at the Bestway on Walker and explained to the woman on the telephone that the only FOR SALE sign on the property had her agency's phone number on it.

"I'm sorry, but we don't show an active listing for that address."

"What about a passive listing?"

"I'm afraid I don't understand what you're—"

"I don't really care who's listing it, ma'am. You have real estate agents there, right? And real estate agents are able to look up the ownership of property and tell buyers—namely me—who the owner is and whether he wants to sell and if so for how much. Does any of this sound familiar?"

"No need to get snide with me, sir."

"Sorry, I didn't mean to offend, ma'am. I just want to find out about this property and it wasn't me that painted your phone number on the sign."

"Hold please."

He held. He had to put in another quarter, he held so long. And then another woman came on the phone.

"This is Cindy Claybourne, can I help you?"

"Are you a real estate agent?"

"I sure hope so." A cheerful voice, gratefully heard.

"My name's Don Lark, and I'm interested in a derelict property on the corner of Baker and Motley. The FOR SALE sign had your phone number on it, but the sign was old and it fell down a long time ago. The receptionist said you didn't have a listing for it. An active listing, anyway."

"Well, it sounds like a mystery."

Don remembered Reverend Gardiner from his childhood, who used to answer Don's endless questions by saying, "Well, I guess that's a mystery."

Smiling, Don said, "Will we need a divine messenger to solve it?"

"No, more like Sherlock Holmes. I'd be glad to look up that property for you. Can I have your number?"

"You could if I had one."

"Business phone, then?"

"Like I said. I'm a legitimate buyer, cash in the bank, don't worry about that, I just don't happen to have a phone. So I'll have to call you or stop in and see you."

"Mysteriouser and mysteriouser," she said. "Tomorrow afternoon at five? Here at the office?"

"Where's here?"

She gave him directions. He thanked her and hung up. Then he got back into his truck and drove back to the Bellamy house.

Don Lark didn't see what most people saw, looking at Calhoun Bellamy's dream house. The weedy yard, the weather-chipped paint, the boarded windows, the half-painted-over graffiti, those were almost invisible to him. What he saw was a pretty good roof—almost miraculously good, considering the house's obvious neglect. That meant that the interior might not be water-soaked and warped. And neither the roof nor the porch was sagging—this suggested a sturdy structure on a solid foundation. It was a strong house.

He walked the property again, looking for signs of termites, break-in sites that would need to be closed off, and practical information like where the power and water entered the house. A coal chute at the back told him where the alley used to be; as for the ancient coal furnace, Don assumed that it was still in the cellar—who could move such a monster?—but that it hadn't been in use for fifty years at least. Good riddance. Nobody better get nostalgic for those old days of coal-fired furnaces. On one house Don had fixed up a few years back, he got curious, brought in a small load of coal, and stoked up the furnace. Besides the black filth all over him by the time he got the thing going, an astonishing amount of soot spewed from the chimney. Flecks of it fell like ash from Mount St. Helen's, or so it seemed to him. No wonder people stopped using coal the minute gas or heating oil became available. This stuff made car exhaust seem clean and healthy.

The more he saw of the house the better he liked it. The wood trim was beautifully made and, despite the fading of the paint, very little of it would need to be replaced. Where a board or two had weathered and sagged away from the windows, he could see that the original glass was still intact. Where were the neighborhood boys with rocks? Apparently the boarding up had been done before the vandals could get to work. The work this house required was enormous, but it was also worth doing. Whoever built this place had used only the best materials, and the workmen had clearly made it a labor of love. Restoring it to its former glory would be hard, intense labor, months and months of it. But when he was done, the house would be magnificent.

I want this place. Don hated to admit it to himself—he knew that this meant he would probably pay more than it was worth. But then, after so many years of neglect, it was possible the owner would be glad to get it off his hands. The price might be low enough for Don to pass the threshold: He might be able to pay cash for the place instead of borrowing from the bank. He had walked away from his last fixer-upper with almost a hundred thousand dollars. If the house came in for under fifty, he'd have enough left over for materials, the occasional subcontractor, and his own meager living expenses during the year it would take to renovate the place. No more borrowing, no more banks, no more money poured down the interest rathole.

And then, as always when he started feeling too good, he remembered one pair of eyes that would never see this house, one pair of feet that would never walk its floors and stairs, one voice that would never be heard calling out to him through the high-ceilinged caverns of the rooms or outside in a newly landscaped yard.

He walked back to his truck. Dark was coming on. He drove to a truckstop out on I-40, paid a couple of bucks for a shower, ate a lousy meal in the restaurant, and slept in the camper on the back of his pickup truck, bedding down among his tools.

3

Motivated Seller

It took a bit of research—more than the possibility of a sale warranted—but Cindy Claybourne found herself interested in the project and so she pursued it. Why else had she chosen a field in which she could pretty much set her own hours, if not to have the freedom to spend a few of those hours doing something for its own sake, and not just for money? She had no appointments that morning. The agency's files and the property records in the Guilford County offices were open to her. And so she began to discover the history of the Bellamy house.

The recent history came first. An owner who was anxious for a quick sale of a deteriorating property—the students renting apartments there were notified that the house would not be available starting in the fall; by midsummer, all were gone. But there were no takers, not at the price asked. The owner moved to Florida. At first he phoned now and then. But the agent who first got the property moved with her husband to Atlanta; the next agent got fired for general lousiness; and the agent after that was a hotshot who lost interest in property that couldn't sell quickly. No staying power. Cindy knew the type, didn't like them much, and resented the damage these fairweather agents did to the profession. They skimmed off the cream, sold the houses that any fool could sell, and then left the tough projects to the real agents like Cindy. The result was that the most shallow, ruthless agents made the most money. What a system.

And the Bellamy house was a prime example of what could happen to a property handled that way. The owner didn't want to sink more money into the house in order to fix it up. But he also didn't want to lower the price. Each time he finally dropped the price it was by too little and way too late.

All that was before 1992, when Cindy joined the firm. For years now the file had lain undisturbed. The owner might be dead, for all Cindy knew. So . . . she called him.

To her surprise, he not only wasn't dead, he even answered his own telephone. "That old piece of junk?" said the old man. "Every year when I pay the taxes on it I just want to spit."

"Well, we have a potential buyer."

"You've got to be kidding. The house hasn't blown down? Didn't Hurricane Hugo finish it off?"

"Still standing."

"Well, ninety thousand dollars and not a penny less."

"You already dropped the price to eighty-four nine back in '89."

"Did I?"

"And it didn't sell then at that price."

"I'm quite aware of that! Don't tell me my business. That's a valuable property!"

With a smile in her voice, Cindy ignored his warning. "A property is worth what someone will pay for it. If no one will pay for it, then it's worth the value of whatever you produce on the land. If you produce nothing and nobody will pay for it, then that property is worthless."

"Are you determined to insult me by taking me back to college?"

"You've been paying taxes on that house for ten years now, earning nothing from it and never getting closer to a sale than a price quote. Do you want to sell this house or are you planning on taking it with you when you die?"

For a moment Cindy thought the man might explode, he was so furious. She let him rail on about her rudeness and stupidity for about fifteen seconds. Then she set down the receiver on the cradle and took a drink from the Poland Spring bottle she kept at her desk. One minute. She glanced at the *News and Record* on her desk, flipped to the Word Jumble, worked it in about two minutes, and then picked up the phone and pushed the redial button.

"You hung up on me," he said.

"Was that you?" she said. "It sounded to me like a man who didn't want to sell his property. But why in the world would such a man be talking to a real estate agent?"

The man chuckled grimly. "Well, aren't you the clever one."

"Not really," said Cindy. "I'm the one who doesn't much care. I don't get a commission if you get angry at me and fire me as your agent. But then, I also don't get a commission if the property just sits there because the owner has a completely unrealistic view of its value."

"Well, what do *you* think the value is?"

"I think the value is whatever the buyer offers."

"Are you crazy? You're going to take the first offer?"

"Let's not get into the question of who is or isn't crazy," said Cindy. "Let's just be realistic about it. There hasn't even been an inquiry on this house in years. Every week you wait to sell it, the less value it has. For all I know, this man's only interest in it is to tear the house down and build something new on the lot."

"A beautiful old house like that? It would be a sin!"

"No worse than letting it die slowly, the way you're doing."

"All right, I'll tell you what. You drop the price as far as you want below eighty thousand. But for each thousand you drop the price, your commission drops by a percentage point."

"I have a better idea. My commission on this is a flat eight thousand dollars no matter what price the house goes for."

"What? Are you insane?"

"You keep asking me that," said Cindy. "But you're the one who decided to start changing the rules on commissions. So let's compromise and stick to the original agreement on my commission. What do you say?"

"It's a good thing I'm a gentleman, or I'd tell you right to your face what I think of you."

"When you get your check and you stop having to pay taxes on that empty house, then what you'll think of me is that I'm a damn good agent who finally did what *no* other agent has been able to do: get you free of that house. You may even realize that the main obstacle I had to overcome was a stubborn owner who has no idea what's going on in the real estate market in Greensboro."

"How do I know the buyer isn't you? How do I know you aren't knocking down the price yourself to cheat me?"

"I'll tell you how you know. Because when you start insulting me like that, I won't stick around to take it." And, once again, she hung up on him.

At the next desk, Ryan Bagatti grinned at her. "I can't wait to see the motivational tape that taught you *that* technique. Sean Penn and Zsa Zsa Gabor star in the video *You Can Make Millions in Real Estate by Hanging Up on Clients!*"

"Hey, I didn't slap him."

"I'm not sure but what he has a bruise from the way you talked to him."

Cindy tossed her hair nonchalantly. "What do I care about money and commissions? Poverty is good for the soul. Unemployment is capitalism's way of getting you to plant a garden."

Her phone buzzed. The receptionist told her who it was. She cheerfully stuck her tongue out at Ryan and picked up the receiver. "Hey," she said.

"Do whatever it takes but sell the damn house," said the owner.

"Commission as per our agreement?" said Cindy.

"Take the whole purchase price, just get it off my hands!"

"I'll do my best, sir."

"And don't you *dare* give me that 'sir' baloney. You are not a lady, young woman. I hope you realize that about yourself!"

"I do now, sir, and thank you for helping me make another leap forward in my quest for self-discovery."

"You just don't let up, do you?"

"It's my most endearing trait," said Cindy. "After it grows on you."

"I just better see results."

"Have a nice day."

This time the hanging up was peaceful, and she turned to grin at Ryan.

"You only got away with that because you're a woman," said Ryan.

"I only *had* to do it because I'm a woman," said Cindy. "If I'd been a man, he would have listened to my advice seriously without having to go through all the drama."

"You're really pretty when you're on a feminist rant," said Ryan.

"And you're really attractive when you remember that you're married," said Cindy.

"Not to my wife I'm not."

"Well, she'd know," said Cindy.

She had a few hours to kill and the house intrigued her. The file said it was built in 1874 by a Dr. Calhoun Bellamy. Cindy always liked to tell her prospective buyers the history of a house, even if it was only a few years old. They liked knowing that a mansion was built by an executive with Jefferson-Pilot, for instance, or that a modest house was built by one of the textile mills as affordable housing for its employees. It gave them a sense of connection with the place, a story to tell their friends. Most important, it made them feel as though the house had some personality and that made them connect with it. No way of knowing whether that finally helped them decide to buy, but it couldn't hurt, could it?

So she went to the county offices and spent a couple of hours hunting for the pertinent records and examining all the transactions. Not many buyers. Dr. Bellamy and his wife lived in the house until they both died in 1918—the flu epidemic? Their children tried to hold onto it, apparently, until 1920, but then they sold it for nine thousand dollars. A very good price in those days. After that the place was nonresidential for a while, whatever that meant, and by the mid-thirties it was just one landlord after another renting ever-smaller apartments to ever-poorer residents.

Boring. It was the Bellamy family that would interest the buyer. And so Cindy walked across the street to the main library and got the microfilms of the newspapers from that era. There was no index, but she knew the pages she wanted—society news. Sure enough, there were notices about the Bellamys all the time. They were party hounds. Soirees, balls, receptions almost every week, sometimes two or three in the same week. And apparently there was real cachet to getting an invitation from the Bellamys. The heavy schedule of entertaining continued until the turn of the century, but then tapered off to an annual ball and reception. Well, that would be something, wouldn't it, to tell the buyer that the Bellamy house had been the high society hot spot of the late 1800s.

Her eyes were bleary from looking at the microfilms. As always after one of these research marathons, she mocked her own obsessiveness. How could a real estate agent seriously hope to make a living if she kept, in effect, taking a day off? This buyer seemed eager, the seller had given her carte blanche on price—why did she need to do research when the deal was as good as done?

Because she loved houses, that's why. Loved houses and the people who lived in them and the neighborhoods that grew up out of the ground and sprouted families and children. Houses are the trunk of the tree, Cindy felt, and people are the leaves that sprout from them until the neighborhood is lush with them. Then the leaves age and fall, the neighborhood decays, but the trunk remains, until another generation of leaves can bud and grow.

She almost never said this to anyone, of course, because they either looked at her like she was crazy or mocked her the way Ryan did. And they were right. But she had no intention of changing her mind or her habits. If she couldn't be herself selling real estate, then real estate could go sell itself as far as she was concerned.

Don Lark arrived five minutes early for his appointment. Cindy knew at once that this must be the man from the payphone, and not just because of his workclothes and shaggy hair. He came in and looked around for a moment and said nothing when the receptionist asked, "May I help you?" Didn't even show a sign that he heard her, for a few moments at least. Only when he spotted Cindy watching him from her desk down at the end of the long room did he turn to Leah at the reception desk and say something. Leah pointed a painted fingernail at Cindy and the man nodded and Cindy thought: He doesn't care about making a good impression. He doesn't hurry to ingratiate himself with people. He takes his time sizing up a situation and then finds the least troublesome way to his goal.

Cindy didn't really have a strategy for dealing with people like him. The ingratiaters required her to be visibly impressed with them, to ooh and aah over their taste and judgment. The roughshod type, on the other hand, would have ignored Leah completely and headed straight for Cindy's desk upon spotting her. Those she worked on by being contrarian, telling them why the house she wanted them to buy wasn't really within their price range, or had a lot of extras they didn't want to pay for. Cindy didn't count these selling strategies as hypocrisy. People looking for a house exposed themselves emotionally, and what Cindy did was feed their need. If she ever did a motivational video, that's the phrase she would use. Feed their need.

This man, though, was of that rare type that knew what he wanted but didn't want anything badly enough to demand it or beg for it or hurt anyone else in the process of getting it. Which meant that all she could do was show him the house and answer his questions and, if he decided he wanted to buy, help him put together a deal. No strategies. Instead of dealing with his inner child, she could talk directly with his inner grown-up. Such customers seldom came along, but she was always glad when they did.

So her smile was genuine when she stood up and offered her hand and said her name.

"Don Lark," he answered. His handshake was firm but brief. "That house on Baker."

"Your car or mine?" she asked.

"Let's each take our own," he said.

Cindy glanced at Ryan, who was shaking his head and rolling his eyes. Ryan's theory was that if ever a customer refused to ride in the same car with you, it meant no sale. Cindy's theory was that it meant they had somewhere to go afterward and didn't want to have to go back to the real estate office.

"Fine," said Cindy. "I have to warn you, though. I found a key that I think is the one to the lockbox, but the file's been inactive for so long that I can't be sure it's the right one or if it'll work even if it is."

Don nodded. "If it doesn't fit, what'll you do?"

"Call a locksmith, I assume."

"Let's go," he said.

She was pretty sure that if the key didn't fit, he would have the door open before she could call a locksmith. But he didn't say so right now because that would lead to a needless discussion. Naturally he assumed that she would argue with him and tell him about laws and rules and damaging the client's property. Well, she could be patient, too, and let him find out that she didn't have a bureaucrat's tiny fears and passions when the occasion arose.

As she got into her Sable—ostentatiously modest among the BMWs and Lexuses—she noticed that while his truck looked like it had been used for real work, the engine started smoothly and quietly. It reaffirmed her impression of him: Doesn't care how his tools look, but makes sure they work perfectly. And for the first time it crossed her mind: He can't possibly be married if he doesn't have a phone.

4

Inspection

Cindy had driven by the Bellamy house on her way back from the library, but she hadn't had time to stop. Now as she drove up, she tried to see it the way a man like Don Lark would. He'd ignore the shaggy yard. The peeling paint and boarded-up windows and clumsy graffiti would mean nothing to him. Beyond that, the house actually looked pretty good. Nothing sagged. The trim was mostly intact. The roof was old but not a ruin. Don Lark had an eye that could see a good house beneath a faded exterior. A middle-aged divorced woman could get naked with a man like Don Lark.

Don't think like that, she told herself sternly.

By the time she got out of her car, Don was already talking to a man on the front lawn.

"Cindy Claybourne, this is Jay Placer. He's an engineer who looks over houses for me."

Cindy smiled and shook Jay's hand. He was a little younger than Don, and his soft hands and body showed that he had an indoor job and didn't do anything in his free time that would toughen him up. That was fine—Cindy kept a clear distinction in her mind between men who were tough because they had real jobs and men who were tough because they had the money and the ego need to spend many hours doing expensive manly activities. Cindy's father was a fireman who hung wallpaper on his free days. She respected a man like Don whose rough hands were earned by hard work. She also respected a man like Jay, whose soft body also came from hard work at a different kind of job. Respected him, but unfortunately was never attracted to his type. It was the tragedy underlying the Dilbert cartoons, which made it so she couldn't really enjoy them. She always wanted to scream at Dilbert: Get out of the office and pour some concrete somewhere!

Cindy led the way to the front door. The lockbox wasn't too rusted—a surprise, considering how many years the thing had been out in Greensboro's weather, which ranged from intense rain to oppressive humidity, but always involved corrosive amounts of moisture. And the key she found went right into the lockbox and opened it.

"Well," she said. "Success."

From the lockbox she took the key that hung there and then discovered that it didn't fit the heavy Yale padlock that hung from a hasp on the front door. She was baffled.

Don reached for the key. She handed it to him. He bent and inserted it into the deadbolt keyhole on the door itself. It fit perfectly and the lock clicked open. Unfortunately, that did nothing for the massive padlock.

"I can't believe they'd put the key to the door in the lockbox but not the key to that padlock."

"Seems obvious the padlock went on after people stopped using that lockbox," said Jay. "Probably the owner had it put up to keep vagrants and vandals out."

Don was already heading for his truck. He came back with a wicked-looking wrecking bar, whose bladed end he slipped under the edge of the hasp on the door. He rocked it back once and got one side up; he slid the blade farther under the hasp and levered it off in one move. The screws tore chunks of wood out of the door coming out.

"So much for the locksmith," said Cindy.

"I'll fix it whether I buy the place or not," said Don. "Wasn't a very secure lock anyway."

He put his hand on the door and pushed it open easily.

"Is that the same technique you use with women, Don?" asked Jay. "Show 'em the wrecking bar and they open right up?"

So Jay was the kind of man who felt the need to make macho dirty comments in front of women. Too bad for you, Dilbert, thought Cindy. Not that Cindy was actually that bothered by the joke, but in this era of political correctness a man who talked like that in front of women was either deliberately trying to give offense or so oblivious to the culture around him that he should be checked for brain activity.

The entry hall was dingy, with a door on either side leading into the two ground-floor apartments. The whole back of the entry hall was filled with a wide stairway, forbiddingly high, that swept straight upward to the second story. The carpet on the stairway was worn to the underlying fabric in the middle.

Jay turned around and around, sizing up the layout. He patted the wall on the right of the stairway, the north side. "With the door off-center the way it is, this has to be the load-bearing wall cause it runs close to the center of the house. The other one was added in to divide off the other apartment, probably back in the thirties, judging from the transom over the door."

"Original stairs?" asked Don.

"Got to be," said Jay. He jumped up onto the first step, the second step, the third step, landing hard each time. "No way would some cheapjack landlord put in a stairway this wide or this solid. The thing's still like a rock! Somebody knew how to build back when this house went up."

"Dr. Bellamy was an amateur architect," said Cindy.

"Who?" asked Jay.

"Calhoun Bellamy, the man who built the house. He designed the place himself for his new bride. It was ready just in time for him to carry her across the threshold in 1874. I imagine he kept a close eye on the contractors as they built the place."

"If he had to," said Jay. "Back then people took pride in their work. Didn't have to watch 'em all the time to keep them from cheating or skimping. A man would be ashamed to put up a staircase that creaked or sagged."

"Still had to put the money in it," said Don. "What do you think, three carriages or four?"

"My money's on four," said Jay. "Or three really thick ones. Nowadays you put up a stairway that heavy, you get accused of gouging the customer by putting in needlessly expensive materials. So you put in a light one and they complain that the stairway bounces when they run up and down it. Go figure."

The apartment doors were not locked, and the apartments behind them were just what Cindy had expected. Ancient shabby furniture that had obviously been used by vagrants or small animals—or both—probably leading to the installation of the padlock on the front door. Faded rectangles on the walls showed where paintings or posters had been. The paint had been lazily applied over wallpaper, which had been applied over even older wallpaper, all of it put up with overlapping edges so that ugly seams ran up the walls under the ugly paint.

"Was this place remodeled by a blind person?" asked Cindy.

"Paint wasn't this color when it first went up," said Don. "It's cheap stuff that fades so fast you have to finish painting it in one day or you can see the dividing line."

"What color was it when it was first painted?" she asked.

"Even uglier," said Jay. "I'm betting it was painted in the seventies. We're just lucky the owner was too cheap to recarpet, or we'd be looking at green or orange shag."

"Is that mildew I smell or a dead animal?" asked Cindy.

"Just the smell of bad taste liberally applied," said Jay.

So maybe he wasn't a macho pig. Maybe he was just a guy who liked making jokes.

They were in the north apartment, which Jay decided must have been the original parlor, while the front room on the other side might have been a consulting office or a library or a study or even a groundfloor bedroom if there was a mother-in-law or a nephew or something. Don led the way through the door leading into a dark, cramped hallway. Small narrow bedrooms opened off the hall.

"The hall and the bedrooms aren't original, of course," said Jay. "This must have been the dining room. Kind of a grand one, too—

four windows, no less!" And at the back of the apartment, a large old-fashioned kitchen with a massive table dominating the center of it. A bathroom had been carved out of the back inside corner of it, and beside the bathroom was the stairway leading down into the cellar. Don and Jay started down the stairs immediately.

"Don't you want to look at the kitchen cabinets?" asked Cindy.

"They're all cheap ones anyway," said Don. "I'll be building nice ones when the time comes."

Well now. That sounded like a man who had already decided to buy. Cindy refrained from comment as she followed them into the dark cellar.

Naturally, both Jay and Don had tiny flashlights with them. No doubt they could come up with any tool or small appliance by searching in one pocket or another. Her grandfather had been like that, and Cindy always thought of a workingman's pockets as a kind of treasure hunt. You never knew what you might stumble across. They trained their flashlights on the unfinished ceiling of the cellar. Here was where the house would reveal its secrets.

The wiring was ancient knob-and-tube, and Jay chipped away the insulation from some of it with his fingernails. "Don't run power through this, not even temporarily," said Jay.

"Don't have to tell me twice on that one," said Don.

"Miracle this place didn't catch fire and burn down when it was still occupied." Jay looked at Cindy. "When did it go vacant?"

"It was last occupied in the spring of '86," she told him. "It was rented by students, so I guess it *was* a miracle there wasn't a fire. What with hair dryers and curling irons left plugged in."

They found the fusebox. Jay gave a little laugh and closed the door immediately. "Give this one to a museum," he said. "A toy museum."

The plumbing, though, was surprisingly good. Jay and Don went on and on about how the cast-iron drainpipes and copper supply pipes were the golden age of plumbing and the workmen who installed it had done a decent job. Only the pipes leading to a couple of the added-on bathrooms were galvanized steel. Jay shone his tiny flashlight on a large patch of rust on the outside of one of the pipes. "Don't touch it," he said. "It's only rust holding it together." Jay sighed. "I guess we'd better figure out where these pipes lead."

"Doesn't matter much," said Don. "Half the bathrooms were added when the house was cut up into apartments, so I'll have to relocate everything anyway."

"Aren't some of these pipes the original plumbing?" asked Cindy.

They looked at her like she was insane. "This place was built in 1874," Don said finally. "The original plumbing was a hole in the back yard."

"And this copper pipe didn't even come into use till the 1930s," added Jay.

"Oh," said Cindy, feeling as though she had failed a test. Or, worse yet, passed one.

Upstairs, in the fading light from the evening windows, the dismalness of the abandoned house became sad and wistful. "This place used to be so beautiful," said Cindy. "Look at the crown moldings, the base moldings."

"Even a picture molding," said Jay. "Took a lot of care with the place. But it's a real fixer-upper now."

They were doing a bathroom-by-bathroom check for old leaks and fixture damage. Soon they were upstairs in the bathroom at the front of the house. "Well, the toilet here is dead," said Don. "But there's a shower and it even has a curtain, if you can believe it."

"The only watertight toilet is that one on the main floor," said Jay. "And the other two bathrooms have those rustomatic pipes, so I guess you'll have to shower up here and use the toilet down there."

"Convenient," said Don.

"You're going to *live* here?" asked Cindy.

"It's what he does," said Jay. "Lives in the house while he's working on it."

"You're going to move in here *before* it's renovated?"

"Saves on rent," said Don. "And that's *if* I take the place."

"Of course," said Cindy. But she knew he was going to offer on the house.

"Time for the acid test," said Jay. "On to the attic."

If you could call it an attic. True, there was a lumber room with unfinished walls, but the other rooms were all finished, with interesting sloping ceilings and large windows bringing in plenty of light. Jay and Don seemed to go over every inch of the ceiling, looking for stains. "I can't believe it," said Jay, over and over. "This place has been empty for a decade and the roof hasn't leaked *anywhere*."

"Still got to replace it," said Don. "Nobody's going to take the place if I can't tell them it's got a new roof."

Again, the assumption that he was going to be selling the place later. And since she controlled the purchase price, it was going to work. Why, then, did she feel more anxiety than ever? It wasn't about the sale. It was Don Lark. Something about him. And not just the fact that he was her type. Her type usually ended up drinking beer and running to the john to pee every few minutes. She didn't really like her type that much. Nor did she find anything romantic about a guy who had no phone and lived out of his truck when he was between jobs. She was flat-out puzzled about why she couldn't take her eyes off him.

In the lumber room, Jay looked at the exposed joists and whistled. "Man, they knew how to build in those days. This is one strong house."

Cindy tried to see what was so unusual about the joists. "Is it just that they're thicker?"

"And closer together," said Don.

"So everything is stronger," said Cindy.

"Stronger but heavier," said Don. "A lot of weight up here, with this roof. Attic floor's bound to be extra heavy, too. The bearing walls on the first floor and the lally columns in the cellar are under an unusual amount of strain."

"It's kind of circular," Jay added. "The stronger you make it, the stronger you have to make it. Add strength up here, you have to add more strength down below to hold it up. After a while, it gets so the ground can't support it."

"Really?" asked Cindy.

Don shook his head. "We're talking skyscraper levels of weight now. You'll never find a house too heavy for the ground here."

"He says that because he's not an engineer," said Jay. "I could tell you stories."

"He could but don't let him," said Don. "Unless you have a sleep disorder."

Jay went into a lame Groucho imitation. "I like to consider *myself* a sleep disorder." He leered at Cindy.

Backing toward the door of the lumber room, Cindy stumbled over a trunk. It must have been empty, because it moved easily across the floor, raising a cloud of dust. Immediately she began sneezing.

"Are you all right?" asked Don.

"Bless you. Bless you. Bless you," said Jay. Cindy hated that custom. Maybe after somebody threw up a "bless you" might be appropriate, but to invoke the powers of the universe because of a sneeze?

"Excuse me but I'd better get downstairs," said Cindy.

The first step she took informed her that she had twisted her ankle a little when she stumbled. She winced and limped.

"You hurt yourself," said Don.

"Nothing, a twist, I'll walk it off."

"Let me give you a hand."

Cindy had such contempt for women who flirted by leaning on men at every opportunity that now, when she would have liked very much to have a hand getting downstairs—especially his hand—she found herself refusing him by reflex. "Really, finish up here and join me when you're ready, I'll be fine."

Don took her at her word, dammit. But in fact she was right—by the time she got out onto the porch, her ankle was working fine again. No pain. But also no Don. His arm must be muscled like iron under that sleeve. He could toss me in the air like a baby.

It didn't take long for the men to get downstairs. Don wasted no time. He did ask if her ankle was all right, but as soon as she assured him that she was fine, he came straight to the point. "If the price is right, then it's worth the work to me. House is solid but I've got to strip out almost everything and start from scratch. So I have to hold on to enough capital to do that."

"If you need time to make an estimate," she began.

"Don't need time," he said. "I already walked the outside of the house and counted the floors and multiplied the square footage. Before I called you. The price has to come in under fifty."

She raised an eyebrow. "Am I to take that as an offer?"

"I don't dicker," said Don.

"*That's* the truth," said Jay. "He can't play poker because he doesn't even bluff. If he bids on a hand, fold, because he doesn't bid unless he's got a sure thing."

"I don't play poker," said Cindy. "I just sell houses."

"What I'm saying," said Don, "is that I'm not saying under fifty so you'll come back with seventy-five and then we'll settle on sixty-two."

"I know," she said. "You're saying under fifty because if it goes over fifty you aren't taking it."

"If it goes over fifty I have to go to the bank for part of the money and then pay interest the whole time I'm working on it. And I'll be working on this one for most of a year. Biggest house I've ever tackled. So I can't afford to borrow. Cash or nothing."

"You have fifty thousand in cash?"

"I said *under* fifty."

"I hear a mistake being made," said Jay.

Cindy looked at him in surprise. "You mean the house isn't sound?"

"Sound as a dollar," said Jay. "Or a yen, or whatever. I just don't think he's going to make back what he's putting into it. Not in this neighborhood, not this year."

"If he's putting in less than fifty thousand—"

"But he's putting in twice that by the time he's done," said Jay. "Plus a year of a highly skilled carpenter's time. Call it a hundred and fifty thousand dollars. And I'll bet nothing in this neighborhood sells for more than a hundred."

Cindy smiled her killer smile at Jay. He was out of his expertise now and into hers, and she was going to enjoy showing off a little. "Actually, most things around here have lately been going in the one-ten to one-twenty range. And part of what's keeping them *that* low is this house—runs down the whole neighborhood. Besides which, this house is something special. Look around. The house next door is the *carriagehouse* to this one, for heaven's sake—and it's the second-nicest house on the street. So when this one comes on the market, it'll sell for at least thirty above the rest of the neighborhood. If you find the right buyer."

"Which is where you come in, no doubt," said Jay. His cynicism infuriated her.

"Yes, Jay, that's where I come in. Because I am to real estate what you are to engineering, except that I can do it without making little dirty references to members of the opposite sex. So when it's time to sell this house, I won't even offer it to anyone looking for a bargain. I'll offer it to someone looking for a jewel and willing to pay top dollar for it. And *if* Mr. Lark is as good as you seem to think he is, I'll bet you right now that the selling price for this house is within five thousand dollars of two hundred thou."

"You'll bet?" asked Jay.

"Stop this," said Don. "I don't use agents to sell my houses. Can't afford the commission."

"If I don't meet that price," said Cindy, "then I won't take a commission."

"That wouldn't be right," said Don. "Your work is worth the price. So I won't have you doing the job unless I pay you for it."

"I've made a bet," said Cindy. "Are you men or what?"

"I'll take the bet," said Jay.

"You've got nothing at stake," said Cindy.

"My reputation as a judge of real estate values."

"You don't have a reputation," said Cindy, "or I would have heard of you."

Don laughed out loud. More of a bark, really, a couple of barks. Almost a warning. I'm amused, but stand back because I'm still ready to bite at any moment. But Cindy liked the laugh. Or at least her hormones liked it. Angry at herself, she realized he could probably take his shoes off right now and she'd probably get all excited by the smell of his socks. Get a grip on yourself, girl.

"Won't take the bet," said Don. "I'm not a betting man. But I will think about giving you a shot at it. Not till after you see my finished work, though. Right now you're buying a pig in a poke."

"She's not buying anything," said Jay. "Realtors take houses on consignment."

"On commission," said Cindy. "If you don't know the difference—"

"Let's not fight," said Jay. "Let's just agree that we don't like each other but we both love Don so we have to get along for his sake."

What did he mean by that? Immediately she put on her business face. "I'll tell my client your offer is forty-six five. You may not like to dicker, but he does. When he settles for forty-nine I'll call you to set up a closing."

"You think he will?" asked Don, looking surprised.

"I know he will," said Cindy. Then she gave Jay her fullcourt smile, which she knew would almost blind him with the dazzling sarcasm of it.

Jay ignored her and turned to Don. "It's your money and your life, Don. If you call it a life."

"I don't," said Don. "But it's the only life I've got." He turned back to Cindy. "When should I call you?"

"Tomorrow at five and we'll set up an appointment for the closing."

"Are you really that sure?" said Don. "It could change the kind of fix I do on that front door."

"Fix?" It took her a moment for her to remember that he had broken into the house with a wrecking bar.

"I mean put up a new hasp, only fastened with a slotless head and inlaid so it can't be pried out the way I did. Or just put on a new frame and door, which is what I'll do if I'm actually buying it."

"Put up the new door," said Cindy.

"And what happens when the owner says no?" asked Jay.

"If the owner says no," said Cindy, "I'll pay for the door."

"Thanks for your help, Cindy," said Don. "Sounded to me like you went to some trouble doing research on the place."

He noticed! "I did."

"Maybe at the closing you can tell me more about Dr. What's-his-name—"

"Dr. Calhoun Bellamy." She couldn't help sounding cold; she didn't like being patronized.

"I'm not doing a restoration here, just a renovation. I'm not trying to get the house back the way he first built it."

"I didn't think you were."

"I'm fixing it up so I can sell it at a profit. But as long as you understand that, then I'd like it if you told me about him."

"I'll do that," said Cindy.

Don brought his fingers to his forehead as if to touch the brim of a nonexistent hat. Then he walked briskly back to his truck and drove away.

For a moment Cindy was annoyed when she realized she had been left alone with Jay. But what was he going to do, really? And he knew Don. He could answer questions.

"How many houses has he done this with?" she asked.

Jay shrugged. "About one every four months for—I don't remember now—however long it's been since his wife died. Two and a half years?"

"Four months. Is he that fast?"

"The other houses were smaller."

Only then did the reference to Don's wife register with her. "He really misses his wife?"

Jay shook his head. "I should have said his exwife, complete with ugly court battles over custody of their baby daughter. She claimed Nellie—that's the little girl—she claimed Nellie wasn't his. *He* said *she* was a drug-pumping drunk."

"Nasty."

"Yeah, but he was right on all counts. The baby was definitely his. And the wife was high on about five different drugs when she piled the car into a bridge abutment. The little girl—she was almost two by then—the mother had her in her safety seat."

"But it didn't help?"

"Might have, except that the safety seat wasn't attached to the car. You can't expect a mother to think of everything."

"My Lord," said Cindy. "He must have been crazy with grief."

"Rage is more like it. We thought at first he might kill himself. Then we were afraid he might go out and kill the judges and lawyers and social workers who decided a baby needs its mother and they shouldn't be judgmental about lifestyle differences when the drug use hadn't, after all, been proved in the criminal courts."

"A baby does need its mother," Cindy said softly.

"A baby needs good parents, both of them," said Jay. "Don't get me started."

"What if I just want to get you stopped?"

Jay looked at her, a bit nonplussed. "*You* were the one asking about Don."

Cindy looked back at the house. "He does these fix-ups to be alone?"

"Oh, he wanted to be alone. Some of us were clinging to him so tight that he finally told us to leave him alone, he promised not to kill anybody, including himself, if we'd just give him room to breathe."

"Good to have friends, though," she said.

"Yeah, well, friends aren't replacements for a lost child, I can tell you that. And there was Don, bankrupt from the expense of fighting to get Nellie back. He barely had enough to bury her. Lost his contracting business. So he borrows to buy a rundown house out in the county, a two-bedroom ranch that wasn't quite as good quality as a mobile home. But Don's good at what he does so . . . here he is now, no debts, cash in the bank, and this is the house he's going to fix up."

"So he turns his loneliness and grief into the restoration of beautiful old houses."

"The ones he started with weren't all that beautiful. You make it sound romantic."

"Not romantic, but maybe a little heroic. Don't you think?" asked Cindy.

"I think Don figures that as long as he can't be dead, he might as well do this."

With that, Jay gave her one last cheesy smile and headed back to his minivan. Cindy went for her car, too, not caring that the house was left unlocked behind her. Don would be back to put on a new door. It was his house now. She'd make sure of that.

It was already almost dark. The wind had picked up and there were clouds coming in over the trees to the west. Autumn coming at last. Real autumn, not just turning leaves but cold weather, too. Cold rain. She hated the cold but she also looked forward to it. A change.

The end of the old year. Christmas coming. Memories. People she missed. Melancholy. Yes, that was it, melancholy. That's what autumn was good for.

But a man like Don, it was always autumn for him, wasn't it? To lose a child and know that if only a judge had decided differently, if only the law was different, your daughter would be alive.

At least he knew that he had spent everything he had to try to get her back. But would that be consolation to him? Cindy doubted it. She thought of her father. A peaceable, law-abiding man. But he worked with his body, his muscled, powerful body. And there were times when she could see that it took all his strength not to hit somebody. She never saw him hit anybody, but she saw him want to, and in a way that was almost more frightening, because she knew that if he ever did, it would be the most terrible blow.

If Don Lark really was anything like her father, it must eat him alive inside, always wondering if he shouldn't have just said screw the law and kidnapped his daughter and gone underground. Even if he got caught, even if he went to jail for it and she got killed anyway, he could live with it better if he knew he had done *everything* to try to save her. Men think like that, Cindy knew. Some men anyway. Take upon themselves the burden of the world. Have to save everybody, help everybody, provide for everybody. And when they can't do it, they can't think of any other reason to live. Was that Don Lark? Probably. A man who had forgotten, not how to live, but why.

5

Doors

Back when Don was a house-builder, the best part of the job was the beginning. Standing there on a wooded lot with insects droning and birds flitting and treerats scampering up the trunks, he saw the slope of the land, the way it would look in lawn and garden, and where the house would crown the lot. He imagined the plan of the house, where he might put a cellar that opened to ground level in the back yard, or how a deep porch might be especially nice on a hot afternoon. He saw the roof rising among the trees—he always saved the best of the trees, because that kept a house from looking naked and newborn. A brand-new house had to look established, had to look as though it had roots deep into the ground. People couldn't feel right about moving into a place that looked like it just came to rest there and might blow off again in a year or two, the next bad storm. Tall old trees gave that feeling of stability even on a house finished just the day before.

Once building began, then the peace of the woods was broken, the dirt torn up and flung into the air as a fine dust that clogged every-thing. The naked frame showed its origin as cut trees—almost obscene to put them up among the living timbers, as if to cow them into submission by showing them what could happen to trees that didn't cooperate. Even when the house was nearly done and Don got his own hands deep in the finish carpentry, the pleasure of working with the wood and of watching it all take shape under his hands, that still wasn't as much of a joy as standing there on the building lot imagining the house inside his head.

Kind of like getting married. Kind of like watching your child make your wife's belly swell. Imagining, wondering, building the finished family in your dreams.

Don didn't build new houses anymore. At first he had no choice. The lawyers' fees ate up his business, his home, every asset he owned except the little bit of insurance that paid for his daughter's funeral. He found a wreck of a property that was worth less with the house on it than it was as bare land. A couple of friends lent him the closing costs and the token down payment and Don moved into the place, a ramshackle four-room farmstead out near Madison, and began to work on it. Three months later it was transformed into what the realtor called "a spic-and-span charmer of a cottage in the woods," and after repaying his friends and the bank and the unbelievably patient credit manager at Lowe's, Don walked away from the place with nine thousand dollars in capital. Three thousand a month. Except it wasn't income, it was another down payment and the expenses involved in fixing up the next place.

Now he had enough that he could build new houses again. He could put Lark Homes back in business if he wanted to. There were people who still left messages for him, passed word along that they weren't going to build their dream house until Don Lark could build it for them, that's the kind of reputation he had. Once Don even went and stood on a building lot, a lovely hill in a development tucked away in an ell of a cemetery so it would always be surrounded by forest. But standing there, he saw nothing at all. Oh, he saw the flies, the birds, the squirrels. He even saw the slope of the land, the drainage. His eye picked out the peripheral trees that would be worth saving, and how the driveway would have to go.

What he couldn't see was the house. He couldn't imagine the future anymore. That part of him had been cut out and buried with his daughter. If the truest dream of your life could be taken away from you and then killed, what were all these houses for? Didn't people know better?

It wasn't Don's job to tell them. But he didn't have to build their houses, either.

So he stayed with the old houses. Abandoned, weathered, derelict houses, or rundown rentals that no one had cared about. Houses that spoke of dead dreams. It was a language Don could understand. And what he did in those houses was not build—someone else had already done that—but rather eke a little more life out of the old place. Make the aging timbers hold another life or group of lives for some brief span of time. Not ready for the boneyard yet.

Now he was starting yet another house, the most ambitious project so far. A house that had been built as a mansion. A house thick with old dreams cut up into tatty little nightmares and finally put to sleep and now his job was to wake the place up again.

The Bellamy house was solid. Jay Placer saw it too, but maybe he hadn't worked with enough old houses to understand how remarkable this one really was. Built in the 1870s, and yet there was no bowing or sagging anywhere. That was more than a matter of good workmanship. This house was a testament to the meticulous care of the original builder. The foundation had been deeply and properly laid. The backfill had been porous and the cellar had stayed dry. Therefore there was no settling. The sill rested on masonry high enough out of the ground that no rot had set in even after more than a century. The walls were solidly tied together and made of the finest tempered wood, and even the roof showed no sign of sagging. Many new homes showed carelessness in the building and it was obvious to Don that most houses being built today would be lucky to be standing fifty years from now. But this one had been built to stand until . . . until what? Forever.

If other people had Don's eye for quality, there's no chance this house would have been available at the price; no way would it have been left abandoned for so long. But what other people saw was the shabby face of the house, the seedy yard, the boarded-up windows, the smell of cheap old carpeting and thick-laid dust. It would take a year and thousands of dollars to get the place back into livable shape again. Other people had neither the time nor the money for it. But Don had nothing but time, and it wasn't half so expensive when you did the work yourself. As long as you knew how to do it.

No doubt about it, the Bellamy house had once been a beauty and it would be a beauty again a year from now. It would go on the market as the leaves were turning. Don would see to it that it looked like a dream of the lost American past. Everybody walking into it would feel like they had come home at last. Everybody but Don himself. To him this place would feel no more or less like home than any other. Walking into it now, the bad smell of it, the dust, the squalor, did not make him shy away; walking out of it a year from now, with gleaming floors and walls and ceilings, with his beautiful finish work everywhere and the autumn-shaded sunlight dancing through the windows, it would not make him yearn to stay. It was a job, and he would live here because he didn't want to waste money paying rent when he already owned a roof and walls that would be good enough.

Not tonight it wouldn't, of course. There was the little matter of the closing, and then the hooking up of water and power. But in a few days he'd move in and sleep where he worked. Better than the back of the truck.

If Cindy Claybourne had known *that*, would she have given him the time of day? Maybe. Some women were drawn to a little bit of wildness, even in a middle-aged man. Trouble was, most women didn't know how to interpret the wildness of men. Don had seen it even in high school. How the brutal guys who thought of women as an easier way to jerk off always seemed to have a pretty girl close at hand. What were these women thinking? He finally came to understand it in a biology class in college, before his dad's death took him out of school and put him in the house-building business. These women weren't looking for danger, they were looking for the alpha male. They were looking for the guy who would subdue the other males, rule the pack. The man with initiative, drive, a will to power. The trouble was, civilized men didn't express their drive the same way the brutes did, and a lot of women never caught on to that. They saw the masculine display, the casual violence, and thought they were seeing just what the estrous female wanted. What they got was only another baboon. While the real men, the kind who built things that lasted, who cared for those under their protection, those men often had to search long and hard for a woman who would value them.

Don thought he had found one. It wasn't until four years into their marriage that he suspected she was having an affair. Only the lover wasn't a man, it was coke, and when she couldn't get that, it was booze. She far preferred what she got from drug dealers and bartenders to what Don had to offer. She called it "having a good time."

Women who were attracted to wildness didn't interest Don. In fact, it had been a good number of years since Don had been attracted to any woman at all. Well, that wasn't strictly speaking true. He noticed them, all right, the way he noticed Cindy Claybourne, how she kept sizing him up, how her smile got extra warm when she spoke to him, how she hung on his words even when he knew perfectly well that what he was saying was empty and boring or so filled with the jargon of his profession that she didn't understand a bit of it. He noticed women, but when he thought of actually trying to see one alone, talk to her, start establishing a relationship, it just made him tired. Sad and tired and a little bit angry even though he knew that not all women were unreliable child-stealing chimps.

Besides, what Cindy Claybourne saw as wildness in Don wasn't vigor and violence at all. There was no man-of-the-woods in Don, no wind-blown hair on the bike or in the convertible. Don was a mini-van kind of guy, a child-safety-seat-toting list-following husband-who-always-says-we-instead-of-I kind of guy who just happened to be living out of the back of a pickup truck because noticing a mini-van or a child safety seat or an actual lived-in family house made him lose control of his emotions all over again and so he stayed away from things like that. He was wild the way a mistreated dog becomes wild, not because it loves freedom, but because it has lost trust.

Don imagined asking Cindy Claybourne: Do you really want to get involved with a man like me? And she would say, Oh, yes! because women said things like that, but when she got to know him she'd end up saying, Oh no! What have I done!

So Don would spare Cindy and himself the time and expense of several dinners out and a feeble attempt at dancing at the Palomino Club or whatever they might do to simulate fun. He would sign off on the purchase and never see her again unless maybe this time he decided to list the house with a realty. And yet, despite this decision, Don found himself thinking of her off and on as he worked on securing the doors.

A guy who lives in a truck can't be sure that his cordless power tools will be charged when he needs them, so Don always did his lockset work with a manual auger. Since he wasn't going to keep these doors, he had no compunction about ignoring the old lockset and installing a new deadbolt higher than any builder would ever put one. Why shouldn't he? He was the only one who would use these locks—when it came time to sell the house, there'd be brand-new doors. Don was tall; for him the deadbolt was no higher than the normally-placed lock would be for a woman of, say, Cindy Claybourne's height.

And thinking of Cindy Claybourne's height made Don think about just how tall she was compared to him. The crown of her head couldn't be any higher than Don's shoulder, which meant that he'd really have to bend down to kiss her and . . . damn!

He put together the deadbolt on the front door, lined up the strikeplate, screwed it in, tested it. Lock, unlock. The key moved smoothly. The door felt solid.

As he stepped off the porch to walk around to the back yard, he saw someone peer at him from a window in the carriagehouse next door. What he was doing on the front porch had to be the most interesting thing that had happened on this block in a while. With the house and yard abandoned for so long, everybody would be grateful to see him working on it—happened every time, and Don didn't mind the waves, the smiles, even the greetings and the "about time" comments. He just hoped nobody got too neighborly and decided that what Don needed was conversation while he tried to work. He didn't like explaining himself to people.

That had always been one of the nice things about working with houses. The guys you worked with were pretty serious about the job. Men in suits, they were usually shmoozers, talking sports, networking, couldn't leave you alone until they figured you out. But the contractors and workmen, they looked to see how you did your job and if you did it right, they respected you, and if you paid them on time and stuck to your schedule, they even liked working for you. The ones who worked in groups, they could go to Cook-Out together for lunch and they knew each other's wives or at least knew about them. But as the general contractor, Don wasn't really part of that. His free time was for his family, for his handful of friends, for his own thoughts.

Like the Duke Power guy when he showed up. No shmoozing, just a little weather talk and then he's looking at the line in. Underground, that's good. Not a very heavy line, that's not good. Then down into the cellar to the fuse box, saying no more than was needed. Don led the way down with his big flashlight, but of course the Duke Power guy had his own light and pinpointed exactly the things that Don had noticed. The ancient knob-and-tube wiring was clearly visible among the floor joists overhead, and the thirty-amp fuse box was a joke.

"Good thing this house wasn't occupied," said the Duke Power guy. "Somebody runs a hair dryer, the place goes up in flames."

"I won't be running any power through the old lines."

"Good. You want a hundred amps?"

"Already got the panel box I need. I'll put it up when you tell me where."

For the first time, the Duke Power guy showed some pleasure. Almost a smile. Probably wasn't used to people doing part of the work. Or maybe he expected Don to do it wrong and it amused him. But Don wouldn't do it wrong, and it would save him work, so it didn't matter what he thought, and the best thing was, he didn't say what he thought, just kept it to himself and that was right. He went right on and asked the next question. "Might as well run the line in through the same hole, as long as you got no need for the old cable."

And Don answered him. "Good enough for me."

By the time the cable was ready to hook in, Don had the panel box up and the old fuse box out of the way. When the guy started to attach the cable Don stepped back out of the way.

"Ain't hot yet," said the guy.

"And my gun ain't loaded," said Don.

That earned him a grin. "I guess that means you don't need the lecture about having a qualified electrician do all your wiring and shut off all the power before you touch this box."

"You can read me my rights, officer, but I've been through it all before."

The Duke Power guy shook his head and chuckled.

Before he turned on the juice, he watched Don attach a single white electric cable to one of the breakers. Didn't say a word while Don did it, which was high praise among workmen. Afterward he nodded down toward the other end of the coiled cable, which Don had attached to a junction box with a quadruple outlet.

"Hundred feet?" asked the Duke Power guy.

"Hundred and fifty," said Don. "I won't tell you how many extension cords I'll be running off this thing."

"Good thing, cause I don't want to know."

"It'll be code before the inspection." In other words, I won't let you get in trouble for hooking me up with the wiring in this condition.

"I seen one of these jobs once," said the Duke Power guy. "Lath and plaster walls. Hope you ain't planning on saving the original plaster."

"I believe in drywall," said Don. "I'm renovating, not restoring."

"Have fun." And that was it. The Duke Power guy got him to sign off on the job and he was gone. Guys in suits would have done lunch and exchanged business cards and promised each other a golf game.

The cable trailing behind him, Don carried the junction box up the stairs to the ground floor. The basement access was in the apartment on the north side, by far the nicest of the units the house had been cut up into. The stairs led into the biggest kitchen, with a massive table that might have been the finest piece of furniture left in the house, if not for all the initials carved in it. Then there were two bedrooms off the narrow hall that led to the parlor in front—again, the largest of the parlors in the house. Don set down the junction box in that room, plugged a six-outlet power strip into it, and then plugged a worklight into that. He flipped it on and the room was filled with a harsh white light. The words from Genesis passed through his mind as they always did at such a time. Only it was Duke Power, not God, who said Let there be light. God didn't bother much with light and dark anymore, Don figured. It had been a seven-day contract with no warranty. He finished a day early, collected his bonus, and walked away clean to let somebody else live with what he'd made. That's how Don looked at God, at least for these last few years.

Now that he had light, it was time to divide the firmament. Actually that was his dad's old joke, to call furniture "firmament." "Word doesn't have any other meaning that anybody knows of," he used to say, "so I can assign it to any meaning I want." So it was furniture that Don moved, pulling it all up against the outside walls of the north parlor so it was out of the way. The cheap and filthy wall-to-wall carpet wasn't worth saving, so Don had no qualms about taking his utility knife to it and baring all of the floor that didn't have furniture piled on it. The floor underneath was what he expected— a badly beaten-up hardwood floor so solid and well made that it couldn't be replaced today at any cost. This place had been built right.

He rolled up the huge piece of old carpet and carried it outside and laid it on the grass next to the curb. Then he backed the truck up onto the lawn so he wouldn't have to carry his tools so far. It took him about a dozen trips to get all the sacks and boxes of hardware in. He plugged in the cordless tools to freshen the charge.

Three things were left in the back of the truck—the garbage can, the workbench, and his cot. The cot had to be last and the workbench was the heaviest thing, so he pulled out the huge Rubbermaid garbage can he had bought that morning and carried it around the outside of the house.

He picked a spot near the back door. The really massive pile of trash would be established at the front curb where he had left the carpet, of course, but he had to have a place to throw leftover food and any dead animals he might find in the house; whatever would rot needed to be in a can with a lid.

It was a hot afternoon, and all the carrying and walking had given him a light sweat. It felt good. So did the shade of the house and the tall looming hedge that cooled and scented the air and made the carriagehouse next door invisible. And at the end of the tall part of the hedge, there stood an old woman leaning on a rake, her white hair done up in a ragged bun that left strands wisping around her head like a halo, her face creased and cracked from a hundred suntans. A neighbor. And from the bright eagerness of her eyes, a talker. It was starting. But Don was raised right. He smiled and said hey.

"Hey yourself, young man," said the old woman. "Y'all fixin' up the old Bellamy house or tearin' it down?" Her accent was pure hillbilly, all Rs and twang.

"House ain't ready to die yet," said Don.

At once the old woman called out to somebody invisible behind the high hedge. "You was right, Miz Judy, the landlord's gonna make this poor feller fix up the Bellamy house!" She turned back to Don. "I hope you don't think a couple of locks on the doors are going to make you safe. Strange people go in and out of that house. It's a nasty place!"

What was she doing, trying to scare him into going away? That made no sense. The neighbors should be glad somebody was trying to fix it up.

An old black woman now emerged from behind the hedge, leaning so deeply into her cane that Don wondered if she even had a hip. This must be Miz Judy.

"I'll bet you four bits, Miz Evvie, four bits says he's bought the place hisself."

So the white woman was Miz Evvie. But of course those were names they called each other. Don knew better than to call them by name until he was given the right name to call.

"Don't be silly," said the white woman. "People with money never do the work theirself."

Don hated to take sides. He remembered the story of the Trojan War in high school and how it all started because poor Paris got himself trapped into judging which goddess was most beautiful. Never get in the middle of arguments between women, that was the main theme of Homer, as far as Don ever cared—it was the only lesson that seemed to apply to the real world. These two old bats weren't exactly Athena and Aphrodite—or was it Diana? Didn't matter, it wasn't going to be a beauty contest. Don was the only one with the answer to their bet and while he didn't expect a war to start, he had a feeling that he was about to get himself roped into a lot of unwelcome conversations later. Oh well, couldn't be helped. His mother would come back and haunt him if he wasn't polite to old ladies.

Directing himself to Miz Evvie, Don shook his head sadly and said, "You made yourself a bad bet, ma'am. I own the place, or I will as soon as we close."

Evvie turned to Judy and pounded the rake into the grass a couple of times. "Damn all! Damn upon damn!"

At which Miz Judy seemed to take great offense. "Don't you go swearin' at me like some cheap hillbilly whore!"

"Gladys told you, didn't she!" said Evvie. "You're a cheater!"

"I never said Gladys didn't tell me, now, did I?"

"It ain't sportin' to bet on a sure thing!"

"I don't know what you mean by sportin'," murmured Miz Judy. "I'm having fun!"

They were so caught up in their argument that they seemed to have forgotten all about Don. Maybe they wouldn't be such bad neighbors after all—not if they did all their talking to each other. Don touched his forehead in farewell and made his way back to the pickup.

The Black & Decker Workmate wasn't all that heavy, really. He routinely carried loads of lumber or masonry much heavier and more awkward. What made it weigh so much was that he carried with it all the days and weeks and months of work that lay ahead. Sometimes that bench seemed like his best friend; he knew just how to use it, how it held things for him. And, like a best friend, sometimes he hated looking at it so bad he wanted to throw it out a window. Carrying it in meant the job was really going to happen and it made him tired.

He brought it into the north parlor and set it up in the middle of the room where the overhead light would shine down over his left shoulder as he worked. He leaned on the bench and surveyed his new quarters. The jumble of furniture would be gone in a day or so. The room was the largest space he'd had to work in since he started doing old houses. The bare floor brought the warmth of wood to the room. Out the front window he could see the carpet lying between the sidewalk and the street and it looked like progress to him.

The door leading to the entry hall stood ajar but because of a slight angle in the hanging it had creaked half shut every time he passed through it, so it still blocked his view of the front door. That was going to be a constant annoyance, having to open and close that door or walk around it all the time. So Don took out a screwdriver and popped the pins out of the cheap hinges. It was a sure thing this door wasn't part of the original house—no doubt this space had been an arch when the house was first built, and the door was installed only when the place was cut up into apartments. As soon as the door was off the hinges the place looked better. The space flowed better.

Don carried the door out to the sidewalk and laid it down on the carpet. Before, it had been just a carpet lying by the street. Now, with a door lying on it, it had become a junkpile. On another street the neighbors might have objected, but here it meant that somebody was taking trash out of the derelict house. That had to be a welcome sight to the neighbors.

He was about to go back in when a Sable pulled up at the curb right in front of the new junkpile. It was Cindy Claybourne. She got out of the car in a smooth motion that Don found attractive precisely because it did not seem designed to make men watch her do it. It was more like she'd been bounced out of the car and hit the ground walking.

"I'm glad I caught you here!" she said. "Hard to get in touch with somebody who's got no phone."

"Not really," said Don. "I'll be here, mostly."

"That's what I thought." She glanced at the door and the roll of carpet. "Already clearing things out?"

"Just my workspace," he said. "I don't do the hauling. Cheaper to have it done and get the junk out of my way."

"Well, I'm sure you can guess why I came by."

"Closing set?"

"Since there's no bank involved and you're willing to trust the last title search, there was no reason for delay. Our lawyer fit you in tomorrow morning at nine, if that's a good time."

"Fine with me."

"I mean, if that's too early . . . "

"I'm up at dawn most days," he said. "Don't like wasting daylight."

"Oh, right," she said. "I guess it'll be a while before they get the power hooked up."

"Duke Power came today," said Don. "But I'm not using the house wiring so I still need daylight."

She nodded. Their business was done, but she was lingering. And truth to tell, he wasn't all that eager for her to go. She kept looking at the house, not at him, and so he said the obvious thing. "Want to go inside?"

"I don't want to interrupt you if you're busy."

"Done all I'm going to do today." Which wasn't true, exactly, so he corrected himself. "Except do a tour of the bathrooms, see which fixtures look to be usable maybe."

She grinned. "Can I come along on the tour?"

"Not exactly what most women look forward to on their first date," said Don. Then he wondered what she'd make of his joke. And then he wondered whether he was joking after all.

"Don't fool yourself," she answered him. "Since women clean ninety percent of the bathrooms in America, we are endlessly fascinated with how the fixtures are working."

Don thought of how he had insisted that he was going to clean all the bathrooms in the house because no wife of his was going to have to kneel down and clean up any spots where maybe he splashed when he was peeing, but then one day he caught his wife down on her knees scrubbing the bathroom he had cleaned the night before. After that he gave up and left the job to her and just tried to aim straight. He figured it wasn't that his wife liked doing the job, it's that she felt like no man could be trusted to do it right. Never mind that Don was the meticulous one in the family. Must be a woman thing.

He didn't speak of any of this to Cindy, though. Nothing more pathetic than a divorced man who can't stop talking about his exwife. Or was he a widower? When your exwife dies, does that count? Only if you still loved her, Don decided. Only if you grieved. And he was still too angry with her for that. The one he grieved for was his baby. Why didn't they have a word for a father who'd lost his child?

All this reflection only took a moment or two, but he realized that the hesitation had been obvious to Cindy and she was beginning to laugh off her request and excuse herself.

"No, no," he said. "I'll be glad to take you on the grand tour of the plumbing."

She searched his face for a moment. He knew what she was looking for—some sign of interest on his part, some reassurance that his hesitation was not because he didn't want to spend time with her. He had no idea what that sign would be or whether he gave it. He just turned toward the house and said "Come on" and when he got to the porch she was right behind him so whatever she was looking for she must have found it.

Each of the downstairs apartments had its own bathroom, but the tubs were sludgy and filthy and the sinks had the streaking and wear that spoke of constant leaks. He'd leave the water off in those bathrooms, except maybe for the toilet in the north apartment, which would be the one most convenient to his workspace. He showed Cindy how there was no warping or staining of the floor around the toilet, so it wasn't a leaker. "I'll probably have to replace all the rubber parts in the tank, but that's no big deal."

She nodded, but he could see that she didn't much care for the brown gunk that lined the dry bowl up to the old waterline.

"That's not what you think," said Don. He pulled a rag out of his pocket and wiped it away. Didn't even take much rubbing. "I think it's a kind of mildew or something that grew when they left the water standing here for a few years." He tossed the rag on the floor.

"I don't envy you your job," she said. "It looks to be hard and sweaty and unpleasant."

"Wouldn't trade for yours, either," he said. "Having to be nice to people all day."

She laughed. "That just shows you don't know me."

"What, you aren't nice?"

"I'm legendary in my office as a real estate terrorist."

Don was puzzled. How could she stay in business if people didn't like her?

"No, no, don't get the wrong idea," she said. "I'm always cheerful and polite. But when it matters I say what I think—cheerfully and politely."

"And you're in sales?"

"It doesn't require any skills," she said.

"Hardest skills of all."

"You think?"

"I work in wood, I know what I'm getting. I can see the grain, I can see the knots."

"People aren't much different," she said with a shrug.

"Harder to read."

"Easier to bend."

Cramped together in that bathroom, neither of them willing to lean against anything because it was so dirty, they were so close together Don could feel her breath against his shirt, against his face, could smell her, a light perfume but behind that, her, a little musky maybe, but the womanliness of her almost hurt, it took him so much by surprise. He hadn't been this close to a woman in a long time. And not just any woman, either. He liked her.

"You bending me?" he asked.

She smiled. "You feeling bent?"

He knew it as if he was in a play and the script said *They kiss*. Now was the time for him to bend over—not that far, really—and kiss her. He even knew how it would feel, lips brushing lips, mouths melting softly against each other, not passionate but warm and sweet.

"Better check upstairs to see if that bathroom has a usable shower," he said.

He could hardly believe he said it. But in fact, while he was standing there looking at her and wanting to kiss her, his mind had raced ahead: I can't hold this woman close to me, I'm dirty and sweaty and I need a bath, she'll be disgusted. And then he thought: Even if the water got hooked up right now, there's probably not a shower I could use here. And so he blurted out the next thought and the moment passed.

But it was a real moment, he could see that from the amused little crinkle in her eyes. "Sounds like you care about keeping clean, Mr. Lark," she said.

"Live in a truck long enough, a shower is like a miracle," he said.

She laughed. "A miracle with a drainhole." Then she brushed past him and led the way out of the tight hot bathroom.

Upstairs, the three apartments were smaller than the downstair ones, and they all shared a bathroom. Even when the house was first cut up into apartments it would have been an old-fashioned, cheap arrangement. By the time the house went vacant, it must have been hard to find anybody willing to put up with sharing. The bathroom was at the end of the hall, right at the back of the house.

Don guessed that originally the back stairs had been there, narrower than the wide front staircase, and when the bathrooms were put in that staircase was taken out and the plumbing was run up through the space where it had been. Modern people needed toilets and showers a lot more than they needed a stairway for the kids to get down to the kitchen without being seen by guests in the front room. So the back stairs wouldn't be restored.

This shower still had a curtain hanging in it, spotted with ancient mildew but not disgusting. And the tub was pretty clean, not even as dusty as he would have expected. No sign of leaks in the tub; he'd be able to use it as soon as the water was hooked up and he replaced the rusted showerhead.

"This where you're going to put the Jacuzzi?" asked Cindy.

"No, I'm going to keep it simple up here. I'm making the back of the south apartment into the master suite and the fancy stuff goes there."

He didn't even have to squat down to look at the toilet. A big crack in the bowl and serious waterstains around the base of it were all the information he needed.

"Toilet doesn't look good?" she said.

"It ain't a toilet anymore," said Don.

"What is it?"

"Sculpture."

She laughed. "I can see it on a pedestal downtown in the Arts Center."

He liked her laugh. He wanted to listen to it again. He wanted to see if that moment would come again, when he'd actually want to be close to a woman, when the memory of his wife would disappear and he could see Cindy Claybourne as herself. "Listen," he said, "you want to meet sometime, not in a bathroom?"

"I don't know, I was just thinking that you bring a special *je ne sais quoi* to the discussion of plumbing fixtures."

"OK, how about dinner in a place with really nice sinks?"

"The bathrooms at Southern Lights really have character," said Cindy.

Don had taken his wife there the first time they went out to eat after the baby was born. He didn't think he could go there without picturing that baby seat on the floor beside their table, the little face in repose, breathing softly as she slept. He quickly ran down the list of restaurants that he had gone to with clients but not with his family.

"Cafe Pasta," Don said. "Art Deco."

"I'll go there, but only if you promise to share the sausage appetizer with me so both of us have garlic breath."

Again she stood in front of him, looking up at him, smiling, and this time he seized the moment, reached up and touched her cheek, bent down and kissed her lightly, so lightly it was almost not a kiss, more of a caress of her lips with his. And then again, just a little more lingering, lips still dry. And a third time, his hand now around her waist, her mouth pressing upward into his, warm and moist. They parted and looked at each other, not smiling now. "I was just thinking that there's more than one way for us both to have the same breath," said Don.

"Who's bending who, that's what I'd like to know," said Cindy.

"Bet you say that to all your clients."

"After we close tomorrow, you're not a client," she said. "In fact you never were—you were a customer."

"So what will I be when we go to Cafe Pasta?"

"A gentleman friend," she said.

He liked the sound of it.

"When?" she asked.

"I'm not the one with an appointment book," said Don.

"Tomorrow night?" she asked.

"Shower won't be running by then."

"Come over and use mine," she said.

That startled him. It sounded like a come-on, and not for anything he thought of as romance. "No," he said, perhaps too sharply. "Thanks, but let's just make it Friday, OK?"

"If it's Friday we'll have to make a reservation."

"You're the one with a phone."

"Glad to do it," she said. She led the way out into the upstairs hall, and as she preceded him down the stairs, she said, "By the way, my offer to let you use my shower—that's all it was. I'm not that kind of girl."

"Good thing," he said, "cause I'm not that kind of guy."

"I know," she said. As if she liked that about him. Maybe she wasn't looking for the alpha baboon after all.

At the front door she stopped and held up a hand. "Don't walk me to my car," she said. "I'd just want you to kiss me again and we wouldn't want to give the neighbors anything to talk about."

"Fine," he said. "See you in the morning."

"Come by my office and we can drive to the closing together. The lawyer's on Greene Street downtown and it's hard enough to find one parking place, let alone two."

"Eight forty-five," said Don.

"Nice doing business with you," she said with a grin. Then she bounded down the stairs and walked across the lawn. He stood in the open doorway and watched her all the way to the car, watched as she got in, started it up, and drove away. And then just stood there a while longer in the open door.

6

Lemonade

Without a building permit or title to the house, Don had about reached the limit of work he could do. Yet he wasn't interested in sitting around the house the rest of the evening, and he had no place he wanted to go. He had long since learned that movies and books were either stupid or not. If they were stupid, it made him impatient and angry to spend time with them. If they were not, then they had the power to unlock emotions that he had no desire to face again. Work was the solution, and so work is what he did.

If he couldn't do anything with the house, there was always the yard. This being North Carolina, anything that you mowed became a lawn, so under the deep scraggly weeds on the property there was a lawn just waiting to be uncovered. It took all his extension cords to get his Weed Eater out to the front of the property, and there was no way he'd get it all the way to the back, but anything he did would be an improvement. Maybe he should have bought a gasoline-powered machine, but he didn't like carrying flammable liquids around with him.

The afternoon had turned hot, and he was soaked with sweat by the time he finished with the front and side yards and as much of the back yard as he could reach. He was also covered with flecks of weeds, most of which he was probably a little bit allergic to, so he itched as well. What a great job to do when you've got no shower, he thought. As he coiled up the cords and put everything away inside the house, he tried to decide whether he should go get a shower and then put on some of his dirty clothes, or go do a laundry while he was still so filthy that touching clean clothes would only get them dirty again. It was getting on toward dusk when he locked the front door and headed for the truck.

"Hey! Hardworkin' man!"

It was the old white woman from next door. She was standing behind their picket fence, holding a plate with a checkered cloth over it.

"Look at this!" she said.

Dutifully he went over to the fence and waited for her to pull away the cloth with a theatrical gesture. It was a loaf of hot fresh bread, and even though he was more thirsty than hungry, and too hot to wish for anything but cold food, there was no resisting the yeasty smell of the stuff.

"I don't know why that smells so good to me," he said. "My mother never baked bread."

"Jesus had to tell us not to live by bread alone because if we had our druthers we'd try," she said. "We also got stew, which I know is too hot to sound good to you right now, but you need something to stick to your ribs. And we got lemonade."

"I'm in no shape to be decent company, ma'am," said Don. "There's no water working in the house yet and I'm filthy as a field-hand."

"I've sat at table with fieldhands before," she said, "and there's nothin' to be ashamed of in it. Now don't give me no argument. I seen you lock that door, so you can't pretend you ain't done working for the day."

"I just couldn't put you out." He almost told her that he had to get some laundry done, but stopped himself in time—the mood she was in, she'd snatch the laundry right out of his hands and insist on washing it herself.

She raised a quizzical eyebrow. "If I ever seen a hungry man it's now, so what are you afraid of, that we'll talk you to death? Maybe we will, but we won't make *you* talk, so you can just shovel in the food and pour lemonade down your throat and pay us no heed, we're used to that since we hardly listen to each other anymore."

Don laughed in spite of his effort to keep a courteously sober face.

"There," she said. "Besides which, if you got no water in that house then you sure as hell need to pee."

That was the clincher and she knew it. She turned her back on him and was halfway to the house before he'd straddled his way over the fence. "Beg pardon, ma'am," he called out to her, "but I'll go around the back way so I don't track this mess through your front rooms."

She called over her shoulder. "I'll have the back door open before you get there, unless you run."

He didn't run and she was as good as her word. If the bread had smelled good, the smell in the kitchen should probably have been a controlled substance. The black woman—Miss Judy?—was sweating over the stove, but she smiled at him as he came in though she didn't have a free hand even to wave.

"I hate to put you to so much work," he said.

"We were going to eat no matter what," she said. "And we were going to have to cook it ourselves, too, so you didn't cause us to do a thing we weren't planning to do anyway. Now go wash those arms up to the elbows, boy, and maybe wash your face while you're at it."

Once he saw the dainty guest towels, he had no choice but to scrub his face and neck and hands and arms for fear that if he didn't wash well enough, he'd mar the perfect cleanliness of the towels. And while he was at it, he took them up on the offer of a toilet. He had a copious bladder but its capacity wasn't infinite, and he was glad when he was done because he could stop thinking about how his first kiss since his wife left him was in a bathroom during an inspection tour of the plumbing fixtures. *This* bathroom might have been romantic; the other one should have been condemned. But the ways of love are hard and strange . . . he had read that somewhere, in one of those books he ended up wishing he hadn't read.

When he got out the kitchen was empty of people and the pots and pans were empty of food. He had brushed himself off on the porch, but he was still embarrassed about coming in to the dining room, what with the carpets and the plush upholstery.

"Don't be shy," said the white woman, who was pouring lemonade from a sweating silver pitcher into three tall glasses.

"You're going to have flecks of grass and weeds wherever I sit."

"Then it's a good thing we know how to clean house, isn't it," said Miss Judy. She had just set down the tureen of stew and was folding up the dishtowels she had held it with as she carried it in. "Let me see your hands."

He walked in and dutifully showed them, palms and backs. He half-expected her to demand to see his neck and behind his ears, but instead she picked up a huge serrated knife and told him to slice the bread. "It's fresh so slice it thick."

Don was good with tools and he got the knack of working with hot bread on the first try. A smooth back and forth, but only light downward pressure so you didn't mash the soft part of the bread. Before he had a chance to ask where to stack the slices, Miss Judy had one of the bread plates right to hand and he flipped the slice deftly onto it. A moment later three thick pats of butter were melting into the bread, and the same happened with the next two slices.

Only when they all sat down did Don get a chance to glance around the room. The china was elegant and fussy, and so were the knickknacks and doilies on every surface in the room, but the overall color scheme and style of furniture were not exactly grandmotherly. It was so plush in red velvet and mahogany that it looked for all the world like a bordello. Naturally, he kept this observation to himself. Maybe this was the only decorating style that could be agreed on by a white woman whose accent made her from Appalachia and a black woman who had the eastern flatlands in her speech.

"It occurs to me," said the white woman, "that you never mentioned your name."

"I think the introductions have been lacking all around," said Miss Judy. "I'm Miz Judea Crawley."

Ah. So "Miss Judy" was definitely a name for only her housemate to use. She'd be either Miz Crawley or Miz Judea to him. He took a guess, deciding on the more affectionate title. "I'm honored, Miz Judea. I'm Don Lark."

"And this is Miz Evelyn Tyler," said Miz Judea.

No correction, so his use of her first name had been acceptable. He smiled at the white woman and said, "Honored to meet you, Miz Evelyn."

"Don Lark," said Miz Evelyn. "What a lovely name. Like the first birdsong of morning. Dawn. Lark."

She said the words as if they were music. Don found it disconcerting. What had been a source of schoolyard teasing now sounded charming. Maybe he had finally grown into his name.

"I got to say, you ladies take neighborliness farther than I ever saw before."

"Then it's a sad world," said Miz Evelyn, "because we've hardly done a thing."

"Folks can't be too neighborly," said Miz Judea.

That was a philosophy that Don knew wasn't true, at least not for him. And while he knew it was ungrateful of him, for the sake of the next year's work, he had to lay down some boundaries. "I got to tell you, ladies, I'm not a very neighborly kind of guy. I'm sort of . . . standoffish."

They glanced at each other. "That's all right," said Miz Judea. "Standoffish is fine."

Miz Evelyn chimed in cheerfully. "In fact, that's sort of what we—"

"Hush, Miss Evvie," said Miz Judea. "That's for later."

For the first time it occurred to Don that maybe there was more here than gregarious old ladies giving a lesson in kindness and manners to the whippersnapper working next door.

Miz Judea lifted the lid off the tureen and steam rose up into her face. She sat a little straighter, closed her eyes and breathed it in. "You smell that?" she asked.

Oh, yes, he smelled it.

"What does that smell like?" she demanded.

He didn't even have to search for an answer. "Like I've died and gone to heaven."

"Don't just smell it, Miss Judy. Serve it!"

Don would never have said anything, but he felt the same impatience. Even after a hard day's work, food always seemed like just another duty, shoveling in something out of a grease-spotted paper sack. Today was a day of unexpected pleasures. And in this case, it wasn't even a forgotten pleasure. Nobody in Don's family was really much of a cook, and certainly nobody on his wife's side. That wasn't just sour grapes after she left him, either. She managed to simultaneously undercook and scorch Kraft macaroni and cheese, and once he opened up a lunch she packed for him and found potato-chip-and-mayonnaise sandwiches. He'd almost gagged. It made him appreciate his mother's very, very plain cooking. His mother always acted as if Chef Boyardee spaghetti was maybe a little too spicy.

The stew heaped high on the ladle and Miz Judea served it without spilling a drop. She passed him his bowl. He waited as the other two bowls were served, while steam and the smell of pepper and beef and spices he'd never heard of rose around his face. Finally they each were served, and since nobody was taking a bite they must be waiting for him, as the guest, to begin. He picked up his spoon and dug in.

Miz Judea laid a hand on his arm. "Don't forget to give thanks."

He almost thanked them again, before he realized what they meant. It made him feel stupid, since he'd said grace every day as he was growing up, and he and his wife had seen to it that they raised their daughter with prayers at meals and every night before bed. But for the past couple of years, there'd been nobody to pray with and, more importantly, nobody he much wanted to pray to.

The ladies bowed their heads. "Dear Lord, for this food we give thanks," said Miz Evelyn, "and for this strong young hardworking man who earns his bread by the sweat of his face. Bless him to be smart enough to get the hell out of that house before it eats him alive."

Don wasn't the only one startled. Miz Judea gave a little cry and apparently kicked Miz Evelyn under the table, since she gave an equally sincere cry in response. "Evvie!" said Miz Judea.

Miz Evelyn steadfastly kept her eyes closed and intoned with all deliberation, "A. Men."

"Amen, you silly old tart," said Miz Judea. "Say amen yourself, young man."

Bewildered as he was, Don had nothing better to say. "Amen."

"Now eat before she says something even stupider," said Miz Judea.

Don was grateful to obey. The food was good, but there was an element of craziness about them both—no, call it simple strangeness—that disconcerted him, precisely because they didn't seem crazy at all. They seemed like his kind of people, earthy yet elegant, gracious yet plain. He liked them. They were generous. They were funny. But when it came to the Bellamy house, they were, in fact, loons.

The conversation stayed on safe subjects through the rest of dinner—how the Bestway on Walker Street was the only survivor of an onslaught of supermarket takeovers that brought in the big boys and drove out the small ones; how outraged everyone was when they changed the names of a half-dozen of Greensboro's historic old streets so that Market and Friendly would have the same names along their entire length; how ironic it was that now they couldn't even remember what the old names had been . . . Hogarth? Hobart? Hubert? No, that was the vice-president back in 1952, wasn't it? Or was he the one who got impeached? It was like being caught up in a history lesson in which the teacher had no notes. They remembered everything, had lived through everything, and yet they remained hopelessly vague about all the public events.

But not the private ones. They could still tell stories about their childhoods. For Miz Evelyn it was Wilkes County, not quite the heart of Appalachia after all, but still true hill country. "I learnt to smoke before I turned five, and nobody whupped me for it either, they just slapped me when they caught me filling my pipe from some grownup's stash."

"My mama caught me smoking when I was ten and I thought I'd never walk again," said Miz Judea.

"And don't it beat all—*her* folks was tobacco farmers, and mine raised chickens and pigs and bad corn." Miz Evelyn shook her head over that one.

"Well, it wasn't cause my mama wanted me healthy, I'll tell you that, cause her whuppings took a lot more out of me than the tobacco ever did."

"I notice you don't smoke now, either of you," said Don. If either of them did smoke, the smell would linger on everything in the house, and there wasn't a trace of it.

"Well, that's Gladys," said Miz Judea.

"Can't abide smoke," said Miz Evelyn. "Can't say as how I blame her, either, all shut up indoors like she is. Not a breath of fresh air. Can't go filling it up with smoke now, can we?"

"Gladys?"

"I should say *Miz* Gladys but she's younger than us so, you know," said Miz Evelyn.

"My cousin," said Miz Judea. "Six years younger."

"She lives here?"

"Upstairs," said Miz Evelyn. "Bedridden, poor thing."

"But let's not talk about Gladys," said Miz Judea. "She *doesn't* like being the subject of talk."

"Says it makes her ears burn," said Miz Evelyn.

After dinner, they tried to make Don sit at the table or in the parlor while they straightened up and got Gladys's dinner tray ready, but Don insisted. "All the good company is out in the kitchen. You wouldn't make me stay alone in the parlor, now, would you?" So he ended up with a dishtowel drying while Judea washed.

"It's not right for us to make you help," she said.

"It's my pleasure," said Don again. "Beautiful china."

"Used to be in the Bellamy house," she said. "Used to be a set of twenty-four places, nine dishes per place. We've only got three complete settings left. The cereal bowls are always the first to go."

"I wasn't expecting to eat so well tonight, I'll tell you, or off of porcelain as fine as this, either."

"The laborer is worthy of his hire, that's what the Bible says. Though what that has to do with this I'm not sure, it just seemed the right passage to quote."

"If I'm the laborer, then what have you given me wages for?"

"If that was your wages, then we cheated you. You hardly made a dent in that stew."

"You made enough for a whole work crew! You'll be eating that stew for a week."

Miz Evelyn came back downstairs with Gladys's dinner tray. Don realized that she had carried up, not a bowl of stew, but the whole tureen, and now it was empty. So was the pitcher of lemonade, and there was nothing but crumbs on a plate where there'd been half a loaf at the end of dinner. Gladys couldn't have eaten it all, could she? How much appetite could a bedridden woman work up?

"Gladys is so crabby tonight," said Miz Evelyn.

Judea plunged the pitcher into the dishwater, and then the tureen, not even seeming to notice the fact that Gladys had already almost polished them both, they were so completely empty.

"I'm not surprised," said Miz Judea. "Wouldn't you be?"

Miz Evelyn spoke confidentially to Don. "She's on a diet."

At once Miz Judea rounded on her. "He doesn't need to know personal things like that about her, Miss Evvie. You *are* talky tonight, aren't you?"

That seemed unfair to Don—it was Miz Judea, after all, who had told him that Gladys was bedridden. Don didn't like it when the two of them crabbed at each other. Especially the names they called each other—names his mother had taught him never to use even with his friends, let alone with women. So Don changed the subject to the one that he knew they couldn't resist.

"You ladies have been talking around something all night and never quite hitting it on the nose. Now we're about done with the dishes and I'm heading back over to the Bellamy house. My house."

His plan to stop their argument worked, except that it focused Miz Judea's scorn on him. She rolled her eyes. "My house, did you hear him?"

"Well, it ain't ourn."

"Ours."

"Oh, you're the one to correct my grammar."

"I'm the only hope you got of not sounding like a hillbilly whore."

"What *about* the house?" Don said, again trying to stifle the argument.

Suddenly the two of them grew quiet. Miz Judea put the dripping tureen in the dish drain. "You just let that dry by itself," said Miz Judea.

"I can dry it," said Don.

"You're tired and I don't want that tureen in your hands when you hear what Gladys said."

Apparently they had no idea Don wouldn't be hanging on every word that came from the mysterious Gladys.

"It's those locks you put on the doors," said Miz Evelyn. "They're *strengthening* the house." She said it as if this were an appalling idea.

"That's the idea," said Don. "I've got all my stuff in there."

"But you just can't," said Miz Evelyn. "The house was finally beginning to fade, don't you see? Any time now, the termites was going to get in and . . . oh, Miss Judy, he's just not listening."

"Yes I am."

Miz Judea laid a hand on his arm. "What Miss Evvie is trying to tell you is that it's out of the question for you to renovate that house."

"I'm sorry, ladies, but it's too late. That house isn't a historic site and I've got all my money tied up in it."

"You said during dinner you haven't closed yet," said Miz Judea. "You can still get out of it."

"But I don't want to get out of it. It's a beautiful old house, strong and in better condition than it looks."

"That's what we're telling you," said Miz Judea.

"Just let the house die a natural death," said Miz Evelyn.

They were definitely crazy.

"He thinks we're crazy," said Miz Judea.

"No I don't," said Don.

"And now you're lying." She was smiling when she said it. "But we're not crazy, and you've got to stop repairing that house. It's very dangerous for you to go on."

Don had no idea how to take this. If they weren't two little old ladies in a decaying neighborhood of Greensboro, North Carolina, this could very well be a shakedown. "Are you threatening me?"

"No! Not us!" cried Miz Evelyn.

"You'll just take our word for it," said Miz Judea with the finality of a gradeschool teacher.

"Ladies, I'm grateful for the meal you fed me, and I hope we'll get along as neighbors while I renovate the house, but I got to tell you, every penny I have in the world is sunk into that place. I'm going to fix it up and sell it."

Their eyes grew wide and they looked at each other in horror.

"Sell it!"

"Oh, Miss Judy, he's not even going to live in it himself, he's going to find some unsuspecting family and . . . "

"It's wrong of you to do that, Mr. Lark!" said Miz Judea.

This was too much craziness for him. And what made him most uncomfortable was that he felt downright ashamed of being so rude as to disbelieve their heartfelt warning. They had been generous to him, and he wasn't complying with the simple favor they asked in return. And what was his real reason? He hadn't signed anything yet. He could walk away. And the only reason he wouldn't was because it would make Cindy Claybourne think he was a flake.

Wait a minute! The *only* reason? It was none of their business, that was the biggest reason, and it was the perfect house for him because all it needed was him and his skill and vision and labor to make it a beautiful place to live, to give it some meaning again. Just because a trio of nutcases lived next door was no reason to feel bad about getting such a good deal and maybe even starting a relationship with a nice woman after all these years. A good dinner didn't entitle them to *that*.

Don folded the damp dish towel. "Ladies, I'm sorry, but I got a lot of work to do tomorrow and I better get to bed."

He took a couple of steps toward the door, but at once Miz Evelyn laid a hand on his arm and slipped in between him and the door. And when she spoke, her voice was strange. "You don't have to leave so soon, do you, Mr. Lark?" She played with the fabric of his sleeve.

She was flirting with him! She was somewhere between eighty and eight hundred years old, and she was playing the coquette. He didn't know whether to laugh or flee.

"Let him go, Miss Evvie, you're making a fool of yourself."

She let go of his sleeve at once. But she didn't stop trying to keep him. Her face brightened and she turned to Miz Judea.

"I know! Why couldn't we let him have *this* house to sell?"

"Will you just think for a minute, Miss Evvie? He doesn't sell houses, he fixes them up, which this house doesn't need. And even if it did, what about Gladys?"

"Ladies, I don't want your house. I've got *my* house over there."

"You think it's your house," said Miz Evelyn. She was still arguing, but she was also moving out of his way so he could leave.

"I'm going to make it my house by my own sweat," said Don. "And when I fix up that eyesore it's going to increase the value of the whole neighborhood. I have no idea why that bothers you, and I'm sorry it does, but . . . "

The sink was drained and Miz Judea's hands were dry. She came over to him, shaking her head, and began to push him gently out the door. It took some quick action on Don's part to get it open before she pushed him through it.

"No need to apologize," she said. "You do what you got to do. Just remember—that house gives you any trouble, you come ask us."

Don found himself on the back porch of the carriage house, the screen door shutting in his face. The two old ladies crowded each other in the doorway, each trying to speak one last word to him, make one last plea.

"We used to live there, you know," said Miz Evelyn. "Back in 1928 till Gladys fetched us out in '35. We're very, very old. We *know* what we're talking about."

"Just ask us whatever you want, whenever you want," said Miz Judea. "Now go on over there and sleep as well as you can!"

That was the last word. Miz Judea closed the door and left him on the porch with the moths and mosquitoes. Only then did he realize that he was still holding the dishtowel. He thought of knocking on the door but couldn't stand the idea of having them think he had had second thoughts. So he draped the dishtowel over the porch railing and walked around the house. He didn't swing himself over the picket fence—he knew better than to try even minor athletic feats in the dark, not when he was this tired. Instead he walked out to the curb and studied the dark Bellamy house. The nearest streetlight was partly blocked by leaves that shifted in the breeze and the moon was flitting in and out behind the clouds, so the house kept changing as he watched. Changing, but it remained unchanged. The lines were clean, the structure sound. If the work he did today somehow made the house stronger, he was glad of it. That was as mystical as he was going to get.

He took out his key, unlocked the front door, and walked carefully into a room only somewhat lit by the streetlamp. He found the hanging worklight by feel more than sight, then followed the cord with his hands to the switch about four feet down. The light was blinding at first, and even when his eyes got used to it, everything in the room still looked oddly shadowed because the worklamp hung so low and kept swinging and twisting a little. The pile of furniture against the far walls looked especially forbidding in the strange light.

Don walked back to the front door and locked the deadbolt, then pocketed the key.

His cot was leaning against the south wall, the bearing wall that divided this room from the stairs. He took it down and unfolded it in just a couple of moments, then unrolled his sleeping bag and flung it out over the cot. It was warm enough tonight that he'd sleep on top of it, but cool enough that he'd stay in his clothes. He sat down on the cot, pried his shoes off his feet, emptied his pockets onto the workbench, then switched off the light and lay down on the bed.

But now he couldn't sleep, tired as he was, full of food as he was. He could only lie there and listen to the breeze moving the leaves outside and the cricking of the crickets and the small sharp sounds of the house contracting as the night cooled it from the outside in. What did these women think this house *was*? They said they'd lived here back in the late 1920s—but how could that be true? Segregation was strict then, and the chance of a neighborhood putting up with a black woman and a white woman keeping house together . . . unless they weren't keeping house, except in the sense of being housekeepers. Had they been servants here? Had something nasty happened? The owner murdered his wife or something? And now they had convinced themselves it was the house that was evil, and not the people they worked for.

What am I doing? Making up lives for these people. How can I possibly do that when I can't even make up a decent life for myself?

"Crazy women," he murmured.

Making me crazy. That's what he couldn't say out loud. I've slept alone in so many derelict houses now, and here I've let a couple of old ladies give me the willies. Well, it wasn't going to go on. The worst thing in the world had already happened to him. He had lost his daughter, lost his wife, and then buried them both. He wasn't going to get scared of house sounds. If any of them got too obnoxious, he'd find the source of the creaking and with a few long wood-screws he'd quiet it down again. This was his house, or would be by this time tomorrow. It was also a good house and he was going to make it better. If there was something wrong with the house, he'd heal it. When it came to houses, he was the physician. By the time he was done, the old ladies would come over for a tour of the place just like everybody else and they'd ooh and aah about how gorgeous he'd made it.

Or else they'd sit there in their house and stick pins in a doll with "Don Lark" scrawled on it in crayon. He didn't really care which.

He rolled over on his side and did what he always did to go to sleep. He imagined rooms and estimated the dimensions and calculated the floor area and the wall area in order to figure out the cost of carpet and wallpaper and how much wainscoting he'd need and . . .

It never took long. He slept.

7

Squatter

Don didn't like dreams because they were even worse than his real life. Either they were meaningless, uncontrollable fantasies, or they were memories, which in his case were just as uncontrollable and fraught with unbearable meaning. And they came night after night. He woke up with them, sometimes as often as an old man with prostate trouble, and it had gotten to the point where during some dreams he knew the whole time that he was dreaming, that he'd soon wake up, that it was either unreal or too far in the past to change. Even knowing that, he couldn't stop the dream, couldn't even stop it from frightening him or enraging him or grieving him all over again.

Maybe it was anticipation of the closing next morning that made lawyers come to mind as he lay asleep. In his dream he sat across the desk from Dick Friend, who had a reputation in Greensboro as the lawyer nobody wanted to mess with. The lawyer you wanted on your side, if only out of fear that if you didn't hire him your opponent would. Don came to him as a man with some money and respect in the community. He heard himself explaining his whole story, ending as it always did: I want my daughter back. She's not safe with my exwife.

And then Friend, beetle-browed and dominating, explained to

him that as long as the mother hadn't been charged with any crime, the courts would have little sympathy with him. "Hire a private investigator, get evidence on her." As if he hadn't tried it. The pictures he got didn't prove anything, the police said, and unless he could let them know when she was going to do a buy and they could get the seller, they weren't interested. He spent almost ten thousand dollars finding that out. "Just to mount a serious case will mean bringing in experts. And when you lose, the appeals cost more and more. This can break you, Don."

"It's worth it."

"Not if the expenses of the suit cost you so much that you can no longer prove that you can provide for the child, or even keep up your child support payments."

"Which she uses to buy drugs."

"Which you can't prove. The weight of presumption in favor of the mother is enormous."

"But there's a chance."

"There's a chance the moon will fall into the sea with a gentle splash," said Friend. "But is it worth betting on?"

"My daughter is worth betting on," said Don. "Get her away from that woman, Dick."

Suddenly a loud creaking sound made Don and the lawyer both turn around and look toward the door. It swung open, but there was nobody there. A thrill of fear ran through Don. From being a memory, this was turning into a weird fear dream. Come on, Don, why do you put up with these dreams? Wake up now, before you end up imagining the car smashing into the concrete and the babyseat rocketing forward through the windshield and headfirst into the cement.

Don opened his eyes. He lay on his cot in the parlor of the Bellamy house. The wind had died down outside. The house was still.

And then he heard it again, the creaking step. It wasn't a normal house noise. It was someone walking on stairs.

Don sat up and reached for his shoes in the dark. If he had to run—toward someone or away from them—it'd be easier with his shoes on. Another stealthy step, another, and then another. In the dim slanted light he found his flashlight and his favorite hammer, the one his exwife called "The Singing Sword" back when they still liked each other. Massive, long, it would make a formidable weapon. Against anything but a gun.

Armed now, Don decided to give the intruder a chance to get away. Who needed confrontation? As long as his tools were undisturbed, there was no harm done, except for whatever they did to a window or his new deadbolts in order to get into the house. He turned on the flashlight and walked over to the foot of the stairs. As he suspected, it wasn't this main front stairway creaking. Whoever it was must be on the stairs up to the attic.

As Don started up the stairs, he called out loudly, "Whoever's in here, I'm unarmed and I'm not going to hurt you." Surely it was all right to lie to intruders in the night. And a hammer wasn't a real weapon, was it? "I just want you out of my house."

In the upstairs hall, he opened each of the doors and shone his light into every room. There were places to hide. He stepped in and looked into closets, behind beds and dressers. Nobody. Room after room.

"If you leave quietly, no harm done. I won't call the cops or anything."

The sounds had stopped. Wherever the intruder was, he wasn't moving now. Lying in wait? Or just lying low? Who should be more scared?

The sound of metal scraping on metal. It took a moment for Don to realize what it was. A shower curtain with metal hangers being drawn across a rod.

He headed straight for the bathroom at the end of the hall. The door was almost closed. If the intruder had a gun, Don didn't want to make an easy target. He stood up against the wall on the hinge side of the door and reached around to push the door open. No sound, no reaction from inside.

"Look, don't be scared, nobody's going to get hurt." He wasn't sure if he was talking to the intruder or to himself. He stepped away from the wall and, from a few paces off, shone the flashlight into the bathroom. Nobody was standing there, but the shower curtain was drawn, and when Don and Cindy were in there that evening, when they kissed in there, Don was quite sure the shower curtain had been open, bunched up against the wall. The curtain wasn't even hanging inside the old clawfoot tub. If water had been running it would have made a mess on the floor. He thought of the movie *Psycho* and wondered which part he was playing.

As he stood there, his feelings changed. The fear faded. Anger took its place. How dare somebody break into his house while he was sleeping there? And then hide in an obvious, stupid place like this? It was outrageous. He didn't have to put up with it.

This is how guys get themselves killed, he thought. Losing their fear and getting mad enough to act.

But he couldn't stand there all night waiting for the shower curtain to open by itself. So he finally took action. In four quick strides he was at the tub, reaching up, flinging aside the curtain, all the time holding the hammer at the ready in case he needed it to defend himself.

The intruder was there, all right, a woman in a scruffy dress, huddled in the far corner of the tub, staring up at him with wide, terrified eyes as she screamed, thus answering the question of who was more frightened. She screamed again, and Don stepped back, letting the hammer drop to his side.

"For Pete's sake, shut up. Nobody's going to hurt you," he said.

Her eyes followed the hammer as he lowered it. Her screaming subsided to a whimper, then to heavy breathing. But she still stared at him in wide-eyed fear. Immediately, male guilt settled in: I made a woman scream in fear of me, I've done something wrong. He tried to stifle the feeling—after all, she was the intruder here. Or was she? From the look of her she was a street person, homeless. Maybe she'd found some way in through a window somewhere, and had been using this house as a safe place to hide out. She wouldn't know that someone was finally buying the place. His voice must have come as more of a shock to her than her creaking footsteps on the attic stairs had been to him. And then he appears, throwing back the curtain, standing there with a hammer upraised in his hand.

"How did you get in here?" Don asked.

She looked at him in puzzlement. "I live here," she finally said.

So he was right. She was a squatter. "Maybe you did, but you don't now," he said. "How did you get past my locks?"

"I was already inside, of course," she said. She looked at him as if he were stupid.

"Then you had to have heard me working down there. Why didn't you just leave out the front while I was working in back? Or while I was cutting down the weeds in the yard? You could have gotten out any time."

She thought about this. "I don't have anywhere else to go."

"Come on, there are homeless shelters, lady. But this isn't one of them."

"I can't go there," she said.

He and his wife had gone with a church group to help serve dinner at a homeless shelter in Greensboro, back when his wife was still pretending to lead a normal life. Everybody at the shelter was on their best behavior—his wife included—but it still looked like a rough crowd to him, so he couldn't argue with this woman, couldn't assure her that she'd fit right in. The more he thought about it, he couldn't remember seeing any women at the shelter. Maybe it was just a shelter for men and there was another place for women. It should be easy to find out.

"I'll help you get there," said Don. "I'll give you a ride."

"No," she said, shaking her head adamantly.

Her stubbornness annoyed him. "What do you think, I'm going to let you stay here or something? How long would that last? I can see it now, I've got the house all finished, I'm showing it to people, I tell them, 'And here you have your own homeless woman who sleeps in the bathtub on the second floor.'"

The young woman laughed, but there was a hysterical edge to it. Don didn't want to be harsh with her, but he couldn't just leave her in the tub, either. "Come on, don't make me call the cops."

"Don't make me go," she said. "Not tonight."

That was the most terrible thing a woman could do to a decent man: look vulnerable and ask him for mercy. If he refused her he'd be denying all his instincts as a provider and protector. Fortunately, Don understood this—he'd better, after all the books about women and men that he read back when he was trying to salvage his marriage. So he wasn't going to act on his natural impulses, he was going to do the sensible, rational thing. Though she really didn't look dangerous; it wasn't as if he had anything to fear from her. "Do you realize what you're asking?"

"Don't make me go tonight, that's what I'm asking."

That was disingenuous of her, and the way she looked away from him showed that she knew it. She wasn't asking for just one night. How would anything be different in the morning?

"I don't need a roommate," he said.

"You won't even notice I'm here."

"I already did. That's why we're having this conversation."

She stood up warily, still hanging back, virtually sliding up the wall till she was standing. "I used to room here," she said. "Paid rent, the regular thing. In college. But nothing's gone right since then. The place was standing empty, I had nowhere else to go. This is my *home*. Please."

Her neediness almost hurt, it was so deep and real. But she was asking him to give up his privacy. For a total stranger, for the kind of person who hides out in abandoned houses. Though, come to think of it, wasn't he that kind of person, too? The difference was that he paid for the houses he hid out in. "Look, I'm sorry your life's been hard, but so's mine, and this is my house and I'm going to . . ."

Going to what? What could he tell her? I'm going to hang out here alone and wallow in self-pity while you go out and live on the street again without a roof over your head because I can't find room in a mansion this size to . . .

"What *is* this, anyway? Is every woman in the world determined to stop me from . . ." And then he realized that he wasn't arguing with her, or even with his exwife. He was arguing with himself. And he'd already lost. He couldn't bear the idea of letting someone share a space with him like this, but at the same time he couldn't bear the idea of throwing her out on the street. Certainly not tonight. What was it, two, three A.M.? He was tired, he just wanted to go back to bed.

"Listen, you can stay tonight. OK? One night. Got that? Say it after me. One—"

She took two steps toward him—all the bathtub would allow— and spoke angrily right in his face. "Don't talk to me like that!"

"Like what?"

"Like I was your daughter!"

The words stung him. His daughter, his little girl. She would never have grown up to be someone like this, homeless, derelict, squatting in someone's filthy bathtub. He would have raised her to be strong and free and able to stand on her own two feet.

But maybe she got taken away from her father. Maybe she got taken away and raised by an incompetent, negligent . . .

No. He would not let her become his daughter in some dark place in his psyche. "If you don't like the way I talk to you, you're free to leave."

"Talk however you like then." The implication, from her words and from her defiant manner, was that she wasn't going, no matter what. And at whatever ungodly hour of the morning this was, Don wasn't going to ruin his own night by trying to throw her out. Either he'd have to use force, which he hated and which could lead to complications, or he'd have to leave the house to go get help from the police, and that would be even more galling, for her to stay and him to leave, however briefly.

"You can stay the rest of the night," Don said. "In the morning, get out. And make sure you don't touch any of my tools. If anything's missing, I'll call the cops and you'll have a new home in jail. Got it?"

His tough talking didn't impress her any more than it did him.

"You want me to say it after you?" she asked.

"This is where I live and work now," he said. "And I live and work alone."

That was the simple truth, and she seemed to realize that *this* wasn't bluster or anger or fear or waking up in the middle of the night. This was how he felt in his heart. There was no room for anyone in his life, and his house was his life, and that was that. She seemed to realize he meant it, because she said nothing.

But she didn't agree, either. He'd have this quarrel all over again in the morning, if she didn't kill him with a two-by-four while he slept. And if he never woke up, well, then the house *would* be big enough for the two of them.

Yet as he left the bathroom, her continued sullen silence infuriated him until he had to call out to her as he stalked down the hall, "You want to live in a rundown old house, you do like I did, start with a small one! Find yourself a rundown abandoned mobile home somewhere!"

That got a rise out of her. He was halfway down the stairs but he could hear her piercing angry voice just fine, despite the echoey quality from the bathroom. Was she still standing in the tub? "Would you be happy if I found an abandoned rundown cardboard box?"

He thought of answering, How about an old truck tire? but then he thought better of it. He was arguing with her like a schoolyard kid. Like siblings, waiting for Mom or Dad to come in and stop them. It put them on the same level, and they were *not* on the same level. He was a property owner, for heaven's sake, and not by inheritance or dumb luck, either, he had earned this house by the sweat of his body.

Back in the parlor, he sat down on his cot and started taking off his shoes again, cursing himself for a fool. That stupid girl didn't have to argue with him, he was going to flagellate *himself* into giving her a place to stay.

She called down the stairwell to him. "Didn't a friend ever give *you* a hand sometime in your life?"

This stung him. He knew how much he owed to the friends who staked him to start his life over. "You're not my friend!"

"Well how do you know who your friends are, till you see who helps?"

He didn't have an answer for that. Instead, he flung a shoe against the wall.

"What was that!" Her voice was fainter. Where was she now? What room did she sleep in? They had all looked equally dusty and unkempt to him. Well, wherever she slept, she should go and do it and leave him alone. He had a closing in the morning. Thinking of that made him wonder: What would Cindy think if she knew there was a woman sleeping in this house with him tonight? *That* was a complication he didn't need.

He flung the other shoe against the wall.

"What are you doing down there!" she called.

"Whatever I want!" he shouted back. "It's my house! Now shut up and go to sleep!"

He lay back on the cot and closed his eyes. This was so unfair, to throw the burden of her poverty on him. That was what taxes were for, wasn't it? So that the poor would go deal with an institution instead of asking so personally for help. And not even out on the street, like the other beggars. No, she accosted him here in his own house. What should have been a sanctuary.

Of course, she had thought of it as *her* house, *her* sanctuary, and from that perspective *he* was the intruder here.

Madness, all of this. Kissing Cindy in the upstairs bathroom, that was insanity enough for one day, wasn't it? Then dinner with those crazy old ladies next door and their warnings about the house. And now this homeless urchin—well, maybe she was too old to be an urchin—this homeless woman, anyway, daring to ask him, Can I stay? As if it were as easy as asking for a glass of water. Can I set up residence in your house and look over your shoulder and get under-foot all the time? Can I destroy your solitude and take away your privacy and force you to deal with another person all the time when all you really ask of life now is to be left alone? How could he be so churlish as to resent the request?

He muttered it again, like a prayer. "I live and work alone." But like all his prayers in recent years, it went unheard.

8

Closing

Don woke up shivering. He thought of crawling inside the sleeping bag in order to warm up—the faintness of the light told him the sun wasn't up yet, or at least the morning mist hadn't yet burned away. But he knew he wouldn't get warm enough to sleep, and besides, he needed to find a toilet. Not to mention a toothbrush and a shower. He thought of Cindy's offer yesterday. A shower, no questions asked, no strings attached. For some reason it reminded him of Esau taking a mess of pottage from his brother Jacob. He just didn't want to be that beholden to anyone.

This from the man who had taken a free dinner from the Weird sisters last night.

And thinking of last night reminded him of how he had spent a half-hour in the small of the morning. Was she still in the house? He looked around at his stuff, glad that by habit he had put it all in the one room. Nothing missing. Even the Singing Sword was where he had put it last night.

So also were his shoes. He got up and rummaged through his stuff until he found where they had fallen after he threw them against the wall. In the process he found his work jacket, which had once been leather but now had a texture and stiffness approaching granite. Rain and sun weren't good on the old cowhide.

He was at the door before he realized: I'm going to a closing. Which ordinarily wouldn't be enough to put him in a suit. But at this closing there would be a woman he had kissed yesterday afternoon, and maybe yesterday's workclothes and a jacket bought when Bruce Springsteen was singing "Born in the U.S.A." on every radio station wouldn't make the right impression.

Then again, it was the man in the workclothes that she had kissed.

This is how it starts, he told himself. You start trying to guess how she wants you to dress, and pretty soon you bring her home so she can tell you herself every morning, but never until after you've put the clothes on yourself, at which point she can say, "You're wearing that?" Am I really ready for this?

More to the point, am I really ready to say that I never want it again? Despite all his grief, all the pain, all the loneliness, wasn't the time with his exwife better than the time alone? Not every woman took away your child to go die in the road. Cindy was the kind of woman he should have been looking for the first time around. It wasn't marriage that had failed him, nor was it Don Lark who had failed at marriage. The only thing he needed to change was the person he partnered with. And why not try to impress Cindy? Why not try to look nice for her?

He found his suitbag and unzipped it. His court-appearance suit. Only he hadn't needed it for a couple of years and even if it didn't need to be cleaned, it sure needed a good pressing. And what would he do for a white shirt? He'd been putting off taking his nice shirts to the cleaner because where would he put them when they came back? Even if he got them folded, they'd suffer, jammed into a bag.

He rezipped the suitbag. Instead he pulled out a cleanish t-shirt and a pair of briefs that didn't have any particular odor and headed outside.

He stopped and locked the deadbolt, then paused to think. If he locked the door, she could still get out the way she came in. Whatever the route was, she probably couldn't get any of his really expensive equipment out of the house that way. Nobody invited her here anyway, did they?

Halfway to his truck, he had second thoughts. She was already inside when he put on the locks, hadn't she said that? And just because she was squatting in his house didn't make her unworthy of normal human decency.

Back up on the porch, he unlocked the door and, leaning in, shouted up the stairs. "Hey! You! Whatever your name is! I'm heading for McDonald's to pee and get breakfast. Time to go." He'd feed her, then drop her off somewhere and head on out to the truck stop to get a shower.

She came to the top of the stairs. She looked even more forlorn in what must have been a spring frock in some bygone age, but now was faded, limp, sad. Like her hair. Like her tired expression. But she must already have been awake, to appear so quickly when he called to her.

"You go on. I'm fine."

"Look, when I lock the deadbolt, you can't get out unless you break through one of the windows."

She seemed distracted. "Really, I'm fine." He wondered if she was in a condition to understand what he was saying to her. Did she have some stash of drugs somewhere? Was she exposing him to the risk of arrest for having that sort of thing on his property? Don't be absurd, he told himself. It's not the homeless who are dealing and using.

His own full bladder reminded him of one excellent reason why she should leave the house right now. "What, do you pee in the sink or something? The water's not hooked up yet, the toilets don't flush. Haven't you noticed this?"

Her face darkened. A flush of anger? Or embarrassment? She walked out of view.

Don stepped farther inside the house, to the foot of the stairs. He shouldn't have spoken so crudely to her. Would he ever have spoken so bluntly to Cindy? "Look, I'm sorry." The way Don was raised, you didn't talk about toilet things with ladies. When had he stopped following that rule? "When you've had a kid you learn to talk about bodily functions." Still no answer from her, but he didn't hear her footsteps walking away, either. "I didn't mean to embarrass you."

Her voice came from directly above him. "Please just go on. I'll be fine."

He stepped up onto the third stair, where he could look up and see her leaning over the railing. "I can't lock you in here. What if there was a fire?"

She leaned over the railing. "Then leave the door unlocked. I'm not going to steal anything."

She had addressed one of his fears directly, so he might as well answer as plainly. "Everything I've got in the whole world is here."

"Me too," she said.

"But you've got nothing."

The words seemed to sting her. "Yeah. And except for all your stuff, same with you." Her eyes were dark with anger. And then she was gone, walking away from the railing. A moment later he heard her footsteps on the attic stairs. Fast now, clattery, not the stealthy creaking tread from last night.

Sorry if I offended you.

Again he closed the front door. Out of habit he already had the key out, poised to lock the deadbolt. He wasn't going to trust her to protect his stuff, that's what the lock was for. That's how he did things.

His own words came back to him. If there was a fire, and she couldn't get out, if she died, then his locking of this door would have been murder. Like murder, anyway, even if it wasn't the fullblown crime. What's the worst that could happen if he left the door unlocked? She could get some streetliving buddies to come over and help her steal all his stuff. There was nothing there that he couldn't buy again. And if she robbed him, she'd have to move out, so he'd be rid of her. Worth a few thousand dollars to get rid of her without a fight? Probably not. Worth it to remain the kind of man who doesn't throw out a homeless woman, who doesn't lock her in an old aban-doned house? Yes. That was reason enough.

He carried his shirt and briefs down the porch steps. On his way to the truck he caught a bit of motion out of the corner of his eye and looked over to see Miz Judea clipping the hedge while staring right at him.

Not clipping the hedge after all. Clipping the air near it.

Where was Miz Evelyn? Ah, there she was. Peering around the

hedge, between the leaves and Miz Judea's arms. Ashamed to be caught spying, apparently, as she ducked back out of sight. But Miz Judea wasn't ashamed. She just kept on gazing at him, cold as you please, clipping the air.

What were they looking for? He didn't have any secrets for them to uncover—nothing they'd learn by watching him go in and out of his house, that was for sure. Or was that business with the hedge-clippers a warning? Get out of that house or we'll come after you with garden implements!

I'm surrounded by women, he thought. One upstairs, two—no, three—next door, all conspiring to take away my privacy, all wishing I'd just go away and leave this house to them. And where am I going?

To see another woman who might very well have her own plans for doing away with his privacy and getting him out of this house. But at least she wanted to give him something in return.

He got into his truck and headed straight for the truck stop. He wasn't that hungry and he really needed to wash off the dirt and sweat of the day before. He also needed to do a load of laundry—it would have been really nice to have a clean shirt this morning. But there wasn't time to get everything through all the washing, rinsing, and drying cycles before the closing.

There were only a couple of cars at the realty. Don pulled in next to one of them before noticing that it was Cindy's Sable. If he believed in omens, he supposed that would have to be considered a good one. Getting out of the truck, however, his door swung wide and tapped Cindy's door a little, and when he closed it he saw that a bit of the Sable's paint was on the rim of his truck's door, and there was a nick on Cindy's door that didn't rub off with his finger. What would that mean—if he believed in omens?

The realty wasn't officially open, it was so early, but there was an agent inside. Don knocked on the door. The agent didn't look up. Don knocked again. The agent raised a wrist, pointed to his watch, and then look down again. If Cindy was inside, she wasn't where Don could see her from the door. Maybe she was in the bathroom.

Don waited a moment, considering how important it was to get in right now. He had some phone calls he needed to make before they left for the closing, and why should he go down the street and feed quarters into a payphone when he could sit inside the office of a realty that was going to make some money from him when he forked over his check at the closing this morning? With the flat of his hand he struck the door three resounding blows.

Now the agent looked up angrily, saw it was still him, saw also that he was raising his hand to strike the door yet again, and rose to his feet so quickly his chair rocketed back against the desk behind his. He charged to the door, his face turning red, and unlocked and opened it. "We don't open till nine o'clock!"

Don knew not to answer an angry man directly. "Is Cindy Claybourne here?"

"Does it look like she's here?"

"Her car's in the parking lot."

"She walks home," said the agent.

So that's how she kept that girlish figure. Must be a good agent, too—all the neighborhoods within walking distance consisted of very nice houses on large wooded lots with winding lanes. Don had built several of those houses, back in an earlier life.

The man had been as helpful as he intended to be. "Now I've got work to do, if you don't—"

"She wanted me to meet her here so we could ride together to a nine o'clock closing downtown."

Don knew the magic words: Closing. Ride together. No matter how annoyed, a decent agent wasn't going to queer a colleague's sale. And this guy was a decent agent.

"Sure," the guy said grudgingly. "Come in and wait." As Don came through the door, the agent held out his hand. "Ryan Bagatti. I sit at the desk next to Cindy's."

To Don it sounded like grade school. I sit at the desk next to Cindy's. "Lucky," he said.

Bagatti rolled his eyes. "She should have been here to let you in herself."

"Maybe I'm earlier than she expected," said Don. "You're pretty early yourself." He also noticed that Bagatti had apparently not been sitting in his own place or Don would never have seen him from the door. Bagatti stopped at the desk he'd been sitting at, but only long enough to exit some program on the computer and return the chair to its place. Then he led Don back to Cindy's desk, offered him Cindy's chair, and sat down in his own, glum behind his professional smile.

"Think Cindy'd mind if I used her phone?" asked Don.

"Cindy's real accommodating, if you know what I mean," said Bagatti.

One of those. Macho pinhead who flirts with Cindy to her face, then pretends behind her back that he's had an affair with her. Don toyed with the idea of entering the fray—are you the agent in her office that she calls Tiny?—but decided that would do Cindy more harm than good. "It's only local calls," said Don.

"Be Cindy's guest," said Bagatti. "Everybody else is."

This guy really needs to get beat up someday, Don thought. But not by me. Let it be some drunk who'll get six months for assault, suspended. If I once started beating on somebody, I don't think I could stop till I earned a solid manslaughter charge.

In his pocket address book, Don looked up the number of Mick Steuben at Helping Hand Industries. As he expected, Mick was already at his desk.

"Got a houseful for you, Mick."

"That you, Mr. Lark?"

"Who else?"

"How many rats living in the couch?"

"Five couches. Place used to be an apartment building."

"Oh, we moving up in the world."

"No rats, or at least if there are any they're real quiet and they don't shit."

"Man, I wish I'd married into that family."

"I'm closing on the house this morning so it won't be mine to donate till after noon."

"I'll get a crew together."

Helping Hand didn't officially provide a moving service.

Supposedly you had to have the furniture and appliances you were donating out at the curb. But Mick had figured out that when somebody was emptying a whole house, they weren't going to pay for a crew to haul everything out just so they could give the stuff away. So he had a well-known but unwritten arrangement with several contractors who worked with old houses, that he'd get some volunteers from his pickup crew to do the hauling, as long as the contractor gave his workers some pretty fair tips. That way the contractor saved money on the hauling, and Mick got a houseful of furniture and appliances that otherwise might have been sold or junked. This amounted to aggressive marketeering in the help-for-the-down-and-out trade. "Mick, you'd be dangerous if you ever got into a business with money and power."

"That's why God put me in this place," he said. "Seeya this afternoon, man."

Don pushed a button for another line and called the city to make sure they were really going to hook up the water today. He was still on hold when Cindy arrived. He hung up and stood to greet her.

She looked good, walking the length of the office, and her smile was dazzling. But he saw her glance at Bagatti, saw how her jaw tightened a little under the smile. He wondered how she'd play it—kiss him openly to drive Bagatti crazy, or greet him formally like any other client because it was none of Bagatti's business. There was no need to wonder. Cindy had class, and Bagatti was a bug. She greeted Don with a cool handshake. "Sorry I'm late," she said.

"I came pretty early," said Don, "but I hoped to exploit your free telephones."

"Putting together another deal in Taiwan?" she said. She opened the file drawer in her desk and took out a folder.

"You know how it is, trying to keep all the time zones straight," said Don. "But Mr. Bagatti here said that it was OK just to dial direct, the company would do anything for a customer."

"Haha," said Bagatti. "You only dialed seven digits."

"See you later, Ryan," said Cindy. "This way, Mr. Lark."

Outside the door, Don let himself laugh. "Never thought he could count to seven."

"He's a neanderthal, but he sells houses to a certain kind of clientele."

"When I got here he was sitting at somebody else's desk, using the computer."

"He's a snoop but we all know it, so nobody leaves anything confidential lying around. He thinks he's a real up-and-comer."

They were halfway to their cars. Don slipped his arm around her waist, feeling like a teenager daring to assert a relationship. And like a teenager, he got slapped down. He felt her twist away just a little.

"Sorry," he said, taking his arm back. What was wrong? Was she regretting yesterday's kiss? Or had she already noticed the nick on her car door?

"Let's take my car," she said.

That had been Don's intention, but now he wondered. "I can follow you, and that way you won't have to bring me all the way back here after the closing."

She had walked to her car door and was unlocking it. Don walked between their cars, positioned either to get into her passenger door or into his own driver's door. "Don," she said, "are you trying to avoid me?"

So what was he supposed to read into that look? If she hadn't just rejected his arm around her waist, he'd suppose she was looking at him with hurt and longing, that sort of dreamy-eyed look that he remembered very well from high school, the look that girls eventually realized they probably shouldn't use with guys unless they really meant something by it, because it had the power to make them hover but then they were pretty hard to get rid of. Come on, Cindy, which is it? But instead of having it out with her over the roof of her Sable on the way to a closing, Don decided discretion was the better part of valor and got into her car.

Once inside with the doors closed, she was full of businesslike talk about the closing, how the lawyer was so nice to fit them in before the start of his normal business hours; Don refrained from giving his opinion of lawyers and how "nice" they were, beyond saying, "No matter what time he fit you in, he's still charging you, right?"

She laughed. "I guess you've got a point."

By now the car was out on Market Street, heading downtown. It was a four-lane with no shoulder, but to his surprise she pulled the car tight against the curb and ignored the car behind them that honked and swerved around them, curses coming from the open window. She was too busy leaning over and kissing him deeply and passionately. Then, without a word, she took her foot off the brake and they pulled back into the flow of traffic.

"Nice to see you, too," said Don.

"Sorry if it seemed like I was blowing you off back in the parking lot," she said. "I just can't stand the idea of Bagatti—you know."

"I imagine he'd never let you forget it."

"So if he was watching, what he saw was a client making a pass and the ice princess blowing him off. Sorry."

"Fine."

But was it fine? She could have explained herself right then. Bagatti couldn't have heard. Instead she waited, she let him fret in silence until she decided it was time to let him off the hook. And even then, the kiss was her doing. Maybe she just wanted to be the one to decide when things happened between them.

Then again, what woman *didn't* want to decide that? Most of them simply waited until after the papers were signed before they took control of the schedule. Cindy was honest enough to get the reins in her hands right from the start.

"All I could think about all night was you," she was saying to him. "I told you I'm not that kind of girl, and that's the truth, but that doesn't mean there aren't times I wish I *were* that kind of girl."

It was hard to think how Cindy could have said anything better calculated to make a formerly-married-but-four-years-celibate man replace all conscious thought with pure adolescent horniness. "You shouldn't say things like that to a man about to see a lawyer."

"Oh, lawyers' offices aren't conducive?"

"Pure saltpeter."

She laughed. "Well, we need to keep our friendship on a loftier plane anyway," she said. "Since you're not that kind of boy and I'm not that kind of girl."

She knew exactly what she had done to him. And yet he couldn't quite believe that she was jerking him around. Maybe she was being completely open with him, saying exactly what she thought and not even caring about the consequences. How could you tell, when utter honesty and cynical manipulation would each account completely for the things she said and did?

Despite the warm-blooded prelude, the closing went quickly and smoothly. For the first time, Don realized that most of the time-consuming silliness with closings was caused by the bank. The whole thing was done before nine-thirty. The house was his. It should have felt good, and it did, but Don had no chance to relish it because all he was thinking about was Cindy.

What made sense would be to take her to the house and talk about his plans and get her talking about her life or whatever came up until it was time for lunch. How could it hurt to revisit the scene of their first kiss the day before? But that homeless girl was there and he just didn't want to have to explain the whole situation to Cindy. Not that she wouldn't believe him; it's how she'd judge him that mattered. Maybe she'd see him as compassionate, but that was hardly the truth, since he couldn't wait to get the girl out on the street. And it was just as likely that she'd see him as a wimp, a doormat. Which he probably was. But he didn't want Cindy thinking of him that way.

So the walk to the car was silent—the worst possible course of action, but how could he speak until he thought of something to say? Besides, she wasn't talking, either. What did that mean?

They got to the car and Cindy punched in the code that unlocked all the doors. "So the real estate part of our relationship is over, I guess," she said.

"I guess," said Don. What else could he say? And yet he knew that he had to say something, because she had just talked about their relationship and tied it to the word "over" and he knew she was asking him for reassurance—but reassurance of what? He had no idea where she wanted things to go. Or where he wanted them to go. So all he said was "I guess" and that was the worst thing he could have said because it sounded like he was agreeing that things were over.

She slid into her seat. He ducked down and got into his. She reached up to get her seatbelt. If he left things with "I guess" then it would be over between them before it had a chance to begin and it would be his own stupid fault. Yet a part of him was already acquiescing, already saying, Well, nice while it lasted, but you belong alone anyway, better to have an uncomplicated life.

Something inside him might think like that, but it wasn't the man he wanted to be. So, as she fumbled to slide the seatbelt into its latch, he reached down and took her hand and raised it up to put the seatbelt back in place behind her left shoulder. That put him face to face with her, and he kissed her. Letting go of her hand, he reached down and embraced her, pulling her close to him, holding her against him. It was a convincing kiss.

When it ended they did not let go. She nuzzled his cheek, then whispered directly into his ear, her breath tickling him: "So you're saying you want me even when I don't have a house to sell you."

"And you want me," he answered, "even when you're not getting a commission."

She nibbled his earlobe. "Aren't you afraid our relationship is already too physical?"

"Ask me that sometime when you don't have your lips in my ear."

"You planning to let go of me anytime soon?"

"I don't want to think that far ahead." He kissed her again.

"You think you can keep doing that while I drive?"

"The real question is, can you drive while I'm doing that?"

Then they burst into laughter and the embrace broke. "Welcome to high school," said Don.

"That's how it feels, isn't it? Does this make me your girlfriend?"

"Do you like me, Cindy? Yes, no, check one."

"But what is it I like about you, Don? The way you rip padlocks off houses? Or is it the way you look when you squat down to check out toilets?"

"It's the hungry way I look at you."

"Like a starving puppy."

"So you want some coffee? Breakfast? Lunch?"

"You men," said Cindy. "Always wanting the same thing."

"Food."

"I don't cook, Don."

"Then why am I so hot?" He couldn't believe he had said that. Was there anyplace for this relationship to go but into bed? Was that all that was driving him on, his long sexual loneliness? He didn't know this woman. Did he even want to?

He finally let go of her and faced forward, untwisting his back. "Drive," he said.

"Yes sir," she answered. She put her arm up on the headrest of his seat as she turned to see where she was backing the car. When she was out of the parking place, she shifted into drive with her left hand so that her right hand could slip down to play with the hair at the back of his neck. "I know a place that has great coffee."

"Fine," he said. Though he wasn't much of a coffee drinker. The last thing he needed was something that made him more jittery by day and kept him awake at night.

They talked about nothing. Real estate lore about nasty surprises at closings, about flaws in houses and how some sellers tried to conceal them from potential buyers, and they laughed together like old friends who already know all the real jokes. In the midst of laughing he realized that she had just driven past her office and was turning onto a road that he knew was purely residential. The place that had great coffee was hers.

He got out of her car and followed her to the porch of her house, a large brick nine-window federal with a deep, immaculate yard. A large house for a woman alone. She unlocked the door and he followed her inside. The living room was like a page out of *Southern Living*. There was no sign that a human being had entered the room since the decorator left.

"Have a seat," she said. "Unless you need to use the john. That's what I'm doing, I'm afraid." He heard her jog up the stairs.

He sat down, but then realized the john was a good idea and got up and wandered down the hall. A little half-bath with a bifold door that he could barely close when he was standing inside. There was a framed print above the toilet, a painting of a bunch of raccoons and a pink little pig with a mask over its eyes, and the slogan, "ONE OF THE GANG." He flushed, washed his hands, and came out into the hall. But instead of returning to the living room, as good manners required, he wandered into the large eat-in kitchen. It was as immaculate as the living room. No one cooked here. Cindy wasn't kidding.

He opened the fridge. Leftover takeout cartons and containers of juice and soft drinks. The freezer had some diet and no-fat desserts. He heard her coming down the stairs and decided not to close the freezer door. If he was going to prowl through her house, he wasn't going to pretend that he hadn't done it. "I'm in here."

"Can't keep a man out of the kitchen," she said.

He closed the freezer and reopened the fridge. "Restaurant doggy bags for breakfast?"

"Always tastes better the next day."

"Have I met a woman as lonely as me?"

"Solitary isn't necessarily lonely, Sherlock." She began an elaborate ritual of making coffee, starting with the beans. She had changed out of her business suit into a summery frock, which made her look younger at first glance, but then older, as he couldn't help but notice a little looseness and sagging in the arms, the wrinkles in the neck. He considered these features analytically and discovered that he didn't find them at all offputting. He came up behind her and ran his hands down her bare arms, then back up to her shoulders as he leaned down and kissed her neck.

"Do you want coffee or not?" she asked sternly.

"Don't much care about coffee," he said.

She turned around and kissed him and he held her, body to body. She was soft and yielding, and his hands discovered that there were no straps or elastics underneath the frock she wore. Her own hands were pulling his shirt out of his trousers, and then they were cool as they glided over the skin of his back, up to his shoulders. They parted, but only by an inch or two. "Screw the coffee," she said. "It's too much like cooking, anyway."

Where does this lead? thought Don. What next? He'd only slept with one woman in his life, and there had never been a love scene in the kitchen. Maybe if there had been . . . but that wasn't a line of thought he wanted to explore. He took her hand and led her through a swinging door into the dining room, then around into the living room. "Where are we going?" she asked. In reply, he sat down on the untouchable couch, tossed the pillows onto the floor, and pulled her down beside him.

"Here?" she asked. He could see that she was a little annoyed.

"Who were you saving this room for?" he asked.

"For me," she said. "To come in and see it perfect and not have to do anything to clean it up." The annoyance was in her voice now. He tried to kiss her. She turned her face away.

"Sorry," he said. "I just thought—"

"You just couldn't leave a perfect room undisturbed," she said.

"It wasn't perfect until you were in it," he said. "This couch wasn't perfect until you were sitting there." He took the hem of her frock and spread it out across the fabric of the couch, showing more of her tanned thighs, making her look as posed as a model. "The only thing wrong with the picture is me," he said. "I should be standing over there, in the entry, looking at you with longing. The unattainable beauty of Cindy Claybourne."

She laughed, but she had to turn her face away from him. Embarrassed? He got up from the couch, walked to the entry, and stood there leaning against the front door. She really did look sweet and young and lovely. Heartbreakingly so. "Cindy, are you as sad as I am?"

"Are you sad?" she said. "Right now?"

"The picture's too perfect. I don't want to spoil it."

She reached out her arms to him. "I want you to."

He knew he should walk into the room, sit down beside her again, take that frock off her, make love to her. That's what she wanted. That's what he wanted, too. Yet he stood there, trying to make sense of the woman, of the room. How she fit with the house. Why this room had to be so perfect. Why she barely lived in her own house, cooking nothing, touching nothing. Of course that probably wasn't true upstairs. For all he knew, clothes were strewn around her bedroom and her sink was covered in half-empty bottles and tubes. And besides, what business was it of his?

Yet for some reason he had to ask a question, one whose answer he didn't even care about, and still he had to ask. "Have you ever been married, Cindy?"

She looked at him for a moment, then lowered her arms. "Yes."

"Kids?" he asked.

"Does it look like it?" she asked, sounding a little defiant.

"Does what look like it? Your body? No."

"What, then?"

"This room looks like a place of refuge for someone who's sick of cleaning up after other people."

Why had he said that? It was a stupid thing to say, precisely because he was almost certainly right. She looked away from him, her eyes filling with tears. She swung her legs up onto the couch and hugged her knees. The skirt of her frock draped away so he could see the entire curve of her naked thigh and buttocks, and he was filled with longing to hold her, to please her, to take pleasure from her. But when she lifted her face from her knees, her eyes were brimming over with tears. So when he strode to the couch and sat beside her and put his arm around her and gathered her against his shoulder, it was not to make love to her, but to comfort her. "I'm sorry," he said. "I didn't mean to cause you pain."

"You didn't cause it," she said.

"I meant to love you," he said. "I wanted to try to love you."

"That was your mistake. You should have settled for making love to me."

"You do have children," he said.

"Three." She clung tightly to him, and he could feel her convulsive sob as she began to cry in earnest.

"What happened?" he asked, dreading the story, because he knew it would only make him think of his own loss.

"I left them," she said. "My shrink said it was because I was a caretaker child. My father ran off with his secretary when I was eleven and from then on I was the mom of the house while my mother worked. I cooked every meal, I cleaned, I did laundry till I hated my mother for being a lazy bitch even though I knew she was working her brains out to make ends meet and I hated my sisters and my brother because they wore clothes that had to be washed and left things lying around and complained whenever I asked them to help in any way and finally I couldn't stand it anymore. If I didn't get out

I'd kill somebody or maybe myself, so I married my poor husband Ray and we had three babies, pop pop pop, and there I was again, cooking and cleaning up. I realized I had only traded one house for another and I thought I'd go crazy. I loved my kids but I found myself one day holding a pillow and wanting to press it down on my baby's face so she'd just stop screaming for a half-hour so I could get some rest. Only I wasn't even tired. It wasn't sleep I needed. I took the pillow and put it in the garbage and then I took the garbage bag out to the garage and jammed it into the trashcan because I had actually thought of smothering my own baby, that's how crazy I was."

Don was sick at heart. He still held her, still felt her breath warm through his shirt, but all desire for her was gone. He knew it wasn't fair. She had stopped herself, hadn't she? She had faced a terrible moment of madness and had triumphed over it, but he knew he would never be able to get rid of the imagined picture of Cindy with a pillow approaching a baby's crib, and the baby crying, only it wasn't an infant he imagined, it was his own daughter when he last saw her, almost two years old, and it wasn't Cindy, it was his exwife. Just one more nightmare for him to remember when he woke up in the middle of the night.

Yet he still held her.

"Do you hate me?" she whispered.

"No," he said.

"I knew I had to get out," she said. "I loved my children, I could never hurt them, but for their sake and my husband's sake and my own sake I had to get out before I got carted off to the loony bin or I killed myself or whatever desperate thing happened that should never happen. So I left. And I went to a shrink. And I got my real estate license and worked hard to get enough money to buy a house that has a room for each of my children even though I know they'll never come to see me, I'll never have them living here with me, but I have a room for each of them upstairs, and a bed that's never had a man in it but it's made for a husband. You're a husband, Don. That's what you are. I wanted you in that bed with me."

His body wanted her; his hands wanted to slide down to the bare skin of her hip and seek the body under the frock. But his heart was no longer in this room. Desire wasn't reason enough to share his body with this woman. He could never love her as she needed to be loved. He had too many problems of his own, too many fears, too much history. What she had told him would be impossible to forget.

"Don," she said, "you have to forgive me."

I'm not a priest, he thought. I'm not Jesus. I can't even get forgiveness for myself, how can I get absolution for you? "You didn't do anything wrong," he said. "You gave up everything to protect your children."

"They'll never understand that," she said. "I left them motherless."

"Someday you'll tell them and they'll understand."

"You don't want me anymore, do you," she said softly.

"You don't need a husband to take you on that bed, Cindy," he said. "You need a father to tuck you into it."

She burst into sobs as he slid one arm under her legs, the other behind her back, and rose from the couch holding her. She wasn't all that small or light, but he was strong and it felt good to carry her up the stairs, to have the stamina to do it without panting for breath, without even feeling tired. It felt good to have some strength to give to someone who needed it. He carried her to the master bedroom, with its kingsize bed; not a feminine room at all, but a masculine one, a man's bedroom. No frills, a bold pattern in the bedspread, earth colors instead of pastels. He set her down on the edge of the bed. "Where do you keep your nightgowns?" he asked.

"Second drawer down, left side," she said.

"Take off that dress," he said. He took the top nightgown from the folded stack and brought it back to her. She sat there naked and forlorn, the frock tossed onto the floor. Her body was still sweet but he had no desire for her. He took the nightgown and gathered it around the neck, as he had so often gathered his daughter's tiny gowns and dresses, and slipped it over her head. She reached her hands up and he guided them into the sleeves like a child's hands. Then, as the nightgown dropped over her breasts and down to cover her lap, he turned down the covers of the bed. He picked her up again and laid her down on the sheets, helped her slide her feet down under the covers, then drew them up to her shoulder and tucked them in. Tears were flowing from her eyes onto her pillow. "Don't cry," he said softly. "You're a good person and you've done right." He kissed her cheek, patted her hand. "Don't go back to work today. You've earned a little rest."

"I've lost you, haven't I, Don, before I even had you."

"You didn't need a lover, Cindy, you needed a friend, and you've got one."

"What do you need?" she said.

"I need all the friends I can get." He kissed her cheek again. She raised a hand to touch his cheek. Maybe she was thinking of trying to kiss him like a woman. Maybe she was thinking of making one last try to get him in the bed beside her. That's how the moment felt to him, anyway. But she saw something in his eyes, saw something as she searched his face, and she didn't try to kiss him, just stroked his cheek and said, "You're too good for me."

"Not good enough," he said. "But sometimes you just have to let somebody cry herself to sleep."

He walked out of the room, down the stairs, and out the door, making sure it was locked behind him. He stood on the porch for a moment, looking for his car. But of course he didn't have one. Never mind. His truck was parked at her office, and it wasn't more than three-quarters of a mile to walk. A neighbor in a car was watching him as he walked down the driveway to the street. Don stared back at her defiantly. None of your damn business, he said soundlessly. The woman started her engine and pulled away from the curb. Don walked on down the street. It wasn't even noon yet, and maybe autumn had broken the back of summer, because the day was still cool and there was a breeze even though the sun was shining and there wasn't a cloud in the sky.

9

Helping Hands

It was hot inside the cab of his truck, and now that he'd worked up a little sweat walking in the sunlight, he wanted a drink of something. They'd put in a new McDonald's up at Friendly Center and a Coke would do as well as anything.

Cindy Claybourne. He ached with sympathy for her, and, to be honest, sympathy for himself as well. He remembered one of his contractors quoting an old saying: "Never eat at a place called Mom's, never play poker with a man named Doc, and never sleep with a woman who's got more troubles than you." Till today he never would have thought there could be such a woman. But now he knew. At least he had never even thought of raising a hand to harm his own child. At least he hadn't been the one to abandon her. He had done everything that he could do short of murder to get his little girl back. So no matter how much pain there was in thinking about her, he was better off than Cindy. Maybe.

He had come so close. To what, he wasn't sure. To sex, of course; he hadn't realized how much he missed that part of his life until Cindy Claybourne woke his body up again. But it would have been more than that, and when he chose to walk through her front door, it wasn't a roll in the hay he was looking for. Not *just* a roll in the hay, anyway. Turned out Cindy needed a friend a lot more than she needed a lover. But what did Don need? Was Cindy right? Was he the kind of man who was just naturally a husband?

Not to hear his ex-wife tell it. Whatever it was that Cindy thought, whatever it was that he himself had unconsciously wanted when he led Cindy to the couch in her living room, he was certain of this: He was not ready to get back into the whole marriage business all over again. The last time had only built him up in order to tear him all the way down to nothing. It wasn't going to happen again.

At the McDonald's drive-up, it occurred to Don that maybe the girl back in his house would like a Coke, too, so he ordered a couple of large ones. He thought of getting something to eat, too, but he wasn't hungry. Still working off last night's feed, probably. Maybe the girl was hungry. He should get her something. So he ordered a Big Mac and fries and only snitched a couple of them on the way back to the Bellamy house, and then only because the smell of them was so strong inside the cab of the truck even with the windows rolled down. That must be deliberate. They must have figured out a way to make the french fries give off a hunger drug that you absorbed through the nose.

When he got to the house, the Helping Hands truck was already backed right up to the porch, with a ramp stretched like a bridge from porch to truck. A couple of black guys made the ramp bounce as they carried a couch across. They were only a few hours early. The guys were coming back out of the truck by the time Don got up the steps.

"Hey," said one of them, which instantly branded him as the driver. "You the owner?"

"Mick got you guys going early," said Don.

"Yeah, well, your wife told us take whatever look good as long as we don't take any of your tools."

Wife? It took a moment for Don to realize that they couldn't possibly be referring to his dead exwife. The homeless girl must have let them in. It irked him that she would dare to pass herself off as his wife. But there was no reason to explain the whole business to these guys. "She did, huh?"

"Be nice when you get your water hooked up, won't it? You both lookin' like you could use a shower." The driver smiled, big and toothy. He knew he'd put Don down, and Don wasn't altogether sure it was without malice. But Don didn't mind, especially considering that the comment was true. His revenge, if he had needed any, was the way the driver and his assistant looked at the sweating cups of Coke Don was carrying into the house.

It was the assistant who spoke up. "You gonna drink both of those?"

"Just the bottom half of this one," said Don. "Already drank the top half. Where *is* my 'wife'?"

"In the kitchen," said the assistant. "Thirsty work out here."

"Sure is," said Don. "Wish the water was on, I'd offer you some."

"You cold, man," said the driver.

Don grinned at him. "I'll be back with something for you guys. I didn't know you were gonna be here, so I only got something for her and me, you know how it is. Less you want to finish mine." He offered his half-empty Coke.

They both held up their hands to ward it off. "No, no, just teasing, man."

"I'll get you something. Whatever you want."

"Nothing, man, we just teasing."

Don shrugged and went on into the house.

In the parlor he took a quick inventory, purely by habit—he'd never had the Helping Hands people take anything he needed, but his new "wife" was complicating things. All his tools were there. But something felt out of place. It nagged at him for a moment. Maybe it wasn't in the parlor. Something he'd seen outside? He'd check it later. He carried his half-drunk Coke and her full one and the bag of food into the kitchen. There she was, looking into the open cupboards. As soon as she heard him, she turned and took a step and touched the massive kitchen table.

"I didn't know if you wanted them to take this," she said. "All the other kitchens have cheap crummy furniture like landlords buy, but this one might have been here when it was a real house. Solid."

It was solid, all right, but had no other virtues to recommend it. Plain as a board fence, that's what it was. "House has to be empty," said Don. "I want everything gone." He slid the full Coke and the bag closer to her. The sight of her there, prowling through the cupboards, "helping" with decisions, infuriated him. He knew, in the back of his mind, that his rage was completely unreasonable. That she had had the full run of every cupboard in the house for months, maybe years, for all he knew. That he was mostly angry because of his frustration over the whole business with Cindy. Because for a few minutes today he had actually thought maybe he was ready to start looking for a wife, but the venture had ended in failure, and now this waif presumed to call herself by that title. As if a wife of his would ever be so hungry-looking, so ill-provided for.

I want everything gone, he had said, and now, with firmness, he added: "Including you."

She took a step back from the table. "Aren't you glad I was here to let them in?"

Might as well tell her the truth, personal though it was. "Not when you tell them you're my wife. My wife's dead."

She looked at him with disgust. "I never told them I was your anything. I found them opening the door and looking around and calling for Mr. Lark and I told them to come on in and get started and don't touch any of Mr. Lark's tools in the front parlor. If the place were cleaner they might have assumed I was your housekeeper."

Of course that's the way it happened. Of course they'd jump to that conclusion. He felt embarrassed at his anger. Now it seemed stupid to him. And yet some of the anger remained. She was still trying to destroy his solitude. If he couldn't have a woman like Cindy Claybourne, why did he have to put up with a girl like this? "I brought you a burger and fries."

"I'm not hungry," she said coolly.

"And a Coke. Drink it and go." He hated himself for being so rude. But this had gone on long enough.

"That was nice of you," she said. There was not a trace of irony in her voice. But that didn't mean it wasn't snide all the same.

"The 'drink it' part was nice of me. The 'and go' part makes me a scumbag." Might as well be honest. He knew he wasn't being noble here.

She shrugged, bent over the cup, and Don saw the brown liquid rise through the straw. After a moment's sip, she stood up, swallowing as if the Coke were the elixir of youth. "Oh, that was nice."

"Hot day," said Don. He looked away from her, toward the window, where daylight peeked through the boards. He thought of the bright windows in Cindy's house. Cindy's immaculate, unlived-in house. Who was the homeless one, really?

Don himself was never going to be anything more than a camper here, a temporary resident, a workman, a servant of the house. It was only the law that gave him the right to throw this girl out of her home. And no one knew better than Don how unjust and arbitrary and sometimes downright cruel the law could be. Don wanted the house to himself because that's what he wanted and he was ready to use the law to get his way no matter what it cost someone else. So how was he different from his exwife?

Maybe she understood his silence. Maybe she felt his ambivalence, his shame at insisting that she leave. "Listen," she said, "it's your house. You got work to do."

She sounded understanding. She was giving him permission to throw her out. But it didn't take away the sting of knowing he was the kind of man who would do it. Damn her for forcing him to discover things like this about himself. "You've got no place to go," he said.

She shrugged.

He thought of the empty rooms, wall after wall, floor over floor. He thought of the tragic emptiness of Cindy's house. "It's not like I'm using most of this space."

He knew she was using reverse psychology on him, but that didn't mean it wasn't working. He didn't want to be the kind of man who threw people out into the . . . well, not snow, but autumn, anyway. Onto the street. He thought about what that might mean for a woman. No money, no place to stay. Didn't a lot of these girls end up turning to prostitution just to live? And then to drugs so they could live with what they'd become? Did he want that on his conscience? He couldn't take advantage of Cindy Claybourne when she was so vulnerable, but he could send this girl out maybe to be raped, just because he preferred to be alone?

"I'd just get underfoot," said the girl.

"Yeah, but you could stay out of my way while I'm working, if you wanted to." He knew even as he said it, though, that she wouldn't. What he was doing would be interesting to her. She'd have to watch. She'd look over his shoulder. She'd drive him crazy. Maybe he could give her some money to get cleaned up, new clothes, get an apartment, get a job. But if he did that, he wouldn't be able to finish the house without borrowing.

"I might even be useful now and then," she said. "What if you had to run an errand but somebody was coming by to make a delivery or something?"

It was already starting. She was already trying to find a role for herself in his life.

"I can't hire you as an assistant," he said. "I don't have the money for that."

"I can fend for myself," she said. "I did before you came."

How *did* she fend for herself? Rummaging through garbage cans? Or had she already been turning tricks? He knew nothing about her. What was he getting himself in for?

"As long as I don't have to leave," she said. Pleading.

"But you *do* have to leave." She had to understand this. "When I sell the house you can't be here."

"Till then. Please."

The begging sound in her voice grated on him, shamed him. He couldn't stand holding someone else's future in his hands. It made him want to get shut of her just so he didn't have to feel her desperation, her subservience. "Don't ask me," he said. "As long as you don't ask me, I'll talk myself into letting you stay. But when you start begging it just makes me want to throw your butt on out of here."

She looked puzzled, maybe a little appalled. "Why should it bother you for me to ask?"

Because it makes me feel like The Man, and I'm not The Man, I'm just a guy. "Shut up and stay. Pick the bed you want to sleep in and tell the Helping Hands guys to leave it for you."

He felt sick at heart the moment he said it. He had given in to his own weakness and her need, and he should probably feel virtuous about what a Christian he was, but all he could think about was having somebody behind him all day, watching everything he did, expecting him to be chatty or even civil, both of which were way beyond his ability. He wanted to walk out of the house himself and just keep on walking. He'd been struggling with this ever since the last hope of getting his little girl back was gone. The longing to shuck off the last vestige of responsibility, to cease caring even for himself, and just go out on the street until somebody killed him or he withered up and died of cold or hunger, he didn't care which.

At least this girl wanted something. At least she wanted to stay here in this house. What did Don want? To be left alone. They couldn't both have what they wanted, and it seemed damned unfair to him that he, who wanted so much less than she did, was the one who couldn't have it. That his own sense of decency had been used against him. People without a sense of decency never got exploited like this. If his exwife or his exwife's lawyers or the judges in every court he pleaded in had had a sense of decency . . . but they didn't. Only Don was burdened with such an inconvenience.

You jerk, Don said to himself. Now you're whining to yourself that you're the only decent person in the universe. What a simp.

Disgusted with himself, Don stalked out of the kitchen.

Maddeningly, she followed him. As they walked down the narrow hall to the parlor, she asked, "I can stay?"

Unbelievable. Hadn't she been in the room when he told her to pick a bed? He stopped and turned so abruptly to face her that she almost bumped into him.

"What," he said, "can't you take yes for an answer?"

He had expected to tower over her, but standing so close he realized that she was taller than he had thought. The top of her head came up to his chin. She was so slight of build that it gave the illusion she was tiny.

She looked him steadily in the eye. "My name's Sylvie Delaney," she said.

He almost snapped back at her, Why would I need to know that?

But in fact he did need to know her name, if only out of simple human courtesy. "Don Lark," he said.

Her gaze never wavered. Brown eyes. "Thank you for letting me stay, Don Lark."

Her gratitude made him almost as uncomfortable as her begging. "Just leave me alone when I'm working. And don't touch my tools. Touch *nothing*."

She held up her hands as if she had just touched a burner on the stove. "Hands off. Like a crystal shop." She grinned.

He wasn't amused. She had followed him down the hall, she had embarrassed him, and now she was trying to joke him into smiling at her. He wanted to hit something, he was so frustrated. "Why don't I feel better? I felt guilty throwing you out, and now I feel stupid and angry about letting you stay." He turned away from her and slapped the wall. "When's the part where virtue is its own reward?"

Behind him, she spoke softly. "Let me practice staying out of your sight for a while."

"Eat the burger and fries before they get cold," said Don. He stalked on down the hall, feeling even stupider because now that she was respecting his need for privacy, the need itself seemed childish to him. He imagined himself as a little boy, running into his room and slamming the door, shouting I hate you, I hate you, leave me alone.

He stopped when he got to the end of the parlor wall and glanced back up the narrow hallway. She was still there, spinning down the hall toward the kitchen in little-girl pirouettes, touching the walls as she went. Between and behind the noises made by the Helping Hands guys carrying some big piece of furniture along the upstairs hall, he heard her intoning, almost singing, "Thank you, thank you, thank you." Then she suddenly stopped and pressed herself against the south wall, one arm up as high as she could reach, so the whole length of her body was touching the wall. "Thank you house."

She was as nuts as the women next door.

Well, what did he think? Why else would she be homeless? A college graduate, living in a boarded-up mansion full of corroded furniture? Of course she was a loon. And he had just given her permission to live under the same roof with him.

Not that he hadn't shared a house with a madwoman before. At least this particular loon, this Sylvie Delaney, had never looked at him with that blank stare that said, I know you're talking but all I care about is how am I going to score some more blow? So he was living with a better grade of lunatic.

He wandered out onto the porch. The Helping Hands truck was almost half full. He could hear the guys starting down the stairs with whatever it was they were carrying. He opened the door all the way and walked around it so he wouldn't be blocking their path. As he waited for them to get down the stairs, he glanced down at the dead-bolt he had put on, still shiny and new, and ran his hand along the smooth wood below it down to the old latchset.

The movers were at the foot of the stairs, stopping to catch their breath. He heard Sylvie's voice and stepped around the door to watch as she spoke to them. They were leaning on a huge bureau, which they had moved with all the heavy oaken drawers inside it. Trying to save extra trips up and down the stairs.

"Just so you know," Sylvie was saying, "my husband and I have decided you should leave the bed in the front corner apartment." She pointed up, indicating the room directly above the north parlor.

My husband and I. Don's blood boiled.

"Whatever," the driver said. "This is pretty crummy old stuff."

"You should look so good when you're that old," said Sylvie. "And we're keeping the big table in the kitchen back there. There's a Coke on it, if you want it before the ice all melts. And a burger and fries but they might already be cold."

"Hey, thanks," said the assistant.

"Oh, you think it's *your* Coke now?" said the driver. "Come on, let's go." They picked up the bureau. The door was wide, but the bureau barely fit through without smashing their hands.

When they were past him, Don looked back into the entry. Sylvie was standing on the first step of the stairway, draped against the wall again in some parody of a girlish pose. He glared at her. She winked at him, grinned, and then turned and ran up the stairs.

He made the conscious decision not to be angry. If he let her teasing get under his skin already, it was only going to get ugly and that wouldn't make either of their lives any better. He leaned his head against the edge of the door and took a couple of deep breaths. Behind him the Helping Hands guys were jockeying the bureau into position inside the truck. He looked down the smooth expanse of the door and then realized what it was that had bothered him before, when he first got back after the closing. The door was smooth.

There should have been ragged screwholes where he had pulled off the hasp to get into the house when Cindy first showed it to him and Jay. But there was no sign that there had ever been a hole in the wood. He looked closely. The holes hadn't been puttied and stained. The woodgrain was smooth, continuous, unbroken. All the way above and below the deadbolt.

He remembered what the Weird sisters had said about the house. A strong house. And getting stronger, with the work he was doing on it.

He tried for a moment to doubt his own memory, to insist to himself that the lock had been on the back door, or that he had drilled the hole for the deadbolt right where the screwholes had been. Wasn't that possible?

No it wasn't. He had noticed at the time that the screwholes were too widely spread to be covered by the deadbolt, and so he had drilled a little farther down, though still well above the original lockset. No, somehow this door had healed itself.

He looked over at the carriagehouse. There were Miz Evelyn and Miz Judea, on their knees in the front yard, digging dandelions. If they noticed him, they gave no sign.

Well what was he supposed to do now? Run screaming into the street? The house was strange or he was crazy, and he was betting on the house. But strange or not, he'd just closed on the deal and there was no backing out now. And it *was* possible that he was simply remembering things wrong. Your mind could play tricks on you, everybody knew that. You remember things one way but in fact it happened completely differently. That's all this was. Just a memory thing. He could live with that. He had only been spooked because of the crazy things the Weird sisters told him.

The city van pulled up to the curb, and Don walked out to meet the guy and lead him to the water meter. All he needed now was to have the new water heater installed and there'd be hot and cold running water in the house. Flush toilets and hot showers without having to go to McDonald's or a truck stop. Life wasn't all bad.

10

Tearing Up, Tearing Down

He couldn't accuse her of following him around the house, but that's what it felt like. Half the jobs he set out to do, Sylvie just happened to be waiting right there when he arrived with his tools. It always made him want to turn around and go find something else to do, but he couldn't work that way, ducking out of sight whenever she was around. Yet he couldn't bring himself to bark at her either. She always seemed so glad to see him. It must have been lonely here, hiding out in an empty house behind boarded-up windows. Maybe when the novelty wore off she'd leave him alone.

The water was hooked up and it was time to run the faucets to check for obstructions and leaks. Some fixtures he wouldn't even try—the cracked toilet would never have water in it again. But the upstairs bathtub, where he first found her, that one would probably end up being the one they used.

He caught himself thinking: We'll have to use this tub. It came too naturally, to think "we" instead of "I." And there was nothing wrong with it—as long as Sylvie was in the house, she was going to use the same tub and sink and toilet as him. So why not think of them as "we"?

Because that's how I thought of me and my exwife and our—*my* little girl. My child, my house, my tub. I'm alone here, despite the presence of this uninvited guest. And all the more alone because she's here, to make me say "we" and remember how empty that word is, what a nothing word, impermanent. How it evaporates and carries everything away with it.

There she was, doing situps in the hall outside the upstairs bathroom when he came up to run the water. So of course she quit and stood in the door, then at the foot of the tub as he turned on the cold water faucet.

"Oh, good, a bath," she said.

"Not till we get a hot water heater."

"Cold showers, then?"

"Whatever turns you on," he said. The faucet sputtered and knocked. Brown gunk squirted out, splashing all over his pants. She shrieked and backed up.

"It's just water and rust," he said. "You won't melt."

"How do you know I'm not the Wicked Witch of the West?"

"Because she was green."

"So's that stuff. Gross."

It was as gross as she said. Deep brown, a sickening color. Don stepped over and turned on the cold water tap in the bathroom sink. It did its own knock-and-sputter routine, and then choked out even nastier-looking gunk that splattered them both.

"Oh, this is an improvement, all right," she said, looking at her clothes.

"Nobody asked you to stand in here when I'm working."

She said nothing and he didn't look at her. The water wasn't getting any clearer in the sink or the tub. He didn't like the silence. But why should he let it make him uncomfortable? She needed to learn not to hover.

Instead of leaving, though, she broke her own silence. "You sure they didn't hook these pipes up backward?"

"It's just been standing in the pipes. Run it for a while, it'll clear out."

"Looks like the house has dysentery," she said.

"Don't use this toilet," he answered. "Look at the crack. I'm not putting water in it."

"Is there one I'm supposed to use?"

"Downstairs in the north apartment."

"Will the water look like this?"

"Till the pipes clear."

"If they ever do."

"Water heater should be hooked up tomorrow. Let it fill and heat, then we can bathe."

"Sounds indecent."

He looked sharply at her. She was joking, probably, but even so it was repugnant, having a woman so dirty and unkempt acting flirtatious. There was a reason people became homeless. In her case, it could easily be her bad taste.

He left the bathroom.

Sylvie called after him. "When do I turn this water off?"

"When it looks drinkable."

"I will never drink this!"

He was already halfway down the stairs, so he didn't bother answering. He didn't want to establish the precedent of shouting through the house. He could just imagine her screaming, "Don! Oh, Dah-ahn!" for the whole neighborhood to hear.

He went downstairs and turned on the toilet and sink in the bathroom he intended to use. Those and the outside hose were all he'd need, so there was no point in testing them until he had new fixtures hooked up to the plumbing. The drain in the downstairs bathroom sink was plugged up, so he did a little work opening the trap to drain into a bucket. A real stink. Wouldn't you know it. A mouse had gotten caught in the trap and drowned. But once it was cleared and reattached, the sink drained fine. Which was good, because in cold water with no soap it took three scrubbings before his hands felt clean again. He didn't put the mouse corpse in the garbage can in back—the last thing he needed was to attach that smell to anything that was going to stay around. Instead he flung it off the edge of the gully in the back yard. It flew ten yards out and twenty yards down, pitching lazily end over end as it fell, till it fetched up about halfway down the gully wall.

As he came back into the house, he knew there would be no more delaying it. He had to choose which section of the house to renovate first. Of course, ideally he would do the whole house at once. All the stripping, then all the breaking down of walls he didn't want to keep, then breaking open the rest of the walls for wiring and plumbing, phone lines, intercom, maybe lines for a computer network if he thought the money would hold out for a luxury like that. It was easier and cheaper to do each job for the whole house all at once. But that wouldn't give him a place to live while it was going on; and just as important was the fact that he needed the small payoffs of having finished this room and that room to keep him going.

Not the main floor. Couldn't do the north side upstairs, because that's the side Sylvie's apartment was on. South side upstairs, though, would be fun. Tear out the add-in walls, and it went from being two lousy bedrooms, a living/dining room, and a kitchen, to being two large bedrooms. They wouldn't do at all, of course, since they were too big to be practical and ended up wasting a lot of space. So he would open up the wall between them and put in a bathroom and two wide, deep closets. And in the back bedroom, which didn't have the fancy bay window the front one did, he'd open a ladder to a part of the attic, which he would make into a loft. In a house like this, every room should have individuality. No, more than that—it should have panache.

Armed with his prybar and a tough carpet knife, he went upstairs and began stripping the floor. It was a tough, durable carpet but it had been installed a lot of years ago, and under it the padding was a mass of decomposing filth. Dead insects made another carpet under that.

"How did all those bugs get under there?" Sylvie stood in the doorway.

Don stopped pulling the carpet. "What do you need?" he asked.

"Just curious. I've been walking on those bugs, I just wonder how they got there."

This was not science class, it was sweaty, nasty labor. What made it bearable was the trance of concentration he drifted into while his hands worked on. She had broken that, and for what? And after how many requests that she stay away from him? "I work alone," said Don.

Sylvie shrugged as if to say, Who, me? "So, I'm not trying to help you," she said.

"Exactly my point," said Don.

"All I did was ask how the bugs got there."

"The crawlers crawled, the wrigglers rigged. Now I've told you, let me work."

She looked angry for a moment, but then she backed away out of sight. Not for a moment, though, did Don imagine the struggle was over. She was a shmoozer. He was going to have to be rude to her again and again, just to get some peace, and he hated being rude for any reason. But this woman just couldn't keep a promise or follow instructions. What did he expect? If people like her had skills like that, they most likely wouldn't be homeless.

He got the carpet rolled up and tried to hoist it up onto his shoulder. He could have done a clean-and-jerk with more weight than this, but there was no good handhold on the thick carpet roll, so he ended up having to drag it. This got tricky at the door, where he had to bend it to get it out into the hall and down the stairs. For a moment he thought of calling Sylvie to help, but then realized that if he ever asked her for something, that would open the floodgate. She would be sure that he needed her and she would hover until the house was finished.

So he went back and forth from end to middle to end of the carpet, bending, pulling, bending more, pulling more, until it was finally out in the hall and headed down the stairs. From there it was a simple matter to drag it out the front door, off the porch, and out to the junkpile on the curb.

Coming back in, he glanced over at the carriagehouse. There on the porch sat Miz Evelyn and Miz Judea, eating delicate little triangles of cucumber sandwich with the crusts cut off. He imagined a huge bowl of bread crusts and cucumber peelings being carried upstairs to Gladys, who for all he knew was an omnivorous crocodile or a large fat sow, eating whatever slops came her way. They waved cheerily at him. He waved back, not cheerily.

Dismantling kitchen cabinets was always a pain. It was easiest, of course, to remove each piece as a unit, but not always possible.

Though the kitchen in the south upstairs apartment was a dark, narrow, makeshift affair, whoever installed the cabinets was apparently trying to make them tornado-proof. Don crawled into the cabinets every which way, removing every screw and nail that connected the cabinets to the back wall and to each other, but still they wouldn't come out. Finally he had to resort to the wrecking bar, and even then the cabinets didn't come away clean. Someone had replaced the lath-and-plaster walls with two-by-four studs and glued the cabinets directly to them, in addition to nailing and screwing them. Fortunately, the studs weren't structural, so it didn't matter if his wrecking bar chewed them to bits. By the time he had the last cabinet detached from the wall, the upstairs kitchen looked like a tornado had struck after all. Studs were broken, gouged, or sticking out like snaggle teeth. Didn't matter. He'd be taking them all out. He would entirely take down the new wall that separated the kitchen from the parlor, rejoining them into one room; the studs between the original timbers he would replace with new ones on 12-inch centers. Don's standard of sturdiness was even higher than that of the guy who installed the cabinets.

He'd never dismantled an upper-story kitchen before, and it was backbreaking work to get the cabinets down the stairs without dinging anything. He could have used another pair of hands and a strong back to help, but dammit, he worked alone.

Standing at the junkpile, which now looked like a madman's kitchen, Don wanted to go back inside and lie down and sleep. Wasn't this a whole day's work? Hadn't he done enough?

But it was only three in the afternoon, and he knew that the temptation to knock off early and take a nap or go for a walk would be with him more and more if he ever gave in to it. There was always another job to do. He had to put in at least eight hours no matter how tired he got. That was the rule. And most days he tried for ten. That's how he could get the house finished even though he worked alone.

That was the main thing an assistant was good for anyway. In Don's experience you usually ended up having to redo the assistant's work or supervise so closely you might as well have done it yourself. But having someone there, watching, was an incentive to keep plugging away. Didn't want to look like a slacker in front of somebody else. Don couldn't stand the thought that he might only be working for show, to impress someone or keep their good opinion. He worked for the job's sake, or for his own self-respect. And so he did not, could not lay off early, take a day off, or even call in sick. Who would he call? He had the sternest boss in town—breaks he would routinely give to an employee he never allowed himself.

Except there by the fence stood Miz Evelyn, holding up that metal pitcher with water beading on the outside so fast it looked like it was raining, all those drops forming, running down the sides, dripping off the bottom. Whatever was in that pitcher must be really cold. And even though it wasn't all that hot of a day, no more than eighty-five degrees, he wanted that pitcher right then with all his heart and soul. Enough to accept it from a crazy woman.

"Yoo-hoo!" she was calling. "Mr. Lark!"

He sauntered over to the fence, trying not to look too eager. She held out a tall metal glass, which was sweating almost as much as the pitcher.

"I've never seen a body work so hard," she said.

"Helps me sleep at night." He drained the glass almost in one draught. It was lemonade, just a little tart, not too tart: just a little sweet, not too sweet. It was a good thing neither of these ladies was his grandma. He'd have moved in with her long ago.

"You can take the whole pitcher if you want."

He wanted. "Thanks," he said, and now, drinking from the rim of the pitcher, he tanked it down so fast it gave him a headache. But the headache wouldn't last, he knew, while the lemonade rushed through his system so fast it caused sweat to bead up on his brow almost as fast as water had beaded up on the pitcher. The pitcher empty, Don wiped his mouth on the upper part of his sleeve, which was marginally cleaner than the forearms.

"Oh my," said Miz Evelyn.

"Sorry. I've got a working man's manners."

"Not to mention a working man's appetites."

He patted his stomach, which now sloshed with liquid. "Nice of you to share that with me."

"We're just glad that you came to see it our way."

Uh-oh. "But I didn't," said Don.

She gestured toward the junkpile. "It looks like you're tearing it all apart in there."

"Just clearing out the ugly stuff." She looked a little disappointed. "I'm going to knock down the added-in walls, too. But the structure of the house—I'm not touching that. In fact I'm restoring it."

"Oh."

"So I guess I got the lemonade under false pretenses."

"You got the lemonade because you needed it and we're Christians."

"Well thanks. I did need it." One good turn deserves another, that's how Don was raised. So: "As long as I'm here, if you ladies need any work done on *your* place, let me know."

"The only thing we need is for that house to come down." She pointed a bony old finger at the Bellamy mansion.

"Then you should've bought it and hired a demolition crew."

He drained the last bit from the pitcher and handed it back to her.

"Thank you kindly, ma'am," he said. He touched the brim of an imaginary hat as he had seen his father do, as salute or farewell, whichever. Then he turned and headed back for the house.

"Don't you think we would've done it if we could?" she called after him.

Why didn't they just put up signs on houses like this? BEWARE OF STRANGE OLD LADIES AND DISAPPEARING SCREWHOLES. WATCH OUT FOR THE DEADLY LOOMING HOMELESS WOMAN. And—mustn't forget—NO KISSING IN NONFUNCTIONAL BATHROOMS.

Once inside, he had to decide what to do next. Strip off the remaining lath and plaster? Take down the stud wall dividing the upstairs kitchen from the rest of the room? He still didn't feel much like heavy work, though the lemonade had refreshed him.

Maybe it refreshed him too much. He headed for the bathroom at the back of the house.

He was still in there when he heard a loud, insistent knocking on the front door. Hang on a minute, for pete's sake. Stubbornly he rinsed his hands instead of running for the door. Had to remember to buy soap, pick up a couple of towels. He came down the hall dry-ing his hands on his pants when he heard the door opening and Sylvie greeting whoever was there. By the time he got to the parlor where all his tools were, Cindy's next-desk neighbor at the realty was peering around to look for him.

"Hi, Mr. Lark," the guy said. What was his name? As if he heard the question, the man said, "Ryan Bagatti, remember?"

"Who could forget?" said Don. He walked past Bagatti to the entry-way, where Sylvie was standing on the third and fourth step—poised to flee. "Thanks for letting a total stranger into my house," he said.

"Nice for you," said Bagatti. "Having your housekeeper living here while you pile up junk on the lawn."

"I'm not the housekeeper," said Sylvie.

"She's the nothing," said Don. "She came with the house. But she's got things to do."

"Cindy know about her?" asked Bagatti, all wide-eyed innocence.

"Bet she will in about fifteen minutes," said Don.

"Aw, man, you're too judgmental," said Bagatti. "I came here because I'm Cindy's friend, you know."

"In other words, she doesn't know you're here?"

"I got a call at the office, she was out. She's been out sick, you know. Ever since you closed on this house."

"Sorry to hear that. Hope she gets better."

"Yeah, send a card or something."

"You got a call," said Don. Whatever this was about, he knew it would be nasty, and he wanted Bagatti just to get on with it.

"From the guy who used to own this place. Actually, from his lawyer. Seems he was suspicious about the way Cindy was handling the sale and how low the price was that she was insisting on. He wanted eighty, you know."

"House isn't worth eighty."

"Well, I guess that's for the courts to decide, don't you think?" Bagatti shook his head. "I mean, that's how the guy's lawyer puts it. He put a detective on her. Got pictures of you going into her house. Coming out of her house. Kissing in the car. Figures it'll prove collu-sion."

"You seen the pictures, Bagatti?" asked Don.

"Why would I have seen them?" said the realtor.

Don picked him up by the shoulders and jammed him against the wall. His head made a kind of bounce against the plaster, and he lost his silly smirk. "I guess I didn't ask sincere enough," said Don. "You take those pictures, Bagatti?"

"Like I said, a private detective. This is assault, you know."

"Got pictures?" said Don.

"All the guy did was call me."

"So why you telling me and not Cindy?"

"He's gonna name both of you in the suit. But he said, like, maybe it could all go away."

"He said? Or you say?"

"What do you think? What are you talking about?"

"Blackmail," said Don. "Extortion."

"Not me," said Bagatti. "But maybe him."

"Maybe?"

"He said twenty thousand. You still get the house for ten thousand less than he asked for. It's a bargain, right?"

"But I bet he doesn't want to go back and adjust the price on the records, right?"

"Why screw up everybody's taxes?" asked Bagatti. "You'll still get a profit on the house."

"And you came to me?"

"Cindy's got no money," said Bagatti.

"How do you know that? She wouldn't tell you where to point your dick when you pee."

"Like I said, the guy has a private investigator. Man, you're hurting my shoulders."

Don let him slide down the wall to stand on his feet. But when Bagatti made as if to go for the door, Don bounced him back against the wall again. And, again, his head did that little rebound from the plaster. "Careful," said Don. "This is a bearing wall, I don't want to have to replace it just because you put a dent in it with your head."

"Look, Mr. Lark, I'm just a messenger."

"Tell me the lawyer's name."

"He didn't say. He said he'd contact you."

"I don't want any lawyer dust in this house. I'll go to his office and we'll work this out, or he can go ahead and take us to court, because nothing illegal happened."

"I'll tell him."

"No, I'll tell him. Give me his number."

"He said he'd call me back. Didn't give me a—"

This time his head didn't bounce as much. "Don't hold your neck stiff when I do that," said Don. "It'll just make it hurt worse later. Stay loose."

"You're hurting me, man."

"His number."

"Let go of me and I'll write it down."

Don stepped between Bagatti and the door and watched while he pulled out a business card and with trembling hands struggled to write the phone number.

"Memorized it, huh?" said Don. "From calling it so much?"

"What do you mean?"

"I mean you're the office sneak. You're the one tipped him off that maybe Cindy and I liked each other. And he must have got you to hire the detective. Fast work, getting those pictures only a couple of hours later."

"So what? The ice queen starts getting lovey with a client, I get suspicious, and it turned out I was right, wasn't I? Getting a thirty-thousand-dollar discount on the house. So don't get all righteous with me, calling me a sneak when you're a thief."

Right then. That was when Don could have crossed the line. All these years of self-control. All those months when he wanted to go kidnap his daughter and hide her in Bulgaria or Mongolia and he didn't do it. All those months, all those years afterward when he wanted to find his exwife's lawyer and smash the sanctimonious snake's head into splinters against a lightpost, and didn't do it. All the violence that had gone unexpressed, he wanted so badly to let go . . . and didn't.

Bagatti must have guessed at the decision he was making, because he cowered, watching Don's eyes. And when Don finally stepped back against the outside wall, letting Bagatti pass, the realtor bolted like a squirrel, out the door, down the porch steps.

Don held the card with the lawyer's number. Another lawyer. Another attempt to destroy him. When you kill, Don, kill the right guy. Life in prison for killing a realtor? Come on. One dead lawyer is worth ten dead realtors any day.

He locked the door, got in the truck, and drove. At first he thought of driving to Cindy's. But what would that accomplish? Either she knew about the threat from the previous owner, or she didn't. Either she would be embarrassed about their near-tryst or she wouldn't. No possible meeting would work out happily for either of them.

So he drove. Up to some of the new housing developments around some of the lakes north and west of the city. Houses for doctors and lawyers, executives and car dealers. Big houses, on huge wooded lots, designed to have great views and to give them, too. From the road over there where the common people drive, this house would look like a slavery-era plantation house, and that one like a Federal mansion, and this other one like a Hollywood extravaganza, and that last one like an escapee from the ugliest part of the 1950s. Taste didn't come with money. Nor restraint. Nor even common decency. I used to build their houses, thought Don. I used to try so hard to please them. Excellence that they didn't understand and didn't want to pay for. I built their house as meticulously as I would hope they did surgery, or handled legal cases, or whatever. Was I the only one who cared that much? The only one who wanted to do good work even where it wasn't on display?

He came out onto Lake Brandt Road, and then took the left fork onto Lawndale. He stopped at Sam's and got out and used the payphone to call the lawyer's number. He recognized the name of the firm when the receptionist said it. They didn't have the best reputation in town, but extortion was a new specialty for them.

"He's with a client," said the receptionist.

"Get out of your chair," said Don, "and go tell him that either he talks to me on the phone or he talks to me in person ten minutes from now."

"We do not respond to threats, sir."

"It says a lot about your law firm that you have a policy about that," said Don. "Don't waste my time, I'm calling from a payphone."

It only took a moment for the lawyer to get on the phone. "Most people make appointments," said the lawyer.

"What you and your client are doing is extortion," said Don.

"No it's not," said the lawyer. "It's fair warning."

"But if I give you twenty thousand, the whole problem goes away."

"It saves everybody a lot of unnecessary legal fees and court costs," said the lawyer. "It's called settling out of court."

"Then in exchange I get a quit-claim that specifies the amount I paid you."

"No you don't."

"Then go to court, and I'll testify that only your unwillingness to have a legal document with the amount of money on it stood between us and settlement."

"That's a privileged matter."

"There's no privilege because you're not my lawyer," said Don. "I'll be at your office at eight-thirty in the morning. The check will be made out to your client."

"It will be cash."

"No it won't. Again, I'm happy to testify in court that your client wanted to leave no paper trail."

"Cash or no deal."

"I'll be there at eight-thirty with the cashier's check. You be there with the quit-claim specifying the amount of money and making no assertions about any kind of relationship between me and Ms. Claybourne. Or you can sue your brains out."

"Apparently you don't know what a court action like that will involve, Mr. Lark, or you wouldn't talk so blithely about getting into one."

"I spent a quarter of a million dollars on assholes like you, trying to get my daughter back. And other assholes who were even assholier than thou managed to keep me from getting her back until my exwife got them both killed. What exactly do you think I'm afraid of now?"

"You're afraid of Cindy Claybourne losing her job."

"Not really," said Don.

"So chivalry is dead?"

"No, I'm just not afraid of her losing her job. You and your client picked the wrong targets here. Ms. Claybourne and I have both lost about all we have to lose. You don't have it in your power to do more than inconvenience us."

"So why are you agreeing to the twenty thousand?"

"Because if I don't get this whole thing to go away right now, I'll probably end up losing control and killing somebody."

"Now who's the extortionist?"

"Yeah, that's it, I'm trying to force you to accept the twenty thousand dollars you demanded from me. Eight-thirty in the morning. Check made out to your client. Quit-claim. No mention of Ms. Claybourne or of any improprieties."

"I won't accept anything but cash."

"Fine. I'll have a dollar in cash, too. The check or the buck. Your choice. See you in the morning." He hung up. He was shaking as bad as Ryan Bagatti had been. It did no good to talk tough with a lawyer, he knew that. They just smirk at you and think of new ways to make your life a living hell. But Don's life was already a living hell. Lawyers had lost their last hold over him.

He went to the bank where his renovation money was and withdrew the twenty thousand in the form of a cashier's check. On the bottom of it he wrote, "For quit-claim on Bellamy house and all related matters." Then he put the check, folded, into his shirt pocket and returned to the house.

The front door was locked, just as he had left it. Of course. Sylvie didn't have a key.

Sylvie didn't have a key, but she had let the Helping Hands guys in.

No. He must have forgotten to lock the house up. That was the morning of the closing, after all. He left the door unlocked.

Okay, so maybe he did lock it. She picked it, that's all. It's not like he'd paid Lowe's for some fancy unpickable lock or anything. She was a burglar, probably, that's how she paid money to support the drug habit she doesn't have.

He thought of the missing screwholes in the door. This house was going to get to him pretty soon.

He took the check out of his pocket, tucked it under the screwdriver he'd used on the kitchen cabinets, and then, wrecking bar in hand, went upstairs and tore off lath and plaster until he was covered in white dust and sweat.

It had been a hot day. The water wouldn't be all that cold. He went down the hall to the bathroom, stripped off his clothes, shook off as much dust as he could over the tub, then got into the shower and rinsed himself off. The water was running clear now, but that just increased its resemblance to a mountain stream. He took it as long as he could, then turned it off and stood there shivering and shaking off the water until he was as dry as he was likely to get. Only then did he remember that he wasn't alone in the house. He hadn't seen Sylvie since he got back from his phone call and from the bank, so he'd forgotten about her. But he couldn't very well parade naked through the house. But he also couldn't put back on these clothes covered in plaster dust. So he compromised. He put back on his briefs and carried the rest of his clothes downstairs.

Of course she was standing in the entryway to watch him come downstairs. "Water's pretty cold, isn't it?" she said.

Wordlessly he passed by her. The fury of his confrontations with Bagatti and the lawyer swept over him, and he wanted to shake her and scream at her to give him some privacy. Instead he walked to his suitcase and got out what was now his cleanest set of clothes. He had to do a laundry, there was no doubt about it.

"What was that guy here for?" said Sylvie. "He sure took off out of here. But then, so did you right afterward."

He didn't owe her any explanation. Especially when he was doing his best not to erupt in fury. So he turned his back to her and hooked his thumbs under the elastic of his briefs and said, "I'm changing my clothes. I prefer to do it alone, but I can't seem to do anything alone in this house." Then he pulled off his briefs and turned around. She was gone. Finally.

He got dressed in clothes that were pretty rank, even for him. It was nearly seven, and even though it was still daylight savings time, it would be dark soon. He took everything but his dirty clothes out of his suitcase and left the house. This time he didn't bother to lock the door behind him. That way he wouldn't have to wonder how she got it open, if he found she had let yet another person into the house in his absence.

When one batch of clothes was washed and dry, he picked a pair of underwear, some socks, and a pair of pants and a shirt, went into the restroom at the laundromat, and changed into them. Then he came back out and put the dirty clothes he'd been wearing into a washing machine together.

A tired-looking middle-aged woman in a grocery checker's outfit was the only other person in the laundry, and apparently it irked her to see a man put underwear and socks in with blue jeans and a red shirt. "Didn't anybody ever tell you to separate whites and coloreds?" she demanded.

"They did, but America is past that now," he said. When she finally realized he had deliberately misunderstood her, she huffed a little and left him alone. If only a little snottiness would work as well on Sylvie.

When everything was clean and dry, it was nearly ten. He stopped at Pie Works and got a pizza and took it back to the Bellamy house. It was late for him, the house was dark, and he wasn't even sure he was hungry, just knew he had to eat in order to keep working again tomorrow. He came in, turned on the worklight in the parlor, and went to set down the pizza on his workbench when he saw the check. He had left it folded, tucked under the screwdriver. Now it was open, tucked under nothing. Sylvie just couldn't stand not prying, it seemed. And she didn't even have the decency to hide the fact that she'd done it by refolding the check and putting the screwdriver back on top of it.

Twenty thousand dollars. Now he'd have to redo his budget. But he could juggle the figures till he was blue, there wouldn't be enough money. He'd have to borrow against the house after all. Not till near the end, though. To buy the countertops and chair rails, the carpet and window treatments. Twenty thousand dollars. That was the most expensive love affair he ever heard of that didn't actually include any sex.

Why am I doing it?

Not for Cindy. Nothing chivalrous about this. I'm just buying my way out of death row. I really am ready to kill somebody. I'm paying them to get out of my life so I don't have to kill anybody.

He sat on his cot eating the pizza as mechanically as if he were driving nails. He heard the telltale footsteps on the stairs. She was making another foray into his territory. She seemed determined not to learn.

But instead of barking at her he just closed the pizza box and slid it across the floor. It stopped right in the doorway between the parlor and the entry. He saw her appear behind it, looking at him gravely.

"Nothing special, just pepperoni and sausage," he said. "I've had all I want."

"Thanks," she said.

"Yeah yeah."

"Why can't I say thanks and you just say you're welcome like a normal person?"

"Why can't I just . . ." He had meant to say, Why can't I just say leave me alone and have you go away like a normal person.

"Why can't you just what?"

"Finish the pizza, it's still warm."

"No thanks," she said. "I'm not hungry."

"Then don't eat it," he said.

"I just came down to say I'm sorry."

"For what?"

"For always wanting to watch what you're doing. I can't help it, nothing's happened in this house for so long."

"I ought to sell tickets."

"And the work you do, it's kind of dangerous, isn't it? Like you're tearing up the house."

"It's safe enough." Especially if you stay out of the room while I'm working.

"No, I mean, dangerous to the house. It feels like it's being knackered, you know? Cut up and boiled down for glue and fertilizer."

"I know what knackering is," said Don.

"You're not hurting it?"

"The lath and plaster is nothing. It has to come off so I can bring the house up to code. I'll put new studs in between the timbers to take nails for, like, hanging pictures or whatever. And for outlet and switch boxes and TV cable outlets. Then I'll put on wallboard and it'll be good as new. Better."

"I don't know how it could be better than new," she said. "It was so beautiful then."

"You weren't there," said Don.

"But can't you just feel it, here in the house? How he loved her?"

"Who?"

"Dr. Bellamy. He built this for his bride. I looked it up in the library, back when I was a student here. That's what I majored in, you know. Library science. I was going to take a job in Providence, Rhode Island. I was about to get my master's degree."

"And?"

"Oh, I found all kinds of wonderful things about the Bellamys. They were so much in love, and so much a part of life in Greensboro. Soirees, parties, dances. Not a month went by without some mention of him or his wife or their house in the newspaper."

"Any pictures?" asked Don.

"Some lovely ones. When they were young. And later, too, when they were getting into late middle age. Not a one when they were old. When they died they ran youthful pictures of them. I think that's the way everyone thought of them their whole lives. Forever young."

"I meant, any pictures of the house. To help in my renovation."

"No," she said. "Except the outside, but I don't think that's changed all that much."

"I suppose not. No obvious add-ons, anyway."

"Sorry I couldn't help."

"No, it's fine. I'm not restoring the place anyway, I just thought if there was some special touch or something—doesn't matter."

"There are all kinds of wonderful things in this house," she said. "But the house keeps its secrets." Then her face darkened. "I'm sorry I've been bothering you. I know it drives you crazy, but I just can't seem to stop myself. My old roommate Lissy used to do that to me.

Sneak up behind me while I was studying or something. And all of a sudden I'd sense she was there and nearly jump out of my skin."

"Well, you've never done that to me."

"Of course not, but you know, looking over your shoulder—that drives you crazy."

He waved it off as if it were nothing. Then cursed himself silently for being a hammered man. Grow up Southern, and you just can't help but do the polite thing even when you've already decided not to do it.

"Drives everybody crazy," she said. "Lissy was just . . . difficult."

She had been going to say another word. Something nastier.

"So why did you room with her?" said Don.

"Younger girl, took her under my wing," said Sylvie. "She was a senior, and I don't think she would have graduated."

"Would have?" asked Don.

"She left," said Sylvie. "She was never that serious about school."

"But you didn't finish either?"

Sylvie shook her head.

"So you were close after all? I mean, why else would her leaving cause you not to finish your program and go take that job?"

Sylvie shook her head. "My life story is too boring for anyone to waste a minute on it." She smiled wanly. "I hated her at the time, but you don't know how often I've wished I could just see her again. Now that she's not annoying me, you see. I miss her a little. She was so exuberant. Headstrong. She found this place. The owner was going to close it down, but she was able to talk him into letting us stay here till we both graduated at the end of the next year."

"What did your family think when you dropped out?" asked Don.

"They did what they always do. They stayed dead."

It sounded like a joke, and then it didn't. "Do you mean that?" he asked. "They're dead?"

"I'm an orphan. Put myself through school. I had a scholarship, but housing and books and food and all that, I earned it all. And grad school, I worked for every dime. And I wasn't in debt, either. I paid my way."

Well, not anymore, Don thought churlishly.

"Dr. Bellamy and his wife lived here until they died in the flu epidemic in 1918. But they were so old by then it wasn't sad, really, it was kind of sweet that they went together, so neither one had to stay behind and grieve."

Don had nothing to say to that. How often had he wished he could have died in the same car that killed his baby?

"But how awful of me," said Sylvie. "I was forgetting. Your wife and daughter."

"What do you know about them?" he snapped at once. Then relented: "I'm sorry. I just don't talk about them usually."

"No, I just . . . your engineer friend told that realtor lady the first day you came here. How your exwife got custody of your daughter and then they died in a car accident."

"What the newspaper didn't tell you was that my wife was so drunk and drugged up she didn't even fasten the car seat to the car."

"Was it in the papers?" asked Sylvie. "I don't get a paper."

Don could hardly imagine how isolated her life in this house had been.

"How many years have you been living like this?" he asked.

"I don't know. A long time."

"What happened to you? I mean, you were in grad school, you were going somewhere. You had a job lined up."

"They were expanding the children's section of the city library, starting some new programs with grade school kids. That was my thesis project, kind of. The effects of competitive versus cooperative reading programs for children in community libraries."

"So why didn't you finish your degree and take the job?"

"For a man who lives and works alone, you sure have a lot of questions."

"Look, I didn't start this conversation," said Don.

She glared at him, then turned and stalked upstairs. Don looked at the pizza box on the floor. Keep up your strength, even if you're surrounded by hypersensitive crazy people. He got up and brought it back to the cot and ate another bite. It was cold now and tasted nasty.

Why should he feel bad because he offended Sylvie Delaney? She was the one who kept intruding on him.

Yeah, right, it's always other people's fault, isn't that right, Don.

In frustration he took the biggest surviving piece of pizza and flung it against the wall. He had expected it to stick, at least for a minute. But it didn't even leave a stain, just bounced off and fell down among his tools.

Got to stop throwing things against the wall.

He went over and found the piece of pizza, put it back in the box, and carried the whole thing outside to the garbage can. It was late. He had to get up and pay off an extortionist in the morning.

11

Hot Water

In the event it turned out to be no big deal. The lawyer was in a suit, a youngish guy who looked like his life was full of disappointment. As if his smile had once been eager, but now it was wry, and soon it would be cynical. He wasn't going to live like the dudes in *L.A. Law*. He was just going to meet working-class guys in parking lots and take their hard-earned money from them as a payoff to ensure they didn't get sued by some faceless jerk in Florida. Not much of a career, really.

The lawyer had the quit-claim. It said the right things. No tricks as far as Don could see. The lawyer didn't even mention cash. Extortionists generally don't want trouble. Nobody knows better than a lawyer how much pain a lawsuit can be. Twenty thousand without a court struggle is better than a hundred thousand with. Such was Don's upbringing that when he handed over the cashier's check, having satisfied himself that the quit-claim was legitimate, he actually said, "Thanks very much," before he could stop himself.

Yeah, that's why my mama taught me to say yes sir and no ma'am and please and thank you. So I could show grateful courtesy to a lawyer who's helping somebody take away my independence.

Back in his truck Don found that for some reason there was a lump in his throat and his eyes were filling with tears. He had to pull into the parking lot at Eastern Costume and sit there till he could see straight.

It made no sense for him to cry now. What was this, just twenty thousand dollars? He'd cry over that? He'd lost a hell of a lot more than that. He'd cried when his daughter died, cried off and on for days, cried till he could only just sit there with bloodshot eyes wishing he could cry but there was nothing more. His diaphragm ached from sobbing. He couldn't go out in the sunlight, his eyes were so raw. He honestly thought, when that time was over, that he'd never cry again, that there'd never be cause again for tears, compared to that. And now here he was, crying over twenty thousand dollars.

No. He was crying for his freedom. He had thought this was it, he was over the top. That house was his return to life. No debt. When it was done, when it was sold, he'd have enough, free and clear, to start a business, to start a real life. And now, what had he lost? Not everything. So he'd take out a twenty-thousand-dollar mortgage. That was nothing compared to the value of the house when he was done with it. Pay some interest, but he wouldn't get the mortgage till it was almost ready to sell, so he could handle that, too. He'd come out of it OK.

Why did it hurt? Because he had been beaten. And how had he been beaten? Because he let himself go. He let himself maybe start to almost love a woman. She didn't mean him any harm, and she didn't even cause it, really. But it was because he was drawn to her and she to him that he was beaten today. Even though his romantic feelings toward her were gone he still felt protective toward her, and they had used that against him. The way this world worked, the decent people had to live by the rules of honor, while the sons-of-bitches could run around biting them on the butt every chance they got. And yet when he thought of becoming like them, becoming a real son-of-a-bitch himself, it just made him sick inside. It came down to this: If his daughter was still alive somehow, in heaven if there was one, and if she knew what he was doing, or if he was maybe going to see her again someday, he wanted her to be proud of him. A woman needed him to protect her. A decent woman being treated badly because she dared to reach for love. Then she needed money and he had some, and so he shared. If his daughter lived with Jesus like they said, then maybe she knew he did that and she was proud of him.

So he did it for his little girl. And now that he knew that, or at least could talk himself into almost believing it, it was OK again. He didn't feel like crying anymore.

When he got home the Carville Plumbing and Heating van was parked in front. This time, though, Sylvie hadn't let him in. Young Jim Carville—young only compared to his seventy-year-old father— was sitting in the front of his van, smoking. When he saw Don, he put the cigarette out and sauntered over to the pickup. "Not many guys I'd wait for," said Carville.

"Sorry I kept you waiting," said Don. "You couldn't possibly be early, could you?"

"Yeah, job fell through."

"Well, mine didn't, and if you got the time I'd like you to inspect the pipes and tell me what I need to replace."

"Plenty of time," said Carville. "You want to give me a hand bringing in the new water heater?"

Don went up and unlocked the deadbolt, then went back to help him get the water heater out of the van. It wasn't really all that heavy. Carville could've done it alone, but why not help? On the way in, Carville said, "That girl you're letting stay with you, you sure have got her scared to do wrong."

"Oh?"

"I told her who I was, but she wasn't letting me in without your say-so. Next time you ought to tell her when you got a contractor coming."

"I knew I'd be back two hours before you were scheduled."

"When you're dealing with Superman, you better plan on him showing up early."

When they had wrestled the thing down the cellar steps, Carville checked out the old installation and pronounced that this would be a breeze and no, he didn't need any help till it was time to carry the old lime-silted water heater out of the building. "And for that you might need three more guys, a winch, and a thousand-pound chain."

"It's that old?"

"And none of the water ever softened. I'd be surprised if this old heater can hold more than a cup of water at a time. The rest of it is one big stalagmite."

Don went back upstairs and thought of doing some sweaty job and then realized that when this one was done, there'd be hot water for a shower. So maybe he should go now, before he got himself all filthy, and buy a few little things like soap and towels and, since he had company in the house and the working shower was upstairs, a bathrobe.

Friendly Center had most of what he needed, between Harris Teeter and Belk. Then he trucked up to Fleet-Plummer to buy a couple of soapdishes and a shower caddy and to get an extra key made. When he got home, he stocked both bathrooms with soap and laid out the towels, a set of them for her, a set for him. He put up a new shower curtain, laid down a bath mat. Downright domestic. Then he went in search of Sylvie to give her the key.

She wasn't on the ground floor or the second floor, and she wasn't in the cellar. But when he got into the attic he didn't see her there, either. Not that the light was all that good, coming in slantwise through the filthy porthole windows in the gables. "Sylvie?" he said. "You here?"

No answer. Called again, no answer. Had she left? Just when she'd finally got it through her head not to let people in, now she slips out of the house when he's downstairs or out shopping? It shouldn't have bothered him, but doggone it, he'd just gone and bought some towels and a bathrobe he didn't need if she wasn't living there. People ought to be consistent, at least, even if they were consistently annoying.

He was about to head back down the steps when he heard her voice from the darkest of the four wings of the attic, the one with no window at all. He hadn't looked real close back there because he didn't think she'd be there in the dark. She picked her way through the scattered junk—even Helping Hands didn't want this stuff—so quickly and deftly that it was like she could see in the dark. But come to think of it, she'd had plenty of time to memorize where everything was.

"You were looking for me?" she asked. He couldn't blame her for sounding incredulous.

"I wanted to tell you the water heater's being installed and after the water has a chance to heat up, you can get a real shower."

"I bet I need one."

"It'll feel good whether you need it or not." As if there was a chance she didn't have years of sweat and grime caked on her. "Got soap there, if you don't mind sharing a bar of it with me."

"No problem," she said.

"And you can take your pick of towels, I'll just use the other set."

"You got me a towel?"

"Can't very well hang you out the window to dry, can I?"

"All I meant was. Thanks." Again, that tone of surprise.

"Also," he said, pulling out the extra housekey. "It isn't safe for you to be in here with the deadbolt fastened and no key. Plus if you went out, you shouldn't have to knock or wait for me to get home."

She looked at it without taking it. "It's not my house," she said. "It's yours."

"I got title to it," said Don. "But I could've lost that just now, if some lawyer really wanted to go to town with me. So the way I see it, we're both squatters here, really. House still belongs to that Dr. Bellamy guy."

"Oh, he's forgotten all about it by now," she said.

"I expect so," said Don. "Him being dead and all."

"Funny how he made such a strong house out of love for his wife, but that's the thing, the house didn't really have a hold on him at all, ever, because it was her that he loved. I think that's romantic."

"Are you taking the key or not?"

"I don't know. I don't know if it's right for me to have it."

"I say it is." And as he said it, he found that he pretty much believed it. "Now that you're following the rules. Not letting people in."

"Would you mind setting the key by the door to my room?"

He looked at her for a minute. What was this game? Didn't she recognize victory when she had it? Did she have to rub it in by making him deliver the key?

"Really," she said. "I don't know if I could even hold the key. I'm kind of shaking right now. I guess what I'm saying is, please take the key and leave it there for me because I don't want to cry in front of you, I'm shy about that."

"Didn't mean to make you cry."

She shook her head and turned her back. He went down the attic stairs and laid the key in front of her door and then headed on to the cellar to see how Carville was doing.

Only when he got down the stairs to the entry hall, he could see through the glass in the door that somebody was standing on the porch, pacing nervously. In the attic he wouldn't have heard any knocking. He opened the door. It was Cindy.

"Hi," she said.

"Sure," he said. "Come in." He had a sinking feeling that she had heard what he did for her and she was there to thank him and he didn't want that scene. But he'd rather have that one than the scene where she tries to pick up the romance where it was when it got sidetracked back at her house.

"You can relax," she said, coming inside. "I know it's over between us."

"I suppose maybe so," he said.

"You have no idea how I've replayed that day in my mind, wishing I could . . . "

"No point in that, Cindy," he said.

"And now I've cost you money."

"They had no business telling you about that."

"Ryan doesn't know how not to tell what he knows. He doesn't understand that that's why he's not a very good spy. It doesn't give you any advantage to know a secret if you blab it as soon as you find it out."

"Ryan needs to have his head shoved up his butt."

"Might as well," she said with a wan smile. "It's always up somebody's."

He couldn't argue.

"Anyway, Don," she said. "I'll pay it back to you. You have to let me."

"You've got other places for that money to go."

"But I know what having this house free and clear meant to you."

"It's OK," he said. "The thing is, I'll only have to borrow for a few months and that's nothing. And I kissed you for the camera as much as you kissed me."

"But you didn't know how I'd bullied him into dropping the price."

"But see, here's the thing, Cindy. You did it because you liked me. So when it comes right down to it, the owner was right. I was getting a special advantage. I would have bought this house anyway, even at seventy thou. It would have taken me a few days to decide, maybe, but I would have bought it. So in a way, the only loser is you, because you didn't get your whole commission."

"Don't you dare even think of paying me a—"

"I got kissed by a beautiful lady," he said. "I found out I could feel things I thought I couldn't feel. That's not about money."

"That's it," she said. "That's how I feel too. And please don't think for a moment I'm upset that you already have a girl here."

"There's a girl here," said Don, "but I don't have her. She came with the house."

"No, no, you don't have to explain anything. I know whatever you did, it was the kind of thing a kind and generous man would do. For all I know, she's just another broken-hearted woman like me. Maybe you're just a trouble magnet, Don."

"Or maybe there's no such thing as a person without troubles, so I'm just lucky to know somebody like you."

She shook her head, holding back tears. "You know too much about me to believe that, Don."

He went to her and put his arms around her and held her again. She clung to him, tight, and now with her body against his he couldn't help but feel some of what he'd felt before, that longing for her.

"You can hold me when you know what I did?" she whispered.

"What you almost did," he said. "What you made damn sure you would never, ever do. That's all that counts. What we do, not what we think of doing or even want to do."

"But see, I lied to you," she said. "I did put the pillow over her face."

It struck him like a blow; his knees gave a little.

She pulled away from him, studying his face, tears flowing down hers.

"Did you . . . hurt her?" he asked.

She shook her head. "Only for a minute. And that's the truth this time. Now that I know you already have somebody else, I can stand to tell you that last little bit. That I *was* doing it."

"But you stopped."

She nodded.

"And your baby wasn't hurt at all."

"She cried cause I scared her, but no, she wasn't hurt. It really was only a minute. Less than a minute. But that's how close I was. It's awful, Don, knowing I could come that close."

"We can all come close to something ugly," he said.

"Not that, though," she said. "You could never even come within a thousand miles of that. And that's why you can't love me."

"I think . . . that's not fair, Cindy. Don't judge yourself by me. I lost a little girl. I've got scars of my own. That's all that's happening here."

"No, I know better, Don. The kind of man that's the only kind worth loving, when I tell him that story, he'll never be able to love me."

"You don't know that."

"Because how could he ever trust me? How could he ever leave our kids alone with me, without wondering? And a man like that, Don, he's going to want kids. A man who's a natural husband and father."

"I don't know, Cindy. I know we mean something to each other. That's better than anything I had for the last couple of years."

"Me too."

"So there," he said. "That's love too. It ain't sex, and maybe that's too bad, but you know, Cindy, when a man and a woman care for each other, that doesn't always mean they have to sleep together or live together."

She nodded, then glanced toward the stairs and gave a little half-smile.

He didn't bother to answer her, to insist that there was nothing between him and Sylvie. Because how did he know? Maybe there was something between them. Maybe he was finally back to a place in his life where he could mean something to people and they could mean something to him. He didn't owe Cindy any explanations. And she wasn't asking for any, either.

"Anyway," said Cindy. "I'm going to start another account. I'm going to fill it up with money till it's at twenty thousand dollars. If you won't take it from me, then I'll call it my Don Lark fund and I'll try to use it as kindly for someone in need as you used it for me."

"That money was as much to get me out of hot water as it was for you," he said.

"Yeah, right." She laughed. "You wouldn't have lost your real estate license."

"Well, just so you don't think I'm too noble, Cindy, I got to tell you that right now what I want more than anything in the world is to kiss you."

"Me too."

"A better man than me would just let that feeling pass."

She stepped to him, put her hands on his chest, let him enfold her in his arms again, and gave back a warm sweet kiss. Not like she kissed him in the bathroom or in the car, none of that hunger. It *was* good-bye. But it was also love, and he had needed that from her and she gave it, and she needed it from him, too, and they were maybe just a little bit more alive, a little bit closer to happiness because of that. So the kiss lasted a long time. But when it ended, she was out the door really fast.

And there, leaning on her car, was Ryan Bagatti. All smiles. "Interesting diner you found for your lunch hour," said Ryan. "What's on the menu? Must be fast food." He was looking at Cindy. Maybe he didn't even realize Don was standing there. Didn't matter. He'd gone too far this time. Don was down the porch stairs before Bagatti could hold his hands out and insist, "Just kidding! Just kidding!" And then he cowered as Don loomed over him.

"Don, don't!" cried Cindy.

Don didn't need the warning. He had the desire, but not the intention of harming Bagatti. But he did stand close, as close as he could. Bagatti straightened up a little, but found himself forced to lean flat against his car or he'd have had Don's chest in his face.

"Hey, back off, man," said Bagatti. "Can't you take a joke?"

Don just stood there, looming. Waiting for Bagatti to act.

It didn't take long. A guy like Bagatti, when someone didn't fight back, he assumed they were afraid to hurt him. So now he started acting cool again. "Get a sense of humor, man," he said. And then he laid his hands on Don's chest and pushed, just a little. "Give me some space."

That was what Don needed. He snatched both of Bagatti's hands and held them, using his own hands like pincers, his thumbs in Bagatti's palms, his middle fingers pressing the other side. And he squeezed. Bagatti yelped. In reply, Don held his hands out to both sides, spreading Bagatti like a crucifix and bringing his face right up against Don's chest. Bagatti struggled to get his hands free, but the more he resisted, the tighter Don squeezed. "You're killing me!"

"Not yet," said Don. Then he bent his head down to speak directly in Bagatti's ears. "Listen tight," he said softly. "I'll say this once. No more jokes, no more teasing, no more following Cindy anywhere. You see her at work, you treat her politely. You never criticize her or even discuss her with others. No nasty tricks, no rumors, no sneaking, no telling tales about her. You getting this?"

"Yes," said Bagatti.

"You're the kind of bully who picks on somebody just because they can't fight back. Well, you were right about Cindy. She can't fight you. But now she doesn't have to. Cindy and I are not now and never have been lovers, not that it's your business. But we *are* friends. And I take care of my friends, Mr. Bagatti."

"Right, yes," said Bagatti. "I'm getting this. I got this."

"I'm not sure," said Don. "You seem to me to be a slow learner."

"I'm a quick learner."

"But the minute I let you go, you're going to forget."

"No, I'm not."

"The minute I let you go, you're going to start yelling about how I've been threatening you and assaulting you and if I think I've heard the last of this—"

"No, I won't say that."

"Then I can let you go?"

"Definitely. Yes. This would be a good time."

Don released Bagatti's hands. It surprised him how much tension had been in his grip. The lad was going to have bruises. Indeed, Bagatti slumped back against the car and cradled one hand in the other, then switched them, then held them both in front of him as if they were stumps. "Look what you've done to me."

"As far as I'm concerned," said Don, "you did this to yourself. If you hadn't come here to taunt Cindy Claybourne, your hands would not be in pain right now."

"This is a crime you committed here, buddy," said Bagatti.

Immediately Don seized the man's hands and Bagatti shrieked and tried to snatch them back. "You promised me," said Don.

"Yes. Yes, I did. I do. No crime. It's fine."

"What you have to remember is that I'm crazy," said Don. "Whatever I do to you, I'll get off."

"Yeah. You won't have to do anything to me. Please."

By now Don wasn't squeezing his hands or anything. Bagatti could have pulled them back. But he wasn't trying to. He was submitting. Don had won. It should have felt good. And it did, a little. Because Bagatti might actually leave Cindy alone. Maybe he had done what it took to protect her.

What didn't feel good now was how good it had felt to squeeze the man's hands, to hurt him. Don had squeezed harder than he meant to. Hands that had worked pipe wrenches and hammers, hands with an iron grip, and he had found a fleshy gap between the long finger-bones in the hands and driven his fingers into that space like nails and while he was doing it he had felt so good.

And Cindy had watched him do it. Had watched him use that kind of violence. What did she think of him now? He was ashamed.

Bagatti slid out from between his car and Don's unmoving body. Without looking at either Don or Cindy, he scurried around the front of his car, got in the driver's side, and drove off. Quietly. No aggression left in the man. For now, anyway. Don noticed that he was steering with the edges of his palms. Those hands were going to be sore for a while.

Cindy stood off near her car. Looking at Don.

"I'm sorry," he said. "You told me not to hurt him, and then I did."

She took a few steps toward him. He met her halfway.

"It's been a long time," she said softly, "since anybody stuck up for me." She took his hands, one at a time, and kissed them.

"Tell me if he gives you any trouble."

"He won't," she said. "You can be pretty scary."

"You heard what I told him?"

"I didn't have to. I watched his face while you whispered in his ear."

"I'm not a nice man, Cindy. That's what you didn't know about me till now."

"A man who stops a bully from picking on somebody who's down? I call that nice."

"What you don't know," said Don, "is how much I wanted to smash his face into his car. Just use his face to make dents until the bodywork on the car would cost more than the deductible."

"I know I'm not what you wanted, Don," said Cindy. "But I've got to tell you this, you are what I wanted. But that's OK. Now that I know I'm ready to try, I'll find somebody else. I can settle for less than the best. I help my customers do it all the time. They all want perfect houses but sometimes all they can afford is a fixer-upper."

"There's a lot of guys around who are better for you than I am."

"Well, that's good to know," said Cindy. "Maybe I'll get lucky and meet one of those." She smiled. She even laughed. "In a pig's eye!" she said. Then she got into her car, gave him one last little wave, and drove away.

He watched her out of sight. As he did, he could feel a kind of tingling in his hands, in his legs. Not like a tickle or an itch or a trembling, not even the prickly feeling when your leg's gone to sleep and it's waking up again. This was deeper, right to the bone, just a hunger to do something. It was maybe his rage at the owner of the house and his pet lawyer. Or rage at Bagatti. Or rage at the death of his daughter and all the things that had gone wrong and the people who had screwed up. He needed to kill somebody, to tear them apart, only there wasn't anybody to kill.

So he charged back into the house, picked up his skillsaw and his two longest extension cords, and ran a powerline up to the room he was working on. Then he went back down and got a sledgehammer and brought it up, too. Time for this added-in wall to go. He set to work with the wrecking bar, peeling back the drywall on both sides, hacking it away, exposing the studs and the lousy wiring job that had been done to hook up the fridge and the stove. Should've been a fire years ago.

With the studs exposed, it was time for the skillsaw. He plugged it in, turned it on, and it began to roar. Then he bit it into one of the studs at about chest height, and the roar became a whine, the sound of wood being killed.

Down in the parlor, Sylvie was sitting on his cot when the skillsaw started up. She often sat there, leaping up and hiding in the other room when she heard him coming, so he wouldn't find her there, wouldn't accuse her of snooping. Because she wasn't a snoop. She just liked to be here. It was as if some of his warmth, some of his life clung to the cot after he slept there and lingered all day, fading slowly until he returned and replenished it with another night of his dark, hot sleep. He was a strange sleeper, this Don Lark. Not that she'd seen many men sleep in her life, but Sylvie Delaney had never felt such intensity in anybody who was sleeping. She'd stand there sometimes at night and watch him from the doorway, careful not to make any noise and waken him.

It was so confusing since he came to the house, because sometimes she could walk around as soundlessly as ever, and other times it seemed like every move she made echoed through the house. But watching him sleep, she was silent then. She could hear how he sort of panted and gasped in his sleep. Bad dreams. She knew about bad dreams. She had had a few of those herself. Lived in one for a long time, come to think of it. But she couldn't sleep like this man. It was like he attacked sleep, a frontal assault, took it by the throat and forced it to yield him the rest he needed. Rest, but no peace.

So there she was soaking up his warmth like some people soaked up a suntan, when that roaring began from upstairs, and then a second later a high-pitched whine like a scream, like the house was screaming, and she could feel the house around her suddenly flinch. It didn't understand. How could it? It was like surgery without anesthetic. All that tearing down Don had been doing, ripping out cabinets, extra studs, lath and plaster, the house was writhing with the pain of it like having its teeth pulled, and now this, whatever he was doing, this new sound, the house was in *pain*.

Don's toolbox slid across the floor, then stopped abruptly; his favorite hammer toppled out of it onto the floor.

"Stop it," she said.

The hammer trembled and rattled and danced. She knew what the house was telling her to do. After all, she'd done it before, hadn't she?

"He's making everything right again, don't you see? You've just got to trust him."

The hammer bounced upward, then clattered back to the floor. Behind her the workbench slid slowly, then rapidly toward her, stopping right at the edge of the cot. "Cut it out!" she demanded. "I'll see what he's doing, I'll make sure he isn't doing anything bad."

The hammer leapt into her hand. She gripped it, then deliberately dropped it back into the toolbox. "And stay there," she said. Then she ran for the stairs.

Don had cut through most of the studs when he saw Sylvie burst into the room, looking as agitated as if the house were on fire. He took his finger off the trigger of the skillsaw. The blade howled and moaned on down to nothing.

"What are you doing?" Sylvie demanded.

Was he supposed to clear his day's assignments with her? "Working," he said.

"It feels like you're tearing the house down," she said.

He wanted to blow her off, but she looked really upset. "Look," he said, "this isn't even part of the house. The real walls are timber-framed with lath and plaster. This is a modern wall, it was just added in by some landlord trying to squeeze a few more bucks out of the house by splitting this room in two. See? It just butts up against the ceiling. A real wall would be joined to the joists above, but this one is just tucked in under the plaster of the ceiling."

"Oh," she said.

"So I'm putting the house back the way it ought to be."

"I've never seen anyone do this kind of thing before," she said. "Please can't I watch?"

"Not if you're going to go on some save-the-two-by-fours kick."

"I'll be quiet. I just want to see."

But he didn't want her to see. He was using this destruction as therapy. With her watching, he'd have to act professional and cool. But what could he say? Sure, he could tell her, Get out, I work alone. But they were already past that. He'd given her a key. And it's not like this job took any concentration. "Watch if you want," he said.

He turned on the skillsaw again and polished off all but the two end studs. With them there was the danger of biting too deep and damaging the structural timber behind them. When the studs were reduced to a row of stalactites dangling from the ceiling and a row of stalagmites rising up from the floor, Don set down the skillsaw and picked up the sledgehammer. Positioning himself like a golfer, standing between studs, he took aim and swung, striking a stud low, near the floor. The nails gave way and the stud flew, clattering against the kitchen wall. He struck again, again, again, ducking and dodging the dangling studs as he went. To get the last few, though, he had to face the other way. "You got to move now," he said, "or one of these suckers is going to hit you."

"I'm quick," she said. "I can dodge."

"Nobody's that quick and just humor me, OK?" He felt the anger building back up inside him.

Maybe she felt it too, because she ducked back into the doorway. That was enough for a margin of safety. He knocked out the last two stalagmites. Then he started in on the dangling studs, swinging high like a lousy Little Leaguer who hasn't learned not to try for obvious over-the-head balls. Each stud clattered across the floor until they were all gone. Now what remained were two long strips of wood screwed to the floor and spiked to the ceiling, with bent nails sticking out of them where the two-by-fours had been attached. Don pried them away from the house with his wrecking bar, then peeled the two end studs away from the walls, and the room was one big space again.

Don stood there, panting a little, sweating. He looked over at

Sylvie. She smiled at him and said, "The superhero saves the room."

"Just call me Hammer Man," he said.

She walked into the room and turned around, arms wide as if reaching for the walls. "It's so big."

"This is the room that Bellamy built." Don looked around at the timbers, denuded of lath and plaster. "Of course he meant it to look a little more finished, but the size is right."

"So from now on," she said, "you'll be putting things back in this room instead of tearing it apart."

"A little more tearing," he said. "Here and there. Get the lath and plaster off the walls. Remove the moldings, get the drywall up. But yes, when I'm done it'll look as good as it did when Bellamy brought Mrs. B. upstairs for the first time."

"There," she said. "I thought so."

Yeah, she was still a loon.

He gathered up two-by-fours and carried them down in armfuls and heaped them on the junkpile. As for the ones with nails sticking out, he took the time to remove what nails he could and hammer the others flat. No point in getting sued by the parents of some kid who got a spike through his foot because he couldn't stay off the junkpile.

It was probably his next-to-last trip to the curb when he came back into the house to find Carville in the entryway, sitting on the bottom step. "I'm ready to haul that old water heater out," he said. "Actually, I was ready a while ago, but I been inspecting the rest of your plumbing and heating while you calmed down some."

"Calmed down?" asked Don.

"When I came to the door to get you a while back it looked like you was having a scene out there with some guy in a suit. Admit it, you was just showing off for the woman."

Don was embarrassed. Cindy hadn't been the only one watching. "You just saw what I do when I don't kill a guy."

"There was a minute there when I thought maybe he wished you would."

"I just don't know my own strength."

"Good thing, cause I was right about that water heater. So limed up we oughta have a winch to get it out."

"Instead you've got the Man of Steel." Hammer Man, he thought, and almost smiled.

"Batman and Lark."

"Funny."

Down in the basement, the old water heater lay like a corpse on the floor. Carville shone his flashlight around the pipes amid the joists overhead. "These are solid. You might as well keep using them, because taking them out wouldn't be worth the pain."

"They're strong then? Nothing corroded through?"

"If a nuclear bomb flattened this whole town, these pipes would still be hanging up there in the air."

"Yeah, they built this place solid."

"Any new pipes, now," said Carville. "Some of these bathrooms and kitchens was put in more recent than the others. Got cheaper pipes running along here and over here."

"Yeah, but I won't need those now, they'll come on out."

"You didn't need me to tell you this stuff."

"Wanted to make sure I was right," said Don. "And I'm not a furnace guy."

"Yeah, well, this gas furnace, don't ever hook it up, it'll kill you the first night."

"Bad, huh?"

"I sealed off the line till you can get a new one installed." Carville walked over and rapped his flashlight against the ancient coal furnace that must have been put in when the house was first built, because there was no way it could have been brought down the stairs. "This coal furnace," said Carville. "Man, it's big enough to heat one of those college buildings."

"Yeah, I figured I'd just leave it down here."

"Good choice. You know, I bet it would still work great. If you could stand shoveling the coal."

"Or find anybody to deliver it," said Don.

"Oh, they still do, you know. There's still a few coal trucks in the world." Carville walked around behind the furnace. "What I can't figure out is what this was for."

"What?" asked Don. He followed Carville and saw at once what he was indicating. There was a gap in the foundation behind the furnace. It was filled with rubble, but not haphazardly—somebody had plugged a hole. No, a doorway.

"I never actually looked back there. I mean, who'd break the foundation behind the furnace?"

"It was probably a root cellar or something," said Carville.

But Don knew that nobody would put a root cellar where you had to walk behind a blazing furnace to get to it. "Couldn't be a coal bin either, could it."

"No, the chute's over there. Oh, well, you never can figure out some of the weird things people do with their houses."

"It doesn't weaken the foundation, does it?"

"Not with that beam over the gap. Looks to me like this was here when the house was originally built. It wasn't added in later."

"Well, someday when I'm feeling more ambitious I'll dig it out and see what's behind there," said Don.

"Tell you what, don't call me in on that job."

"I wouldn't dream of it. All that's back there is Al Capone's vault anyway."

"Nice working with you, Geraldo," said Carville. "Now pick up your end of this chunk of limestone and let's get it out of here."

They were both strong men but they had to rest twice, getting the old water heater out. And getting it onto the junkpile had them both dripping with sweat and panting like fat old men jogging for the first time.

"I've been younger," said Carville.

"Yeah, but you were stupid then."

"But I didn't know I was stupid," said Carville. "I knew you were stupid, though."

"Go home, man, you've given me half the day, I can't afford any more."

"Hot water'll be ready in an hour or two."

"You did the electrical too?"

"I'm a full-service heating and plumbing and air-conditioning guy."

"That's why you're such a babe magnet."

"Naw. It's my pipe wrench."

"Take your tiny little pipe wrench and go," said Don.

A few more dumb jokes and Carville was on his way. It was a friendship that began in high school, and that was the level it was still at. Which was OK. That was all he needed from the guy.

The shower was all he'd hoped it would be. The new shower head didn't pulsate or anything like that, but it delivered a stream of water so intense it tingled and that was fine with Don. It was nice to shower in a tub he'd cleaned himself, instead of those truck-stop showers, which always felt kind of clammy and slimy and fungusy.

And then to pull back the shower curtain and dry off on his own clean new towel and put on a new bathrobe and slippers—it was downright domestic. From now on living here wouldn't feel like camping anymore.

Down in the parlor, he was just finishing buttoning his shirt when he heard Sylvie's voice from the hall. "Knock knock?" she asked.

"I'm decent," he said.

She came in. He sat down on the cot and started putting on socks. "Clean clothes," he said. "You ought to try it sometime."

"The dress isn't as dirty as it looks," she said. "After a while, the old grime builds up so thick the new grime just brushes right off. Sort of Teflon clothes."

"Bet we can market *that* and make a killing."

She smiled wanly.

"I left the soap and shampoo in the shower. Be careful 'cause it gets really hot now."

"I can hardly wait," she said. "You clean up nice."

He didn't know what to say. "Thanks." And then he had to change the subject. "Now that I'm cleaned up, I'm going over to call on those old ladies next door."

"I thought you said they were crazy."

"Yeah, but they really cook. Want to come, see if we can wangle two snacks for the price of none?"

She shook her head. "I'll stay here."

"They told me I could ask them if I had any questions about the house. They used to live here. Before you."

"What question are you going to ask them?" asked Sylvie.

"There's a gap in the foundation behind the old coal furnace. Might have been a root cellar or something."

"It's nothing."

"People don't leave a gap in their foundation for nothing, Sylvie." His shoes now tied, he got up and headed for the door. "I'm locking up behind me," he said. "You've got your key?"

She took it out of the wilted little pocket in her sad blue dress and held it up for him to see. "Thanks," she said.

He stepped out and closed and locked the door.

Sylvie listened to the deadbolt close. She didn't need the key. She knew the house would open for her whenever she asked. But it still mattered to her. The key meant that he was admitting she belonged there.

But just because she felt better about things didn't mean the house did. She had tried and tried to calm it all afternoon, but the removal of that wall had been traumatic. "It's cosmetic surgery," she explained. "That wall was a goiter. It hurts to have it removed, but you're glad it's gone. The room is beautifully proportioned now, and the windows are in just the right places on the wall."

She heard a sliding sound and turned to see Don's wrecking bar creeping toward the hall. "Stop it," she said. "He'll just find it anyway, and he'll think I moved it."

The wrecking bar stopped.

"I've got to look into this shower thing," she said. "I vaguely remember that cleanliness was next to godliness. But will it ruin the bounce in my hair?" She walked out of the room, up the stairs.

As soon as she left, the wrecking bar slid on out of the room and down the hall. And the workbench moved even closer to the cot, butting right up against it, sliding it an inch or so out of position. Then all was still in the parlor once again.

12

Garlic

The Weird sisters acted as if Don's coming over that afternoon were a visit from royalty. Well, to a point—presumably they wouldn't have had Prince Charles sit down in the kitchen with a cup of tea while he watched them prepare bread and a bean-and-bacon soup for that night's supper. But apart from the setting, they couldn't have fussed more over him or spoken more solicitously if he had been the prince himself. Don couldn't decipher their game, other than his certainty that they still hadn't given up hope of him abandoning his renovation of the Bellamy house.

"The secret," Miz Evelyn was saying, "is to use only a *dash* of seasoning, just the faintest hint of it. That way you don't smother the natural flavors of the stock and the vegetables."

"Miss Evvie," said Miz Judea, up to her elbows in bread dough, "will you be a dear and put away the flour and sugar bins for me so I have room to lay out the loaves?"

Miz Evelyn stepped away from the stove and picked up the two bins from the table. As she headed for the pantry, she went on with her commentary. "If I let Miss Judy here make the soup, she'd drown everything in garlic and peppers."

While Miz Evelyn was out of sight, Miz Judea rushed to the spice rack, grabbed a jar of garlic powder, popped off the shaker top and poured about a third of it into the soup. Then she replaced the top, set it back in its place on the rack, and returned to her bread before Miz Evelyn came back in from the pantry.

"Miss Judy's a wonderful cook," said Miz Evelyn, "but she has no subtlety."

Miz Evelyn stirred the soup pot, then lifted the wooden spoon to take a taste. "There," said Miz Evelyn. "Just the right amount of garlic. You can only just barely taste it."

"That's why Gladys likes Miss Evvie to make the soup," said Miz Judea. "Garlic makes her fart, the poor dear." She looked at Don with a steady gaze—did not so much as wink.

There is no untangling the complicated webs they weave in this house, he thought. Maybe it was time to get down to business. "You ladies told me that if I have any questions about that house . . ."

"Oh, we'll know the answer," said Miz Judea. "Or Gladys will, anyway."

"Well I was down in the cellar with the heating and plumbing contractor, and we noticed there was a break in the foundation behind the old coal furnace. It's all plugged up with rubble, but I wondered if maybe it was a root cellar or—"

"He found it!" crowed Miz Evelyn with delight.

"Took you long enough," said Miz Judea.

"Well I wasn't looking for it," said Don. "What is it?"

Miz Evelyn's voice got low and conspiratorial. "A rum runner's tunnel."

"That house was a speakeasy during Prohibition," said Miz Judea. "They'd sneak the booze up the tunnel from that gully out back."

"And whenever the cops raided the place," said Miz Evelyn, "they'd sneak the city council *out* through the tunnel."

The two of them broke up laughing at the memory.

"Oh, those were the days, those *were* the days," said Miz Judea.

"You were here then?"

Miz Evelyn answered him. "Both of us came here in '28. Shared a room upstairs."

"The one you been tearing apart," said Miz Judea. "Feels *so* good."

"You lived in a speakeasy?" asked Don.

"We weren't in the speakeasy part," said Miz Judea.

"We were in the bordello part," said Miz Evelyn.

Don couldn't think of a thing to say about that. But his silence was an answer all the same. Miz Judea laughed and hooted, while Miz Evelyn clucked her tongue and shook her head.

"What's so shocking?" said Miz Judea. "We were ladies of the night. It got me out of a sharecropper's cabin and it got Miz Evvie down from the mountain."

"Sorry," said Don. "I . . . you just don't look like . . . "

"He can't imagine us being young and pretty enough," said Miz Evelyn.

Judea slapped another loaf into shape and dropped it into a well-oiled pan. And another—slap slap slap slap *slop* and she slid the breadpan aside and pulled over the next.

"It was fun at first," said Miz Judea. "An adventure. All those men with money, clean-smelling. You got to remember where we were from. But when we got tired of it, lo and behold, the house wouldn't let us go. Prohibition ended and it became just an old whorehouse and the men got worse and worse and we were *stuck*. Then my young cousin Gladys came looking for me."

"It was Gladys who got us out," said Miz Evelyn.

"The house still holds onto us, though," said Miz Judea. "We could never get farther than this carriagehouse."

"Not for long," added Miz Evelyn.

"Once a strong house like that gets hold of you, it takes real power to get free. Gladys, now, she—"

Don set down his teacup. "Ladies, I'm sorry, I don't mean to be rude, but have you really been living next door to that house all these years because you believe it has some kind of magical hold over you?"

"Oh, he's an *educated* man," said Miz Evelyn, as if this were a well-known joke.

"I know, I know," said Miz Judea. "Young and skeptical."

So they were back to the mumbo-jumbo. Well, Don knew what he had come to find out—that gap in the cellar wall was a secret back door with a tunnel leading down to the gully. Someday it might be worth digging out the rubble and exploring it, but in all likelihood it had long since collapsed inside and what he really ought to do was seal it over so it didn't make a prospective buyer nervous. He pushed back his chair. "Thanks for answering my question, ladies. And for the tea."

Miz Evelyn was crestfallen. "Are you sure you won't stay for some of this soup?"

"No, sorry," said Don. "Too much garlic. Makes me fart."

Miz Evelyn looked shocked and offended. Out of the corner of his eye, Don caught Miz Judea's glare—she could no doubt cook a goose in flight with a look like that, and baste it, too. So Don grinned at Miz Evelyn and rose from the table. "I was joking, Miz Evelyn. I have no doubt your soup would be so good I'd eat it all and leave nothing for the two of you."

"Three," said Miz Judea, a bit of acid in her tone.

"Oh, Mr. Lark, you joker!" said Miz Evelyn. "What a caution!"

Don tipped his nonexistent hat to Miz Judea, then to Miz Evelyn. "Ladies, you are a constant marvel and I'm glad to have you as neighbors, even if only for a year."

Miz Evelyn giggled, and as he left Don heard her saying, "He makes a pretty speech, don't he, Miss Judy." He didn't hear Miz Judea's reply.

Don was hungry and he figured Sylvie must be, too. Whatever she'd been scrounging for food over the years, it was about time she stopped and got something decent. As long as she was his tenant, after a manner of speaking, he couldn't very well let her starve or risk food poisoning. So he drove down to the new standalone Chick-Fil-A on Wendover south of I-40 to buy a few dozen nuggets. Which wouldn't be as good as the Weird sisters' soup, maybe, but also wouldn't leave him beholden to anybody, which was just as important.

He couldn't get over the old ladies being prostitutes. What kind of perversity was it regarded as, in those days of deep Jim Crow, to have a black whore and a white whore sharing a room? He couldn't help wondering if men paid to get them both at once, or if the room was partitioned off somehow. But then the very thought of those old ladies naked or, worse still, prancing around in merry widows or negligees made him faintly ill, and he drove the image from his mind.

Or tried to. Why did they always have to tell him things he didn't really want to know? However things went in the Bellamy house during its bordello days, it was still a fact that they had come out of the whole affair as friends, and if there was a little underhanded conflict between them, like that garlic business, it didn't make them any less close. And Gladys got them free somehow. That's the part he couldn't understand. These ladies were sensible. In fact, they were smart. Yet they still believed in magic and houses having a hold over people and . . .

And he remembered the missing screwholes on the front door. And how Sylvie, who didn't seem crazy at all, had somehow decided she had to stay in that house rather than go out and face the world. Maybe they were the sensible ones indeed, and he was the one so superstitiously bound to the folklore of science that he couldn't admit the obvious. Those old ladies had been stuck and were still tied to the house, and Sylvie was stuck right now and couldn't get free. The way she ran into the upstairs room when he was butterknifing through the two-by-fours—did the house send her to find out what he was doing, cutting into it that way?

Could the same thing happen to him? Could he also get stuck in that house?

I'm surrounded by crazy people and now crazy is beginning to seem normal. Houses don't hold people, and I covered those screwholes with the deadbolt and just remembered it wrong.

When he got back with the bag of nuggets, having snitched only a few, he went through the house calling Sylvie's name, but she didn't answer. Not even in the attic. It was the first time he'd been in the house that she hadn't also been there. So he sat down and ate the nuggets himself. He was hungry enough to polish them off without trouble, and the fries, and both lemonades. Then, because he hadn't really done his day's quota of work yet, he went room to room tearing up carpets and hauling them out to the curb. No reason not to bare the floors everywhere in the house, get the carpets all hauled away with the first load. When he tore up the carpet in the room that had Sylvie's bed in it, he couldn't help noticing that the bed was all she had. No other furniture. Not so much as a book to read or a nightstand.

It was dark when he finished. He was sweaty and dusty and worn out. So much for his shower. But he didn't have the energy for another one tonight. Besides, his towel wouldn't be dry yet.

When he came into the house from the junkpile out front, he heard water running in the house. So she had come back while he was outside. Must be using the back door. Or . . . the tunnel? Was there room enough to squeeze through over the top of the rubble, if somebody really wanted to?

Tired as he was, curiosity got the better of him and he went down the stairs into the cellar. He had left a worklamp hanging in the cellar, but even after he found the power strip and turned on the overhead, he still needed his flashlight to see behind the coal furnace. The rubble didn't quite reach to the top of the gap in the foundation. Depending on how skinny Sylvie really was, maybe she could do it. But there was no sign of anybody climbing there—not that he knew what such a sign would be. A footprint? Not likely. Fallen rocks? It was a pile of rubble, for heaven's sake. How could he tell which rocks were fallen because of somebody climbing over? So what did he know now? Maybe she used the tunnel, maybe she didn't. And what did it matter?

He was tired. It was dark outside. Time for sleep, so he could be up at dawn. He stopped in the bathroom at the top of the cellar stairs in order to use the toilet and to wash his hands and face, then ducked his head down to splash water onto his hair to rinse out the worst of the dust, then toweled his head so he wouldn't soak his pillow. He still felt filthy but at least his face didn't feel cemented over with carpet dust. The water was still running upstairs. He wondered if he might have caused Sylvie's shower to turn cold when he washed up or hot when he flushed the toilet. It had been thoughtless of him not to wait till she was done. But then, it was kind of a long shower she was taking and he needed to get to bed. He'd ask her in the morning whether the downstairs bathroom affected the upstairs shower.

He went into the parlor without switching on the light—he could see well enough by the streetlight to take off his shoes and socks and lie down on his cot. So he followed his ritual and pried each shoe off with the toe of the other foot, then sat down to take off his socks.

But when he leaned back, he cracked his head hard against something. It was so painful, so sharp a blow that he almost blacked out. He had to lie down until he could see again, and when he felt the back of his head it was wet. Which meant he had just got blood all over his pillow. Of course he knew at once what he had hit. Lying there on the cot, the workbench fairly loomed over him.

He tried to stand up but again almost fainted. So he crawled to the power strip and turned on the light. The workbench was almost malevolent in its placement, right up against the cot, at exactly the middle, where he sat every night to take off his shoes. Why did she move it? And why to that exact spot? It was impossible to imagine that she actually meant him to hurt himself, and yet it couldn't have been more perfectly placed to achieve that end.

His head was clearing. When he looked at the pillow he could see that there really wasn't much blood, just a dot of it. His fingers had felt the liquid, but of course his hair was still wet from the washing up he did. That's what he had felt. Mostly. But there was a goose egg growing on the back of his head.

He pulled and then pushed the workbench away from his cot. The strain of moving it made his head throb. Damn her anyway for touching his stuff. Didn't they have a deal? He wasn't going to let this pass. He wasn't going to be calm and reasonable about it, either. She had drawn blood, for pete's sake.

He strode to the stairs and started to take them three at a time. The pain in his head immediately let him know that this was not a good idea. One step at a time he finished the ascent, then walked to the bathroom door.

It stood ajar by a couple of inches, and inside he could see fog swirling. He raised his hand to knock—or to push the door open?

What was he thinking? She was taking a shower, which meant she was naked in there. Just because he had bumped his head didn't give him the right to violate her modesty. Time enough for this discussion in the morning.

He made his way downstairs gingerly, because each jolting footstep rang through his head. This was going to slow him down tomorrow, he knew it. He rummaged through his suitcase and found some extra-strength Tylenol, then went to the bathroom and took four of them with a few handfuls of water. Had to get some paper cups.

Back in the parlor he switched off the light, then felt the back of his head to see if it was still bleeding. It felt like it had scabbed over. Not much of an injury, really, though the swelling was pretty high. If he was suffering from concussion, how would he know? He should go to the hospital. But what would they do? Tell him to take Tylenol and go to bed. He could do that without paying for a doctor and waiting for three hours in the emergency room.

Maybe he'd die in his sleep tonight. So what? Let Sylvie figure out what to do with his body. Let the Weird sisters cover him with garlic and bury him in the back yard. He was too sick and tired of everything to care what happened. You help somebody a little, and look what happens. Twenty thousand dollars because of Cindy. Now concussion and possible death because of Sylvie.

Don't be such a baby, he told himself. You're going to be fine.

He lay on his side, his head throbbing. Come on, Tylenol, don't fail me now.

The water stopped running. How nice. Sylvie had apparently drained the hot water tank and would now go blissfully to bed, clean for the first time in years, no doubt, while he suffered alone downstairs because of her negligence.

A few moments later, he heard soft footsteps on the stairs. Was she coming down to inspect the damage? No, he shouldn't leap to conclusions. No doubt she'd have some reason why she moved the workbench and then forgot to put it back. He should be fair and hear her out.

Like a good father.

The words in his own mind made his head throb even more. He wasn't her father. He wasn't her anything, not even her landlord, since she wasn't paying rent. And yet he was thinking of her as a daughter, wasn't he? Because when he knew that she was taking a shower, when he stood there at her door, it was her modesty that he cared about, that he wanted to protect. What he didn't feel was desire. She was not in the category Cindy Claybourne had been in, when Don kissed her, when he felt himself swept away with desire for her. He and Cindy had met as equals. Sylvie was a waif; Don had her under his protection. The way Cindy was now. Off-limits.

Only he had still felt desire for Cindy today. It had taken willpower—not a lot, but some—to keep from trying to reopen that closed door.

It didn't matter. Sylvie was coming down the stairs and he'd have to deal with her now whether she was in a daughter role in his unconscious mind or not. Painfully, slowly, he rose to a sitting position.

She emerged from the shadow of the entry way into the light slanting in from the streetlamp. Her hair hung straight and wet, with just a hint of curl in it where a few strands had dried. She had apparently decided against the bathrobe he bought for her—she was back in the same faded blue dress. But in this light, cleaned up, the hair no longer stringing across her face, she was almost pretty in a forlorn, dreamy sort of way.

"You're still awake?" she asked softly.

"Don't you mean still alive?" he asked.

"What?" she said. "I just thought I heard you upstairs when I was showering. Did you want something?"

"You were gone when I got back with dinner," he said. "Nuggets from Chick-Fil-A. I called through the house but you didn't answer so what can I say. We don't have a fridge or a microwave and they're nasty when they're cold. So I ate them."

"That's OK."

No, it wasn't OK. That wasn't what he meant to say to her at all. He was going to chew her out about her carelessness. It was the headache. He couldn't think straight.

He reached down and held out the pillow. Not that she could see it in the dark.

"What is it?" she asked.

"Nothing much. Just my blood."

"You hurt yourself?"

"No," said Don. "*You* hurt me. By moving my workbench right up against my cot."

"No," she murmured.

"Smacked my head on it when I sat down to take off my socks. Almost knocked me out."

"You should go to the hospital."

"No, I've decided to die at home," he said nastily.

"Concussions can be dangerous."

"So why didn't you think of that when you moved things around down here? I thought I asked you not to touch my tools."

"I didn't," she said.

"Who else, the tooth fairy?" he asked. "Come on, you can't move the workbench halfway across the room and then forget you did it. It's heavy."

"I didn't move your workbench," she said. "I'm sorry you were hurt."

She turned abruptly and left, pattering up the stairs.

He had no sympathy for her. Imagine denying it. How stupid did she think he was?

Couldn't deal with it now. Thinking about her only made him angry, and that made his head hurt worse, and he didn't need that. Had to sleep this off so he could get to work the next morning.

At the top of the stairs, Sylvie slapped the newel post. Without a sound she formed words and spoke them. "Stupid, nasty . . . what are you doing? What are you *thinking* of?"

She walked into the room Don Lark had stripped and opened up. "How many times do I have to tell you, he's not hurting you?"

She strode to a bare timber, a thick vertical post, one of the ancient bones of the house, and pressed her head against it. "No more of this. No more hurting him. Ever." The house seemed to her like a little child going to the doctor. Lashing out in terror of the needle. You couldn't get angry, you just had to explain. "Don't you see he's going to make you whole again? It hurts now, but soon he'll make you stronger. You have to trust me."

13

Daughters

Tearing out walls, ripping up carpets, stripping lath and plaster off the old timbers, those were the dramatic changes, requiring hard labor and little skill. But those jobs were soon done, for the moment at least, for that first upstairs room. Don paid to have the junkpile hauled away; then he settled in to the routine of turning that upstairs room back into the graceful, comforting space it was meant to be.

He went back and forth over whether to add another bathroom upstairs. Now was the time to do it, or at least to rough it in between the back bedroom and the front one. On the one hand, plumbing it would be expensive and difficult, since no pipes ran to that region of the house. And it would cut into the nice proportions of one room or the other—or both, if he made it into a huge, two-window bathroom. So his inclination was to leave it out.

On the other hand, Americans seemed to be in the middle of an intense love affair with the bathroom. Not only were bathrooms getting larger in both size and number, people weren't even frosting the glass anymore, and often didn't even allow for window coverings. Heather and Chuckie next door could look out their window and watch whatever you were doing in the jakes. Don didn't get it. Some of the bathrooms he'd seen looked like water shrines. One bathroom he saw, in a development just off the Algonkian Parkway in northern Virginia, was exactly as large as the master bedroom. All the normal accoutrements were scattered around the edges of the room, and in the middle was a huge jacuzzi that looked like an altar to some pagan god. He could imagine some priest in gold lamé sacrificing a virgin or a sheep.

For people who needed porcelain temples, would one small bathroom cut into the hall at the head of the stairs do the job for the entire second floor? He could hear the househunting couples already. "The children would fight constantly over the bathroom. And what about guests? It would be so awful trying to get the kids to keep their bathroom clean enough for company."

Even money wasn't a reliable guide. Putting in more bathrooms would make the house easier to sell, especially since the original bedrooms were so large that there was room to tuck a good-sized bathroom in every one of them. But *not* putting in more bathrooms would save him a lot of money, which he wouldn't have to borrow from the bank, and that would allow him to charge maybe a little less for the house, which would make the house easier to sell. He couldn't lose. Or couldn't win, depending on how you looked at it.

In the end he followed his own preferences and opted to keep the simple purity of the original design. In other words, he saved himself a lot of bother and expense. He would still cut into the bedroom space to put in a beautiful closet that would look more like fine furniture than architecture. But it wouldn't rise to within three feet of the eleven-foot ceiling, so the proportions of the room would still be visible and have their effect on the dweller. As for the cost, building an elegant closet was entirely a matter of carpentry, which he would do with his own hands.

The decision was made, and he set to work.

The rough framing always went fast, even working alone. Then wiring to bring the whole thing up to code—that took time, but the payoffs were immediate, as he was able to get rid of the extension cords running up the stairs and plug things directly into the new outlets. The wallboard got the fastest results of all, making things look so close to being done.

But that was just when the real work began. Any hardworking, careful guy could put up a stud wall and wallboard, then mud it and prime it. Any competent electrician could install a slew of outlets. But there weren't many people left in America who still knew how to make elaborate wood trim out of fine hardwoods, which were stained, not painted, so the grain showed and no knots or other flaws could be tolerated. Crown moldings, a picture rail, wainscoting, and baseboards were all turned out by Don's own hand.

With Sylvie watching.

There was no escaping her and he no longer tried. Partly because he was trying to be decent about it, but even more because she really wasn't intrusive. Most people who watched others work were extraverts, insisting on constant engagement, asking questions, offering opinions, or, worst of all, trying to carry on involved conversations about things that had nothing to do with the task at hand. Sylvie just sat there, virtually unnoticeable. When she did speak, it was to ask questions that—to Don's surprise—were worth answering. Like, How did carpenters make moldings before the invention of the router? Why wasn't wallpaper put on first so the moldings and chair rail could cover the edges and keep them from peeling? Because the questions came rarely, they were a pleasure to answer.

And now and then Don would ask a question of his own. He began to build up a picture of Sylvie's life. An only child, orphaned in her teens, she got a friendly foster home with the parents of a friend, but it was always more a room-and-board arrangement than a family relationship, and after high school graduation they quickly drifted apart. Sylvie had no money—either to inherit or from insurance. She earned a scholarship to UNCG and worked hard to pay her own living expenses. It was a solitary life; between work and school she had no time for dating and no particular interest in it, either. "If I met a guy who seemed like he might be as good a man as my father, then I started comparing myself to my mother and realized I wasn't worthy of a guy like that." She laughed over it, but Don understood the pain under the laughter. Squatting here in the Bellamy house hadn't been that big a change for her, except for matters of personal hygiene.

Felicity Yont changed all that. Lissy was the extravert Sylvie wasn't. They were close enough to the same size that they could trade clothes, but mostly Lissy made Sylvie borrow her more stylish outfits so she wouldn't look so mousy. Lissy changed Sylvie's hair, drew her into some double dates, even got her to sleep in t-shirts instead of her dowdy flannel nightgowns. Never mind that Sylvie's t-shirts were all shapeless oversized men's shirts, while Lissy always managed to find shirts tight and short enough that she couldn't have scotch-taped a rose petal to her skin without making a bump. It was still a lifestyle makeover for Sylvie.

Except it didn't take. Sylvie was older, had a keener sense of responsibility. Maybe she had always been older. But she knew her grades had to be good enough to win her a solid job offer upon completing her master's degree. So despite many changes in Sylvie's look and habits, Lissy couldn't change the big one: Sylvie's need to work every possible moment. Sylvie thought it was a big deal to go out and frolic once a month. Lissy thought her life was over if she only went out on weekends. "Oil and water but our life was exciting," said Sylvie. "Mine was certainly more interesting than the average librarian-to-be."

So after that first year as friends, when Lissy proposed they share a large apartment on the ground floor of a decaying but gorgeous old house, Sylvie was game. What could go wrong?

"What *did* go wrong?"

"You're going to laugh, but it was when she started watching every move I made. It used to be she was so free and I was the stay-at-home stick-in-the-mud. But then that last semester she stops seeing her boyfriend Lanny so much and there she is hanging around the apartment, looking over my shoulder, reading my textbooks. It's as though she suddenly realized she was about to graduate with about a C average and nobody was going to want to give her a job worth having. While I had a couple of offers, including that Providence job. I think she wanted to learn how to study, only it was too late."

"You miss her."

Sylvie looked away. "She wasn't a nice person. But no worse than me."

From then on it was impossible for Don to see Sylvie as a homeless waif. She was a person with a past, with friends found and lost, with emotions that could be stung into life by a memory.

Conversations like that were pretty rare, though, during the couple of weeks Don worked on that one room. Mostly Don just worked as Sylvie watched from across the room. Mostly he forgot she was there.

In fact, they evolved a kind of signal. Don plugged in his cheap boom box during the jobs that didn't involve power tools. Music gave a kind of rhythm to the work, made it feel like he was flowing a little faster through the minutes and hours of the day. He tuned to 98.7, which used to be a hard rock station but now played the new-country format. First time it drove Sylvie out of the room, which annoyed Don a little. Couldn't help but take it as an insult to his taste. But then she gradually sidled back in, listening to the music. While the music was playing, she never talked. But when Don was tired of the station and turned the boombox off, she usually had a question or comment stored up. Often enough it was country music she wanted to talk about it. "Once you get used to the twang," she said.

"Some of us don't hear it as a twang," said Don.

"Don't tell me John Anderson sounds natural to you."

"I give you John Anderson."

"'Swangin','" she sang.

He laughed.

Gradually he got a feel for the kind of music she liked, and one evening after work he went to Borders and came back with a fistful of CDs. Garth Brooks was too plastic for her; Lyle Lovett was too weird. But she liked Martina McBride and Lorrie Morgan, Trisha Yearwood and Ronna Reeves, liked them a lot. Don tried to figure out what it was that she liked so much about their music. Heaven knows they were twangy enough, and pretty plastic too, sometimes. She couldn't put it into words. "It's like their lives are full of tragedy and yet they can sing about it with so much energy. Instead of being depressed, they turn it into music."

"Is that what you are?" asked Don. "Depressed?"

"No. I'm just plain old-fashioned sad." And then she got up and wandered off. He couldn't figure out why she left when she left. There didn't seem to be a pattern to it. Sometimes she'd answer the most personal questions—not that he asked her anything *that* private. Other times the most innocent, general comment would make her wander away. Now and then Don would feel a little stab of annoyance at her moods, but then he remembered how he let his own moods control her, too, what with turning the radio on when he didn't want to talk and taking off to run errands when he needed to be alone.

The longer he worked on refurbishing that upstairs room, the more she warmed up. She finally started taking a little food now and then. Never more than a bite or two when Don was looking. She'd chew it like it was the best thing ever cooked. But she'd leave the rest. "You're going to waste away, you keep eating like an anorexic."

"You can't eat like an anorexic," she said. "You can only *not* eat like one."

"Well pardon me while I go puke like a bulimic."

"That's the room that's missing from this house. A vomitorium." Then, because he had no idea about Roman culture, she explained to him how the Romans would feast and feast, then duck into a vomitorium to puke it up.

"How does the chef tell the difference between a compliment and a criticism?"

"If you go back for seconds."

Times like that, there was a lot of silly joking, easy laughter. The kind of chatter that could go on while Don was working, without him missing a stroke or a cut.

One time after they heard Ronna Reeves sing "Man from Wichita," Sylvie started talking about her parents. "I don't know why that song reminds me of them. The song's got nothing to do with parents."

"It's got to do with missing someone so bad you want to die," said Don. "My folks didn't die on me when I was young, but it still hurts."

"I know," said Sylvie. "You fight with them because they're always trying to control your life, you want to break free. And then . . . I was free. And I thought: Why isn't this more fun? Isn't this what I always wanted?"

"Of course it wasn't."

"I don't mean them being dead, I mean the freedom. I wanted freedom. But it was . . . what. Empty."

"Me too," said Don. "It's like, anything you do when your parents aren't there to watch, it didn't really happen."

"People aren't supposed to lose their parents so young."

"In the old days most people lost one or the other. Childbirth. Sickness. Industrial accidents. Every time I cut myself on something, I think, there but for antiseptics and modern hygiene would be my last injury. Gangrene."

"Half the people I knew in school had lost a parent."

"Yeah but that was divorce, right?"

"My parents fought sometimes," said Sylvie. "But I don't think they would have gotten divorced, even if they hadn't died."

"Mine were solid, too."

"I had to keep imagining my mother was checking on me," said Sylvie. "The whole time I was working on my schooling and all, I'd keep imagining her just out of sight, watching." She laughed derisively. "Turned out it was only Lissy."

"But why shouldn't your mom be watching you from . . . wherever she is."

"Heaven is the word you're looking for," she said.

"I didn't know if you, you know, believed."

"In what?"

"The afterlife."

"Maybe the word 'belief' is too strong," she said. "I hope."

"Me too."

"It ain't your parents you're missing, Don Lark."

"Careful, Sylvie. You're starting to talk like a hick. 'Ain't,' indeed. Too much country music. It's getting to you."

She ignored his attempt to change the subject. "I try to imagine what it would be like to have a child, and then lose it."

"I didn't *lose* her," said Don. "She was stolen away from me."

"I try but I can't do it," said Sylvie. "Either one. Can't imagine either one."

"Having one is the best thing in the world. Losing her is the worst. After that, you've seen the best, you've seen the worst."

"So you're scared of nothing?"

"I look like a damn fool to you?"

"Only when you're holding up a slab of wallboard with that toe-lever thing and pressing your whole body against it to get it set in place. Then it looks like you're praying to the wall."

"Or flirting with it."

"What you do is way beyond flirting."

"Way beyond praying sometimes, too," he said.

"See, Don, what I wanted to say was this. Even if you get mad at me. I've got to say it. Your little girl. She had from you the thing that matters more than money or 'quality time' or anything. She knew she was *seen* and *known* and admired and loved and . . . *respected* by you, she knew that, didn't she?"

"I don't know. She was so young."

"She knew. You think a kid has to be able to talk before they can know?'

And they got off on something else and then after a while fell silent and that moment was over. There weren't many of those times, but there were enough of them that by the time Don was pretty much through with that room, he didn't feel like he'd really finished it until he had Sylvie come in for a formal inspection and guided tour. "You're my surrogate parents," Don said. "I need to have you look at what I did so it will all turn real."

"Bibbity-bobbity-boo," said Sylvie. "You're now a real boy."

"You're thinking of *Pinocchio* but quoting *Cinderella*."

"I'm thinking of the sequel. Pinocchio tries to put the slipper on Cinderella and she gets splinters in her foot."

"I don't leave splinters," he said.

"So show me, and I'll make the room turn real," she said.

He led her to the room and opened the door, feeling silly as he did it. Hadn't she seen this room every day while he was working on it? But she came inside and turned around and around, like a child dancing, seeing it all as if for the first time. "Oh, Don, it's so beautiful."

"It was a well-designed space to begin with," he said. "All I had to do was keep from screwing it up."

"It makes the rest of the house look so drab."

"That's why I finish one room before doing anything else. I like to see the contrast."

Sylvie ran to the closet and opened the doors. Though on the outside it looked like an armoire, it was deep, a walk-in, with gentle lights that came on as soon as a door was opened. She turned around, reached out, and closed the doors. He stood in the middle of the room, waiting for her to reopen them. Waiting. "Sylvie?" he said. Then he began walking to the closet, wondering what could possibly be keeping her inside it so long. Couldn't she figure out that you opened the doors just by pushing them?

Just as he was about to reach out for the handles, the doors were flung open and Sylvie bounded out, right in front of him, and shouted, "Boo!"

Don made a great show of clutching his heart, but that was only to cover the fact that she really had frightened him. She almost collapsed with laughter, and he couldn't help laughing with her. Then she ran to the window and touched the natural-wood frame, the blinds, the fabric texture of the wallpaper.

"You can almost feel the house getting younger," she said.

Then, because she insisted on it, he gave her the guided tour, explaining what he had done—and what some builders might have done but he chose not to, so the space would be better proportioned or truer to the original concept or more functional. The inside story. And she listened to him. The way a daughter might have done, if she had lived long enough to grow up to be a homeless student of library science living in an abandoned mansion.

This idea stopped him cold, his thoughts spinning.

"What?" she asked, looking at him with some concern.

"What what?" he said. Then he realized that he must have been standing there in sudden silence. "Don't worry, when I have a heart attack I'll clutch my chest and grunt and fall down."

"I was thinking more of a stroke. Paralyzed on the spot. Turned to stone."

"A pillar of sawdust."

"What were you thinking?" she asked.

He hesitated a moment. His normal impulse would be to fend her off with a joke. But instead he found that he wanted to talk openly to her. No jokes. "I was thinking that this was like, you know . . . that showing you this room, I might have done that with my . . . daughter, if she had lived. Shown her my work like this."

She took a step back from him. "I'm not your daughter," said Sylvie.

So it had been a mistake to open up that far. It always was. "I just meant that I was imagining what it would be like if you were."

"I'm nobody's *daughter.*" She said the last word with such vehemence that Don wondered if there might be something more to her relationship with her parents than their early death.

He almost apologized, but then stopped himself. What had he actually done to *her?* "What do you care if I think of you as a daughter?"

"I don't need a father," she said coldly.

"And I don't need a houseguest," said Don. "I've got no room in my life for what you actually are, but I do have this huge empty space for a daughter and if that's where I find a little room for you, what do you care?"

"My father left me, and my mother, and I did just fine."

"Oh, yeah, look at you, you've done *so* well."

His words visibly stung her and he regretted saying them. But he wasn't going to apologize. *She* was the one who decided to turn a contemplative moment into a quarrel.

"What happened to me in college has nothing to do with losing my parents," she said.

"Yeah, well, my letting you stay here has *everything* to do with losing my daughter, so learn to live with it, kid."

"What are you, the ancient of days or something? I'm twenty-four, not four years old. You can't be my father."

"Give me a break," said Don. "Twenty-four? How old were you when you got your doctorate?"

"I never got it," she said. "Remember?" But then she realized what he was asking. "I meant—I mean, I was twenty-four when I would have gotten my degree. But now I'm . . . even older."

"How much older? Don't you even know?"

"Look around, how many calendars do you see?"

"There are seasons, you know. You go outside, there's snow or ice, think winter. It gets like an oven in here with everything boarded up, you can figure you're having summer."

"I was going to get my degree in '87." She looked away from him, and he could see that she was afraid of what he was going to tell her.

"Ten years," said Don. "You've been squatting here for ten years."

"It's 1997?" she tried to look nonchalant. "My how time flies."

"You don't even know who's president, do you?"

"They never invite me to the White House anyway, so what do I care?"

"Doesn't this bother you?" But he could see that it did, that she was frightened by what had happened to her, the years lost in whatever funk had kept her in this place.

"I had no idea," she said. "All those years." She gave a little cry, maybe a sob, then gasped, trying to calm herself.

Don reached out his hand, rested it lightly on her shoulder. It dawned on him that it was the first time he had ever touched her. Have a woman living in your house, it wouldn't do to touch her; but Sylvie needed comfort, not the tongue-lashing Don had been giving her. He was thinking: What kind of father am I?

But she recoiled from his touch as if he were some sort of disgusting amphibian. "I told you!" she screamed at him. "I'm not your daughter!"

"Damn right you're not!" he snapped. "There's not a chance in hell I would have let a daughter of mine end up like *this*, trapped in an abandoned house so you don't even keep track of how many *years* you've been wasting your life!"

"How old are *you*, Mister Wisdom, Mister I-Would-Have-Made-Everything-All-Right-No-Matter-How-You-Screwed-Up?"

"Younger than you," said Don. "And a hell of a lot older."

"Well, *Daddy*, don't swear at me." She made *daddy* sound like an epithet.

"Don't call me that," he said.

"I thought you wanted me to be your daughter, what happened to *that*?"

"When she called me Daddy it didn't sound like that." And then he heard her voice in his mind, the voice of his little girl when she was barely a year old, just walking, just able to say *Mama* and *Daddy*, before she was taken away from him. Daddy. And the floodgates opened. Sobs took over his body like a convulsion and he sank to the floor, trying to twist his body away from her so she wouldn't see how the tears leapt from his eyes and splashed on the light lustrous finish of the delicately whitewashed wooden floor.

But she saw, of course. He heard her step toward him. Felt her hand on his head, patting him. A light touch, like a child's. It burned through him, lightning through his body. "Don't touch me like that!" he cried.

"I'm sorry," she whispered.

"You're not my daughter, all right?" He tried to get control of his voice. He couldn't look at her, couldn't show his face contorted, tear-soaked like this. "She's dead and I'll never see her again and you're not her so get out! Get out!"

She left the room. If she went right on and left the house, that would be fine with him too. He should never have let her stay. He should never have let anybody get this close to him. He lay down on the floor, curled up like a child, crying, saying her name over and over. He hadn't let himself think of her name in years but he had lost control anyway, and so he might as well say it, over and over like a prayer, like the refrain of a sad half-forgotten song, "Nellie, Nellie, Nell."

It didn't last long, really, considering how many months, years, his feelings had been pent up. He lay there for a while, then rolled onto his back and stared up through sore, wept-out eyes at the ceiling he had finished only a few days before. The warm natural-wood molding. The closet that looked more like an armoire than a built-in. He turned his head to the windows. The wooden venetian blinds sliced the afternoon sunlight into thick buttery bands. A room for playing, for dreaming, for resting, for life.

After all the rooms he had created out of nothing, out of junk, with this room he finally understood what it was he was making.

Safe spaces. Comforting refuges. He was making rooms for Nellie.

Only Nellie would never set foot in any of them. Never in this room. So what was it for?

He got to his feet, a little sore from lying on the floor. He walked out into the hall, down the stairs, out the front door without ever seeing Sylvie. Maybe she was gone. Good.

No, not good. Not good that he could build a place like that and then drive her out of it. Surely that wasn't what he had intended. Surely it was for her that he had built it. When he was through showing her the room, he had meant to tell her that it was hers until the house was sold. Her bright safe place, after all these years in a dark, dirty, hot-or-freezing house. Not that he had admitted this plan even to himself. But that was where today was heading before it turned into that stupid, meaningless fight, into this emotional disaster.

The leaves were all turned to autumn colors now, and they still festooned the trees, except for a copious sprinkle across the lawns. But there was a wind picking up and the sky was lowering. The leaves would go tonight, the bulk of them, blown off the trees and then matted down to the ground by cold, pounding autumn rain. He walked in the chilling air, breathing in the smell of impending weather, letting the color wash over him. He had spent too long indoors. And even indoors he had not looked out the window half enough. Running errands, he hadn't seen the world he was moving through.

It was Sylvie's room. That's who he had made it for. He knew that Nellie was dead and would never live there. He knew that Sylvie wasn't his daughter. But she was someone who needed his protection. He hadn't wanted to take her into that place, but she was there, and the room was for her, had always been for her. For herself, not for some imagined surrogate of his daughter.

When she moved into that room it would no longer be his. He would knock at the door if he wanted to speak to her. If she invited him in then he would go, but as a visitor. That was the way of it, for a builder like Don. You made beautiful spaces, you built with your whole heart, and then you invited someone else into the space you had made and gave them the keys and locked yourself out of it forever. But you were still there, that was the secret. Don was still there in all the houses, watching out for the people, enclosing them, sheltering them. He was still there, soothing their eyes, stilling the sounds of the outside world, framing their lives so that all their dreams could be contained in a place where they had only to reach out and touch them and they would come to life again.

He headed back to the house. Jogged back, the tape measure and wallet and keys bouncing in his pockets. He had left the front door unlocked; he burst through it, calling out to her. "Sylvie!" His voice echoed through the house. It sounded so empty. "Sylvie, are you here?"

He ran up the stairs, tried all the doors on the second floor. Up into the attic. "Don't hide from me in here, Sylvie," he said. No answer, she wasn't there, or if she was he couldn't find her.

She'd come back. She'd hidden before, stayed out of sight for a while. But she came back. Ten years she'd been trapped in this place, it's not likely that one quarrel would drive her out, was it? He tried to fill himself with confidence as he went back down the attic stairs, then down the wide staircase to the main floor. Maybe she was in the cellar.

No. She was in the parlor. Lying on his cot. Asleep on his cot. Hadn't she heard him calling? He'd been so loud. Nellie had been like that. When she slept, she slept.

He thought of waking her, apologizing to her, telling her what he had realized, that the room was for her all along, that she was welcome here as long as the house belonged to him. But he couldn't bring himself to disturb her.

He went upstairs to the bedroom she had been sleeping in, to the one shabby bed remaining in the house. He took the mattress off the bed, blankets and all, and dragged it into the new room; the sagging box springs came next. Then he knocked apart the bedframe and carried in the four parts and reassembled them, put on the springs and mattress, and neatly made the bed. It looked so small in that large space, like a child's bed, though it was a regular twin. And so tatty compared to the glowing perfect finish of the room. He thought of buying her a new bed, a queen-size perhaps; a canopy bed, or a brass one, or a four-poster. But no, that would feel too permanent. A waste of money in a house he was going to sell in a year. This shabby old bed would have to do. It was the space around the bed that mattered. What she would see in the morning when she opened her eyes. The bands of light through the windows. The closet where she had already played like a child. She owned nothing with which to fill this space. So instead she would own the space itself.

He heard a sound from the hall outside the room. A footstep. He turned around and there she was.

"My bed," she said.

Suddenly he was shy about what he had done. "I needed to have your stuff out of the other room before I worked on it."

She stepped into the room and looked at all of it again, turning around once, twice. "I get to sleep in here?"

He nodded.

"I've never had a room like this." She laughed, a low sound, deep mirth; and then another laugh, cascading, the music of delight. "I know, it's only for a little while, but—thank you."

And with that the room was no longer his. He had bestowed it. He smiled at her, tipped his invisible hat, and went away downstairs.

14

Wrecking Bar

Don went to sleep that night feeling better than he had for a long time. Embarrassing as it had been to break down like that in front of Sylvie, he knew that it had been a good thing. A wall inside himself had been broken. He could think of Nellie's name again, say it to himself. Something had been given back to him. And because Sylvie had been part of it, there was something between them now. A bond of loss, if loss could bind. He could share this house with her, for the months ahead, because they were no longer strangers.

In the morning, though, with the emotions of the day before faded, he began to think of other things. Bleaker things. Had the sight of his weeping diminished him in Sylvie's eyes? He remembered standing there watching Cindy weep. Touching her as Sylvie had touched him. It had meant the end of his relationship with Cindy. Not that the situations had been analogous. It was the passion that ended between him and Cindy. There had never been any such feeling between him and Sylvie. On the contrary, there had been suspicion and hostility and dread. The transformation could only be for the better.

Yet his suspicion grew as he climbed the stairs, heading for the shower, and glanced at the door to her new room. Closed. Getting her own room—that was a victory he had simply handed to her. Now could he ever get her out of there? Why had he done something so foolish? Yesterday, caught up in emotion, he had felt protective, expansive, even grateful to her for her show of kindness. Today, the emotions spent, he could see that he had only complicated things worse. She was still a stranger. But now she was a stranger who was bound to think she had a hold on him. Loneliness had driven him to do foolish things, and now he would have to face the consequences.

Sooner than he imagined, in fact. For once he was showered, ready for the day, his first task was to look for his wrecking bar. He hadn't needed it since he tore out the walls in the room that was now Sylvie's. Which meant it should have been where he always kept it, in the long green toolbox. It wasn't there.

At first he thought perhaps he had put it away somewhere else. But it didn't take long to eliminate all the possibilities. Don was meticulous about putting his tools away. There was no reason to think he had done anything unusual with the wrecking bar.

He didn't want to suspect Sylvie, but what if she had moved it awhile ago, before their reconciliation? It was still annoying that she might have been doing things like that, but at least it wouldn't be a complete repudiation of the kinder, gentler relationship that was established yesterday. He wouldn't hold such a prank against her. As long as she gave the wrecking bar back to him.

He went upstairs and knocked on her door.

"Yes?" Her voice came only faintly through the closed door.

"Have you seen my wrecking bar?"

"Just a minute."

He waited. After a few moments, she opened the door. Wearing her dress, as usual. He wondered if she slept in it. Probably not; it was faded but not terribly wrinkled. So she must sleep in her underwear or in the buff—on bedding that couldn't have been washed more recently than her dress. "Listen," he said, "I'm going to do a laundry today, you want me to take those sheets?"

Her face brightened. "Sure. Thanks."

"Um, I could . . . that dress. If you wore your bathrobe while I'm gone, I could take that dress and wash it."

She shook her head. "No thanks. Really. It's all right."

"It wouldn't be any trouble. Or I'd get it dry-cleaned."

"I don't . . . that's kind of you, but I just . . . it's not dirty."

He didn't bother to argue. "Whatever," he said. "But anyway, what I actually came up here for, I wondered if you knew where my wrecking bar is."

"Wrecking bar?"

"That black metal prybar I used for popping off wallboard. All-purpose breaking and ripping-up tool."

"I don't remember it."

He drew it in the air. "Shaped like this."

"OK, yes, I think I remember. What about it?"

"Where is it?"

"Where did you put it last?"

"I put it away in my long green toolbox."

She gazed steadily at him for a long moment before answering. "Don, you told me not to touch your tools and I don't touch them."

So much for a more forthright relationship between them. "What was it, killer moths? Fairies? Elves?"

She sighed and leaned her head against the doorpost. "Please," she said. "I thought we were friends now."

"So did I. But I need my wrecking bar. I've got to start on another room. Tearing out a stud wall and stripping the old lath and plaster."

"I'll be glad to help you look, as long as we don't start from the assumption that I know where it is but I'm just not telling you. Because I don't know. If I knew, I'd tell."

Don turned away from her, exasperated, then turned back. "All right, play it how you want. Help me look for it. Just remember that I really need it. This isn't the only room I have to finish."

"Now that *my* room's done, what do I care?" she said. And then, because he no doubt looked outraged, she reached out and touched him lightly on the arm. "A joke, Don. That was a joke."

"Please, just . . . help me look."

"OK," she said. "Let me guess. You want to search in my room first."

"Why not?" he said. "We're already here."

She led the way, opening the closet, making a show of looking in ludicrous places, like the light fixtures and the venetian blinds. "Not here. Not here. Not here."

"OK, so you're offended," Don finally said. "But the wrecking bar didn't just walk off, somebody had to move it."

"Why is that? What makes you so sure of that?"

"So sure of what?" For a moment he had no idea what she was asking him.

"That somebody had to move that wrecking bar?"

"Because objects made of solid metal don't move unless something moves them."

"Some*thing*."

Now it dawned on him. "Oh, some supernatural force did it. The house did it."

The sarcasm stung her. "I don't care what you believe. Why should I help you look? If I'm the one who finds it, you'll assume I put it there."

"Put it where?"

"Where I find it. *If* I find it. Promise you won't accuse me of that."

"I promise."

"I don't believe you." She wasn't joking. But then, neither was he.

"I just want my wrecking bar!"

"And I want to be trusted."

He thought of a lot of rejoinders that would have made him feel a little better while making the situation quite a bit worse. Instead he answered, quietly, "Please help me look for my wrecking bar."

"If I find it," she said, "it will be because I've lived in this house long enough to know where stuff collects."

"Collects?"

"Where it drifts to. Lost stuff."

"This isn't a lake. Things don't drift."

"Then we won't find the wrecking bar in any of those places." She sounded amused, but her eyes were on fire.

"This is worthless," said Don. "I'll just hunt for it alone."

"Do you want my help or not?"

"I want my wrecking bar. If you can help me find it, please do.

Otherwise, stay here with your bizarre fantasy life. It's done you so much good up to now."

He headed out of the room.

She called after him. "Maybe you better make sure you know what reality is before you start talking about *my* fantasies!"

He kept walking, into the hall, down the stairs.

"How do you know you didn't just put it somewhere yourself and forgot where?"

That was too much. "Because I always put my tools away."

"Always?" She was standing in the hall, leaning over the banister to look down at him on the stairs.

"Always."

"Your mom must have loved raising you. All of Don's little toys put neatly away. A place for everything and everything in its place."

"Exactly," said Don. He headed back into the parlor and began rummaging through all his toolboxes again. He heard her coming down the stairs. If he turned around, he knew he would see her leaning against the doorframe, her arm flung up high, like a dancer, like a drawing from the flapper era. Oh, wait, it's the Weird sisters who were flappers. Sylvie is from the eighties. Got to keep my insane women straight.

He had to look. And yes, there she was, leaning on the doorframe, her arm up over her head, stretched along the white-painted wood. Then she bent her arm at the elbow and it arched over her head like a dancer's or a skater's. The image of grace.

"I thought you said the wrecking bar wasn't in your toolboxes."

"I already looked," said Don. "So I'll look again."

"Unbelievable."

"What?"

"That you actually have enough self-doubt to check. I thought you were above such weakness."

"What exactly have I done to you that I deserve to be mocked? Did you think I was the kind of guy who'd accuse you before I checked up on myself? The back of my head is still tender from the time you moved the workbench, but I'm not supposed to wonder if you touched my wrecking bar?"

Her face darkened. She ducked away from the door. He took a few steps after her. "That's right, hide from me, that's mature of you. Don't face up to anything. Isn't that what your life in this house is all about? Hiding!"

When he got to the entry, he saw her leaning against the other doorjamb, the one leading into the apartment on the other side of the stairs. Only this time it wasn't in that carefree, graceful pose. She was facing the wall, her face turned down, the top of her head in full contact with the wood, her body angling away. Like a goat charging. As if she were trying to push her head into the wall.

"There's maybe something in the cupboard in the kitchen," she said. "Far right, up high in the back corner. The cupboard over the fridge space."

"Which kitchen?"

"Lissy's and my kitchen. The one with the big table."

Don strode down the narrow hall to the kitchen at the back of the house. The top shelf of the cupboard was up high, and because it was over the refrigerator gap, there was no counter under it. Don had to stand on the counter next to the gap and lean over, holding onto the cupboards, and even then he had a hard time reaching in. How did she know what was up here? More to the point, how did she get it here?

He got down and pulled the heavy table over to the counter. It was hard to move and it scraped noisily on the floor. Once he was standing on the table, there was no need for leaning. He could reach right in, could look in.

No wrecking bar. But there were several boxes of nails and screws. The Lowe's price tags were still on them. He got them down, set them on the table, then opened them up. Each one was filled with a confusing assortment of all kinds of hardware, including a lot of old nails and screws that Don had taken out of the walls. What infuriated him, though, was the number of shiny new screws and nails that had obviously been pilfered from his supplies in the parlor.

"Sylvie!" he called.

From the door of the kitchen she answered softly. "It wasn't there?"

"What are these doing here?" he demanded. "What *is* this?"

She came over, peered in the boxes. "A nail and screw collection?"

He wanted to scream at her, but he kept his voice low. "Is this a joke?"

"I don't know," she said. "Is it funny?"

He held up a bent nail with plaster still clinging to it. "What did you expect to do with this?"

"I thought you threw all of those away," she said.

"You didn't scavenge this and hide it away?" he said sarcastically.

"Why do you bother asking, when you know the answer and you also know you don't intend to believe it?" Her face was sullen now. Defeated.

Well, he was pretty near defeated, too. "Sylvie, where's the damn wrecking bar?"

Her answer was a whisper. "I don't know. There are some places I can't see."

"So tell me the places you can't see and I'll look there."

She turned her face to the wall to hide from his wrath. Touched her forehead to the wall. "The old furnace," she whispered.

"I've got to get inside that?"

"Behind it," she said.

"Why couldn't we just have started with this?"

No answer. She just stood there, looking beaten. Well, she *had* been beaten, hadn't she? Though truth to tell he had no idea what the game had been.

Don clattered his way down the basement stairs. "I don't like wild goose chases," he said, not loudly, because she looked too defeated for him to want to rub it in; but not softly, either, because he was really annoyed.

He hadn't brought a flashlight, and of course the worklight didn't cast anything but black shadow behind the old furnace. He'd have to go back up. But when he turned, there she was, standing on the bottom step, clinging to the two-by-four banister as if it were the only thing standing between her and disaster. He didn't want to go near her right now. If the wrecking bar was behind the furnace he could find it by feel. He stepped into the darkness. And sure enough, the moment he disturbed any of the rubble, he heard the clang of metal on stone. Or stone on metal. Unfortunately, some of the rubble fell on top of it, so he had to do some rummaging, but at last he got the wrecking bar out.

Now he was filthy with clammy dust. Whoever stacked the rubble did a lousy job. It hadn't taken anything at all to dislodge the pile and tumble enough of it down that it was spilling out around the furnace on both sides. The gap at the top must be bigger now, though he couldn't see it in the darkness. One thing for sure: He couldn't ignore the tunnel forever. If he wanted it sealed off, he'd have to remove the rubble and build a proper masonry wall.

Well, that wasn't the job for today. He had the wrecking bar. He was going to take out a wall. And man, would it feel good to hack into the lath and plaster. He was in the mood for some serious hacking.

When she saw him come out with the wrecking bar, Sylvie visibly relaxed. "Oh, good. You found it."

"Why couldn't you just tell me in the first place?"

She turned away and started up the stairs. "I knew you'd accuse me if I helped."

"Or better yet," he said, "why didn't you just leave it where it was?"

She stopped on the stairs, her head hidden now by the ceiling. "I didn't take it. And if I did, I wouldn't have put it *there.*"

"You have better hiding places?"

She sank down and sat glumly on the landing. Now he could see her face again. She looked really upset. "I don't go there."

"Why? It's nothing. The old ladies next door said it was a rum runner's tunnel. They said this place used to be a bordello." He slapped the wrecking bar against the palm of his other hand. It felt good to have it in his hands.

"How interesting," said Sylvie, not sounding interested. "A tunnel. Who would have guessed it."

"Sylvie, what is it with you? Why can't you just say you're sorry you hid my wrecking bar and you won't do it again?"

She looked up at him with anger in her eyes. "When I do something wrong, I say I'm sorry."

In disgust, Don pushed past her to go up the stairs. "Then I guess you must have done this just right." A few steps above her, he stopped and turned. "Aren't you a little old to be playing the bratty little sister?"

"I'm nobody's sister!"

He continued up the stairs. He heard her calling after him. "I'm not your daughter! I'm not your sister! I'm not your anything!"

Time to get rid of the wall separating the stairs from the south parlor. This one had been built earlier than the other dividers in the house. Probably dated from the twenties, from the bordello days. So it wasn't a stud wall, it was as thick as the wall on the other side, with the same kind of molding. And it wouldn't be drywall, it would be lath and plaster. A messy job, but he was already filthy from the dirt behind the furnace.

He swung the wrecking bar and it went deep into the wall. He pulled it away, and laths gave way and chipped out like broken ribs, with plaster dust flying back into his face. He ought to have his safety glasses on, but he was too mad and it felt too good to be tearing at something. He took another swing at a spot about a foot over, but this time the bar rang against thick hard wood. It surprised him, to find a timber only three feet from the end of the wall. Nobody put vertical posts that close together, not even in bearing walls. He moved farther over, swung again, and this time a huge chunk of plaster gave way and shattered onto the floor. The laths behind it were easy now to pry away from the timbers. Sure enough, it looked as though there were heavy timbers every three feet. Ludicrous. What were they thinking?

"What are you doing!" cried Sylvie. She stood in the doorway, panic on her face.

"What does it look like?"

"You can't tear down that wall! It's the . . . it's the spine of the house!"

"Look, Sylvie, it's a nothing wall. See how the front door is off-center to the house? That's so the load-bearing wall can run right down the middle of the house and hold the floor joists for the second story. This wall isn't holding anything up, it was just added so they could put a door between the entry and this apartment. Or maybe so they could get customers up the stairs to the prostitutes without everybody in the parlor seeing them."

"You're wrong," said Sylvie. "It's holding everything up! If you break that, you'll—you'll *paralyze* the house, you'll—"

"You ought to give lessons to those loons next door," said Don. His patience was gone. "This is a house, not a person." He tore out another lath.

Sylvie ran over and gripped one of the thick vertical timbers. "Feel this! Can't you feel the tension in it? It's holding up the whole weight of the house. It's trembling under the weight."

"The engineer said the other one was the—"

"He didn't look, he assumed. Like you did." She touched one timber after another; four of them were exposed now, at his shoulder height, so she had to reach up to touch them. "So many of them. Why would they put in so many timbers? Like the masts of the ship. Why would they put them in if they weren't holding up the house?"

She was right. It made no sense. And Jay Placer hadn't actually inspected the walls. He just pronounced the north wall to be the load-bearing one and that was that.

Well, there was one way to be sure. Don walked past her, grabbed a flashlight out of the north parlor, and soon was back down in the basement. This time, though, his attention was to the east. The basement was under the back half of the house; the front half had only a crawlspace, and it wasn't easy finding a place to get over the masonry foundation and up under the front of the house. When he did, he regretted it. This was spiderweb country, and all the crawling things that had lost their homes under the carpets in the old house had apparently moved down here. It would take a couple of showers before he felt clean again. But this was part of the job. You didn't rebuild a house without getting filthy and disgusted.

Once he got to the place, it was obvious. The heavy timbers from the south wall were the ones that came down to stand on a foundation of huge cut stones, a row of masts, just like Sylvie said. A bed of stone like the shoulders of the earth. Whoever built this thing understood the terrible strains he was putting on that way-off-center wall, and he made sure the foundation was up to the task. Eight posts, but not evenly spaced. The first one was set back far enough from the front of the house to allow for the entryway. Then there were four posts, three feet apart. The other four were spaced at a more normal but still extra-sturdy six feet. Then, just before the crawlspace opened up into the basement, the whole load-bearing foundation shifted over to the exact center of the house. Well behind the stairs, Don realized. But back here apparently there was no need for the extra-long and extra-heavy floor joists.

Don crawled back out. Once he was out in the basement, he tried to brush away all the webs on his skin, but he couldn't wipe away that creepy feeling. His own dripping sweat felt like insects crawling on him. Get a grip, he told himself.

On the way back up the stairs Don realized how close he had come to stripping out the backbone of the house. If he had cut through those timbers, the whole thing would have come crashing down around his ears. He should have realized it the moment he saw how closely the timbers were spaced. If he hadn't been so angry, if he hadn't been so eager to sink that black iron tooth into the house, he would have stopped and thought about it and checked it out.

And he would have realized it anyway, eventually. Using the skillsaw, he would have felt the tension in the timbers. Wouldn't he? He would have sensed that these were load-bearing posts.

Or maybe not. The one certain thing was that *she* had sensed it.

He set the flashlight aside and walked back into the south parlor to retrieve his wrecking bar. She was still there in the room, but in the far southeast corner, sitting small against the bare walls. He said nothing to her. She said nothing to him. He took the wrecking bar out of the room. That was a clear enough message about what he had found.

He pulled his stuff away from the wall that he had thought was load-bearing, pulled his bed out of the way, too. Didn't want plaster dust where he had to sleep. When he had a good fifteen feet clear, he swung at the wall. He still expected lath and plaster. But no, the bar bit into wallboard. And when he had pulled enough of it away, he could see that this false wall had been built a good eight inches away from the stairway. This was what had fooled him and Jay Placer both—it made the wall look as thick as the bearing wall on the other side of the stairs. No, thicker. But why? Since the wall ran right up the stairs, it meant using twice the materials to build this wall as were needed. Why leave the gap?

Because there was something there, that's why. Don got the flashlight again and shone it through the hole he had made. And gasped. Because now he could see the face of the stairway. It was polished walnut, deeply and delicately carved. Pillars about two feet high, stepping up the stringer, and behind them, in deep recesses, beautifully carved classical figures, sculpted to suggest Italian Renaissance paintings. Venus on the half-shell, or whatever it was called. Adam reaching to pull God's finger. All the jokes from college art appreciation class came back to him. Only this was no joke. This was a million-dollar staircase. This was the treasure of the house. And even though some landlord was stupid enough to cover it, at least he wasn't so callous, so barbarian that he let anybody nail directly to this masterwork. He had boxed it in, kept it from being touched. He must have known that someday this house wouldn't be a cut-up rental. Someday it would be a house again, and this stairway would be the walnut jewel in its crown.

There was no more swinging of the wrecking bar. Don worked very carefully, prying away wallboard, pulling out nails. No skillsaw and sledgehammer this time—he took each stud out of the false wall one at a time, then worked his way up the stairs, removing the wall on the other side, which was seated on the steps rather than touching the carved stringer. He should have seen that too, how the banister could not be the original, how the box around the stairwell had been extended inward by four inches, how the cheap molding could not have been the original. Why hadn't he seen it?

Because it was pretty well done, that's why. And he wasn't looking for it. This was where the bearing wall should be, so a bearing wall is what he saw.

But she had known.

"Sylvie," he called. "Sylvie."

He heard her padding across the floor in the other parlor. Coming through the entry. Then she was in the north parlor. He pointed to the beautifully carved stringer. To the polished wooden bench around the walls of the alcove under the stairs. She touched the pillars, looked in at the figures behind them. "You," she said to each one. "You."

She had seen all she could see at her height. "Want a boost to see the rest?" he asked.

She nodded. He knelt down under her, got her sitting on one shoulder, and stood up. She was so light. So small. Like a child. "You," she was saying. "Hiding here all this time." To help her see the last ones, he gripped her thighs and got her standing on his shoulders like an acrobat. Not dangerous, because she was leaning for balance against the stairway. When she said to, he took another step, another step, sidling along in front of the alcove, until she had seen all the carvings. Fourteen-foot ceilings. An extravagance, Don had thought. Useless, meaningless in rooms this size. But now, as he helped Sylvie glide along the stairs until she was bent over enough that he could hoist her down, he began to wonder about the rest of the room. It made no sense, it had never made sense, for the ceilings to be so high down here. This stairway now ruled the room. It was beautiful, but it was also too much for a room this size, just as the ceiling was too high. Nothing else in the house was so badly out of proportion. What was the builder doing?

Sylvie couldn't take her hands off the wood. She walked around under the stairs now, into the alcove. She sat on the wooden bench, slid along it like a child trying out every possible place to sit. Then she swung her legs up onto the seat and gripped her knees.

Exactly the pose that he had seen Cindy take, there on the untouched couch in her living room.

"I dreamed about this place," said Sylvie softly. "And candles everywhere." She reached up and touched the sloping underside of the staircase. Don stepped into the alcove behind her and saw that set into the wide expanse of walnut was a painting, one that could only be seen by someone sitting in the alcove. A double portrait. A man and a woman. Youngish but not young. The style of the painting made it of the era of Gainsborough. Or at least in imitation of that period. Sentimentalized. But Don knew, looking into the eyes of the woman, that it was for love of her that this house was built. And looking at the man, whose eyes were turned to look at the woman, Don knew that he was the builder. "Dr. Bellamy, isn't it?"

"And they left it here," she said. "Even when it was a whorehouse. That was an awful thing to do, to make them watch what their house had become."

"But it would have been worse to tear them out of it," said Don.

"I guess."

"And the whorehouse was upstairs. Down here it was just a speakeasy."

"I wonder if my father loved my mother like that," she said.

"Nobody ever knows the truth about their mother and father. What they really felt. Easier to see Elvis than to know your parents' hearts."

She chuckled. He liked that low chuckle.

She laughed, a cascade of mirth like water over mossy stone. He liked that, too.

"How do you know this stuff?" asked Don.

"What stuff?"

"How did you know that was the bearing wall?"

"Live here long enough, you get a feel for the house," she said.

But that wasn't it. He knew now. The Weird sisters were right. You could get caught by this house. It could hold you. That's why Sylvie was here. The house had her and she couldn't get away. But in return, the house talked to her. The house revealed itself to her. She knew where everything was. She didn't put it there, she just saw it.

I'm falling into their madness, thought Don. I'm getting caught myself, but not by the house.

Then he laughed at himself. "Why am I so certain of my doubt?"

"What?" she said.

"Why is doubt the one thing we're never skeptical of? We question other people's beliefs, and the more sure they are the more we doubt them. But it never occurs to us to doubt our own doubt. Question our questions. We think our questions are answers."

"We?"

"Me. I. I think that. I'm sorry."

"For what?"

"For thinking you were crazy."

"Don't apologize for *that.*" She smiled wryly.

"For what then?"

"For thinking I was lying."

"I'm sorry."

"You're welcome." She giggled. "Or whatever I'm supposed to say."

Sitting there beside her in the alcove, the painting above their heads, he suddenly wanted her to lean back against him.

Instead she swung her legs off the bench and turned to face him. "I think I *am* crazy, Don. I think I really am."

He shook his head. "Like that makes you different from the rest of us."

She buried her face in her hands. "You like me now, don't you, Don."

"Yes."

"Because I stopped you from wrecking the house."

"No. I liked you a long time before that. Now is just when I could admit it to myself."

"But you shouldn't," she said. "You shouldn't like me."

"Oh, right. OK. Whatever."

She laughed a little. But maybe it wasn't a laugh.

"If you knew what I did. What I've done. You wouldn't like me."

He could feel it coming. Another confession. Like Cindy's.

"Well then don't tell me," he said. "I don't want to know."

"I don't want to tell you."

"So don't, then! Why do people have to confess things? I'm not a priest! I'm just a guy with an incredibly screwed-up life who's trying to maybe fix it up into something, and every time I turn around somebody's laying their own screwups on me, and I don't want to hear it!"

She was starting to cry. Dammit, he didn't want to make her cry.

"Look, I'm sorry. I'm sorry I didn't believe you before. I'm sorry you've been shut up in this place for—ten years? Why did you stay here for ten years? You had everything going for you. A degree. A job. Providence, right? It was a job you wanted, right?"

She nodded.

"But here you are. What is this, then? Penance? What crime did you commit that was so terrible you should be put away for ten years? In solitary confinement, it's a miracle you *didn't* go crazy. In this house, prowling around, letting it get under your skin, letting it get into you. What did you do that deserves *this?*"

In reply, she bent over and buried her face in her hands and wept.

"Your turn now," he whispered. "First me, now you." The family that cries together ... what? Dies together? Fries together? Lies together? He shook the thought out of his mind. We're not a family. We're the opposite of a family. We're people so lonely that when we're together we make a black hole of loneliness and everything else gets sucked down into it and is never seen again.

Black hole.

He thought of the tunnel under the house. The one thing she didn't know about. The one place she couldn't see.

15

Tunnel

"Okay, look, I'm not doubting you now," he said quietly. "I think this house does some weird things. OK? And you have this sense of the house, right? Like—what, like it's part of you, right? Or you're part of *it*."

She nodded.

"But you really didn't know where my wrecking bar was, did you."

She shook her head.

"The stuff high in that cupboard over the fridge, you knew about that. It sort of washed up there. Washed to shore, so to speak."

She nodded.

"So why couldn't you see behind the furnace?"

No answer. No movement.

He'd have to try another tack. "Why didn't you ever get to that job in Rhode Island? Why didn't you go? You were so close."

Still no answer.

"And you never got your degree. After working on it for so many years."

"Some of us don't suffer from completion anxiety."

Good. She was talking. She was joking a little. "What held you here, Sylvie? There were other people living in this house that last year before the landlord closed it down. I bet some of them even lived here longer than you. *They* were able to leave. The house didn't hold *them*. Your roommate, Lissy. *She* left, right? Got her degree?"

Sylvie shrugged.

"But you stayed."

"I guess I washed up here." She wasn't crying anymore. That was good, too.

"The whole house, you feel it, the shape of it, the strong points, the weak points. All the . . . moods. Of the house."

"Maybe. I feel things, anyway. Nobody knows everything about anything."

"Why not that tunnel in the basement?"

"I don't like the cellar," she said. "So sue me."

"It's more than that, Sylvie," he said.

"The house wants to be beautiful again. The tunnel doesn't have a thing to do with that."

But it did. He knew that. Whatever was holding her here had something to do with that tunnel. She couldn't go near it, but she couldn't get too far from it, either. He thought of how the tunnel had been closed off. The rocks piled up, yes, but placed lightly, balanced, not a solid barrier, not enough to contain anything large or strong. Just enough to keep from having to see what was down there. Or to keep something down there from seeing in.

"I thought for a while you were getting in and out of the house through that tunnel."

She shook her head. "Please just forget about that. It's nothing."

Forgetting it was the one thing he couldn't do. He was already filthy from plaster, from the dust of the rubble. He might as well do it now. He was going to have to do it eventually. "Look, just stay up here, OK? Nothing down there can hurt you." He got up from the bench and stepped through the newly disarranged piles of his tools until he found the pick.

"What are you doing?" she asked.

"Like you said, it has nothing to do with you. I'm going to walk the tunnel, see if it's caved in. See if it's a hazard. If it is, I have to seal it off for real."

"It's no hazard."

"Forget about it. It's nothing. Like you said." He grabbed his flashlight and headed down the hall for the cellar stairs.

She ran after him down the hall. "Please," she said. "Leave the tunnel alone."

He didn't pause in his stride. "I have a feeling that tunnel's the most interesting feature of this house."

"It's not. It's just damp and dirty."

"So you *have* been down there." He jogged down the basement stairs.

"Yes. But I stopped going because it isn't safe, it could cave in on you."

Don reached up and switched on the basement worklight. "Fess up, Sylvie. What are you hiding down there? You keep your stash down there?"

He meant it as a joke, but she wasn't laughing. "There's nothing down there that belongs to me," she said.

"Then stand back and watch the rubble fly."

Now, with a light, he could see how much the barrier had collapsed from his previous foray here, searching for the wrecking bar. The gap at the top was now several feet high. He could crawl over. But he didn't want to do that. He'd have to clear the rubble away to seal up the gap or to open it permanently. Either way, the job needed doing.

He set to work with the pick. Mostly he just used it like a scraper, drawing the stones away from behind the furnace. As he cleared them away, more fell from the barrier. "Look at this," he said. "Easy. Not much of a barrier at all."

He turned to face her. She stood half-hiding behind the furnace.

"Flimsy," he said. "Like it was built by somebody little and not very strong."

Finally it had collapsed as much as it was going to. Then the work got tedious and slow as he bent over and picked up the stones and pitched them or hiked them across the cellar out of the way. Sylvie backed out of range. He was vaguely aware of her waiting by the stairs.

By the time the job was done, his back was aching from holding that bent-over pose. But the door into the tunnel was clear. Taking up the flashlight, he took a couple of steps into the tunnel.

"Wait!" Sylvie called from behind him.

He turned back, found her standing between the furnace and the foundation.

"I'm begging," she said. "Don't go." She looked almost frantic, and yet she spoke quietly.

"Tell me why not," he said.

"Because I like you."

"What, there's something terrible down there?"

"Yes."

"Some kind of monster?" He said it mockingly. "I'm not much afraid of a monster that couldn't get through that barricade."

"There's no monster now."

His patience was wearing thin. "Stop the mysteries and tell me!"

Sylvie started crying and leaned against the furnace, her head bowed.

This again, thought Don, too tired now to be sympathetic.

"I'm going, OK? I'll be fine."

"I know you'll be fine," she said, trying to control her crying. "My roommate's down there, all right? Lissy's down there."

If there was one thing Don didn't expect, it was that. And yet it fit. Why she couldn't leave. Why she hated the tunnel. "I don't think you mean she's *living* there."

"She was cheating," said Sylvie. "She spent all her time that last semester with her stupid boyfriend, she was going to flunk out. So she started stealing *my* work and copying it to write papers for her own classes. If she got caught we'd *both* be kicked out! Nobody would believe I wasn't helping her cheat."

"You killed her for cheating?"

"I didn't mean to!" Sylvie turned to face him. "You think I'd plan something like that? She was always in the tunnel. Our apartment was the only one with access to the basement. So she did keep her stash there, *her* stash, I never used that stuff. But she had pot, some- times coke, and she and her boyfriend would go down there to get high and . . . so I knew where she was. I was just going to talk to her. Lay it on the line. She had to stop or I was going to the dean with it."

Sylvie didn't like to go down the tunnel when she knew Lissy was there, mostly because she could never be sure Lanny wasn't there too. He often came up the tunnel the other way to join Lissy there, so Sylvie had no way of knowing if they were together or not. That was a scene she didn't want to walk in on. Sex didn't bother her, or even the idea of seeing people doing it—you don't go to college for this many years without getting an eyeful now and then. What she didn't like was to see Lanny and Lissy doing it. She'd heard it often enough in the next bedroom. Lissy was a squealer and Lanny was a grunter. It sounded like a pig farm and it nauseated her. She couldn't shake the memory of Grandpa's pig farm, back when she still had family. She stood on the second rail from the top, with her daddy holding her up to make sure she didn't fall into or out of the sty. She must have been all of four years old. The pigs were all bigger than her. Like elephants, that's how they seemed. Huge fat muddy pink backs lurching and trotting around in the mud, muzzling the trough, making hideous noises, grunts and squeals. And there was Papaw, teasing her by telling her not to fall in, those pigs would be just as happy to eat little girl as slops. In memory she knew he meant well enough. He'd forgotten the terrors of childhood, the credulity. But at the time she had no perspective. She believed in the danger, and for weeks after that she had nightmares about the pigs looming and grunting over her. They'd be trotting past, back and forth, and then all of a sudden one would notice her and start to squeal. Mud sharks, that's what pigs seemed like to her. So the sounds she heard from Lissy and Lanny, they weren't erotic, they were disgusting and, when she admitted it to herself, terrifying.

But tonight was the last straw. Lissy wasn't even bothering to paraphrase now. She had taken Sylvie's old paper on the system of filing active documents during World War II—her senior thesis, for heaven's sake—and turned it in for a history class. She probably thought it was safe because Sylvie was in library science, not history, but there was a history professor on her evaluating committee and the paper was on an eccentric enough topic that it would be remembered. She had to find out if Lissy had already turned the paper in. If she had, then she had to withdraw it. If she hadn't, then she could take the incomplete and write another. That was it. There would be no compromise, no sweet-talking, no tears that could soften the hardest heart. It's not *my* heart that's hard, anyway, thought Sylvie. It's hers. Having no concern for what she's doing to me, the risks she's making me take against my will. My whole future down the toilet. She can marry Lanny, but my career is all I've got. My education and my career.

Midway down the tunnel, in the level stretch, Lissy had her candles lit, four of them, perched up on the two stone walls that lined the tunnel. She was alone, lying on a dirty old mattress, wearing only a t-shirt. Hadn't she worn more than this to come down here? But there were no other clothes visible. The things Lissy did when she was high.

"You missed the party," said Lissy. She started to laugh.

Don listened to the story, liking Lissy less and less—but how else could Sylvie tell the story? Turn the girl into a saint or something? Still, he believed her. Believed her, but also hated hearing the tale. He didn't need another dark story rinched out of somebody's humid conscience.

"I confronted her about cheating," Sylvie said. "About how she had no right to put my whole life at risk, everything I worked for . . . I got emotional. That never worked with her, but I couldn't help it."

"Lighten up, Sylvie," Lissy said lazily. "You take it all too seriously." She settled back down on the mattress as if she meant to go to sleep.

Sylvie was used to Lissy's selfishness. It used to be that was part of her charm. Her unconcern, her childlike innocence of the complicated moral questions that plagued more responsible people—Sylvie used to admire it, back before they lived together. Used to laugh *with* Lissy about some fretful teacher or heartbroken ex-boyfriend. "Why do they have to get so *intense?*" Lissy would always ask.

Well, now Sylvie knew. They got intense because Lissy was so destructive. She wasn't childlike, she was devilish. Because she knew exactly what she was doing. She enjoyed it. Sylvie understood that now. Lissy had used Sylvie's senior thesis, not because she didn't know the harm it could cause, but because she did know. She liked the risk. She loved dragging Sylvie into it.

"You've got to live more on the edge," that's what Lissy always said. But Lissy herself, she never seemed to get near the edge. She lived on *other* people's edges. And when they fell off, she'd admire how pretty they looked as they fell.

So Sylvie lost it. She'd spent her life being quiet and well-mannered. She had to, with no parents to look out for her. If she pushed people, they slapped her down. But if she was quiet and endured all things patiently, yes, they took advantage of her, but they also tolerated her. Didn't throw her out. Let her stay in places where they didn't really want her. That strategy had suited her fine, for many years, until Lissy. Quiet endurance was over.

Sylvie had slid down the furnace and was sitting on the floor, her toes pressed against the basement wall. She didn't look at Don as she told her story.

"I screamed at her and finally she sobered up enough to scream back at me and one thing came to another."

"It always does," said Don. But the truth was it didn't always. As Sylvie talked about reaching the end of her rope, Don wondered: Why hadn't he ever reached the end of his? Sure, yesterday he had broken down and cried, but when did he ever just lose it and start screaming? Maybe if he'd gone a little crazy, he could have broken through the barriers that kept him from justice.

Of course, look what "losing it" did for Sylvie.

"She accused me of the most terrible things," said Sylvie. "She called me everything, she said no wonder my mother died, no wonder my father died, anything was better than living with me. She wasn't my friend anymore, you know? She wasn't even human. Her face all twisted up, screwed up, her mouth open, her teeth like—it was like the monkey island at the zoo. An animal. She didn't justify herself, she didn't argue, she just went on the attack, saying I was worthless and boring and nobody liked me till she took me on as a project, to try to prove that there was nobody so lame and hopeless that she couldn't bring them out and give them a life. I tried to scream back at her about how she wasn't giving me a life, she was taking it away, but she never heard me. She wouldn't shut up and listen at all, and I admit it, I was an animal too. We were both animals right then. And there was a loose stone. Lots of loose stones. I just wanted to shut her up, to hurt her. But I'd never hit anyone before. In my whole life, Don. Never hit anybody. And I'm not very strong. So I didn't know how hard to hit. I just swung with all my might. The rock hit her in the side of her head."

"Bet it shut her right up," said Don.

Sylvie nodded. "You see people get knocked out on TV all the time. They go unconscious and then they get up and in the next scene they aren't even groggy."

"I take it she wasn't groggy, either."

"I shook her and shook her and she didn't wake up. It was terrible, what she'd been doing to me, the things she said to me, but she didn't deserve to die."

"You're sure you killed her?"

"There was so much blood."

"There always is, from head injuries. But it's usually just from the skin."

"You think I didn't try to feel her breath? Her pulse? I screamed at her, I slapped her, I got her blood all over me trying to wake her up and nothing worked. And then it finally dawned on me what I had done. My life was over, too. I couldn't live with it. Don't you see?"

"No, I don't. Why wasn't there an investigation when she disappeared? Why weren't you arrested?"

"Nobody knew. She didn't have any family, either. Just like me. And her boyfriend, Lanny—he never came back. Can you believe it? What a jerk. She disappears and he doesn't even look for her. Doesn't even *ask*."

"And you never left this place."

"The landlord gave up on the house that summer. It stood empty.

What could I do? Go out and live my life as if I hadn't committed murder? Take the job? I didn't have the heart for it. I couldn't even go pick up my diploma. I already defended my dissertation. I was done. But I couldn't bear to go out there and . . . be alive. When I had killed her."

"So you stayed there by her body? You checked her? You buried her in the tunnel?"

She looked horrified. "Of course I didn't," she said. "When I knew she was dead I ran out of the tunnel. I . . . put up that barricade. From stones near the entrance. I was crying the whole time, it kept collapsing, I kept piling it up. And then suddenly the stones started staying where I put them. Balancing themselves. The house was helping me, you see. Because now I belonged to the house. I was never going to leave."

"So how do you know she didn't wake up two hours later and go out the back way?"

"She was dead, Don!"

"That would explain why the boyfriend never came back. She went and met him and told him how you were going to turn her in for cheating and they split."

"It didn't happen that way. I wish it had!"

"But how do you *know* it didn't happen?"

Sylvie looked at him, horrified at a possibility she had never considered. "She had to be dead. I had hit her so hard."

"Like you said. You never hit anybody before. You're not very big. Getting blood from somebody's scalp is easy. Killing them isn't." Don knelt in front of her. "She isn't down that tunnel, Sylvie. She's out there, alive. For ten years she's been out there having a life and you've been in here doing penance for a murder that never happened."

"She *is* dead! How would you know anything! You weren't there!"

"But I'm here now," he said. "And I'm going to go down that tunnel and see for myself."

She started to cry again. "She haunts me, don't you get it? When I sleep, I dream of her coming for me, dragging me down in the tunnel, strangling me. I wake up, I can't breathe, because she's come to get even with me."

"She doesn't haunt you, Sylvie, you haunt yourself. You're doing all this to yourself." He picked up the flashlight and started down the tunnel.

It felt old to him. Dank, heavy, cool. No, cold. It had been sturdily built. The stones formed into walls on the left and right weren't structural, they were more like a retaining wall to keep the sides of the tunnel from eroding when it rained. The real structure was wood as thick as railroad ties, vertical posts every four feet or so, bridged by wood the same thickness, and then the whole tunnel spanned by more railroad-tie-sized beams forming a continuous ceiling. This was a lot more tunnel than any rum runners would need, he thought. Like the house, it was built to last forever. But why would Dr. Bellamy need a passage like this? It made no sense.

He could hear Sylvie behind him. She was coming down the tunnel after all. Well, good. She should see for herself. If Lissy had really died, there would have been an investigation. Policemen would have come to the house, asking Sylvie questions. Since that never happened, Lissy didn't disappear. It was Sylvie who disappeared, hiding out for years. But no one came looking for her because the diploma really doesn't matter. In fact they probably mailed it to her. They probably thought she was off in Providence, Rhode Island, starting her new job. Maybe some professor was a little hurt that she never wrote to him. Maybe at some professional conference, years later, somebody from UNCG met somebody from Providence and asked how Sylvie was working out and found out that Sylvie had never shown up for the job. But by then where would he start looking? The house where she used to live was boarded up. She had no family to write to. And in the end there was no reason for anyone to search for her.

She sacrificed her life for nothing.

The tunnel had sloped downward rather steeply, but now it began to level out.

"Don, please!" she called from behind him.

He stopped to wait for her. "Come with me if you want," he said. "Or not. But I think it's about time you faced what you did. Or what you didn't do."

She came into view, stumbling in the darkness. "Don't project your own problems onto *me*. You're the one who's eating himself alive with guilt over what he *didn't* do. You didn't get your daughter away from your exwife legally, and you didn't kidnap her in time, either."

Lissy wasn't the only one who went for the jugular. "Don't talk about things you don't know anything about."

"It's *you* who needs to face the fact that you couldn't help what happened, you didn't do anything wrong. Not me! I killed her!"

"I haven't seen a body anywhere down here," said Don. He turned away and continued down the tunnel. Four candles up on the stone retaining walls, right? That's what he was looking for now.

And there they were. The flashlight beam found the burnt-out stub of a candle, and a quick pass of the light showed the other three candles. For a moment he couldn't bring himself to point the flashlight downward, or even to look down in the spilled light. For all his bravado, he wasn't at all sure what he'd find.

Then he looked. And now he was sure. There was the mattress lying on the packed dirt, and on the mattress was a desiccated body, skin like parchment, lying on its back, rictus smile staring upward.

"Oh," he said.

He heard Sylvie coming up behind him, picking her way through the darkness again. He moved the flashlight away from the body.

"Sylvie, I was wrong," he said. "She's here. You don't want to look."

"After all these years, I've come this far. It's time. Show me."

How could he have doubted her? She said she knew what death was. And she was right. He was the one who had never faced death. It happened at a distance for him. It happened on the TV news. She had held death in her hands.

Even in the darkness, she knew where to look. He turned from her and shone the flashlight onto the corpse.

"Listen, Sylvie," he said. "Whatever you did, you've been paying for it, don't you see? Trapped in this house. It wasn't first-degree murder, it was in a rage, I'm no lawyer but it was probably only manslaughter, you would have been out of prison before now."

She didn't say anything, just panted. Then groaned, a sound torn from the depth of her soul. Was she all right? He turned the flashlight from the body on the mattress to Sylvie's face. It wasn't grief or guilt that he saw there. It was horror. As if she were seeing this scene for the first time. She pointed at the corpse.

"What is it?" Don said. "She can't hurt you now, Sylvie."

"What she's wearing," said Sylvie, her voice weak. "Look what she's wearing."

Don shone the flashlight back on the body. He looked closely this time. The clothing was dark with tunnel grime, but as he stepped closer he could see that it wasn't the t-shirt Sylvie had described. It was a dress. A faded blue dress. He turned the flashlight back on Sylvie. She was plucking at her skirt like a little girl. The identical skirt.

"Same dress," said Don stupidly, trying to make sense of it.

"That's not Lissy," said Sylvie.

She sank down against the stone wall.

"It's me," she whispered.

16

Ballroom

It took Don a moment to realize what she was saying. "How could it be you?" he said lamely.

"I thought it was a dream," she said. She was shaking, leaning against the stone wall of the tunnel. The flashlight in his hand made her look like she was on stage, with a tight but feeble spotlight picking her out of the darkness. "I dreamed I came back down the tunnel and I was shaking her again, trying to wake her even though I knew she was dead, and then her hands . . . *shot* up and took me by the throat and I tried to apologize, I said I was sorry, sorry, I didn't mean to hurt her, but then I couldn't breathe and it hurt and I kept thinking, any time now I'll wake up, any time."

"She strangled you."

"Her face. So hateful. I thought it was what I deserved. I thought it was her ghost, haunting me. I've dreamed it a thousand times since then. I thought I was dreaming then. Because. Because it all went black, and then I woke up and it was dark because the candles had burnt out but I tripped over a body, lying on the mattress, a body right where I had left her body, I tripped over my body." She turned and looked over toward the corpse on the mattress. "Show me," she whispered. He turned the light toward the body. She crawled over. Touched it. Touched the parchment skin of the bare leg. Touched the damp rotting fabric of the dress. Then touched her own dress, the same dress, but not rotting.

"How can a . . ." How could he ask her this?

Her head sank. She didn't look at him.

"How can a ghost *trip* over a dead body."

She shook her head.

"You touched me. I touched you." He reached out to prove it to her.

"No!" she cried, recoiling from him, scurrying back to the wall.

"You're real," he insisted.

She cried again.

He reached out to touch her and this time she endured it. And yes, there was resistance, he could feel the skin of her arm.

And then he couldn't.

And then he could, but his finger was about a half-inch deep in her arm. He cried out in horror and pulled his hand away. She raised her face to look at him. "The house," she said. "I've got to get back inside the house."

"No, you've got to get away from this house."

"We're not in the house," she said. "Shine the light, show me the way back. I'm losing it."

He shone the light up the tunnel toward the basement. Sylvie got up. Too far up—she rose from the ground and drifted. She wailed in fear.

"My hand," he said. "Take my hand."

"I'm not here, Don! I'm not real, I can't—"

"You *are* real," he said. "You're Sylvie Delaney and you live in the old Bellamy house. In that new room, you've touched the walls of that room. You hid in the closet that I built and . . . "

And he felt her hand in his. He didn't look. He simply led her up the tunnel. He didn't want to see if she was walking or floating or if there was anything of her but that hand. That living hand.

They came out into the rubble-strewn basement and now he could hear her footsteps. He turned around and faced her. "You're all right," he said.

"I'm inside the house again."

"It sustains you."

"The stronger the house is," she said, "the realer I am."

"So if you know that," he said, "how could you not have known it was your body down there? That you were—Sylvie, you're dead. How could you not *know?*"

"I was still here, that's why I didn't know. The house held on to me." She walked toward the stairs. "But there were times when I felt . . . soft. Unreal. *Puncturable.*" She walked up the stairs. Her hand was so solid on the two-by-four banister. He couldn't help it, he had to reach out and touch her again. She stopped walking. Stopped and waited, his hand touching hers.

"Sorry," he said, thinking she was offended.

"Oh, no, please," she said. "Oh, please, you're so warm. Don't let go." She burst into tears again and turned to face him, almost fell into his arms. He gathered her into an embrace; she wept against his shoulder. Her tears soaked through his shirt. How could she not be real? He got one arm under her legs, lifted her, carried her carefully up the stairs.

"Take me to the nook under the stairs," she said. "The heart of the house."

So once again they sat on the bench, with the portrait of the Bellamys looking down at them. She would not let go of his hand. "She left me there, Don."

"It explains why you never had any inquiries about her death."

"But what about *my* death?"

"She must have told them something. That you left. Went home. Went on to that job in Providence."

"When I thought I killed her, it destroyed me."

"Maybe it destroyed her, too," said Don.

"Now I know why I couldn't leave the house," she said. "I tried, early on. When they were closing it all down. I hid from them but then when they left I tried to leave. I'd get out onto the porch. Or out in back. And I'd get so faint."

"Faint?"

"I mean like I was going to faint. Light-headed. It frightened me. I thought it was my guilt holding me. I couldn't face the world. I had no right to be out there if Lissy couldn't go too. But she *did* go. So I *did* have the right."

"But the house held you."

"Held me, but it also kept me alive. Without the house I'd just be . . . gone. I think I was going anyway. All those years when the house was weakening. I was weakening too. Till you came. The sound of you walking through the house. As if it woke me from a long sleep. I was in the attic, listening to you talking to that guy and that woman. And she left because the dust was getting to her. Talking about how strong the house was. And how you could fix it up again. You don't know how that . . . it filled the house with hope. *Me* with hope."

"So you were there," he said.

"But maybe I wasn't even . . . visible? Maybe I was . . . sometimes I felt like I *was* the house. Like the timbers and beams, they were my bones, and the outside walls were my skin, and this place, this invisible place was my heart, beating, beating. Can't you feel the pulse here?"

He reached over and laid his fingers against her throat. The pulse was pounding there. "A ghost can't pump blood like that."

"Imitation of life," she said. "Mimesis. That's all I am. Plato said we were all shadows. Me more than most."

"Not as long as you stay here."

"Now when you sell the house, do I have to leave?" She laughed, but it quickly turned to crying again. Again he held her, his arm around her shoulders, her face turned in to his chest. "I've really screwed things up now. You can't sell a haunted house, Don."

"You think I care about that?"

"Yes."

"Sure, yes," he said. "But not as much as the fact that your body is down there. And she got away with it."

"I think I always knew," she said. "I knew I was dead. My life was over. I knew I wasn't hungry. I kept thinking, sometime along about now I ought to get something to eat, I'm going to die if I don't, and then I just never . . . I never even got thirsty. You think I didn't wonder about that? But then I'd think, Don't think about it, you'll just make it worse if you think about it. So I didn't. I'd sleep. Inside the bones of the house. I hid from it. Because if I knew the truth, then I'd fade. If I knew I was a ghost, I'd start having to live like one. Invisible. Going through walls. Appearing and disappearing."

"But you did that anyway."

"But I didn't *know.* I could still believe. And now I can't."

"Yes you can. You *are* real. How else could I know you if you weren't real?"

She looked up into his eyes. "That's true," she said. "You aren't by any chance dead yourself, are you?"

"Despite my fondest wish on many a dark night, no, I'm not dead."

"Maybe the house kept me here so there'd be someone living in it. Maybe it kept me alive so I could keep *it* alive."

Don reached up and touched Dr. Bellamy's face. "OK, buddy, what did you put in this house? What's the plan?"

"It won't answer," she said. "It doesn't talk. It doesn't think. It just *is.*"

"It's been keeping you alive all these years, trapped here, for a reason."

"Reason," she said scornfully.

"Purpose," he said. "I'm not saying it's rational, but maybe if we could figure out what the house *wants,* it would let you go."

"It isn't a letting-go kind of place," she said.

"So you'd rather stay here? What if you're supposed to be in heaven?"

"Don't be silly," she said. "God's forgotten me, if he ever knew I was here."

"Maybe you're the lost sheep, and he's out looking for you."

"Maybe you're the one he sent to find me." She giggled.

"The repairs I made," he said. "The room upstairs. The house didn't want me to do that. But when I finished, it made the house stronger, didn't it? It made you more real and solid, didn't it?"

She got up, took a few short steps out into the room. "I took a shower, Don! I felt the water against my body! I *washed.* And that Coke you brought me, I tasted it. Oh, Don, I felt it in my mouth, fizzing. I felt the sheets of the bed you moved for me. I ate that pizza. A bite of it, anyway. I chewed it. The cheese was stringy, Don. How would I feel that if I'm not alive?"

She turned around slowly, around and around.

"How would I dance here in this room if I weren't real?" She closed her eyes, her face upturned, spinning slowly. "O house, big old house, why did you keep me alive? Why didn't you let me go?"

He saw her turning and turning, and he imagined seeing her by candlelight, reflected in mirrors between the windows. A very clear picture. Why would he imagine something like that? Then it suddenly came to him, the reason why this house was shaped so oddly.

"It's a ballroom," he said.

"What?"

"This room. Look. It isn't a parlor. It never was."

"But it's too small."

"No," he said. He ran to the back wall of the room, thumped it with his hand. "It's plaster," he said. "But that doesn't prove anything. When it was a speakeasy, they didn't need the ballroom. They needed more walls, more private rooms. The two bedrooms—they're both part of this. That narrow hall, it's part of the ballroom."

She walked over to join him. She touched the wall. "When I read about the Bellamys, back in college, when I read about them they were having dances all the time. They had ball after ball. It's what they did. Dancing."

Of course. It was dancing that they loved. It was for dancing that the house was built. "The wall's *not* tied to the house, is it? Nothing's resting on this wall."

She leaned her head against it. "You're right," she said. "It's just . . . it's nothing. This wall is in the way."

"And the next one? Between the bedrooms?"

They went down the hall, verifying that the bedroom walls were add-ins, just like the north wall of the passage. But the south wall was real, as was the wall between the kitchen and the back bedroom.

"It was a huge room," said Don.

"He built it for her," said Sylvie. "Can't you feel it? She loved to dance, and he built her a dancing place."

"Well, now we know," said. "Why the house is so off-center. I can't believe I'm worrying about that right now, though. I mean—what does it matter? After what happened to you?"

"But I'm tied to the house," she said. "Now that I'm facing the truth, I might start fading. So the house needs to be stronger."

"If you want to stay," said Don. "The Weird sisters next door, they kept telling me to let the house go. Leave it alone or tear it down. What if they were trying to set you free?"

"Free?" said Sylvie. "I don't want to be *free,* Don, I want to be *alive!*"

"But I can't do that."

"Yes you can," she said. "The stronger the house, the realer I get. Tear out these walls, Don. Please."

He studied her face. Her body. Incredible that this might be only spirit. He reached out and touched her again. Her cheek. She brought up her hand and held his.

"Let me dance in this room," she said. "Make me real."

He let go of her and went in search of his wrecking bar.

It took until well after dark. Past midnight, into the small of the morning. Tearing down huge chunks of plaster, then prying out every lath. Then the skillsaw through the timbers—though these were nothing like as heavy as the great masts of that bearing wall beside the stairs. The sledgehammer blows shivered him to the shoulders, to the spine, but the timbers came free of the ceiling, came up from the floor, and he hauled it all outside, a huge pile of junk out by the curb.

Still he wasn't done. He gathered up all his tools, his boxes of supplies, his suitcases, his cot, and moved them all into the south parlor. The real parlor. So nothing was left on the floor but the fragments of plaster and a few eight-penny nails from the laths.

And still there was a job to do. He found his broom and swept the whole floor, it felt like acres of wood, but he swept it all till it was clean.

Only one more job. He found all the nailholes where the new walls had been fastened down to the polished wooden ballroom floor, then filled them with putty and sanded them smooth. It was three in the morning. He was exhausted. He turned to her, there in the alcove, where she had sat as she watched the whole job, her eyes shining.

"How's that?" he asked.

In reply she smiled at him. "Aren't you going to ask me to dance?"

He laughed. "I'm a sack of sweat right now. I must have chalkdust sticking to me all over."

"It just makes you all the more real."

"I'm not the one who felt unreal," he said. But the moment he said it, he wasn't altogether sure it was true. How real *had* he been, before he found this house?

He walked over to her and held out a filthy hand. "Miss Sylvie Delaney, would you be so kind?"

"I think it's a waltz," she said.

"Could well be."

"I'd love to waltz with you."

He pulled her up from the bench. Her hand was solid in his. So was her delicate hand resting lightly on his shoulder, her girlish waist under his hand. He pressed with the heel of his right hand, to let her feel which way they were going, and she followed his lead. One-two-three.

"We need music," she said.

"So sing," he said.

She began to hum, then to sing wordless tunes. He recognized them. *The Emperor Waltz. Blue Danube.* And others that he didn't know. They danced around and around. He should have been too tired to dance. Or maybe he was only just now as tired as he needed to be, to forget his exhaustion and go on dancing and dancing.

And in his mind, in his weariness, he began to hear, not Sylvie's voice, but an orchestra. And to see, not the light from the worklamp, but the light of a hundred candles in sconces on the walls, in three great chandeliers overhead. Around and around the room, great sweeps of movement, and Sylvie's dress swayed as if there were a bustle under it, exaggerating the movements of the dance. So did all the other dresses in the room, all the men in tails, whirling, whirling. No faces, Don couldn't see any faces because everything was moving so fast; nor could he see the musicians, though he caught the movement of a bow, the flash of light on a trombone slide every time he passed the bandstand against the wall separating the ballroom from the serving room. Servants moved in and out of that room with drinks on trays, hors d'oeuvres on platters. Onlookers smiled and laughed, and Don wasn't just imagining it, they did look up whenever he and Sylvie danced past them. Thank you for this party, they were saying with their silent eyes. Thank you for inviting us. For the lights, the food, the champagne, the music, and above all the grace of the dancers, skittering over the floor as lightly as the crisp leaves of autumn, around and around, caught in a whirlwind, *making* a whirlwind, churning all the air of the world . . .

And then they clung to each other, no longer dancing. The room still turned dizzily around them, but then even that held still. The music was over. The orchestra had disappeared, and all the onlookers, and the other dancers. Only Sylvie and Don remained, holding each other in the middle of the room. Don looked at the windows and saw that a grey light was now showing.

"We danced until dawn," he said.

She said nothing. He looked down at her and saw tears in her eyes. "They danced again in their house tonight," she said.

"And the house is strong," he said.

She nodded. "It's the Bellamy house again. It has the right shape for its real name."

"And you," he said. "You're strong, too." Her face so ethereal, her skin so pure, so translucent. Her lips still caught in the memory of a smile. He bent and kissed her lightly. She laughed, a low chuckle deep in her throat.

"I felt that," she said.

He kissed her again.

"I felt it to my toes," she whispered.

He wrapped his arms around her, picked her up, spun around and around. Her legs swung away from his body. Like a child, around and around, flying. Then he carried her to the threshold of the front door. Reached down and opened it.

"Don," she said.

"This is the only test that matters, Sylvie," he said.

"No, it's the one that *doesn't* matter."

"If you can leave, then you're alive," he said.

"Isn't it enough that I'm alive inside?"

"No," he said. "It's enough for me, but it's not enough for you. Unless I can give you back what Lissy took from you."

"You can't," she said. "Put me down, Don."

"Flesh and bone," he said. "Heart's blood and mind's eye."

"Oh, Don," she said. "Is it true?"

In answer, he opened the front door and stepped out onto the porch. It wasn't true dawn yet. Just the faintest of the early light. No lights shone in the neighborhood except the streetlights, and they were shrouded in the morning mist. Don stepped down, one, two, three steps. Onto the mown weeds of the yard. Out toward the junkpile, out toward the street. She clung around his neck.

And then she didn't.

There was nothing in his arms.

"Sylvie!" he cried out.

Almost he let his arms drop, because he couldn't see her. But he knew: If she was anywhere, she was here, in his arms. He had to get back to the house. "Sylvie, hold on to me! Hold on!" He ran back.

"Don!" he heard her call. As if from a distance.

He looked and couldn't see her. Not in his arms, not anywhere.

"Don, wait!"

He retraced his steps, felt with his arms. Brushed against something. Nothing he could see, but *something*. "Hold on to me," he said.

"Slow," she whispered. It sounded like her voice was in his ear. "Slow."

Trying to gather her like wind, he walked backward, slowly, toward the house. And the closer he got, the more he could feel her. Her hands, clawing at his sleeves, her feet dragging in the weeds. Now he could get his arms around her. Could hold her. Draw her along, then get his arms under her, lift her up again, carry her up the stairs. He could do that, he did it, he brought her to the front door and took her inside and closed the door and then they collapsed on the floor, exhausted, clinging to each other, crying, laughing in relief.

"I thought I lost you," he said.

"I thought I was lost," she said.

"The house can't make you real except inside."

"That's enough for me," she said.

"Not for me," he said. "Not while *she's* alive."

"Who, Lissy?"

"She killed you with her bare hands. Not just one blow struck in anger. It takes a long time to strangle somebody to death, five minutes of tightly gripping your throat. She could have stopped any time, Sylvie. But she never stopped. She hung on even after you were unconscious. She hung on till she *knew* you were dead."

"So what can we do about it?" she said. "We have this house."

"I want you to have your life back."

"How?"

"I don't know," he said. "But I know who might, if anyone does." He got up and walked to the door.

"Where are you going?" she asked.

"Next door," he said. "The Weird sisters." He turned away, started through the door, then stopped, turned back inside.

"Please," he said. "Be here when I get back."

"Cross my heart," she said.

17

Questions

Don walked around the fence, then slogged through the damp mass of leaves that covered the front lawn of the carriagehouse. Autumn had struck with a vengeance. He was a little surprised they didn't have the door open for him before he mounted the porch. What, were they slacking off on their spying?

He rang the doorbell. Nothing. Knocked. No answer.

He waited, knocked, rang, knocked again. Nothing.

Around the back it was the same. The curtains were drawn. No sign of life within. These were elderly women. Was something wrong? He tried the doorknob, just to peer in. It was locked.

Back to the front porch. That door was also locked. He knocked again, louder, rattling the windows. "Miss Judea!" he called. "Miss Evelyn!"

Then he realized. It was barely dawn. Old people didn't sleep all that much, he knew, but maybe they still slept past first light. And he couldn't keep shouting, he'd wake the neighbors. He shouldn't be here. And yet he had to ask them what they knew. What they understood about the house. What hope there was for Sylvie cutting loose from the place.

One last ring of the doorbell, and he turned away to head back to the Bellamy house. Naturally, that was when he heard the door being unbolted behind him.

It opened only a crack. No one peered out at him.

"Go away," said an aged, weary voice. He couldn't be sure which of the Weird sisters it was. It didn't sound like either of them.

"I need to talk with you," he said. "You told me if I had any questions—"

No answer.

"About getting somebody free of that house. I have to talk to you."

"Talk," she said scornfully. Now he knew the voice. Miz Evelyn. Probably. Maybe.

"Are you all right?" asked Don.

"What do you care?" she asked.

"Of course I care," he said. "Can I get you something?"

"Are you really that stupid?"

No. It was definitely Miz Judea.

Her voice came again, a whisper now, fierce but broken. "Don't you know you're killing us?"

The door closed. The deadbolt turned.

Don turned away and surveyed the front yard. Covered with leaves. These ladies spent every waking moment either fixing food for Gladys or working in the yard. And yet the yard had been so neglected that not a leaf had been raked.

Why? The answer was obvious. Now that he believed in the power of the house, he also had to believe what these women had told him about it. Every bit of work he did on the house had sapped their strength. They had begged him to tear it down, for their sake. He had done the opposite, restoring it closer and closer to its true shape. What would happen when he finished? Would they come feebly staggering around the fence to knock at his door and beg him to let them come inside their prison? Or would they remain stubbornly in the carriagehouse until they were too weak to feed themselves?

Who would the killer be then?

And yet if he weakened the house now, what would that do to Sylvie? Now that she knew the truth about herself, now that he also knew, their ignorant faith could no longer help them maintain an illusion. They depended on the strength of the house to keep her there, to make her real, until . . .

Until what?

He couldn't think. He was too tired. He hadn't slept at all last night, had done two days' worth of work, and there was nothing left.

He turned back to the door and shouted through it. "Can I bring you something!"

But there was no answer.

He walked back around the fence and into the Bellamy house. To his surprise, his cot had been moved back into the ballroom. It looked small, almost pathetic compared to the vast space around it. He remembered dancing with Sylvie, how the room had sparkled with the memories of the people who had danced here. Did the house hold all these memories? Had the breaking down of the false walls released them? Why was this house so powerful, when others had no such power? What magic had been done? And how, how could it be undone without hurting Sylvie?

Or maybe it was being here that was hurting her. Maybe if she had gone on she'd be happier. Instead of being trapped here. Maybe he should tear down the house, burn it right now, let her go, and free the Weird sisters.

Even the thought of wrecking the house made him sick with grief. He couldn't bear the thought of losing her.

Is this what it comes down to? My need for her? Is that more important than what the ladies next door need? What Sylvie herself might need?

He would gladly do whatever it took to set everything to rights. But what was the way things should be? Simple: Sylvie not dead, the Weird sisters free. But Sylvie *was* dead, except for the power of the house. And the Weird sisters were trapped because of the house. He could not save one without harming the other.

And somewhere Lissy was free as a bird, unharmed by any of this. He knew that, even though he had no evidence, even though for all he knew she was tormented by guilt and living in a hell of her own making. He knew that she was unharmed because that's the way the world worked. A decent person like Cindy lived in hell for a crime she only *almost* committed. While Lissy, a selfish, lying, conniving murderer, was probably doing just fine.

Wasn't there something he could do? Wasn't there some choice that didn't lead to somebody's destruction?

There was no one to ask. All he could do was lie down on the bed Sylvie had prepared for him and sleep at last.

He dreamed that he was a house. He dreamed that he felt the bones of it when he moved his hands, his arms. That he knelt to form the foundation, strong and steady, that the wind blew across his body, and inside him a heart was beating strongly, and it was his daughter there. She was in the most beautiful alcove in his body, playing, laughing. He heard her laughing. And then . . . silence. She was gone, and no heart beat there.

He grew cold. Snow piled on him, the wind tore at him. He bowed under the blast of the storm, empty. He did not understand why he was still kneeling there, why he hadn't simply ceased to exist. Why he was not dead, with his heart no longer beating.

And then it beat again. His heart was alive again, only he looked and there was still nothing there, nothing at all, and yet he was coming alive. Where was his heart? Why was he alive when he had no heart?

His eyes flew open and there she was, sitting in the alcove. Sylvie.

Why hadn't he been able to find her in his dream?

Because she wasn't there.

She did not know he was awake. She sat there, holding her knees, her head leaning back, her hair free, as she looked straight above her at the apex of the alcove. Was something carved there? What did she see?

For that matter, what did *he* see? What was it, exactly, that he wanted from her? With Cindy there had been no doubt about what was driving their passion. But what kind of passion bound him to Sylvie? Certainly he had taken her under his wing—reluctantly at first, but completely. So there was that fatherly, protective element. But she wasn't his daughter. When he thought about it, she might be a year or two older than he was. Except that she hadn't aged these years in this house, so she was still younger. Oh, but what did their ages matter? A man has his children under his protection, and his wife also, and his parents—it's part of what defines a man, to provide and protect. It's what you do when you grow up.

It was partly Sylvie's beauty, he knew that. It wasn't a traditional beauty, not the beauty of models or the fresh-faced beauty of the cinematic girl next door. She had a moody face, and her hair, while it couldn't possibly hold a coif, he was sure of that, had a kind of freedom to it, a contrariness that echoed her elusiveness. What was the beauty of her, really? Was it the line of her slender neck? Was it, in fact, how lean she was? A beauty that would be lost if she filled out to a more womanly shape? He didn't think so.

At last she sensed his eyes on her, and turned to look at him. She smiled. "What are you looking at?" she said.

"Beauty," he said.

"I laugh." But she didn't laugh.

"I'm trying to figure it out myself," he said.

"Thanks."

"I start with the beauty, Sylvie, and figure from there."

"Truth is beauty."

"Is that it?"

"I was just quoting Keats," she said.

"Are you the truth?" he asked. "That's pretty heavy. The truth is dead but still beautiful, haunting us but always out of reach."

She rose lightly to her feet and came to kneel beside his cot. She kissed his cheek. He touched her face and kissed her lips, warm and sweet and slow. "Not out of reach," she said.

"Oh, Sylvie," he said. "Don't you know how tempted I am just to live here forever with you? Keep the place up, leave only to earn enough money to come home to you?"

"Then do it," she said. "Oh, do it, please."

He rolled onto his back, looked at the ceiling. "For how long?" he said. "Until I'm sixty and you're still whatever age you are now?"

"I won't mind."

"I will," he said.

"Then you'll die and we'll be together."

"This is a good plan?" asked Don.

"*The Ghost and Mrs. Muir*," she said. "Did you ever see it?"

"There are some old ladies next door who are being destroyed by this house."

"Only because they fight it."

He turned to her. "They should come and live with us, too? Is that what you're saying?"

"I don't know why this house is so strong, Don. I didn't make it that way. They were trapped before I was born."

"I want to do the right thing, Sylvie."

"The right thing for whom?" she asked.

"The right thing."

"The greatest good for the greatest number? Did you ever take ethics?"

"Sylvie," he said. "I'm blocked. I'm stopped cold. There's nothing I can do that doesn't ruin somebody's life."

She kissed him. "I know."

"And if I don't do anything, that also ruins lives."

"Beginning with your own."

"Maybe," he said.

"Because you need children," she said.

He shuddered.

"Don't you?" she asked.

"I don't know if I could ever do that again. Now that I know what it does to you when you lose one."

"Is it any worse than losing a parent?"

"Yes."

"Worse than losing yourself?"

"I've never lost myself, Sylvie. Neither have you."

"I must have," she said. "Because it feels so good now that I've found myself again."

"You think because we danced, because we kissed, because we love each other—we do love each other, don't we?"

She kissed him again.

"You think," he said, "that this means our problems are over. But they're not."

She sat crosslegged on the floor. "Something's still wrong."

"Right. But what is it? What's the thing that if we fix it, everything will be all right?"

"It's not the house," said Sylvie. "The house isn't aware, really. It's strong, but it doesn't know anything. It . . . holds people. That's all it does. It makes them yearn for this place. It's a home."

"And that's not bad."

"That's not bad if you want to be here. My point is that the house isn't what's wrong. It just *is*."

"The ladies next door don't feel that way."

"You know what the problem is? She's still out there."

Don's mind was on Miz Evelyn and Miz Judea and the mysterious Gladys upstairs. "Who?"

"Lissy. My roommate. My murderer."

"Don't I know it."

"I know I can't live here forever, Don. If you can call me alive."

He squeezed her hand.

She smiled at him. "I know that if you're really going to be happy, you have to love a living woman."

"I do," he said. "You."

"I know that maybe if I could let go of this place, if I could drift away. I mean, think about it. Who is it the house holds onto? Not the Bellamys. When they died, they drifted away."

"True," said Don. "And why didn't their children get caught up the way the ladies next door did? They grew up here and yet they could leave, they could even sell the place."

"That *is* odd, when you think about it. Why would two prostitutes be tied here, and not the others? Why me, and not the others who died here?"

"Maybe because you lost something here. Maybe you all lost something."

"My life," she said. "What about them?"

"I don't know. Their innocence? Their trust?"

"Their self-respect?"

"I don't know them that well," said Don. "But they lost something and so they can't leave the house until they get it back."

"Maybe it's not something in particular at all. Maybe it's just—loss."

"Other people have to have lost things here, too."

"Well, then, maybe it's need."

"What do you need?"

"A life," she said, laughing.

"But that's not a joke, is it?" he said.

"No," she said. "Even before she killed me, I needed a life, Don. My parents were gone. There was nobody to show my accomplishments to. You know? Nobody to watch me sing or dance or whatever and clap their hands when I got through it without a single mistake."

He nodded. "I know what you mean."

"So I believed all that stuff about pleasing myself." She laughed. "Can't be done. You can't please yourself by doing what you want. Because it doesn't mean anything if it's just you. There has to be somebody else it matters to. I think . . . I think that in my heart I needed that to be Lissy. I needed her to care about what I did."

"And instead she cared so little that she was willing to wreck it all just to get a good grade on a paper."

Sylvie nodded. "So it's my own need holding me here."

"Maybe," said Don.

They sat in silence for a while.

"Or maybe," said Don.

"What?"

"Maybe it's justice that you need."

"What's justice? I hit Lissy with a stone. I *could* have killed her. As far as I can tell, my being dead and trapped here may very well be justice. Maybe this is hell, Don."

"Hell is knowing she's out there, thinking she got away with it."

"Not just thinking," said Sylvie. "She *did* get away with it."

"I want to find her," said Don.

"No."

"I just want to . . . I don't know. Send her a note. Just let her know that somebody knows what she did."

"And then?"

"I just don't think she should be happy," said Don.

"Will it bring my body back to life?"

Don thought of the corpse lying on the mattress down in the tunnel. He thought of Nellie's little body—and his exwife's, too. She at least had died for her sins. Lissy hadn't.

"She has to face what she did," said Don.

Sylvie laughed. "You're not going to do that by sending her a note."

"How, then?"

"Bring her back here," said Sylvie. "Bring her back to me."

Don looked at her. What was she talking about? What did she mean to do?

"Maybe now that the Bellamy house is becoming itself again, it's time for it to be haunted."

He thought back to the movies he'd seen with haunted houses. *Poltergeist. The Uninvited. The Changeling.* He thought of Lissy coming into this house and coming face to face with the woman she murdered. And the house . . .

"Oh, man," he said. "What would happen?"

"I don't know," said Sylvie. "But one thing's certain. She couldn't hurt *me* again."

"So she comes," said Don. "We find her somehow and she comes and you face her and she, what, I don't know, runs screaming from the house and never has a good night's sleep again. Or she goes to the police and confesses. Or she laughs at you and burns the house down. Or she dies of a heart attack. Whatever. Then what?"

"Then nothing," said Sylvie. "We know, that's all. We find out what happens and then we both know."

Don thought about this. "Is there really some balance in the universe? Some scale of justice that will bring her here and find some way to set things to rights?"

"She's what's missing, Don. You're the one who kept saying it—she's out there. And she shouldn't be. She committed murder in this house, Don. If anyone should be trapped here, it's her."

"You think the house wants her?"

"The house just wants. But if she comes, I think it might want her."

"And it will let you go."

"Maybe."

"Let you go, but how? By making you disappear? Like you did this morning out there in the yard?"

"Would that be so terrible, Don?"

"I don't want to lose you."

"Don, be honest, please. You don't have me. You never can. And I can never have you. So maybe the best thing, the right thing—remember, you were asking about that?—maybe the right thing is for me to be set free of this place. And maybe if Lissy comes here, that can happen. I can . . . "

"Go to heaven," he murmured.

"Whatever."

Don swung his legs off the cot and got up. "I've got to use the john." Then he laughed. "And I actually worried about whether you'd been peeing in some sink or something."

"Gross," she said.

He walked through the huge ballroom instead of along the narrow hall. When he got to the bathroom he closed the door out of habit. It felt so good to release his bladder. The easing of that pressure.

He thought of the ladies next door. What pressure they felt, what its easing would mean to them. Was Sylvie right? Did it all depend on bringing Lissy back?

When he came back into the ballroom, he could feel a draft. A cool breeze was blowing outside, and the front door was open. She couldn't have gone outside!

No. She was sitting on the bottom step of the stairway, looking at the outdoors.

He sat down beside her. "You know, I'm not some macho guy who avenges murdered girls."

"I know," said Sylvie. "That's what's eating you alive. That you aren't the kind of guy who takes the law into his own hands. You left the law in other hands and it screwed you over pretty bad."

"I was talking about you, not . . . "

"Not your little girl. But that's still part of what this is about. It's *your* hunger, Don. You need to save *some* captured girl before this whole thing plays out."

"So you've got me figured out, huh?"

"You haunt this house just like I do, Don."

"I'm not dead."

"You live in dead places."

"I bring them back to life."

"But then you move on to another dead place."

Don sighed. "Whatever. I wouldn't even know where to start looking for her. She could live anywhere. Under any name."

"Not if nobody's looking for her," said Sylvie. "Not if she thinks no one ever found my body. And even if they did, there'd be no way to tie it to her."

"So I just check every American phone book looking for Lissy— what's her last name?"

"Felicity Yont. But she *has* changed her name, I'll bet. To McCoy."

"Why McCoy?"

"Because that's her boyfriend. Lanny McCoy."

"So I look up Yont and McCoy."

"Lissy was from Asheboro, but her people were all dead—it's one of the things we had in common, that we were both alone. Lanny, though, he was local. He even lived with his parents. She used to laugh about that. How she never thought she'd be with a guy who lived with his parents. She said all that was left was for her to put on Spock ears and go to a *Star Trek* convention."

"You think they might still be living in town?"

"No," she said. "Lissy couldn't wait to get out of North Carolina. She was so jealous of my getting a job in another state. We joked about how she was dying to leave and couldn't, and I didn't care about leaving North Carolina, and I was the one who had the cool job waiting for me in Providence."

"So I start calling directory assistance? That's the way to go through my bankroll, a quarter at a time."

"No, silly," she said. "Haven't you ever done any research?"

"Not lately."

"Not ever," she said, teasing him. But they both knew it was true. "The library has a lot of phone books from other areas. But you won't start there. If Lanny's people still live in Greensboro, all you have to do is find them and they'll probably tell you where Lanny is living now. With his wife Lissy, I'll bet."

"That would be too easy."

"But maybe that's how easy it'll be."

18

McCoy

Plenty of McCoys in the Greensboro phone book. Calling from a pay phone at the grocery store, twenty-five cents at a time, was tedious work.

The same conversation, over and over. "I'm looking for the family of Lanny McCoy. . . . He would have been in school at UNCG back in '85. . . . No, I never met him, but my wife did. . . . Sorry for bothering you. . . . Thanks for talking to me. . . . Sorry for. . . . Family of Lanny McCoy who went to UNCG back in '85. . . ."

Going on maybe four hours of sleep, Don had a hard time staying awake between calls. A hard time listening to what people were saying. A teenage kid walked by talking loudly to his girlfriend. "*The X-Files* is a crock. The government couldn't have secret UFO stuff because the government can't keep a secret, period!" He almost missed hearing the soft voice on the other end of the phone say, "You knew him?"

So there was a pause in the conversation before he realized that maybe he was hitting paydirt. "Actually, not me," he said. "My wife knew him. Good friends with him and his girlfriend in those days, what was her name? Missy? Lissy?"

"Oh, yes, that dear girl, that poor girl."

"Poor girl?"

"So broken-hearted. Oh, you don't know, do you? Of course not. Lanny's gone. All these years."

"Gone?"

"You don't—you haven't seen him, have you?"

"No ma'am, I'm sorry."

"Can't help hoping. Silly, isn't it? To hope that a phone call out of the blue. . . ."

This was it. And he wouldn't get anywhere on the phone. "Mrs. McCoy, I don't mean to intrude, but can I come over?"

"Oh, I wish you would."

As soon as she said the address, Don knew half the history of the family. It was a tiny crackerbox house on a street of crackerbox houses, in a neighborhood built by Cone Mills for their textile workers. A strategy for keeping the unions out. The paternalistic employer provides workers with homes and they're grateful; meanwhile, labor agitators get evicted, not just fired, so their families are out on the street. Very effective disincentive. But when times changed, the company sold the houses to the workers at a better than fair price, and now those factory families or their children or grandchildren kept immaculate yards around those tiny houses, their labor insisting that the size of the houses did not tell you about the class of the people inside. These were solid people, working people, salt of the earth. And for one of these families to send a child to college was still a big deal, even in the days of student loans and government financial aid. Lanny must have been the bearer of the McCoy family honor, their hope, their ambition.

Mr. and Mrs. McCoy were white people in their late fifties, her hair grey, his greying. They ushered him into a tiny living room filled with furniture covered with doilies and throws. The fireplace mantle was covered with knickknacks, including a couple of Hummels and a Lladro that must have been the markers of special occasions. The pride of place in the center of the mantle went to a framed eight-by-ten of a young man with longish hair and a great smile. No sooner had Don sat down than Mr. McCoy took down the picture and handed it to him.

"That's our Lanny," he said. "Senior picture from high school."

"Nice-looking boy."

"He was the first of our family ever to get to college," said Mrs. McCoy. "And he was with that nice girl, too—we were sure they'd get married."

"You just never know," said Mr. McCoy, shaking his head.

"Nice girl?"

"You mentioned her on the phone," said Mrs. McCoy. "Felicity Yont."

"Lissy," said Mr. McCoy.

"Then they didn't get married?" asked Don. "We all assumed that they would."

"It just broke her heart," said Mrs. McCoy. "She came over here crying and crying about how he ran off with her roommate."

Ran off with. . . . This was not the story Don had expected to hear.

"A snake in the grass, that's what *that* one was," said Mr. McCoy. "The librarian steals the man? What a joke."

"And you don't know where they're living now?"

"We've never heard from him since." Mrs. McCoy broke down in tears.

After a delicate pause to show respect for his wife's grief, Mr. McCoy said softly, "I don't expect they're *together.* A woman like that, she's got no loyalty. She probably left him cold somewhere."

What could Don say? What would be gained by telling them that in fact Lissy murdered that very roommate, who certainly did not run off with anyone because she was still haunting the house where they roomed together?

The only sound was Mrs. McCoy's soft crying. Her husband gave her a handkerchief.

"I'm sorry I made you think of your loss again," said Don.

"Oh, young man, we think of Lanny every day," said Mrs. McCoy.

Mr. McCoy nodded sadly. Don suspected he carried handkerchiefs solely to deal with his wife's tears.

Don hated deceiving these people, but it was kinder than the truth. "My wife always assumed Lissy and Lanny must have ended up together."

"Maybe our boy is alive, maybe not," said Mr. McCoy. "I don't know what we did to make him leave us without a word." He stood up to keep himself from crying openly. So . . . maybe the handkerchiefs weren't just for her. "I guess we've disappointed you," he said.

Don could take a hint. Besides, he'd learned what he came to learn. There'd be no address from these people. "I appreciate your time. I'm just sorry that . . . I'm sorry." He got up, shook hands with Mr. McCoy, and took the one step that was needed to get him to the door.

Mrs. McCoy rose to her feet.

"Don't be sorry, young man," she said. "Don't. It's *good* to remember a child you loved, even if you've lost him."

He thought of his own tears, his own rage, his years of hiding in old houses from himself and the whole world. The pain he had suffered . . . and yet she was right.

"I know," said Don. Almost he told them about Nellie. But he couldn't. In this home, there was only one lost child to be remembered. There were other places where Nellie's memory was the foundation of life. After ten years, they still shed tears for their boy. The edge of grief never lost its sharpness. And yet . . . there was a nobility about their suffering. Their child still lived in them as a light of goodness. If Lanny were still around, they would not have the grief; but they would not have the illusion, either. Just as Don would never hear a teenage Nellie shout at him what a terrible hateful man he was, how he was trying to ruin her life. She would never wreck his car, never fight with him over whether she would or would not wear *that* outfit on a date. The lost child remained a dream of a child. A sweet ghost haunting the memory. The tears that came were not bitter for these people. It was a sweet grief they felt. They had lost him, but once they had him, such a good child, they had him and he still gave shape and meaning to their lives.

He hadn't bargained on learning so much from these people.

Mrs. McCoy came to him in the doorway, took his hands, held them in hers. "I believe you do know," she said.

Out in his truck, driving back through the streets of Greensboro, Don got caught up in the traffic of teenagers from Page High School racing to get to the Weaver Center downtown for special classes that no one high school in the city could afford to teach. The kids called it the "Weaver 500," and drove like stock car madmen. Don wasn't exactly moseying down Elm, but they were whipping around him to pass at fifty or sixty on what was, after all, a residential street through this part of town. Miracle that more of them weren't killed.

He imagined talking to Nellie when she got her license. "I don't care how late you are," he'd have said. "You got twenty miles an hour over the limit for three blocks, do you know how much time you've saved? Exactly none. But in the meantime you've put your life, everybody else's lives at risk. Better to be late. Always be late. I'll never be mad at you for being late. Just be safe. Be safe."

It was blinding him, the tears that came when he thought this way, when he imagined the kind of father he might have been. The father he would never be. Even if he married someone and had children, none of them would be Nellie. That ache would never be eased. Besides, look who he fell in love with lately. A woman who couldn't trust herself with her own children. Then a dead woman. Nope, he wasn't exactly picking the child-rearing type. Nellie was it. Because he knew how much it cost to lose one. Couldn't put himself at risk like that again.

It was obvious, of course, that Lanny McCoy was dead. When Lissy told his parents that story about him running off with Sylvie—how ludicrous to imagine even if Sylvie *hadn't* been dead!—it could only mean one thing. Lissy knew that neither of them would ever be showing up to contradict her story. How did it play out? Did she tell Lanny what had happened, and then he got all these crazy ideas about going to the police and pleading self-defense? He could imagine him earnestly telling her, "She hit you with a rock, you had to defend yourself," but Lissy would know that the prosecutor would have an expert testify that you had to hold onto the victim's throat so, so, so long in order to strangle her. Strangling is never a crime of passion, the prosecutor would say. It's a cold-hearted crime. It's a crime of icy hate. So what could Lissy do? She lures Lanny somewhere, maybe even tells him she wants to show him the body, but they're down in that gully maybe, and suddenly there's a rock in her hand, a blow to his head.

Or maybe she never talked to him at all. She knew already that she couldn't afford to have anyone else who knew about that tunnel. The body couldn't be found until she was long gone. Lanny never got a choice. Because a woman like Lissy, she doesn't love anybody. Lanny was good for sex and drugs. But expendable. So she went up to the kitchen and got a knife and was waiting for him when he arrived. For all Don knew, his body was farther down the tunnel.

Then she went to his parents and told them a story that would hold them for a while. A few days. Long enough to get away. Only instead of a few days, it held them for years. Because Lanny had never told them about the tunnel. And since the house was closed, why would they dream of looking there in the cellar? No, Lissy's secret was safe in that old house. Until now.

He had to laugh at his own pretension. Until now? What a joke. Her secret was *still* safe. Sure, he could go to the police and tell them he found a body in the tunnel. But how could he possibly explain anything about it? Everything he knew, he learned from a ghost. The dead woman was not going to be acceptable as a witness. Nobody was going to take her deposition. So they'd have a body and no leads and that would be it. They probably wouldn't even figure out who it was. Sylvie was never reported missing, except to the McCoys, and to them she was missing because she ran off with their son. The story of the body found in the basement could play for a day in the local paper and on the TV news—they'd find a way to sneak footage of that corpse onto the screen—but no one would ever make the connection. Or if they did, nothing would come of it. The trail was too cold.

Lissy actually went to Lanny's parents and *wept* as she told them her lies. Cried as if her heart were breaking, when in fact she murdered the two people she was slandering. Don boiled with rage against her. This Lissy Yont—for sheer gall she topped even Don's exwife when she testified how the baby couldn't be Don's because he only had sex with his secretaries at the office.

He got to Friendly Avenue and headed west, but instead of turning south into the College Hill area where the Bellamy house was, he drove on to the grocery store where he'd been making his phone calls. The huge new Harris Teeter—the local pundits were now calling it the Taj Ma-Teeter–had a pretty good deli. He went in and bought vast quantities of basic food. The soup of the day in a tub the size of a paint can. Another container of potato salad, another of fruit salad. Don remembered how much food could disappear when it was carried upstairs to Gladys. He had to talk to the Weird sisters, and so he needed a serious peace offering. He stopped in the bakery and bought a cheesecake. None of the food would be as good as what they made themselves—but if they were as weary and sick as Miz Judea or whoever it was said this morning, they'd be glad of the break from cooking.

Don pulled up in front of the carriagehouse instead of parking around the corner beside the Bellamy house. He got the bags of food out of the cab and carried them up to the porch.

It took even longer to get someone to answer the door this time. Naptime? Or both of them upstairs with Gladys, and now so feeble that getting down the stairs took forever? He wasn't going to give up, though. He pounded on the door, he rang the doorbell over and over. Finally the door opened, and not a crack, either. Miz Evelyn stood there, haggard, stooped, her eyes bloodshot and angry enough to kill on the spot. "Who the *hell* do you think you are!" she demanded.

"I'm lunch," he said, holding out the bags. "It's only Harris Teeter deli stuff, but it's edible and you didn't have to cook it."

"After what you done—"

"I didn't believe you. I'm sorry now, but I just couldn't believe in it then."

Her face was the picture of scorn. "Fine to be a skeptic when other people pay the price for it."

"Eat the food," he said. "Get some rest. Please let me come back and talk to you."

"Why, when it takes you two damn months to believe what you're told?"

But she took the food. He offered to carry it to the kitchen for her, but her lip curled in disgust. He clearly wasn't welcome in this house anymore.

"Can I come back later?" he asked.

"You can hang yourself for all I care," she said. "In fact, there's rope in the shed out back. Feel free." She smacked the door with her butt and it closed in his face.

Couldn't blame them. But despite her tough words, she had taken the food. And she knew that he believed them now. Sooner or later they'd let him come in and ask his questions.

Only when he got to the front door of his own house and Sylvie opened it wide for him, only then did he realize that he hadn't bought any food for them.

Which was stupid. She didn't need food. He was famished, after all of yesterday's work and missing dinner besides. But he could grab something later. He sat down with Sylvie in the alcove and told her about his conversation with the McCoys. She reached the same conclusion he did. "Lissy killed him," she said.

"She's a nasty one all right," said Don. "If you had any doubts about the moral difference between the two of you—"

"Yes," said Sylvie. "She kills to cover her crime. I hide."

"You hid to cover *her* crime."

"Poor Lanny. He was an ass, but he might have grown out of it."

"I realized something," said Don. "A little fact about murder that you often overlook. It's always somebody's child who dies."

"Not me," said Sylvie. "I'm nobody's child."

He held her hand. You're mine now, he was saying. Not my child, but mine. To miss you when you go, to look out for you, to hope you'll be careful.

"I don't know what to do, now, Sylvie," he said. "I don't know how to find her. I just can't imagine Lissy is still living under her own name. She told her lies to the McCoys and then she took off. She could be anywhere. Any country."

"So," said Sylvie. "So we don't find her."

"But we have to," said Don. "I don't know how we can set things to rights without her."

She stroked the wood of the bench. "So work awhile this afternoon. Maybe some idea will come to you."

He shook his head. "I can't work on the house anymore," he said. "Not till I know what's needed."

She flinched. "Don, it's the house that's making me real. Keeping me alive."

"But it's killing the women next door."

She looked at him searchingly. "Don?"

"Don't ask me to do that, Sylvie," he said. "Think what you're asking. Those old ladies may be crotchety and strange but I can't just forget them and finish the house and it kills them or enslaves them completely or . . . You're solid *now*, Sylvie."

She nodded. "I know, I wasn't . . . I didn't mean for you to forget them, I just . . . I can feel the hunger of the house."

"So can they."

"It wants you to go on. Can't you feel it?"

He shook his head.

"Well that's good," she said. "You're still free, then."

"I've got to find a way to set things *right*. Not to decide between the dead woman that I love and a couple of strange old ladies I like a lot."

She giggled. "Did you ever think you'd say a phrase like 'the dead woman that I love'?"

He stroked her neck, the part of her shoulder left bare by the neckline of the dress. "Nor did I ever think that the most beautiful woman I ever met would disappear if she ever went outdoors."

"Strange times," said Sylvie.

"Strange but good," said Don.

"Good?"

"This is completely selfish of me, but if you hadn't been killed in this house and trapped here and . . . you think a college graduate librarian would ever look at a man like me?"

She shook her head. "But then, think of the hard road you had to travel to bring you here."

"Come to think of it," said Don, "if our meeting and falling in love with each other—that is what happened, isn't it?"

She nodded.

"Well if that was part of some cosmic plan, then I got to say that's one hell of a lousy planner. Somebody should fire that guy."

"Let's be honest," said Sylvie. "If we could undo the bad things—

I wasn't murdered, and you didn't lose Nellie—and the price of doing that was that we never met each other and never loved each other . . . "

Don didn't need to answer. They both knew that they'd do it in a hot second.

"That doesn't mean this isn't real," said Sylvie. "Just because our lives might have gone another way. A better way. Doesn't mean that we don't love each other *now*. I mean, it *did* go this way, and we *can't* trade this for that or that for this, so . . . "

She couldn't figure out how to end what she was saying, so he kissed her and solved that one small problem. Anything that could be solved with a kiss, he could do that. Trouble was, it was a very small list of very minor problems.

"It's Gladys who'll know," he said. "If anybody does. She had the power to get those old ladies out of here. To keep them out this long. If there's any way to keep you alive but get you out of this house . . . "

"There isn't," said Sylvie. "She couldn't even get those ladies farther than the carriagehouse. What can she do for *me?*"

"Hey, it's just a lot of old wives' tales, right?" said Don. "But I'll tell you, everything they told me has turned out to be right. I'm not going to make the mistake of underestimating any of those old wives."

"Think they've finished the food you brought them?" asked Sylvie.

"You had to remind me of food."

"So go eat," she said. "And when you come back, see if they'll let you in and give you some answers. Even if the answer is that there's nothing you can do for me, at least we'll *know*."

He paused at the door. "Do you really think God has anything to do with this?" he asked.

She shrugged.

"I mean religion is all about life after death and right and wrong, right?"

"I guess we know there's a life after death," she said.

"But the will of God and all that," said Don. "I just don't see how the will of God could possibly have anything to do with this."

"I don't know, Don. I wasn't a believer."

"I was raised that way, but when Nellie died I decided that was all the proof I needed that God didn't exist or if he did then he didn't care about us at all." Even saying this much about Nellie brought tears to his eyes and he had to swallow hard. "But now here you are. Here you are. A spirit, alive when your body's dead. So where does God come into it? Is he out there somewhere, working to make it so that in the long run, the really really lo-o-o-ong run, everything comes out even?"

"I don't think so," she said. "I mean, maybe he's out there." She walked to him, touched his chest, right over his breastbone, right over his heart. "But maybe he's in there. Making it all come out right."

Don shook his head. "I don't think God is in there." He lifted her hand from his chest and kissed it. "But you are."

He went out to the car and his legs felt loose and rubbery under him. He was a little dizzy. Either he was very hungry or he was in love. A quarter pounder with cheese would settle the question.

19

Answers

If the idea was to make up with the Weird sisters, Don still had a ways to go. And the start would be that leaf-covered lawn.

Their garage contained no car. Instead, it had the cleanest array of gardening tools Don had ever seen. What did they do, wash them in dish soap after each use? Every tool had a shelf of its own or a clip to hold it to the wall. Nothing touched the ground. The only sign that they had not been maintaining the garage up to their normal standards was a couple of spiderwebs, but these were so new they didn't even have sacs of eggs or more than a couple of bug corpses. If these ladies had stayed in the Bellamy house, the place would never have decayed at all.

The rake was clipped to the wall. Don took it down and toted it over his shoulder out to the front yard. His body didn't like raking, not today, not after yesterday's labors, but he pushed on and after a while the aches and pains subsided and became the trance of labor. His hands were already callused. It felt good to him, to know that work had shaped his body. Back when he was a general contractor, building house after house, real physical labor had been only a hobby for him, fine carpentry in the garage. He had no calluses then. The last few years before his wife left, he had even been developing a little pooch at the beltline. That was gone, too. He didn't have the shaped, constructed muscles of a bodybuilder. He had the body that honest labor made, and he had learned to recognize it in other men, and respect it. And to like his own. He felt good in this flesh.

The job was done. The leaves were piled at the curb. He leaned for a moment on the rake, and the front door opened. Not just a crack, and not just to be slammed in his face. Miz Judea and Miz Evelyn both stood there, waiting for him. He waved. "Got to put the rake away." They closed the door as he walked around the house to the garage in the backyard.

Unsure how they went about making their tools so perfectly clean, Don contented himself with picking all the leaves off the rake before putting it back into its clip. He used that small handful of leaves to swipe at the spiderwebs and clear them away. Then he tossed the leaves over the high hedge into his own yard. Plenty of room for spiders there. They didn't need to go disturbing the perfection of the Weird sisters' garage.

The back door stood ajar, waiting for him.

He went inside. Miz Judea, looking weary and ancient, was slowly washing the plastic containers that had contained the food Don brought for them. "Was it good?" he asked her.

She just looked at him sadly and went back to washing.

Miz Evelyn came in from the parlor, carrying a plate of cookies. "I had this set out for you in the parlor, but then I remembered you didn't like going in there when you were dirty from work." It broke Don's heart to see her walking like an old woman, one step at a time, balancing the plate in one hand.

"Oh, ladies," he said. "I'm so sorry I've put you through all this."

Miz Evelyn shook her head. "All began before you were born."

At the sink, Miz Judea began to hum a melody that Don didn't recognize. At first he wondered why she was singing this song at this point in the conversation; then he realized that she wasn't paying attention to their conversation at all. She was humming because she felt like it.

"Thank you so much for raking our leaves," said Miz Evelyn.

"I had an ulterior motive."

"Oh, and for the lunch, too. But Gladys liked it. She misses store-bought food. Can you believe it?"

"Too much vinegar in everything," said Miz Judea. So she *was* listening.

"Maybe that's how they keep it from going bad in the display case," said Don.

"Maybe they don't know how to cook," said Miz Judea. "Gladys wouldn't know a good meal if it bit her on the butt."

"Now, Miz Judy, don't go talking down your dear cousin," said Miz Evelyn.

"Hungry bitch," said Miz Judea.

"It's the house that's hungry, Miz Judy, and you know it."

Miz Judea nodded. "I'm tired."

Miz Evelyn turned to Don to explain. "The house is so strong now."

"I wake up dreaming about it," said Miz Judea. "Five times a night. Dreamed there was a ball there. Saw you dancing, young man. With a heron."

"A what?" asked Don.

"A heron. Long-legged bird."

"It wasn't a heron," said Don.

"Whose dream we talking about, boy?" she demanded.

"I thought it wasn't a dream," said Don. "Because I was dancing there this morning. Until dawn."

"You too lonely, boy," said Miz Judea.

"You wasn't dancing alone, I take it," said Miz Evelyn.

"No, not alone," said Don.

"Who you got over there?" asked Miz Evelyn.

"She was there when I arrived. A girl. A woman."

Miz Judea looked skeptical. "Gladys never said nothing about no woman there."

"She's not a . . . her body was left in a tunnel under the back yard. About ten years ago."

"Good Lord," said Miz Evelyn. "You telling us she's a haint?"

Don nodded. "She gets stronger along with the house. I didn't understand any of what you told me. But the more I worked on the house, the more solid she became. Until I could feel her in my arms as we danced. But she's only real inside the house."

"You expect us to believe this bullshit?" asked Miz Judea.

"Hush, you silly old goose," said Miz Evelyn. To Don she said, "She's only trying to get even with you for not believing us earlier."

"I don't blame her," said Don.

"Well who the hell else you going to blame?" asked Miz Evelyn. "We may be old and feeble and going through a hard time, but we're still responsible for what we say, I hope! I ain't ready for them boys in white coats, I can tell you that."

"Ladies," said Don. "I need your help."

Miz Judea whirled on him, sudsy water flying from her fingers, she turned so fast. "And how that supposed to work, Mr. Lark? You tell us what you need, and then we go do the *opposite*, that it? That how folks help each other?"

"Come now, Miz Judy," said Miz Evelyn. "Can't you see he's sorry?"

"Look at my hands," said Miz Judea. They were trembling so violently it was a surprise she could wash dishes without dropping them. "You sorry enough to make up for that?"

"All I want," said Don, "is to find a way to set everything to right. I've stopped renovating the house."

"When?" said Miz Judea. "You tore out those false walls all yesterday afternoon and half the night. Gladys was up there crying her eyes out, saying, Don't he have to sleep? When that boy going to sleep! We all so desperate for sleep we almost gave up, we almost just walked on over there and knocked on the door and give ourselves back to that place."

"We weren't even close," said Miz Evelyn. "We just *talked* about it. Nobody was going to do it."

"Gladys *can't* do it," said Miz Judea. "That's the only reason we didn't. Her magic ain't doing much now that the house is so strong. It just goes on day after day, year after year. What you think that poor woman can do?"

"It's not him, Miz Judy," said Miz Evelyn. "It's the house. Don't you go getting that confused."

"There's got to be a way," said Don. "To set you free without destroying Sylvie."

"That the name of that haint you got?" asked Miz Evelyn.

"Didn't you ever think maybe you tear that house down, she get set free too?" asked Miz Judea.

"If that's the best solution, and she agrees to it, then that's what I'll do," said Don. "But neither of us wants to."

They looked at him in silence for a moment.

Then: "Don't that beat all," said Miz Evelyn. And at the same moment, from Miz Judea: "He gone and fell in love with a ghost."

"I didn't know she was a ghost until after."

"After what?" asked Miz Evelyn, all curiosity.

"After I came to care for her," said Don.

"'Care for her,'" echoed Miz Evelyn. "Ain't that sweet, Miz Judy? You hear anybody talk like that anymore these days?"

"Shut up, you silly two-bit tart," said Miz Judea. "There's nothing old-fashioned about plain old love. I'm just glad to know he's suffering a little, too."

"Miz Judy, it pains the Lord to hear you talk like that." To Don she spoke apologetically. "She doesn't really wish suffering on you, Mr. Lark."

"But she's right," said Don. "The way things are going right now, everybody's in some kind of pain except one person."

"Who's that?" asked Miz Judea, as if she meant to find that person and slap him.

"The woman who killed Sylvie."

Suddenly Miz Judea grinned. "Oh, now we got the game going, don't we. That's why you come here. To find a way to get that killer."

Don had no idea what she was imagining. Voodoo dolls? A fatal potion? "I don't know why I came," said Don. "Except that the way y'all talk about Gladys, I thought she might know what I should do."

Miz Evelyn looked shocked. "Talk to Gladys? In *person?*"

"Well, I don't have a phone."

The two women retired to the back of the kitchen and conferred for a moment. Don ate a cookie while he waited. It was very good. When did they have time to bake, as wiped out as they were? And how many of these cookies did Gladys eat at a time?

"We got to ask her," said Miz Judea, when they broke their huddle.

"But it's so hard getting up and down the stairs now," said Miz Evelyn. "Would you mind helping us get up the stairs? You still have to wait outside Gladys's room. And you best call her *Miss* Gladys, even though we don't. We're older than her, but you sure ain't."

"Promise you don't go in till she say so," said Miz Judea.

Don agreed at once, and soon had Miz Judea on one arm and Miz Evelyn on the other, helping them up the stairs, which were wide, but not wide enough to make three abreast easy. They both hung from his arm, they were so weak. It hurt him to feel how light and frail they were. I did this, he thought.

No, age did this, and the house. I only pushed them the next step.

Miz Judea disappeared inside the bedroom to the left at the top of the stairs—the bedroom whose curtains Don had so often seen parted, back when they still had the strength to spy on him. As soon as the door was closed, Miz Evelyn leaned close to him. "You got to be nice to that girl," she said.

"Miz Judea?"

"No, you fool," said Miz Evelyn. "Gladys. Don't you look at her like no sideshow. Because she got that way for our sake. She got to eat to give her the strength to fight that house. Only fighting the house, that don't use no *calories* if you see my point."

"She's fat," said Don.

"Oh, she's way beyond fat, you poor boy. Fat? My land." Miz Evelyn shook her head. "You just remember that we owe her everything. Me especially. She didn't need to take me. She come for Miz Judy, her cousin, don't you see. Gladys, she was only a slip of a girl, fourteen years old at the time. Took the train from Wilmington all by herself, and those was hard times for a black girl traveling alone, you can bet on that. But she comes right in and rebukes that house like a preacher casting out Satan. Then she calls our names and says, 'Come forth,' like Jesus calling Lazarus. And Miz Judy and me, we just feel a load come off our shoulders like as if we're free for the first time since we was born. That little slip of a girl."

"How could she do what the two of you couldn't do?"

"Oh, she learnt the old ways. Some of them black people brought secrets with them from Africa. Passed them along mother to daughter, aunt to niece. Gladys knew them old ways, and found out a few new ones of her own. And I said, 'We're free!' and Miz Judy starts laughing so hard she's crying for joy, but Gladys, she just scorns us and says, 'That spell's the best one I know for what ails you, and it only lasts an hour or so. I got to keep casting it over and over, or this house going to suck you back here.' And I see she's just talking to Miz Judy, not to me, and I understood that. I didn't even ask her to take me along. But I got to saying good-bye to Miz Judy, and naturally I was crying but I didn't ask no favors. And Miz Judy, she's crying too, but she never thought Gladys would care a fig for a hillbilly white girl like me, so she didn't ask either. But Gladys, she ups and says, 'You planning to spend your whole life here?' and I says, 'I pray not, every night and every morning.' And she says, 'This day your prayers be answered.' Just like scripture she said it. 'All you got to do is stay together, close by me, and I can keep you out of this house.' And she kept her word. So you show respect to that girl, Don Lark. You hear?"

"I hear, ma'am, and I'll obey."

"About time you started doing that," she said, without a trace of a smile.

The door opened. Miz Judea shuffled out. "She says come on in."

The curtains were drawn in the room, and in the light of a single lamp beside the bed it took a moment for Don to realize that the mountain of pillows on top of the king-size bed that almost filled the room wasn't pillows at all. It was the vast body of a black woman, her face sagging with chins and dewlaps of fat, her arms sticking out almost sideways, held up by the rolls of fat.

Don tried not to look at the body. Look at the eyes, that's all, see nothing but her eyes.

They were good eyes. Kind eyes. Weary, but well-meaning. And they were gazing at Don.

"Took you long enough to believe us," said Gladys. Her voice was deep and husky. The voice of a woman just roused from a sleep that was not long enough.

"I believe you," said Don. "But I don't know what to do now."

"Tear the damn house down," said Gladys. "We told you that from the start."

"It's the only thing keeping Sylvie alive!"

"Excuse an ignorant girl from tobacco country, but it seem to me that girl already be dead."

"But she shouldn't be," said Don.

"A lot of things is that shouldn't be," said Gladys. "I should be married and have me about forty grandkids by now. Your baby daughter ought to be about four and a half years old. Sure that girl ought to be alive. God's world works that way."

"God expects us to make things right when we can," said Don.

"What do you know about what God expect?"

"I know as much as you know about God," said Don. "What I don't know about is houses."

Behind him, the Weird sisters were whispering, coaching him. "Don't do no good to make her mad." "Careful what you say to her, Mr. Lark."

A slow smile spread across Gladys's face. "I think the word uppity was invented so they'd have something to call you."

Don didn't bother answering that. What mattered was that he had her attention. "Miss Gladys," he said, "what is it about that house? Why is it so strong?"

"You ask me that?" said Gladys. "You, a builder of houses?"

"I've built plenty of good solid houses in my life, but none of them had *that* kind of power."

"Come on now, Mr. Lark. Don't tell lies like that. You know the minute you walk into a house which ones got power and which ones be dead. The powerful ones, they feel like home the minute you go inside. You feel like you already remember living there even though you never did. But the dead ones, they feel like nothing but walls and floor and roof, just slabs of stuff."

Now that she put it into words, he'd felt those things about every house he ever entered. Some made him welcome, and some repelled him. "So what makes the difference? Good design? Workmanship?"

"That's part of it," said Gladys. "That's the starting place. Shoddy don't ever come to life. But the house got to be one of a kind. You build a whole bunch of houses all the same, you got to take one house worth of life and spread it out over all fifty or a hundred of them."

So much for housing tracts. No wonder Don hated working from overused designs. They felt dead before work even started.

"One of a kind, shaped to fit the people who live there. And then the first people who live in a house, oh, that's more important than all the rest. You got love there, you got parents looking out for their kids, you got hardworking folks caring for the house, you got guests coming in and feeling welcome, people in and out all the time—why, that house gets a heart to it, that house gets a soul, it gets a name, *their* name. The carpenter make the bones of the house, but the people breathe the breath of life into it. You get a ugly little cottage, shoddy built, ten thousand others just like it, and if the first people that live there fill it up with good life, then there be some strength in that house, at least a little."

"So it really is the Bellamys' house. Even though they're long dead."

"It has their name, it beats with their hearts. I felt their love the minute I walked into the place. Made me *sad* how the strength of that love got twisted by the ugly things bad folks turn it to when my cousin Judea got to whoring there. Stole that house, turned the name into a lie. That wasn't no love there, that wasn't no joy. It wasn't the *Bellamy* house no more."

"So how did they get stuck?"

"It ain't the house sticking to them, it be them sticking to the house."

"So it depends on the person?" said Don. "But why them?"

"You don't think I be wondering about that myself? I'll tell you what I guess. And this just a guess, Mr. Lark. It be the folks who most need a home that gets stuck in a strong house. Pain and loss, that fetch you up in a place like that. Shame and guilt, that hold you, that make you stick. My cousin Judea, she got herself pregnant by her uncle Mack, and they took that baby away from her before it make a sound, she never see it, and then she run off what with her mama and daddy calling her a low-class whore, and then she fetch up here where they make it true. You got it all there, pain and loss, shame and guilt. That baby didn't get adopted, either. They drown that baby like a cat. She told me before that baby born, she say, Gladys, I better run off, they going to hurt my baby. Only she never did run off, did you, Cousin Judea."

"No," said Judea softly.

"So she stick to that house. Her need so strong, that house so strong, they be two magnets."

Don turned to Miz Evelyn. "What about you?"

"That's nobody's business," said Miz Evelyn darkly.

"Oh, now, Miz Evelyn, we asking this man to help us get shut of that house," said Gladys.

"He don't have to know all that," said Miz Evelyn.

"Let's just say that Miz Evelyn knowed where the shotgun be, and where her husband be, and who he with. Let's just say that. Had to hightail it out of the mountains before the sheriff found the bodies. They still warm when she fetch up here and hide out in that house. Pain and loss and shame and guilt."

"So why am I not caught?" asked Don.

"You got the pain, you got the loss," said Gladys. "But what you ashamed of? What you guilty for?"

"I didn't save my daughter when I could."

"My laws, boy, you know you couldn't save her. You know you did all that Jesus ever let you do. You may think you ashamed, but you not. Deep in your heart, you know you done all."

"You don't know what I feel," said Don.

"I know that if you be guilty, that house suck you in."

Don had to think about this. About what it meant for Sylvie. He walked to the window that faced the house and opened the curtains.

"Please don't," said Miz Judea.

"No, you let him," said Gladys. "Just you don't look."

What about Sylvie? He knew her pain and her loss. But shame? Guilt? She had thought she killed Lissy. So the house held her. But now she knew she didn't . . .

"The girl next door," said Don. "Sylvie Delaney. She thought she committed murder there, and so she had the shame and guilt. But now she knows she didn't. That she was the one who was murdered."

"Kind of slow, ain't she?" said Gladys, looking amused.

"Innocent, that's what she is," said Don. "And now that she knows it, will the house lose its grip on her?"

"Maybe she not telling you, Mr. Lark," said Gladys, "but that house already letting go of her bit by bit. She fading. So you might as well tear that place down. She as good as gone."

Don sat down on the window sill, despondent. "I found her and then I lost her," he said.

"Why you sad about that?" said Gladys. "She going to be free now. She can go home to Jesus."

"Call me selfish, but I wanted her to go home with me."

"You show me where it says in God's plan about a man marrying him a dead girl. You show me that."

"You show me where it says that when a man and a woman fall in love, they shouldn't get married just because one of them's dead."

"I'll tell you where," said Gladys. "It says in the Good Book that in heaven they be neither marrying nor giving in marriage."

"Well what does that prove? Sylvie ain't in heaven." Don got up and walked up and put a knee on the foot of Gladys's bed, so he could look her straight in her squinched-up little eyes. "Miss Gladys, everything about this is wrong. That house is beautiful and filled with love—so why should it snag people because of the ugliness in their lives?"

"Nothing needs beauty so much as ugly do," said Gladys.

"But it's *not* beautiful to them. To Miz Judea and Miz Evelyn. If it was, they'd still be over there, and it would make them happy inside."

"It got twisted," said Gladys. "Man who make it a whorehouse he be six kinds of ugly in his heart. I tell you the *strength* come from the love of that first family who lived there. But after that, the house take on the soul of the owner."

"Well I'm the owner now!"

"Too late," said Gladys. "Too late for us. Maybe ten years from now, you so good that house be decent again. But you think we still alive by then? Besides, Mr. Lark, that's a pretty big gamble. Whether you good enough to unbad that house, or it bad enough to ungood you."

"I don't want to tear it down," said Don. "It's too beautiful."

"Beautiful to look at," said Gladys. "But if it do ugly things, then all that pretty be a lie."

"But it's not doing ugly things," said Don. "No, listen to me. The house was mean enough when it thought I was tearing it down. I still have a sore place on the back of my head to prove it. But then it stole my wrecking bar and when I went looking for it, it was behind the old coal furnace. Right where that tunnel entrance was. That was what sent me down the tunnel. That was why I found Sylvie's body there, and we learned the truth. Now you can't tell me the house is malicious when it did that!"

Gladys shook her head, which moved her whole body, quaking the bed. "You poor man, you try so hard," she said.

"Don't make fun of me," he said, "just tell me what's wrong with what I said."

"It Sylvie's house all these years, Mr. Lark," said Gladys. "House be malicious, all right. It do what Sylvie want. Not what she want in her mind, but what she want in the dark secret places. She want to be blame for her crimes. So . . . the house led you there. Betrayed her."

"But she didn't commit a crime! And if the house knows so much, it knew that!"

"Tunnel ain't part of the house, Mr. Lark. Tunnel be older than the house. A good place. A freedom place. The tunnel showed you the truth. But the house, all it knew was what Sylvie knew. So the house, it trying to make you hate Sylvie. That's what she thought—if you went down that tunnel and saw what it had there, you hate her then. Treachery and malice, Mr. Lark. That's what that house got from all those years with that bad man and his bad sons owning it."

Don thought of how he'd had to pay extortion money to the last owner. "I guess none of the owners were very nice, not since the Bellamys."

"Now that dead girl," said Gladys, "she's nice enough. She been taking the edge off that malice. Made my job a little easier. That's why Miz Evelyn and Miz Judea, they can go out and work in the yard. Till you fix things up over there."

"Miss Gladys," said Don. "I appreciate all you've explained to me. But the big question is still hanging in the air. What can I do to set things right?"

"And my answer still hanging right next to it. Tear down that house."

Don could feel Sylvie slipping through his fingers. "No," he said. "Not till I've done . . . something."

"What?"

"I got to set things right."

"You can't."

"If Sylvie's going to fade from that house no matter what I do, then she's sure as hell not going alone!"

"If you thinking of killing yourself, do the kind thing and tear the house down first, all right?" said Gladys.

"I'm not killing anyone," said Don.

"You're killing me right now," said Gladys. "Me and these ladies. Look how they can't take their eyes off that house."

It was true. Miz Evelyn and Miz Judea had both wandered over to the window and now had their faces pressed against the glass like little children.

"Close that curtain, Mr. Lark," said Gladys.

Don excused his way past the Weird sisters and drew the curtain closed. Miz Evelyn was crying softly, and Miz Judea looked like she had lost her last best hope in life. Gladys was right. This couldn't go on.

"Thank you for your help," he said. And it *was* help. He knew more. Knowing was better than not knowing.

But not by much.

20

Lissy

All the way back around the fence to the Bellamy house, Don was filled with dread. Sylvie was fading already, Gladys had said. Now that she didn't have that aching hole of guilt and shame in her heart, the house didn't have so much power over her. What if she was already gone? At this moment it was an unbearable thought. I just found her, he thought. I didn't ask to be in this swamp, and neither did she, but we found each other, and it's not right that I should already be losing her.

The door wasn't waiting open for him. She wasn't in the alcove in the ballroom. He called her name, striding through the main floor. Called again, again, more loudly, as he ran up the stairs, searched the second floor. Then up to the attic, and she wasn't there either, and now he felt it like another death. How could it happen so quickly?

The basement? She never went down there on purpose.

But then, that was before she learned the truth about who killed whom. Don skimmed down the stairs like a schoolboy, then ran the length of the ballroom to get to the basement stairs. "Sylvie!" he called. "Sylvie!"

She still didn't answer, but now it didn't matter, because there she was, pressed against the foundation wall, almost behind the coal furnace. Near the tunnel entrance.

"Sylvie, what are you doing?"

She smiled wanly. "I don't know," she said.

"What brought you down here?"

"I just . . . wanted to see myself again."

Was it ghoulish to want to see a corpse, if it was your own? "So did you?"

"No," she said. "Part of me wants to go there. Down the tunnel. But the house doesn't want me there. I don't know what's the right thing to do."

"All I know about the tunnel is that it's not part of the house," said Don. "Gladys says it's older than the house."

"You know what it feels like?" she said. "If I go down there again, I'll be free!"

"Depends on what you mean by freedom." He explained to her what Gladys had said about how the house might be losing its hold on Sylvie. "If you want to be free, then go," he said. "I can't ask you to stay."

"Yes you can," she said.

"Then stay," he said. "Please stay."

She launched herself from the wall, ran to him, threw her arms around him.

He held her, but as he stroked her hair, it kept passing right through his fingers. Slowly, but passing through. He couldn't help the tears of grief that began to flow. "You're going," he said.

She pulled away from him, her eyes frightened. He showed her what was happening with her hair. In reply she clung to him all the more tightly.

He lifted her—lighter now, or was it his fear of losing her that made her seem like nothing in his arms?—and carried her upstairs, back to the alcove. "I'll tell you something," he whispered to her. "If I lose you, Sylvie, then you can count on this. I'll find Lissy wherever she's hiding. I'll find her and . . . "

"And what?" she said. "Look, your hair goes through my fingers, too." She shuddered. "Which one of us is disappearing?"

"You don't know how many times I've wished that I could."

"Me too," she said. "And now that I don't want to, the wish comes true." She kissed him lightly. "But you didn't answer my question."

"What did you ask?"

"What you'll do when you find Lissy?"

Kill her, thought Don. But then he knew that it wasn't true. He wouldn't have the heart for it. "There's no statute of limitations on murder," he said. "I'll turn her in."

"Waste of time," said Sylvie. "Don't even bother looking for her, Don. They won't do anything to her because there won't be enough evidence, nothing to point to *her* except you, and you got all your information from the victim's ghost. And they'll say to you, Well, Mr. Lark, where's that ghost now? And you'll say, Sorry, Your Honor, but she faded away."

"So Lissy gets away with it."

"She already got away with it. There's nothing you can do about that."

"That's all I seem capable of, when it really matters: nothing."

Sylvie leaned back. "I think I won't sleep tonight," she said. "I don't want to go to sleep and wake up invisible. So I'll stay awake. I'll watch you all night. I'll hold your hand. And then when your hand sinks through mine and leaves my hand empty, I'll know I'm gone."

Again Don's tears flowed. It made him angry, to have to face grief again. He clenched his fists. "Damn, what happened to me? I used to be stronger than this."

"Fat lot of good it did you. I'm glad you're crying for me, Don. I've been dead for a decade, and you're the first one to shed any tears of grief for me."

"This is just the start, kid."

"You want to hear something pathetic?" she said. "I've had more kisses from you than from every other boy or man in my life combined."

He kissed her again.

"What's that for? You've already got the record."

"Running up the score," he said.

She kissed him back.

"Mm," she said.

He broke off the kiss. "What?"

"Just thinking," she said. "About Lissy. Maybe we're giving her credit for being too resourceful. You know, coming up with a false name. That's not easy to do. I mean, sure, you can get fake ID, but don't you have to know somebody? How do you go buy a fake driver's license?"

"She bought drugs," said Don. "So she knew *some* underground people."

"No, Lanny bought the drugs. Just pot, mostly. I don't think she knew anybody like that."

"She really *did* coast on other people, didn't she," said Don. "He buys the drugs, you do her homework."

"That's the thing," said Sylvie. "When she needed some A papers right away, she didn't write them, she didn't do anything on her own, she just copied mine. Whatever looked easiest. Going underground and changing identities, that's hard. I just don't see her doing it."

"So you're saying she'll be living under her own name?"

"Don't you think?"

"No," said Don. "She knew she had to conceal her crime. That's why she killed Lanny, it's the only possible reason. She didn't know that neither body was going to be discovered. So she couldn't keep her own name."

The idea dawned on both of them at once. "She used mine," said Sylvie, as Don said, "How much did you two look alike?" They laughed for a moment, more at the excitement of the discovery than the coincidence of their talking at once.

"You said you two could swap clothes," said Don.

"Same color hair, nearly," said Sylvie. "Same basic shape in the face. Not that we looked like sisters, but if you didn't know either of us . . . "

"I mean, could she use your ID?"

"She could maybe get a haircut, different glasses, and tell the person at the motor vehicle department that of course she doesn't look the same, it's been years."

"No," said Don. "She just reports your license missing. Says her name is Sylvie Delaney and her purse was stolen."

"She'd need a birth certificate or something, wouldn't she?"

"Where did you keep your birth certificate?"

"In my room." Sylvie nodded. "You're right, she'd never have to show a picture."

"And your fingerprints were never taken."

"Right," said Sylvie. "I wasn't arrested much."

"This feels right, Sylvie. This is it. She took your name, your identity—"

"My savings. She could do my signature. She did that as a joke, but she could do it as well as I could. She used to tell me that I should do a harder signature, any fourth grader could fake mine."

"That's her whole getaway," said Don.

"Getaway," echoed Sylvie. "Don, she took my job."

It took him a moment to realize what she meant. "Providence?"

"They interviewed me over the phone. We never met. She read all my papers. She's a champion shmoozer. She could fake being me well enough to get along until she really learned the job. All the time getting an income."

"That makes my skin crawl," said Don. "To think of her out there in the world, using your name. People asking for Sylvie Delaney and *she's* the one they mean."

Sylvie shuddered. "Well, after killing me, I guess that's only adding insult to injury."

"I'm going to call," he said.

"Call who?"

"Directory assistance," he said. "Providence, Rhode Island."

"And then what?"

"And then I'll invite her here," he said.

"What makes you think she'd come?"

"Come on, Sylvie, give me credit." He put on his Marlon-Brando-as-Don-Corleone voice. "I'll make her an invitation she can't refuse."

"I don't want you hurting her, Don," said Sylvie. "You'd only get in trouble yourself. It won't help me for you to be in jail."

"No, I won't hurt her," said Don. "All I want is for her to face what she did. To face *you*. While you're still here."

"Oh," she said. "Oh, Don, I'm not sure I want to—"

"Why not?" he answered. "What can she do to you? What are you afraid of? Let her face her own shame and guilt."

Those words resonated with what he had told her from his interview with Gladys. "You're hoping the house will hold her," said Sylvie.

"Maybe," said Don. "It probably won't, though. She's guilty and what she did was shameful and she knows it, she can't hide from that. But pain and loss? She's got everything. I'm betting she feels no pain."

"She lost her family," said Sylvie. "Remember?"

"Then the house will snag her. That's justice, Sylvie. To have her trapped here."

"But how will you finish your renovations then?" she said.

He looked away from her. "I don't know if I will."

"You can't afford to walk away from this place."

He shrugged. "I have some money in the bank. I can break the house up a little bit, weaken it so the Weird Sisters aren't so drawn to it."

"But then *she* won't be drawn to it anymore."

"Sylvie, why don't you want me to bring her here?"

"I don't know," she said. "Because . . . because this is *our* place. If I'm going to fade, the only memory I want to take with me is this one. You and me. In this place."

Don got up from the alcove, paced toward the far wall, then stopped. "OK," he said.

"OK what?"

"OK, I won't call her. I'll let her get away with it. We'll have these last days or hours, whatever we've got, we'll spend this time together, and then I'll just . . . I'll just *forget* it all." He turned around and kicked the wall. It was tough and strong. It hurt his foot through the shoe. He slapped the wall with the flat of his palm and leaned there, crying again, *dammit*.

After a while he felt her hand on his back. Lightly, too lightly.

"Don," she said. "I can face her."

"No," he said.

"I want to," she said. "What she did to me, that's done with. But what she's done to *you*—that really pisses me off."

He laughed in spite of himself, turned around, held her. "You mean it?"

"It's less than a twelve-hour drive to Providence if you go straight through," she said. "I had that all figured out. Feels like only yester-day."

"Let me guess. The bitch took your car."

Sylvie danced away from him. "We're such stupid children," she said. She pirhouetted lazily. "We've built up this whole castle in the air, and she's probably married to some executive with Coca-Cola and living in Atlanta under his name."

"Still, it's worth a shot. It makes *sense*," said Don. "I'm going next door to see if they'll let me use their phone."

"Hurry back," she said.

"Stay out of the basement, please."

"Of course," she said. "I'm too busy dancing my life away to bother with basements." She was still turning around and around as he closed the door behind him.

Next door, Miz Evelyn let him into the house. "So have you decided what you're going to do?" she asked.

"Sylvie's fading. When she's gone, I won't leave the house strong like this."

"But all your money's tied up in it."

"I've lost a lot more money than this," said Don. "Lose enough of it, and you start thinking of it as nothing."

"Money's never *nothing*," said Miz Evelyn. "All those years we took in laundry and sewing, living on nothing, growing a garden, saving, saving. All so we could keep living here and never go out of the yard. Money is very *much* something."

"Not compared to saving people I care about."

"Well, all I can say is, if you weaken that house I'll be the first to kiss you."

"Too late," he said.

"There's already a line?" Miz Evelyn laughed. "Should have known, a strapping young man like you."

"Miz Evelyn, you ladies do have a phone, don't you?"

"Oh, you need to borrow one? It's right here in the parlor, right over here on the writing desk."

It was an ancient black dial phone. "You don't know how many years it's been since I've used one of *these*," he said.

"Oh, I don't know how we could ever get along without it. That's how we get our groceries delivered! And lightbulbs and things like that!"

"I didn't mean the phone, I meant *that* phone." She didn't understand. "They have phones with buttons now."

She looked baffled. Then comprehension dawned. "Oh, you mean *push*buttons. For a minute I thought, what in the world would you need to button up a telephone for!" She laughed. "Oh, my laws, I don't get out much." She looked wistful.

Don picked up the phone and dialed 411. He got the area code for Providence and then dialed directory assistance at that number. It was amazing how irritating it could be. The pressure on the sides of his finger. The endless waiting for the dial to return to position.

"For Providence," he said.

Miz Judea walked into the room.

"I need a listing for Sylvia Delaney. Or Sylvie. I'm not sure how the last name is spelled. Delaney."

He realized he had nothing to write with. He flung out a hand toward the Weird sisters, who were eavesdropping unabashedly. "Pen pen pen, please," he said.

Miz Evelyn fetched a pencil for him from a cubbyhole in the writing desk, and took an open envelope from the mail table.

The operator came back on. "Could that be S. Delaney, D-E-L-A-N-E-Y, on Academy Street?"

"Could well be, it's worth a shot."

"Hold for the number, please." After a moment, the computer voice started intoning the number. Don wrote it down and dialed it immediately.

"Am I missing something?" Miz Evelyn asked. "Ain't Sylvie Delaney the name of the haint?"

Don nodded, listening to the phone ringing.

Miz Evelyn went on talking, ostensibly to Miz Judea. "Why's he calling a dead girl in Providence when she's haunting the house next door?"

"Hush and listen, Miz Evvie," said Miz Judea.

Someone picked up the phone. A woman's voice. "Hello?"

"Hello, is this Sylvie Delaney?" He did his best to keep his voice sounding breezy, cheerful.

"Yes," she said. "Who's this?" Bored. Must have a *lot* of unidentified men calling her.

"Forgive me, but I just want to make sure I've found the right person. Did you get your graduate degree at UNC-Greensboro?"

"Who is this?"

Don waited a moment. "When I'm sure you're the right person," he said.

"Yes, I did my graduate work there. Now who are you?"

"We've never met, Miss Delaney," said Don. "But I feel as though I know you. You see, I've been renovating the old Bellamy house."

"I don't know of any such place," she said.

"You roomed here back in the mid-eighties."

"You must be thinking of somebody else. Good-bye."

"Hang up if you want, Miss Delaney, but I've seen what's in the tunnel under the house."

She said nothing.

"You don't seem to be hanging up," said Don.

"Maybe we do need to have a conversation," she said.

Don covered the receiver and whispered to the old ladies, "*Now* she wants to talk." Into the phone he said, "Yes, I think we ought to meet."

"Are you here in town?" she asked.

"No, here in Greensboro."

"Well, you don't expect me to drop everything and go all the way down there, do you? I have a job, I have responsibilities—"

"That's not my problem, is it?" said Don. "I'm betting you can get here by tomorrow at noon. After that, I call the police to check the body. When they figure out that it matches Sylvia Delaney's dental records, they're bound to start wondering who's this woman who's been using Sylvie Delaney's name for all these years."

"You're crazy if you think I'm going to pay blackmail over something that you've clearly concocted out of your own imagination."

"I'm not taping this, so you can skip the innocent act," said Don. "Noon tomorrow, at the Bellamy house. Come to the front door, and come alone."

"This is the stupidest prank I've ever heard of."

"I'm looking forward to meeting you—Lissy."

"Who *are* you?" she demanded.

He set the receiver down on the cradle. Then he sat back in to one of the plush parlor chairs. "That may just be the stupidest thing I ever did."

"What *did* you do?" said Miz Evelyn.

"Is your brain gone, you silly hillbilly?" said Miz Judea. "He just invited the woman who killed the girl next door to come down here and kill him, too."

"Oh!" cried Miz Evelyn. "That was foolish of you, Mr. Lark!"

"I know," he said. "But it seemed like a good idea at the time."

"You mean you don't even have a plan?" said Miz Judea.

"All I know is that Lissy Yont is *going* to face Sylvie one last time before Sylvie fades away."

Miz Judea shook her head. "You best talk to Gladys again," she said. "You bit off more than you can chew this time."

Nothing had changed in Gladys's room, except that Gladys looked even wearier and more impatient. "I wish you'd tell that girl to stop all that dancing," she said. "It wears me out."

"Her *dancing?*"

"Around and around. Like spinning thread. Like knitting. It ties me up in knots."

"Well, don't worry," said Don. "She'll be gone soon."

Immediately Gladys was full of sympathy. "Oh, you poor thing. It never lets up for you, does it?"

Was she mocking him? "Miz Judea thinks I should talk to you."

"Only because you're as stupid as they come," said Gladys. "Of course, I say that with your best interests at heart. Most people are stupid. I don't hold it against them. I just wonder what we're supposed to do for you when you're dead?"

"Why, you can see the future now?"

"Miz Judea *told* me what you did. That woman's going crazy right now, figuring out how she's going to kill you and get away with it."

"Well, if it's any comfort, she's also probably planning how to burn down the house or blow it up to destroy all the evidence against her. So *you'll* win no matter what."

"Burning's the last thing we want. It'll take *years* for the shadow of that house to fade, if it burns. We need it *torn down*. In case you haven't been listening."

"Give me a break here," said Don. "*You* didn't come up with anything. And I'm going to get Sylvie some justice before she goes."

"*Which* Sylvie?"

"Which?" He was confused. "Sylvie. *The* Sylvie."

"The Sylvie who's dead and living next door? Or the Sylvie who's probably buying a gun right now and heading on down here to kill you?"

"That's Lissy Yont."

"It *was* Lissy," said Gladys. "Don't you know nothing about the power of names, Mr. Lark? When I saved these girls, I called them by their soul names—name of their spirit and their body. When that girl started going by Sylvie's name, she didn't know what she was getting in for. When people know you by a name, call you that name and you answer, it ties the name right to you. Now, her *spirit* is still Lissy Yont, but her *body* has been called Sylvie Delaney by everybody for the past ten years. She's been divided. Her soul is split, so her body's name *is* Sylvie Delaney by now."

"So the soul's name is the spirit *and* the body?" said Don.

"Divide the names and you divide the soul. Leaves room for other spirits to try and seize the body, possess it. That woman doesn't know how weak her hold on her own body is. That body don't feel like it be part of no *soul*, it feel like it just be possessed by this spirit named Lissy. It want to get with its right spirit." Gladys cackled with pleasure. "People who don't know what they're doing, they do the *dumbest* things! Like you, calling a killer down to visit you."

"And you think it's funny?" asked Don, irritated now.

"I won't laugh when you dead," said Gladys. Sounding a little irritated herself.

"Not this time," said Don.

"Why? You don't look bulletproof to me."

"Because long before she can get to me, she's going to meet Sylvie face to face, the *real* Sylvie, right there in that house, where Sylvie is strong. Where the house does her bidding."

"Sylvie strong there compared to dead people who got no house. A dead woman's *never* as strong as a live one."

"They're not going to wrestle. Lissy's just going to face what she did to Sylvie."

"Meaning you think that ghost is going to scare her to death."

"She thinks she got away with it. I just want her to see that there's a life after death and someday she's going to answer for what she did."

"Don't it ever occur to you that only good people are afraid of paying for their sins?"

"No ma'am," said Don. "I've known some bad people and some good people in my life, and it's the bad ones who live in fear, all the time. Cause they know their own hearts, Miss Gladys, and they think everybody else is just waiting to pull the same moves on them that they've got planned to pull on somebody else."

"People be more simple than you think, Don Lark."

"You've spent the last sixty years sitting on a bed getting fat while you do spells to keep a big old house from swallowing up your people, and you're telling me that people are *simple?*"

"Nobody simpler than me," said Gladys.

"Well, so, maybe you're right. Maybe Lissy'll get here and see Sylvie and laugh in her face and then come shoot my brains out. If she does, then I won't care anymore, will I?"

"Now look who's talking brave."

"I got to do something for Sylvie before she goes, if she's going."

"She's going, and you already done something. You gave that girl love. What you think anybody want more than that? You think she give a rat's behind about seeing Lissy? That for *you*, Mr. Lark. She do that for *you*."

"OK, maybe," said Don. "Maybe that's for me. Maybe just once I want to look evil in the face and name what it is."

"Only it be using the wrong name. That body be Sylvie Delaney walk through that door. And don't you go expecting her to show up at noon. You think she crazy? You call her what, ten minutes ago? She on the road now. Not the airplane! She ain't putting her name on no plane ticket. She driving, but not slow, no. She flying down the pike. How long from Rhode Island? Ten hours I bet. Pay cash for gas. She get to town at midnight. Then she get scared. Midnight too busy. She wait for you to sleep. She park way up the block. She come by the house on foot. From back there. Maybe she come to the gully, maybe she come up that tunnel. Maybe she try to take that body out. Destroy the evidence, like they say in them cop shows. Obstructing justice."

"I didn't think of that."

"You didn't think of nothing. You acting from your heart now, not your head."

"Yeah."

"No, no, that be good, you keep doing that. Good people can't out-think evil, cause evil think of things good folks can't think of. Can't enter your head what evil do."

"You'd be surprised."

"But the good heart, now, *it* think of good things that evil can't imagine, cause it got no heart. How about that? That be philosophy. That be deep."

Either it was too deep for Don, or not deep enough, he couldn't be sure either way. But he was glad he talked to Gladys again. That back entrance to the tunnel, that had to go before tonight. That had to be sealed off.

"You know I wish I wasn't so fat," said Gladys.

"I hear that from a lot of folks," said Don.

"I wish I could fit through that door. Wish I could go down them stairs. Wish I could be there next door."

"Why? Can't you tell what's going on from right here?"

"Oh, sure I can. But see, I never heard of something like this before. I don't think it ever happened. Somebody been living under a dead person's name for years and years, come face to face with that dead person's spirit. Who know what going to happen."

"What do you mean?"

"Well, that Sylvie spirit, it going to meet a Sylvie body. And back again. They going to know they belong together. If the Sylvie spirit still had its own body, then so what? That happen before, lots. But the Sylvie spirit got no body. What then? And that Sylvie body, it hungry for a Sylvie spirit for a long time. Want to be a *soul* again, not just possessed."

"You're not saying that Lissy's body might capture Sylvie's spirit," said Don.

"I not be saying nothing, I just wondering. I just thinking it be a real good thing if you tell that dead girl not to touch that Lissy when she get here."

"She might get trapped in the same body with the woman who killed her?" The idea made him sick at heart. What had he got her into?

"Just tell her keep away. She a ghost, Mr. Lark. That Lissy girl, she can't touch her if she don't want to be touched."

"Thanks for the warning," said Don.

"These ladies give you lots of warnings, you didn't listen to a one of them."

"So maybe I'm learning to listen better," said Don.

"Maybe but not likely," said Gladys. "But if you ain't dead when this is all over, you come see me, tell me what all happened. I can't see it except with the eyes of magic, and I want to know what it *look* like."

Don held out his hand, then walked around the bed to where she could reach it. They shook on it, though her hand was so puffy with fat that he could barely get a grip on it. "We got us a deal," said Gladys.

"Better than that," said Don. "We got us a friendship."

"Well, that's good news. Cause I know you a man look after his friends."

"No one does that better than you."

"Now you go and don't get killed if you can help it." She waggled her sausage fingers at him.

He tipped his imaginary hat to her. Then to Miz Evelyn and Miz Judea. "I'll let myself out," he said.

They bade him good-bye as well, and he headed back over to the Bellamy house.

21

Reunion

It didn't take long to explain to Sylvie what he had done.

"Why did you call her?" Sylvie said. She looked miserable.

"There's nothing she can do to you now," said Don. "You don't have anything to be afraid of."

"Yes I do," she said. "She can kill you."

"Hey, you're living proof. Death isn't the worst thing in the world."

"Yes it is," she said. "You lose everything."

"You keep your memories," said Don. "In the end, that's all we have."

She held up her hands. "And our hands. And our feet. Our eyes. Our ears. The feel of things, the taste and smell of them." She smiled wanly. "I can't smell anything."

"We have what we have. If I'm still alive when you go, I'll remember you forever. That's how long I'll long for you."

"So I managed to hang on here long enough to ruin somebody else's life."

"Sylvie, you gave my life back to me." He reached for her, to kiss her. She turned her head. "I don't want to kiss you, Don."

"Are you mad at me?"

"I don't want to kiss you and not feel it."

He looked away to hide his face from her. By habit, really, his old habit of hiding his emotions. There was nothing she hadn't seen of his emotions by now. No weakness she didn't already know.

"You need to get some sleep," said Sylvie.

"You think I can sleep?"

"You hardly got any rest last night. This morning. You're still mortal, Don. Don't you think you need to be alert when she gets here?"

"Something I got to do first."

"What?"

"Seal the gully end of that tunnel."

"What does it matter which way she gets into the house?"

"I don't want her messing around with your body." His wrecking bar wouldn't be enough. He got a big old crowbar, almost as heavy as his sledgehammer. Got the sledgehammer, too, and his skillsaw and his two longest extension cords. Sylvie came down into the basement to watch him plug in the saw and string the cords together. But he wouldn't let her come down into the tunnel with him. "The tunnel's outside the house," he said. "I don't want you to disappear on me again."

"So the little woman sits home and waits while her man goes off to war."

"Down into the mine is more like it."

"How green was my valley."

He didn't get it.

"An old movie about Welsh coal miners," she said. "Roddy McDowell was in it, back when he was cute."

"Someday you have to take me to see it," he said. They smiled at each other, even chuckled a little over the bitter impossibility of it. Then he plunged down into the dark tunnel.

The cord was long enough, with plenty to spare. There was no second corpse near the entrance. Whatever she did with Lanny's body, she didn't leave it here. The wooden ceiling came to an end right where the tunnel narrowed down to a twisting passage that showed no daylight. There must be some kind of closure outside, something that kept neighborhood children from discovering and rediscovering this tunnel all the time. Lissy would know how to find it, though, even in the dark, and open it. When she got in here she'd find things changed a little.

Don wore his goggles this time—the debris would be coming from above. He took the safety guard off the skillsaw. Now it was just a naked blade, spinning, deadly. Starting at the board nearest the entrance, he sliced through the rotting old wood pretty easily. Of course, there was no way the blade could get even halfway through the boards, so nothing fell but chunks of sawdust. Exposed to the wet ground for so long, however, there was no chance this ancient wood was dry and termite-free. The miracle was that it had lasted this long. Maybe the tunnel was a structure of its own. Gladys talked about it being a place of freedom. If it was older than the Bellamy house, that could only mean it was used for escaping slaves. Guests coming in and out, leaving happy. A place built by love. It had all the ingredients for strength, didn't it? Maybe that's why it lasted when any other such structure should have rotted away a long time ago.

It's history I'm cutting down here, thought Don. It's a place with a life of its own. I'm a builder, not a destroyer. And yet right now it's destruction that we need.

He didn't want to cut too far. When the tunnel collapsed, he didn't want it to make a sink across the lawn. He only needed to break down enough of it to stop Lissy from coming in. It wouldn't take more than a few yards of blockage to stop her completely. In the dark, she wasn't going to want to dig. She no doubt would be armed—but not with a pick and shovel.

He picked up his sledgehammer and began the arduous work of breaking up the wood overhead. He held the sledgehammer out in front of him, then launched it upward, his arms extended. His muscles weren't shaped to deliver much strength in that direction. Fortunately, the wood was as rotten as he had hoped, and most of the time the sledgehammer sank into wood and when it came away, half the railroad tie crumbled down with it. Dirt began to fall like rain. Now it was time for the crowbar. Don rammed it into the packed earth over the rotten fragments of railroad tie and pried it, tore it loose. More and more of it fell. He backed up and hammered out more wood, pried down more earth. Finally some kind of critical mass was achieved and with a whoosh and a great cloud of moist earth, the roof at the tunnel mouth collapsed completely.

The force of it made him lose his balance. He fell. He tried to scramble out of the way. More of the ceiling was collapsing. His legs were covered with dirt. For a moment he couldn't move them. Then he pulled hard with his arms and his legs came free. Another section of roof sagged, right where he had cut it. Wish I hadn't cut so far, he thought. He scrambled up the tunnel, reaching for his tools, trying to gather them up. The sledgehammer he got; the crowbar was buried and he didn't have time to get it out. He had left his work-lantern on the shelf of stone just a little ways down the tunnel. He could still get it by clambering over the fallen earth just a little ways. But he decided against it. Good thing. Another two yards of roof gave way right then, and the light was gone.

He could hardly breathe in the thick wet dust. He still had the sledgehammer. And the skillsaw had to be around here, lying on the floor.

He felt the cord under his foot, followed it back. It disappeared into a pile of earth. Had he really left the saw so far down the tunnel? Forget it, leave it. It wasn't that expensive to buy another.

No, don't be stupid, he told himself. The part of the ceiling you cut has all collapsed. The saw must be just a few feet under the shallowest part of this earthfall.

He probed with the handle of the sledgehammer. Right. The saw was right there. He reached in, felt through the dirt till he got it by the handle and pulled it out.

Only now he was turned around. He swung with the sledgehammer until it rang against stone. Here's the wall. The left wall, as he headed up the tunnel. He didn't want to stay on the right side, where his feet would stumble across the mattress, across Sylvie's ruined body. He could hear snapping and creaking overhead. Was more of the tunnel going to collapse? Even where he hadn't cut the wood? This was going a little better than planned.

He finally saw the light at the top of the tunnel, just as he heard the rotten wood snapping and tearing like velcro as tons of earth collapsed into the tunnel, zipping toward him. He ran, faster, scrambling. He thought of dropping the tools, but couldn't get his fingers to let go of them, he was holding so tightly. A huge cloud of choking dust blew past him. He couldn't breathe. He staggered, fell. The crackling sound was coming toward him. He couldn't see at all now. He got partway up, crawled, stumbled, until he ran into something hard, right in his path. What could he possibly have run into?

The coal furnace. He was out of the tunnel. But he still couldn't see. The fine moist dust that had blown upward through the tunnel was hanging thick in the air in the basement. He blinked; dirt was in his eyes. They teared up, he couldn't see. Still pulling the skillsaw with him, he picked his way around the furnace, out into the open. Except the skillsaw suddenly snagged. Of course. The cord had been buried. Don grabbed the cord and pulled hard. It came free. But it was only the short cord of the saw itself that he had. The long extension cord was trapped down the tunnel.

"Don!" She was calling his name. She sounded so far away.

"I can't see," he said. "I've got dirt in my eyes."

"I'll lead you." He felt her gentle touch, tugging at his arm. She kept letting go. No. Not letting go. Her hand was sliding free. She was getting less substantial all the time. Less real.

He couldn't think of it that way. She wasn't getting less real, she was getting more free. She would let go of this house that had trapped her for so long. That was a good thing for her. It's not as if he was losing her, because he never really had her. Just the dream of her, the idea of her. It felt so real to hold her in his arms, but in the end she was always a ghost. And here, now, with his eyes closed, surrounded by darkness, he could believe that. This was reality, this choking blindness. What Sylvie was, what she meant to him, was a moment of clarity in the dark. She would be his memory of light. He could live with that.

Barely.

At last they were up the basement stairs. She led him into the bathroom. "I can't turn on the faucets anymore," she said.

"Can't you get the house to do it for you?" he said.

"Oh," she said. Then laughed. "I was getting used to being real."

He was still fumbling with the faucet when he felt it move on its own, and the water gushed out. He filled his hands again and again, splashing it on his face. Finally he could blink his eyes open without pain. His hands were filthy. He soaped them up to his elbows, then washed his face with soap. After he rinsed, as he toweled himself dry, he looked in the bathroom mirror. His hair was caked with mud. His clothing was completely covered.

"I thought you were dead down there," she said. "What was exploding?"

"No explosion," he said. "That tunnel was ready to collapse. I got it started and it didn't know when to stop."

"Well," she said. "I guess I finally got a decent burial."

He shuddered. He thought of her body lying on that mattress, now covered with broken, rotted timbers and tons of earth. Buried was buried, with or without a box. With or without a marker.

"What I need," he said, "is a shower."

But when he left the bathroom, he didn't go out to the ballroom to head up the stairs to the shower. Instead he went down the basement stairs. The dirt had settled on everything. A thin skiff of it covering the whole basement, even clinging to the beams overhead. The light was dim because of moist earth spotting the bulb. He walked over to the coal furnace. Dirt spilled out from both sides like the fan at the mouth of a canyon. Behind the furnace, it was piled up as tall as he was. And daylight was visible above. The tunnel had broken down along its entire length, and what he feared had happened—there had to be a sag in the back yard right behind the house, marking where the tunnel was. If Lissy wanted to, she could sneak into the house through this gap in the foundation. But he didn't think she would. The gap wasn't all that high. She wouldn't know to look for it. If she couldn't get into the far end of the tunnel, she'd assume she had to come through the door.

The plugged-in end of the extension cord still emerged from the tunnel. He unplugged it and started to pull. At first it came easily. The earth that had fallen wasn't tightly packed, and he could straighten out the bends in the cord. It got harder as the cord straightened out and the weight of all the earth of the tunnel began to oppose him. Stubbornly he pulled and pulled. He had some vague idea that he didn't want to leave a cord like a trail, tempting someone to excavate and find Sylvie's body and disturb it. He leaned against the resistance of the cord, putting his whole weight behind it. And then suddenly it came free and he fell down on his butt, like a baby just learning to walk. It hurt his tailbone; the pain really stabbed as he got up. I'm getting old, he thought. All I need now is a broken tailbone.

The rest of the cord came out easily. He found what had given way. The second extension cord had come free. All he had pulled out was the first one. Well, that was fine. No part of the buried cord was sticking out. Nothing was left dangling.

He coiled the cord and walked up the stairs as he finished. She wasn't waiting for him at the top of the stairs. But he heard water running in the house. He gathered up the sledgehammer and the skillsaw. They were caked with dirt. He brushed them off at the back door. I could use the Weird sisters to clean my tools right now, he thought.

In the back yard, the sag of the collapsed tunnel was only visible right up against the house, where the entrance had been. The rest of the tunnel was deep enough that the sag didn't make a sharp line across the lawn.

He looked around. Could anybody see him from the nearby houses? Screw 'em if they could. He stripped off his shirt and pants and chucked them in the garbage can. There wasn't a coin laundry in America that could cope with this dirt without breaking down. His shoes, though, he could clean. He got them off and beat them against the wall of the house until they merely looked dirty instead of encrusted. His socks went into the garbage with his pants and shirt.

Even his underwear was muddy brown from dust that had got through his jeans. That stuff was in his lungs. He'd be coughing up mud for a week, he was sure. He glanced around one more time for onlookers, saw none, and stripped off his briefs and dropped them in the garbage can. Then he picked up the skillsaw, cord, and sledge-hammer, and dodged inside the house. Maybe I take this neatness thing too far, he thought. I'd rather be naked for a whole minute out in front of God and everybody than leave my filthy clothes anywhere but in a closed garbage can, or set down my tools anywhere but in their proper place. He imagined the police showing up at his door with a warrant for his arrest for indecent exposure. Maybe they'd arrive just as Lissy got there with her gun.

Lissy. If he had harbored any ambition of getting her arrested, it had sure faded now. His best evidence was now lying under tons of dirt in a tunnel. He could see the police excavating with pick and shovel, tearing apart Sylvie's body in the act of discovering it. No, whatever happened with Lissy would be private. Just between the three of them.

Don put the saw and cord and sledgehammer where they belonged, then rummaged for some clean clothes. He could hear the water running. He knew it was Sylvie starting the shower for him. Man, was he ready. He felt his skin crackle as the clay dust dried all over him.

Holding his clothes, he turned around to head for the stairs, and there was Sylvie, watching him. Instinctively he brought his clothes down to cover his crotch. "Um, sorry," he said.

"I've seen you naked before," she said.

He raised his eyebrows.

"I watched you all the time," she said. "You were the only interesting thing going on in the house, Don. You can hardly blame me."

He wondered how she watched him. With her own eyes, or somehow using the house to see for her? He didn't understand how this thing worked with a house and the spirit that haunted it. It responded to her, did things that she wanted without her even knowing she wanted them. It watched whatever she wanted to see.

"Well fine," he said. "You've seen me naked, I've seen you dead. We got no secrets."

She laughed.

He jogged up the stairs. His tailbone still hurt and his muscles were sore from all his exertion of the past few days. Hard work was a good thing but he hadn't been giving his body enough rest. He set his clothes on the lid of the nonfunctional toilet and stepped into the shower. It took three soapings before the water finally rinsed away clear. He must have been carrying ten pounds of dirt, from the thick mud that formed in the bottom of the tub. He washed it all down the drain and soaped and rinsed himself a fourth time before he opened the shower curtain to find Sylvie leaning nonchalantly against the door, watching him. He grinned and shook his head, reached for his towel, and dried himself. "They got laws against peeping, you know," he said.

"I don't peep," she said. "I stare."

"That's all right then. As long as you don't point and laugh."

He pulled on his clothes. He tried not to look at her too much, because if he did, he'd see how he could kind of make out the door behind her, right through her. She was fading way too fast.

Sylvie, of course, didn't try to avoid the question. "What if I'm not here when she arrives?"

"That would be a bummer," said Don. "Let's hope she drives fast."

"Believe in me, Don," she said. "Keep me here."

"I have something better than belief," he said. "I know you. I love you."

"Well what do you think belief *is?*" In the doorway he bent to kiss her. He could feel her, yes, but only faintly. Like the memory of a kiss. Like a gentle breeze. He started to cry again. "Damn," he said. "Damn, I'm not the crying kind of guy."

She touched his cheek. "I can still feel your tears," she said.

"I feel like this is just one sadness too many, Sylvie. I don't know. I don't know."

"You'll be fine."

"I don't know."

"You've got to sleep now," she said.

"Sleep? You think I'm going to waste any of the time we have together?"

"She's coming, Don. And you're so tired right now you can hardly stand up. Look at you, stooped over like an old man. What good will you be to me or yourself if you're falling down from exhaustion?"

"What if you're gone when I wake up?"

"I won't be gone, Don. Even if I've faded, I'll still be here. In the house. I'll still be here."

"She has to see you, Sylvie. She has to *face* you."

"I'll hold on. I'm stronger than you think. I've got the strength of the house to hold me here, don't I? And your strength to keep me real. But for now you've got to sleep."

She was right and he knew it. He nodded, unhappy about it, and started for the stairs.

"No, not down there," she said. "You can't sleep down there. What if she sneaks up in the dark before either of us knows she's there, and shoots you through the window?"

"Didn't think of that."

"This isn't TV," she said. "Bad guys don't really stand there and confess everything so there's time for the good guys to get there and rescue you. They just shoot and down you go and they're out of there."

"I don't know, even bad guys like to have somebody hear their story."

"We'll find out tonight, won't we. Here, sleep on my bed. In this beautiful room you made for me."

"I didn't know it was for you till it was done."

"I didn't know you loved me until you gave it to me."

Her bedding had gone unwashed for ten years, but it felt clean enough as he lay down atop the bedspread. Whatever was hers was clean enough for him. Or maybe it really *was* clean. Like her faded dress. Maybe the house had the power to do that, too. All that was missing was flower petals to mark her passage through the house.

With all his aches and pains, with the evening light still coming in through the windows, he thought it would take him forever to get to sleep, or that perhaps he might not sleep at all. But within a few minutes he felt himself fading. For a moment he thought: Is this how it feels to her? To fade like this? But he knew it was the opposite. His body was heavy and real; it was his consciousness that was fading. Her consciousness would stay, locked up in this house until he tore it down and set her free. And that's what he'd do. He'd have ten, twenty thousand left, maybe a little more, after paying the demolition crew. That was enough for a down payment. He'd work his way up to cash purchases again. He'd done it before. His life wasn't over. It only felt that way.

She was still there, sitting on the floor, her back against the wall. "Sylvie," he whispered.

"Aren't you asleep yet?"

"Almost," he said. "Promise me you'll wake me when she comes. Don't try to face her alone."

"I promise," she said. "I've been alone long enough. The house kept trying to draw me in, make me part of the walls, the timbers. I never did. I knew I had to stay separate. Myself. I was waiting."

"For Lissy to come back?"

"No. For you."

She crawled the yard or so to the bed and leaned on it with her face just inches from his. "When Lissy was around, men always ignored me and fell for her."

"I'm smarter than those guys," he said.

And then he slept.

Sylvie watched him for a while, but then she began to wander through the house. As she was fading, she felt the pull of the house on her growing stronger. She could already feel her footsteps as strongly from underneath as from above; she felt through the floor as much as through her own feet.

For ten years she hadn't let herself want anything. Not sunlight, not food, not love, not life. Nothing. She hadn't known she was dead, but at the same time she knew she felt that way. Only when she stopped *being* dead, only these few weeks with Don Lark in the house did she understand how dead she had been. Lost in her guilt, her shame, her pain, her losses. Now that she had learned again to love and hope, now that she was no longer ashamed or guilty, of course it was that very joy that was killing her again. Whoever set up this universe, she thought, it really sucks. If you ever get around to making another one, change the rules a little. Lighten up on your creatures. Give us a break now and then.

She walked the house, feeling like a ghost now for the first time. She could sense the house responding to her. Windows rattling as she passed. Boards creaking because she wanted them to. Doors opening, closing. She walked among Don's tools as if they were a field of butterflies; they rose up and flew out of her way as she walked among them, then settled back down, right where they had been, when she was gone. The flue opened and wind blew up the chimney because she wanted to exhale. She could feel her own heartbeat throbbing in the walls. This house was strong now. Don had made it strong. So now when she faded into the house there would be real power in it. She would *own* this house.

Please tear it down, Don. Please don't leave me trapped here, with timbers for a skeleton and lath-and-plaster skin. Windows are not eyes. This alcove is beautiful, but it's not my heart, not *my* heart.

The sky grew dark outside. The nearly leafless trees whistled in the gathering wind. Cold front coming through—she felt the temperature dropping through the contraction of the clapboard of the house. It would rain, it would blow; the last leaves would be stripped from the trees. Rain would probably pour down into the house through the sag in the lawn, the new opening in the basement. Mud would spread across the basement floor. The beginning of death. She could feel it like a wound. Not serious yet, but it would be infected. Left untended, it would kill the house. She wouldn't let Don fix it. She wouldn't.

And yet she felt the house's need for it to be repaired, felt it like a deep hunger, like thirst, like a full bladder, those strong desires. When she was fully swallowed up by the house, would she have the strength to tell him not to repair it? Or would the house's hungers become her own, the way most people were never able to distinguish between their bodies' hungers and their own. As if their body were their self. They tore their lives apart, all for the sake of giving their body what it wanted, thinking all the time that it was what *they* wanted. Then they looked at the wreckage of their lives and wondered what had seemed so important about getting laid right then by that person; they lay in the hospital tubed up and dying, wondering what it was about each new cigarette that had made it seem so much more important than life itself. It takes death to wake you up, she thought. And then it's too late. And when I'm caught up in the house, will I remember what I learned? Not likely. I'll be mortal again, and die when the house dies, never remembering that its desires were never my own. My love for Don will be a distant memory. And he'll forget me, too.

No. Not so. Never. You don't forget this, any more than Don could forget his daughter. He'll remember me. And I'll feel it. I'll know that I was known, that I am known. That someone holds me in his heart.

If she could have wept, she would have. Instead she let the rain cry for her, streaking down the side of the house, faster and faster. She let the wind sob for her, throbbing against the house, gust after gust.

And all the time she watched. Watched Don sleeping. Watched the street outside.

Midnight. A Saturn drove slowly by. She noticed it. When it passed, she almost let it go.

But it parked just up the block. Just the other side of the gully. A woman got out. A dim shape in the rain. Years had passed, but Sylvie knew the walk. It was Lissy. She had come.

She walked across the bridge over the gully. Looked both ways. No witnesses? If she only knew. She climbed the low fence. Went down the muddy slope. Sylvie lost track of her, but it didn't matter. She wouldn't get into the house that way.

Sure enough, ten minutes later, the rain falling much harder now, a cold rain, the woman came up out of the gully, bedraggled and muddy, her feet sliding. Still holding that purse, clutching that purse. That's where the gun was, Sylvie knew that.

Sylvie glided up the stairs to where Don slept. How many hours had he slept already? He was so tired. She hated to wake him, but she had promised.

"Don," she said. "Don, she's here."

But he didn't hear her. Didn't stir.

Was he that sleepy? She reached out to shake him, but her hand disappeared into his body. For a moment she felt his heart beating, then snatched her hand away. She couldn't shake him. "Don," she said, frightened. But this time when she spoke, she realized that her own voice was very faint now, almost lost against the sound of the wind outside the house, the rain against the windows and walls. "Don!" she shouted, screamed. But he only rolled over, probably putting her voice into his dream.

All right then. What could she do? She had tried to keep her promise. But it was better this way, she had known that ever since he told her Lissy was coming. This was between her and her old room-mate. Don was the catalyst, but not the cause and not the solution. She'd deal with it. She had voice and substance enough left for that. Didn't she?

She flitted to the mirror in the bathroom. She could see the wall behind her, yes, but she was still there, still visible.

Down the stairs just as Lissy reached the front door. Lissy rattled the doorknob. Sylvie went around the corner to the alcove. Then she caused the house to unlock the door. To open it. It creaked open because she wanted it to creak. Let's do the whole haunted house bit, she thought. Let's give Lissy the whole ride.

Lissy came in with her hand inside her purse. Holding the gun, of course. Not a light was on in the house, but the streetlight was no longer obstructed by the leaves of the trees, and the rain did little to block the light. So Lissy could see, but not well, and the shadows were deep and black.

Sylvie watched as Lissy crept through the south apartment first, checking each room. No one there, of course, just Don's tools all assembled in the parlor, where he had put them while he opened up the ballroom. Five minutes, and then she was back at the entryway, looking up the stairs.

I don't want you to go up there, thought Sylvie.

So she made the worklight in the ballroom switch on, all by itself.

At once Lissy came into the room, her gun out of the purse now, naked, exposed. There was murder in her face. But she didn't see Sylvie in the shadowy alcove. Her gaze was taken by the hugeness of the ballroom. She walked out into the middle, looking around her in awe. She had never guessed that there was a space like this hidden in their cramped apartment.

Sylvie spoke aloud. She felt like she was shouting, but she had to make sure Lissy could hear her over the noise of the storm outside. "Not quite like you remember, is it?"

At once Lissy whirled and fired the gun without even looking to see who it was, or whether she was armed. Still a murderer, aren't you, Lissy.

The bullet passed through Sylvie and lodged in the wood behind her. She felt it with her sense of the house, and there was a vague sense of heat in her own shadow-body as the bullet passed through, but that was all. Sylvie laughed at the futility of Lissy's weapon and rose to her feet, stepping out into the light.

"Ouch," Sylvie said.

Oh, it was sweet to see Lissy's eyes grow wide. To see her back away, holding the gun in front of her like a cross to ward away a vampire in an old horror movie. Fear, that's what Sylvie saw in Lissy's eyes. Fear and—could it be?—shame. Guilt? Could she still feel guilt? What was the recipe that would trap her here?

"Sylvie," said Lissy.

"Oh, but I thought that was your name now," said Sylvie. "I thought that's the name you were going by, there in Providence."

"The man who called me," said Lissy. "Where is he?"

"Your appointment was always with me," said Sylvie. She walked closer to Lissy. She remembered that she wasn't supposed to touch Lissy, but she wasn't even close yet. And Lissy's confusion was delicious. Lissy had never been confused. Always so sure of herself. Finally here was something she didn't know how to handle.

"Get away from me," Lissy said, panicking.

Now the gun wasn't a talisman. It became a gun again. She fired. Again, again. Sylvie felt the bullets pass right through the center of her chest.

"Good aim," said Sylvie. "But too late. You already killed me as dead as I'll ever get." But that wasn't quite true. Soon Sylvie would be even deader. Well, she wouldn't give Lissy the satisfaction of knowing that.

"I didn't mean to kill you," said Lissy.

"Sure, I know," said Sylvie in her most understanding voice. "You accidentally fell on my throat and accidentally squeezed it till I stopped kicking and clutching at you and then you accidentally kept squeezing until I was dead. These things happen."

"You hit me first!" cried Lissy. "With a rock!"

"But I didn't kill you, did I."

"So I was better at it than you were," said Lissy. "I was always better at everything."

There it was, the old Lissy. Angry Lissy, tearing at Sylvie, making her question her own ability. But Sylvie knew better now, knew how Lissy was a parasite who sucked her life from the people around her.

"How long did my job in Providence last?" said Sylvie. "I bet it didn't take them long to learn that you just couldn't cut it. You just didn't seem to be the same person who wrote that dissertation."

"Who needs a job like that?" said Lissy. "That was just to get me started anyway. I couldn't live on a pissant salary like that anyway. That was only enough money for the mousy kind of life you lived."

Lissy was moving toward the back of the ballroom, looking through the door to see if anyone was there. Fearing a trap, because she would have laid a trap.

Well, there was no trap. But she also wasn't going to get out that way. Just as Lissy broke and ran for the kitchen door, Sylvie reached through the house and slammed it right in Lissy's face. Lissy screeched and fell against the door, then whirled around and fired the gun again. This time it was wild. It entered the ceiling where the chandelier used to hang.

Sylvie felt his footfalls on the floor above her before she could hear the sound. Don was awake. The gunshots had done what her faint voice couldn't do. And now he was going to run down the stairs, straight into Lissy's gun.

"There he is!" cried Lissy.

"This is between you and me," said Sylvie.

Lissy ignored her and ran the length of the ballroom, toward the entryway, toward the passage to the stairway. This was not going to happen. Sylvie flew to the passageway between ballroom and entry and spun around several times in her fury, trying to make enough of a show to frighten Lissy, to make her back off.

"You've done your last murder, Lissy!" she cried.

"*I'm* Sylvie now! *Me!*" Lissy answered. She sounded contemptuous, but Sylvie could see she was also afraid. "Get out of my way."

"I'm not moving," said Sylvie. "I'm in your face forever."

Sylvie could see how Lissy steeled herself, put on a mask of bravado to hide her fear. "You don't *have* to move. You're nothing. I can walk right through you."

Sylvie backed up as Lissy took a step toward her, holding up a hand to ward Lissy off. Lissy lashed out with her left hand, the one not holding the gun, to slap Sylvie's hand away.

She should have seen it coming, should have dodged out of the way. She knew she wasn't supposed to let Lissy touch her. But the moment the hand touched her, it didn't feel like someone else's hand. It felt like her own hand. Her own self. The room spun insanely, and then everything was changed. She was looking out of eyes again, real eyes. Eyes that blinked, that went wide with panic.

But there was something suffocating her. Something interfering with her heartbeat. Something inside her body with her that had no right to be there, that was trying to control her, screaming at her even though it made no sound because Sylvie had control of the lungs, the throat, the tongue, the lips, the teeth.

This is my body. Sylvie felt it, knew it deep down. And the body knew it, too. Sylvie Delaney, that was this body's name, that was who this woman was. The other was a stranger, with another name, belonging in another place. The whole soul named Sylvie Delaney rejected the interloper. And without saying it, without even meaning to do it at any conscious level, Sylvie screamed silently back at the intruder: Get out! And gave a little *push.*

A little push at some level that she could not understand or feel with the flesh, a little push and suddenly she was alone in this body, this delicious living breathing flesh, this skin, this muscle, these organs, this beating heart. These hands holding a gun, this face with sweat dripping down, this hair tangled around her face, her neck. These clothes binding, pulling, sliding across her skin as she moved. This life, this reborn life.

Don heard the first gunshot, but it was part of his dream. The next three were also in his dream, but they woke him. His eyes opened and he listened but didn't hear anything. And then he did. Voices downstairs. Running feet. A slamming door. Another gunshot. He was off the bed and running along the floor. He heard the voices more clearly now. Someone was running across the ballroom floor. And he thought: She has a gun. What am I going to do, run down the stairs and die?

He ran as lightly as he could down the stairs, knowing that he was heard, but what could he do about that? He could hear their conversation. "I'm not moving," Sylvie was saying. He ducked around the corner into the south parlor, where his tools were. He could have used the big crowbar now as a weapon. "I'm in your face forever," Sylvie said.

The smaller wrecking bar he used for tearing out drywall and lath and plaster would have to do. Truth was, neither tool would be worth much against a gun, but it was his only chance. If she came close without seeing him, he could maybe get in a blow before the gun came into play. The right blow, and the gun would never fire again.

He came back around the corner, tiptoed as rapidly as he could across the entryway, peered around the corner into the ballroom. Sylvie was standing with her back to him, blocking Lissy's path. Lissy, gun in hand, gathered herself up, covering her fear with a mask of contempt. Don had time to notice how much alike they looked, and yet how different. How jaded and world-weary Lissy looked, compared to the fresh beauty, the untainted grace of Sylvie's spirit.

"You don't *have* to move," Lissy said. "You're nothing. I can walk right through you."

She took a step toward Sylvie, who backed away, raising a hand to ward her off. Lissy lashed out with her left hand.

"No!" Don cried.

The hands touched. And to his horror, Sylvie lurched toward Lissy, then suddenly spun around in the air like a kite out of control in a storm, and then was sucked into Lissy's body.

"No!" Don screamed. She was trapped in the body of that murderous bitch and it was his fault, he had brought her here. Don lunged toward Lissy as the woman's face contorted, twisted with—pain? Confusion? She looked toward him but didn't seem to see him. The gun hung by the trigger guard from her hand. She was slackjawed, stupid, empty-faced. Don reached out to take away the gun.

Suddenly Lissy's body stiffened and she moaned, a long moan, rising in pitch, rising to a screech. And when it seemed she couldn't possibly scream any higher or louder, something leapt out of her body, flew up. For a moment it hung in the air, spread-eagled. It was Lissy again, a copy of her, a shadow of her, wearing only a t-shirt. She looked younger. Not like the body that had been called Sylvie for all these years. It was the spirit of the Lissy who murdered Sylvie that night more than ten years ago, now suspended in the air in the midst of the ballroom.

Meanwhile, Lissy's body came to life. The eyes opened. Looked at him. The gun clattered to the floor. The hands reached up to touch the face. The tongue flickered out to lick the lips. And the face changed. Came to life in a different way. No longer weary-looking, no longer cynical and angry. Those lines were still there, but the expression belied them. It was a face filled with wonder. With joy. "Don," she said. "It's me."

If Lissy's spirit had been flung out of the body, if it now hung in the air drifting toward the exact center of the ballroom, then who else could be in Lissy's body?

"Don, don't you know me?"

Of course he knew her. "Sylvie," he said.

The face smiled. And in that moment it was no longer Lissy's face. Oh, it was, by the superficial markers of a face, the bone structure, the lips, the eyebrows, the cheeks, the brow, the chin. The nose longer and narrower than Sylvie's had been, the eyelashes heavy with makeup where Sylvie had not had any such artifice. But the expression of the face, the way the mouth moved, the way the eyes sparkled when she looked at him—it was Sylvie's face that looked at him. Sylvie, in the flesh, in living, breathing flesh. In a body that knew it belonged to her. Sylvie alive. Sylvie whole.

He stepped toward her, reached for her. "Of course I know you," he said. He took her hand. He gathered her into an embrace. Not light now, not inhumanly light; she had the weight and mass of a real woman, the softness of flesh yielding against him as he held her. The breath warm on his chest. "Sylvie," he said.

"Did you know?" she said. "Did you know it would end this way?"

At that moment the spirit hanging in the air began to scream in terror. They parted, turned, looked up to see what was happening.

"I guess it hasn't ended yet," said Don.

The spirit was twisting in the air, turning over and over. But there was nothing simple about the movement. Parts of her were turning faster than other parts. She was being stretched, pulled, drawn out like elastic. Like a victim on the rack. Finally one hand flung itself out and smacked against the ceiling of the room, the arm drawn long and thin like an elastic, and so transparent it was a mere shimmering in the air. A foot leapt to the far wall, another hand to the floor, the other foot to the front wall of the house. The head spun, then leapt to the bearing wall.

What was left in the middle of the air lost all shape. It grew like a balloon, thinning as it grew, till it was nothing but the shining of a bubble, iridescent as it filled the room. Don felt it pass over him, through him, a cold feeling that chilled him to the bone. And then the shimmering reached the walls of the ballroom, the ceiling, the floor. The room glowed for a second or two, no longer. And then everything was back to normal.

"She's gone," he said.

"No she's not," said Sylvie. "The house took her."

"Then she's gone," he repeated.

"No," said Sylvie. "I can't feel the house anymore. This is my only body now. Lissy's got the house."

They could hear it start, far up in the attic. Doors slamming. Windows rising and falling, rattling. The second floor now, the slamming, the rattling. The water turned on. The toilet flushed.

And now the room they were in. A window was flung up by invisible hands. Wind and rain sprayed into the room. The kitchen door opened, slammed, opened, slammed. Under their feet the floor buckled, a wave of it rippling across until it passed under their feet, knocking them down. Sylvie clutched at him; they held on to each other, helping each other as they struggled to their knees, tried to stand.

The vast expanse of the bearing wall beyond the alcove began to shudder, forming a new shape. The shape of a face. Lissy's face, huge, like a bas-relief made of lath and plaster. The mouth moved. They could hear the voice like the sound of a bass drum talking. "That's my body!" moaned the face on the wall.

They were so enthralled in watching the wall that it was only out of the corner of his eye that Don caught the movement at the entryway. It was his favorite hammer, flying through the air straight toward Sylvie. Don leapt up just in time; the hammer struck his back, between the shoulder blades. The force of the blow was vicious, knocking him down to the floor, entangling Sylvie and bringing her down, too. Just as well, for the wrecking bar flew just over them as they fell.

"Are you all right?" Sylvie cried out to him.

"Get out of the house, Sylvie!" he shouted.

"I can't leave you to face her alone—"

"It's you she wants! Get out!"

He got up, looking around desperately for any more flying objects as he helped her to her feet. Stooped over, he half-dragged her toward the entry. The pain between his shoulders was excruciating. Bruised ribs? Or broken ones? Or a bloody wound? No time to worry about that now.

In the passage to the entryway, Don could see into the south parlor, where his tools were sliding and sliding in concentric circles on the floor. In the middle was the workbench. As he stood in the passage, the circles stopped moving, except where they cleared a path leading straight to where Don and Sylvie stood. The workbench began to slide, then hurtle toward them.

"Get out!" Don screamed as he ran toward the workbench.

It hit him at hip level, flipping him over it. But he caught it as he fell, held on to the leg of it, so it had to drag him, so it slowed down as it continued relentlessly toward Sylvie.

Sylvie was fumbling with the doorknob. "It won't open, it won't open!" she cried.

Don got enough of a purchase on the floor to get some leverage. He lifted upward on the leg of the workbench and it tipped and fell on its side. As if the house knew at once that it was no longer half so useful as a weapon, the bench stopped moving and lay there, inert.

Don started toward Sylvie to help her with the door, when he saw the wood of the door below the handle start to deform, to extrude. "Get away from the door!" he shouted, but almost before he was through saying it, and long before Sylvie could possibly have reacted, the extrusion became a human hand made of splintering wood, and it seized Sylvie's wrist and held her.

Sylvie screamed and tried to pull her hand away. To get leverage, she leaned her back against the wall beside the door. Another hand pushed out of the plaster and wrapped itself around her other arm, gripped it. Hands took her ankles, hands made of plaster, hands made of floorboard. And then a pair of hands at her throat.

"Don!" she cried, her eyes filling with panic.

It was going to happen again. Lissy was going to kill her again.

He stood up and screamed at the house. "How stupid are you? If you kill her then you won't have that body, either!"

At once the window in the door deformed and became Lissy's face in rippling glass. The mouth opened and the voice was high and sharp like the tinkling of crystal. "If I can't have it, nobody can."

Another face formed in the floor, the mouth gaping wide, the throat dark and deep. The voice thrummed deeply. "That body is Lissy, Lissy, not Sylvie. Call it Lissy."

"Don't say her name!" Don cried out. "Don't say it, Sylvie! Don't let her have that body back."

She looked at him with frightened eyes.

He didn't bother trying to pry away the hands that held her. He knew that his bare strength wouldn't have the power to get her free. It would take weapons, and instead of attacking these new-made hands at the door he would break this creature's back.

He searched the disarray of his tools for the skillsaw and the extension cord. Found. He plugged the extension cord into the wall, the skillsaw into the extension cord, and then pulled the trigger. It whined into life, the bare blade spitting off dirt from yesterday in the tunnel. The great timbers of the bearing wall still stood partly exposed, and he bit the skillsaw into the first one, making a cut all the way around it like a lumberman girdling a tree.

The glass Lissy-face in the doorway screamed. The wooden one in the floorboards buckled and deformed. What had once been the brow of that face now became a ripple in the floor, then a pair of hands that reached up and fumbled with the junction of the power cord and extension cord. Don was just starting on the second timber when the cords came apart and the skillsaw died.

One timber was cut. That was something. If he could find his sledgehammer he could break it apart. That would start the weakening of the house, wouldn't it?

There was no time, no time to be searching for tools. Sylvie was dying there, pinned like a bug against the wall. He had to paralyze this house, break its back. Kill it and kill Lissy along with it.

He caught the movement in time to fling up his hand. The point of a mortaring trowel pierced his palm. The pain shot through him and he stumbled, nearly fell from the shock of it. But he was too angry now, too frightened to let pain stop him. He took the trowel by the handle and pulled it out. This moved the pain to a new level, and he almost fainted with it as the blood flowed. He had to stop this house before he lost too much blood or he'd end up watching Sylvie strangle to death as the last life fled his own body. Where was the sledgehammer?

It flew through the air straight for his head. He caught it, spinning with the force of it as he did. "Thanks!" he shouted triumphantly. She had put his best weapon in his hands herself.

"I've got to let her have the body back, Don!" cried Sylvie. The hands had loosened around her throat enough to let her speak. "She's going to kill you!"

In answer, he swung the sledgehammer and struck the timber above the cut. It shuddered, but it did not break.

Sylvie screamed. He turned just enough to see the nails rising up like a swarm of bees from their brown sacks, eight-penny nails, ten-penny, twelve-penny. Every one of them an arrow aimed at him. He turned his back on them and swung the hammer again. The hammer struck just as the nails began stinging, stabbing at his back. His neck, his scalp, his arms, all up and down his legs. A hundred bee stings. He groaned, partly from the pain of it, but more because again the timber didn't break free. As he twisted his body to swing yet a third time, he could feel the nails popping out of his muscles, or snagging them, tearing him inside. It wasn't going to stop him. He wasn't going to stand by and let her die just because he was in pain. He swung with all his strength, perhaps with more than his strength. And this time the timber tore apart at the cut. Above the split, the post was dislodged almost completely free of the bottom part; only an edge of the upper part still rested there. A fourth swing as the face in the glass cried out, "No, you're hurting me, you're hurting me!"

He struck the post and it came entirely free. At once a great creaking sound came from the ceiling. The post that had been holding up the second story and the roof was now a weight pulling them down. The house writhed with the injury.

Don looked over at Sylvie. She was struggling to get free. The hands still held her, but were they perhaps a little bit weaker? The hands at her throat seemed no longer to be trying to strangle her. No—it was worse. They had hold of her head now. Twisting. Lissy was trying to use the strength of the house to break Sylvie's neck.

"Don," Sylvie cried. "If I go back into the house she'll leave it, she'll go into the body. You have to be the first to get the gun!"

"Don't do it!" he screamed at her. "Don't let go of that body! Don't go into the house! I can do this!"

He meant it when he said it, but he had no idea how.

Gladys watched with her eyes closed, feeling more than seeing what was happening. Judea and Evelyn could look out the window all they wanted—there was little to see that way. It was Gladys who could sense what was happening. How the spirit of the murderer had taken possession of the house. Fortunately it was still distracted, trying to destroy Don and either get the girl's body back or, failing that, to kill it. But if it once succeeded in doing that, it would turn its attention again to them. To their old bodies, in thrall to the house. Gladys wouldn't have the strength to fight it off anymore, not if it were ruled by such malevolence.

So when the floor rose up and tore apart the power cord, Gladys moaned in despair.

But despair never lasted long. There were things she could do to help. "Quick," she cried out. "Get me that extension cord!"

Evelyn and Judea looked at her blankly.

"From the TV! The extension cord!" The TV had been her lifeline to the outside world. The girls never watched it—it just made them sad. But Gladys had it on a lot, a background to her life, to her struggles with the house. There was only one outlet in this old room, electrified before modern codes. To get the TV across from her, they had had to run an extension cord from the outlet beside her bed.

Judea got it free of the wall and handed that end to her. "Both ends," Gladys said. And in a moment Evelyn had the end from the television plug. Gladys took the male end in her left hand, the female in her right, and tried to put them together. It was like pushing together the north poles of two magnets. They dodged, refused.

Of course they did. Because the spell she was casting linked the extension cord to the skillsaw cord in the house. And the house could feel it, and was fighting her. It was a hard spell in any circumstance. But she had to do it.

"Help me," she said. "Hold my arms. Push. Help me get these together."

They did their best, but it wasn't until Don managed to break open the first timber that the house weakened enough or got distracted enough that they could do it. Gladys felt the plugs touch. She guided them, carefully, forced them with all her strength, all their combined strength, until the prongs slid into the receptacle.

In the parlor, Don held the skillsaw but couldn't get the cord to hold still long enough to grab the power end. It was like a snake, dodging, dodging. And then, suddenly, sparks leapt from the extension cord on the floor, arcing like a welder, blinding him for a moment. The extension cord and the skillsaw power cord still didn't touch, were yards apart, in fact, but the power sparked through the air to join them. A current flowed, dazzling white and blue in the air. Don's finger found the trigger of the saw and it whined into life. He wasted no time, no matter what the house flung at him. He made his cuts, post after post. Of course

only the posts in this room were exposed, but that had to be enough.
Cutting these down had to be enough.

The house's strength was growing feebler all the time. What it
threw at him struck with less and less force. He glanced over to see
that Sylvie still hung in the house's grip, but it was no longer trying
to break her neck or strangle her. It only held her, held on to her.

"Please," moaned the face in the glass. "I didn't mean anything by
it. I didn't mean to do anything bad."

Don had no pity. He knew what Lissy was and what had to happen
to her now. He hefted the sledgehammer and began striking the cut
timbers. It took three blows with the first one, but after that the
house was weak enough that a single blow broke each timber apart.
The whole second floor sagged. The house's back had been broken.

The glass face rippled, thinned, then collapsed back into the original flat surface. Only a shadow of it remained. Only the whisper of a
voice.

"Don't kill the house, Sylvie," said the face. "It loves you."

The ceiling above them, pulled downward by the weight of the
timbers, bowed more and more; plaster in the ceiling cracked.
Plaster dust and fragments began to fall, more of them, faster and
thicker. As the house weakened, its power to heal itself, to hold itself
together faded and its age began to tell on it. Don cared only for
Sylvie, still held by plaster hands, wooden hands. They didn't let go
but they didn't grip her tightly, either. They were dead. The house
had lost the power to extrude them, but along with it had also lost
the power to draw them in. Don used the sledgehammer, aiming
carefully so as not to break Sylvie's bones. He struck once, again,
again. The plaster hands shattered into dust. The wooden ones broke
off in splinters at the wrists. Nothing held her. She was free.

Behind them, the stairway itself, no longer anchored to anything
on one side, groaned, sagged, lurched downward. Sylvie looked at it,
looked up at the cracking ceiling above her as Don fumbled with the
deadbolt. The key was gone from the lock. He had one in his pocket,
but he wasn't going to look for it. "Out of the way," he said to Sylvie.
She moved behind him as he swung the sledgehammer one last time,
knocking the deadbolt clear out of the door. The door itself

rebounded from the blow, falling open. Don grabbed Sylvie by the wrist and half-dragged her out onto the porch. It buckled and sagged under the weight of them. He bounded down the steps, then held out his arms and she jumped to him, he caught her and staggered back, turning around and around, out on the lawn in the rain, in the wind, free of the house. He held her in his arms, dancing again, only this time no dream of old waltzes, now it was real and cold and wet and the woman in his arms was alive and crying and laughing for joy.

He stopped. He kissed her. Her lips were wet with rain, but her mouth was warm, and she held him, not lightly, but with tight, eager arms.

22

Freedom

A voice came from across the yard. "Pardon me, but don't you two have sense enough to come in out of the rain?"

They looked over at Miz Evelyn standing behind the picket fence, holding an umbrella. Even by the light of the streetlamp she looked stronger than yesterday. Invigorated.

"We did it, Miz Evelyn," he said. "We put things back to rights."

"House is weaker now but it ain't dead."

"It will be soon," he said. "And we're alive."

"Just barely! Look at you, bleeding like a stuck pig."

It was true. Blood was still seeping from the wound in his hand. Now that he thought about it, now that the adrenaline was wearing off, he hurt all over.

"Oh," cried Sylvie softly. "There are nails still in your head. Turn around."

"Get over here," said Miz Evelyn. "I can help."

As they walked around the picket fence and into the carriage-house yard, Miz Judea came out onto the porch and waved them over. "Get on up here out of the rain," she said. "Come on, I've got what you need." Steam rose from a pitcher. She held a basket full of bandages and ointments. Some of them looked like the FDA had never certified them, but he figured Gladys knew things that the FDA never heard of, so there on the porch he stood while they pulled nails out of his legs and backside.

"Somebody nailed you good," said Miz Judea. Then she cackled with such mirth, you'd think she hadn't laughed for years.

As soon as he could, he sat on the porch swing and let them strip off his shirt and start anointing his wounds with foul-smelling salves that stung and then felt good. The old ladies introduced themselves to Sylvie and Sylvie smiled and introduced herself back again. Don just sat and watched, deeply weary but also satisfied.

"So you're the haint that's been living in that house all these years," said Miz Evelyn.

Sylvie reached up and touched her own cheek. "Not anymore, though," she said.

"I told Miz Judy here, I said if *any*one can put things to rights, it's that boy Don Lark."

"Said no such thing," said Miz Judea. "You just said nobody could ever put things to rights."

"The memory is the first thing to go," said Miz Evelyn.

They watched as a man in sweats carrying an umbrella padded across the street to them. "What's going on in that old house there?" he demanded. "I thought I heard such a crash. And a woman screaming."

"That was us, I'm afraid," said Don. "I'm the one who's been renovating it. It wasn't as sturdy as it looked. A main load-bearing wall collapsed."

"That house ought to be condemned."

"You're telling me," said Don. "I'm not spending another night under that roof. I'll have a wrecking crew out here to tear it down first thing tomorrow."

"Wait till after eight in the morning, would you?" said the neighbor.

"Count on it," said Don.

"Can I give you some coffee?" said Miz Judea.

"No thanks, ma'am," said the neighbor. "I don't *want* to be awake."

"They barely escaped with their lives," said Miz Evelyn.

"Yeah, well, nobody was hurt, right?"

"All of us are fine," said Don. And, in fact, with Gladys's salves going onto his body and Sylvie there in the flesh before him, it was true.

The neighbor trotted back across the street.

"I think the rain is letting up a little," said Miz Evelyn.

"I love the rain," said Sylvie.

"You'll love the sun, too, come morning," said Miz Judea. "Now let's get this poor boy inside and in to a bed. I'm afraid he's going to have to buy himself some new clothes. Everything he's got is either in that house or full of holes and covered with blood."

"I guess I can go shopping for him in the morning," said Sylvie. Then she burst into tears. "Oh, Don," she said. "I can go shopping. I can go *out*."

In answer he held her hand, and with the old ladies fussing around them, they went inside.

A week later, the demolition was complete. Don never went into the house again. He was afraid that some shadow of Lissy would remain alive in there. He didn't want to hear her voice again. Didn't want to walk into her lair where she and the house might have one last trick up their sleeves. So his tools were a dead loss. The only things he might have missed were his pictures of Nellie, but those were in the photo album in the glove compartment of his truck. So he could lose the rest.

As the house came down, the old ladies brightened and strengthened and began taking walks around the neighborhood. Sylvie got a locksmith to make her a new key for the Saturn, and after Don cleared out every reminder of its previous owner, she began driving everywhere, taking Miz Evelyn and Miz Judea with her. The three of them were soon as thick as thieves. Leaving Don with Gladys in that upstairs room.

With new tools he carefully dismantled the doorway of her room and laid boards and carpet down the stairway to convert it into a long, slow slide. He opened the front door, cutting away part of the wall, and made ramps out onto the porch and down to the lawn. A parade of doctors came to examine her, to judge whether she could make the move. Arrangements were made with a sanitarium, and they rented a truck to move her.

On the day the demolition was complete, everything hauled away, and the foundation hole filled in, Gladys was hoisted from her bed and, with the help of four men from the sanitarium, she passed through the widened doorway of her room and slid very, very slowly down the carpeted slide. On the main floor they harnessed and winched her up onto three gurneys strapped together and rolled her out through the gap in the front wall of the house to the street, where the truck waited.

"We going to the fat farm!" she cried when she saw the truck. "Inside this body be fourteen skinny women dying to get out!"

"Just do whatever the doctors tell you," Miz Judea said.

"We'll visit every day," said Miz Evelyn."

"No you won't," said Gladys. "That get boring for you, and tell the truth I could use a little vacation from looking at you two every day. Of course I mean that nice as can be."

It took another twenty minutes of hard labor but finally Gladys was up inside the truck, sitting on a king-size mattress with an enormous pile of pillows all around her. Two attendants would be riding in back with her, monitoring her vital signs during the whole trip.

Sylvie and Don and Evelyn and Judea gathered around the wide-open back doors of the truck to say good-bye.

"I told you not to visit every day but that don't mean I want you to forget me." Gladys pointed at Don in particular. "I'm charming company and besides, you owe me."

"We'll be there," said Don. "We'll even hold the wedding there if you want, so you can come. Nothing fancy. I figure just the five of us and some preacher or something to make it legal."

"And thanks for tearing up the house to get me out," she said. "Once I didn't have to fight that damn house anymore I thought I go crazy if I stay in that room another minute."

"I understand that," said Sylvie.

"Come on, boys," she said to her attendants. "Get me to the fat farm. Good-bye, Miz Evvie, Cousin Judy! I'm gonna *miss* your cooking!"

They said their good-byes as the driver closed the back door of the truck. Then they watched as it drove away.

Don walked over to the FOR SALE sign on the lawn of the carriage-house, then up at the gaping hole in the front wall of the house. "I guess I got me some work to do before this house can be sold."

"And it's right kind of you to do it for us," said Miz Evelyn.

"No need for this house to end up like the other one," said Miz Judea.

They all looked over at the freshly leveled ground where the old Bellamy house had stood. It was hard to believe that the plot of land was even large enough to hold such a house, or that it had once risen tall among the trees.

"It was a beautiful house," said Don.

"Built in love," said Sylvie.

"Too strong for its own damn good," said Miz Judea.

"But I did love the place," said Miz Evelyn.

"Too many ugly secrets," Miz Judea answered.

"I was content there," said Sylvie. "For ten years."

"Dead but happy," said Miz Judea.

"No," said Sylvie. "*Now* I'm happy."

She took Don's hand.

"How can you be happy?" said Miz Judea. "You two got no money to speak of. All lost when that house came down."

"I got a few thousand left," said Don.

"Now don't spoil it by telling us you got all you need," said Miz Evelyn. She reached into her big purse and pulled out a SOLD sticker. She peeled off the backing and placed it across the FOR SALE sign.

"You've already sold it?" Don asked.

"The boy's a little dim, isn't he?" Miz Judea said to Sylvie.

"I think they're giving us the house, Don."

"No," said Don. "You need the place."

"I've had enough of this house, Don Lark. I want a nice little apartment where somebody else takes care of the yard while I watch TV or go to the movies."

"We already agreed on that," said Evelyn. "I'm still working on getting her to take a cruise with me."

"No boats," said Miz Judea. "No planes."

"She's just an old woman," said Miz Evelyn. "No doubt about it."

"We got plenty of savings," said Miz Judea. "We don't need the house. And we got no sentimental attachment to it, either, so once you get all that damage repaired, you go ahead and sell it yourself and move on, you understand? I know you two won't want to live next door to where all that bad stuff happened. The house may be gone, but the memories ain't."

"But we're OK," said Don. "I'll fix this up but *you* keep the money—"

Miz Evelyn shook her head and reached up and put her hand across his mouth. "Some folks just can't figure out when to shut up and say thank you."

"I feel sorry for folks like that," said Miz Judea. "Don't you, Sylvie?"

She laughed and Don laughed and it was done.

"We'll let you know when we set up the closing," said Miz Evelyn.

A Daniel Keck Co. taxi pulled up to the curb. The old ladies immediately bustled around, telling the driver to put the bags in the trunk and when there wasn't room, into the front seat so they could sit in back. And a few minutes later, they were away.

Alone together now, Don and Sylvie walked up the ramp into the torn-open house they had just been given. Sylvie went around touching knickknacks, pictures, furniture, the artifacts of a half-century of life. "They can't mean to leave all this behind," she said.

"I think they do mean to," said Don. "They're done with it. It doesn't matter anymore."

"I guess you'd know," said Sylvie.

"I've left everything behind before. Lost it all. Only one thing I'm hanging on to now." He took her hand.

"Don," she said. "Look at me."

He looked into her face.

"Now that I look like Lissy, am I prettier?"

He laughed as if it were a crazy question, but she held his hand tighter and insisted. "I have to know, Don."

"Sylvie, I can't tell you, because I only saw Lissy's face for a few seconds before she left and this became *your* face."

"It's still the face I looked at all those years when I saw her. I don't like looking in the mirror now. It makes me sick and sad. And then to know that when you look at me, you see her . . . "

"No," he said, "no, don't think that way. It's not her face, not for a moment. She never smiled like you do. She never looked out of those eyes with your soul. I saw her there in the ballroom, how tired and worn-out she looked, cynical, plain-looking. And then it was you inside that face, and Sylvie, I would have recognized you even if I hadn't seen the transition. All the gestures, all the facial expressions. The way you laugh, the way you smile, it's *you* I'm seeing, and the face will look more and more the way it should as time goes on. Don't you see, Sylvie? The men who looked at her and preferred her to you—they were her kind of men, that's all. I'm not. I'm your kind of man."

She searched his eyes, believing him, not believing him, believing him again.

"Aw, hell," said Don. "I guess I'll just have to spend the next fifty or sixty years reassuring you."

"OK," she said. "That just might work. We're both damaged property, I guess."

"Plenty of time for renovation." He kissed her, there in the gap at the front of the house, with the chilly autumn breeze passing through, where all the world could watch, if they noticed, if they cared.

The kiss ended. "Let's get started," Sylvie said. "I know you work alone, but I'd like to train as your assistant."

"I think the official term is 'helpmeet.'"

"Whatever," she said. "I've got no experience but at least I'm cheap."

They spent the rest of the afternoon framing in the replacement wall and putting up the new door. By nightfall, the house was tight again.